The
Shadow
at the
Door

Tim Weaver is the *Sunday Times* bestselling author of eleven thrillers, including *No One Home* and *You Were Gone*. He has been nominated for a National Book Award, twice selected for the Richard and Judy Book Club, and shortlisted for the Ian Fleming Steel Dagger Award. He is also the host and producer of the chart-topping *Missing* podcast, which features experts in the field discussing missing persons investigations from every angle. A former journalist and magazine editor, he lives near Bath with his wife and daughter.

The Shadow at the Door

*Four
Stories*

*Four
Cases*

*One
Connection*

TIM WEAVER

MICHAEL  JOSEPH

MICHAEL JOSEPH

UK | USA | Canada | Ireland | Australia
India | New Zealand | South Africa

Michael Joseph is part of the Penguin Random House group of companies
whose addresses can be found at global.penguinrandomhouse.com.

First published 2021
001

Copyright © Tim Weaver, 2021

The moral right of the author has been asserted

Set in 13.5/16pt Garamond MT Std
Typeset by Jouve (UK), Milton Keynes
Printed and bound in Great Britain by Clays Ltd, Elcograf S.p.A.

The authorized representative in the EEA is Penguin Random House Ireland,
Morrison Chambers, 32 Nassau Street, Dublin D02 YH68

A CIP catalogue record for this book is available from the British Library

ISBN: 978–0–241–54132–6

This book is dedicated to you . . .
Because without readers, a writer is nothing

Contents

Dear Reader . . .

Believe it or not, this book was never part of the plan.

I'd been thinking for a while about the idea of someone going missing inside their own house. And, of course, I knew who would investigate the case. After all, when it comes to missing persons mysteries, there's really only one guy you can count on.

The problem was, I also knew that, although this would definitely have all the trappings of my usual David Raker stories, there wasn't *quite* enough in the idea for a full-length novel. So, while I considered it very briefly for a subplot in both *You Were Gone* and *No One Home*, in the end I couldn't make it work in either of those books and the idea quickly returned to the backburner.

And then two big things happened.

I finished my first ever standalone novel, *Missing Pieces*, and – as I nervously awaited my editor's verdict – found myself with a little downtime. Usually, in between novels, I try to take a complete break from writing and get out and do some of the things I haven't been able to do in the last months before a book's deadline (like seeing real people and breathing fresh air). But, within weeks of my sending the standalone to Penguin, an even bigger thing happened: a global pandemic shut the world down.

As frightening, stress-inducing and weird as the first coronavirus lockdown was, it also meant I had no choice but to return to my desk. There was literally nothing else to do. And because I wasn't due to start *The Blackbird*, aka David Raker

11, for a while – and, more importantly, hadn't completed the research for it – I went back to the idea about someone going missing inside their own house. And as I started writing, as the idea became bigger and more ambitious than I'd first imagined, but still only about half the size of one of my full-length novels, another idea came to me. What if it wasn't one case, but four of them, all different, all featuring different characters from the Raker series, and each a self-contained, standalone story in its own right – and yet with plot lines tethering all four together? What if, despite each of the stories having a clear beginning, middle and end, there were underlying connections in each that echoed from one investigation to the next? It would mean that the events you read about in Case #1 could reverberate all the way through to the events of Case #4. It would also mean that, unlike in other story collections, these stories would have to be read in order, starting from Case #1, otherwise – just like with any other novel – you wouldn't be able to follow the plot. (Oh, and in case you're interested, and talking of chronology and connections, this book acts as a handy bridge between the events at the end of *No One Home*, via one particular chapter of *Missing Pieces*, to the opening chapters of next year's *The Blackbird*.) Finally, there was perhaps the most important question I asked myself: what if David Raker was in each of the stories, sometimes centrally (as in Case #1: 'The Shadow at the Door'), sometimes in the background (Case #2: 'Bags') and sometimes actively helping and interacting with characters he's worked with before (Case #3: 'The Red Woman' and Case #4: 'Sleeper')?

So, welcome to what I imagine will be a true one-off.

As always, I'm so grateful for your support. Thank you for buying my books, talking about them, sharing them and posting about them – without this, I would never get the chance to try things like the book you're holding now. I so hope you enjoy what you read here, that this special, limited-edition collection looks good on your shelves, and that *The Shadow at the Door* fills a David Raker-sized hole in your life until he returns in a few short months in an all-new, full-length missing persons search.

Tim Weaver, November 2021

CASE #1
The Shadow at the Door

I

When I was thirteen, I discovered an old house in the woods behind my parents' farm. I'd been down there countless times before, into that knot of branches, but I'd never come across the building before. It was like it appeared there one day, emerging from the earth, shaking the dirt from its roots and forming like a tree.

I headed back to the farm, buzzing with excitement, and told my dad everything. He said he would come and see once he was done for the day, but I couldn't wait for him – I had to go and find the house again – so I went into the village and grabbed my friend Lee instead, and for the next couple of days, he and I claimed the house as our little secret. Then, as time wore on, we got bored of just the two of us knowing, so we brought other friends to see it, and the more of us there were, the braver we got.

Eventually, after a week of standing outside, staring at the memory of what it had been – its windows gone, its stone walls blistered and broken – we decided we'd go inside.

There were seven of us in all. We passed through the gaping mouth at its front – no longer a door, just a hole in the brickwork – and found ourselves in a hallway. Most of the wallpaper had been ripped away, the plaster too, exposing the old bones of the structure – its warped wooden struts, its decaying cavities – and as we moved into what would once have been a living room, the whole place seemed to darken. Shadows grew longer. The sounds of the woods disappeared behind us.

We were teenagers, knowing nothing of the world, its

strangeness and danger, but all of us felt something change then: a gentle shift we couldn't put into words. Instinctively, we looked at each other – and then, a second later, we bolted. We ran as fast as we could out of the woods and didn't stop until we made it to the farm.

Four years later, six weeks before I left south Devon for London and university, I was out with Dad, shooting air rifles at targets he set up in the woods, and I stumbled across the house again, completely by accident. It was the only other time growing up that I ever came into contact with it. By then, it was barely visible any more, nature having claimed it back. Its roof had begun to collapse and thin, crooked branches were inching through its façade like skeletal fingers.

Dad watched me stop, seeing that something had caught my attention, and then he moved closer to me, rifle at his side, head turned in the direction of the house. We both stood there in silence, watching it, as if it were coming alive. After a while, when he said nothing, I looked at him. He was staring at me.

'That's the Montgomery place,' he said quietly.

'Who were the Montgomerys?'

'They used to live here – back in the fifties.'

'Why did they leave?'

His eyes flicked to me. *They didn't.*

'Are they dead?'

He still didn't reply, but I knew I was right. They were all dead. In his face, I could see that he was trying to work out how I'd known. But I hadn't. All I recalled was the inside of that building years before and how it had felt to us as kids – its long shadows, its hush, as if the memory of the family were still lingering.

'Dad? Did the Montgomery family all die?'

'Yes.'

4

'How?'

My father's mouth flattened, his lips blanching, and I saw the conflict in him. Did he tell me the truth, or did he sugarcoat it? Eventually, his eyes came back to me, taking me in: the boy he'd brought up, just weeks away from becoming a man.

'He shot himself,' Dad said.

'Who?'

'William Montgomery. The husband.' A pause. 'The father. His wife and children died. They left this place one morning and never came home again.'

'Why?'

'A car accident.'

I frowned at him, unsure of exactly how it all fitted together. But then, suddenly, it snapped into focus and I understood, and it was maybe the first time in my life that I'd ever felt that pull; that emotional connection to the tragedy of others.

'Was William Montgomery the one driving the car?'

Dad's eyes moved back to the house.

'Yes,' he replied. 'His wife and kids all died. He survived.'

I'm not sure I ever gave a single thought to that moment in the decades that followed, not until our final conversation. By then, Mum had been gone for nearly a year, and – because it was clear he'd be unable to cope on his own – I'd helped Dad sell the farm and moved him into an old fisherman's cottage, perched in the hills overlooking the beach in the next village. Dad had been up and down health-wise, heart-sore about Mum's passing, but that day had been one of his better ones. The three of us – me, my dad and my late wife, Derryn – all sat at the window, gazing out at the dark sea.

'Do you believe in ghosts, son?'

Dad had asked it without looking at me, and when I turned to Derryn, she gave a gentle nod of the head and started to

5

get up, as if glimpsing the intimacy of this moment. Once we were alone, I touched Dad on the arm. He flinched, his bones so small against my fingers, his skin so meagre.

'Are you okay, Dad?'

He turned to me.

'Can I get you anything?'

'*Do* you?'

'Do I what?'

'Do you believe in ghosts?'

I smiled at him, but he didn't smile back. His eyes returned to the window, to the sea, evening moving in, the sky beginning to look like it was sketched in charcoal.

'You remember that house?' he asked. 'The Montgomery place.'

It took me a few moments to catch up.

'The place in the woods?'

He looked back at me, his eyes milky.

'The reason Montgomery put a gun in his mouth was because he was haunted by the memories of what had happened to his family.' He stopped and stared into his empty coffee mug, as if searching for the words in there. 'I guess what I'm saying is, you'll realize as you get older that ghosts aren't things that go bump in the night. They're not apparitions. They're *feelings*. They're things you can't let go of. They're fear, and heartache, and regret. Ghosts, they're just things you've done – or haven't.'

I studied him, confused, a little stunned. 'Dad, I . . . uh . . . I don't . . .' I stopped again, unsure what to say. I'd never heard him talk like this in my entire life.

'Ghosts, the ones you should be *really* scared of, they're not haunting the rooms of your house, son.' He took a long, abrasive breath. 'They're haunting the rooms of your head.'

PART ONE

The Watcher

2

The house was tucked away in a narrow cul-de-sac about a quarter of a mile south of Wimbledon Common. It was a modest two-storey, three-bedroom home, but it was set behind a brick wall that separated the property from the pavement and hid most of it from view, unless you were seven feet tall. A wooden door – locked, with a letterbox cut into it – filled a space at the far end of the wall, and at the other end was a set of double gates with an intercom mounted to the side. I knew the house was modest because it had been on the market four years ago and I'd tracked down some photos of the interior in an image search, but from this side of the wall, and with an attractive gabled roof visible, it would have been easy to believe it was larger and grander, and owned by a family much wealthier than the Conisters.

I parked on the street, grabbed my notebook, and then paused as I locked the car. I started thinking about my dad again, about the final conversation I'd had with him at the kitchen table in his home in south Devon, and about the things he'd said to me at the end. *Ghosts aren't haunting the rooms of your house, son. They're haunting the rooms of your head.* I wasn't sure if his voice had resurfaced after so much time because of what I'd found out about the Conister family over the last few days, or if it was still residue from the pain and distress of a case I'd had three years ago and could never forget. But, whichever it was, as I approached the gates, I could suddenly picture my father clearly, light painting one side of a gaunt, exhausted face.

I pushed the buzzer.

After a moment, a female voice said, 'Hello?'

'Mrs Conister? It's David Raker.'

Another short buzz and then one of the gates slowly fanned back to reveal a small, oval-shaped driveway. I stepped through and pushed the gate shut behind me. A five-year-old Astra was parked next to a metal stand to which a couple of bicycles were chained. Beyond that was the front door, shadowed under a first floor that pushed outward from the house and rested on top of two white pillars.

Margaret Conister was standing in the doorway, dressed in a pair of leggings and a vest top. It was a warm day at the start of July and she was a little flushed, but almost as soon as she saw me she started to apologize for the sheen of sweat on her face and arms: 'I went for a run,' she explained, 'and the time just got away from me. I started to panic that I was going to be late.' We shook hands and I told her she needn't have worried. 'That's kind of you,' she said, smiling, 'but it isn't a great first impression.'

'I don't judge people on their timekeeping.'

She smiled again. She was an attractive woman: forty-seven, petite and slim, her dark hair scraped back into a ponytail, her cheeks rouged, her eyes dark as chocolate. 'Come in,' she said, gesturing to the hallway. From the front step, I could see it ran all the way through to a big living room at the back that extended into a conservatory; to the left was a kitchen with an oak table at one end; to the right was some kind of office – poky, dark, cluttered.

'Have you been running long?' I asked, trying to put her at ease. This was always how the families started: a little nervous, a little worried about how every tiny thing they said or did might impact on my attitude, or how hard I worked for them.

'Yes, since I was teenager,' she said.

'I've just started to pick it up in the last couple of years,' I told her. 'I like the way it clears your head.' In the living room, I glimpsed someone on one of the sofas, partially obscured by the door frame: a pair of crossed legs, female. 'That's why I said not to worry about being late. I can't tell you how many times I've gone out for an hour – and got home after two.' She smiled again in response: she'd finally begun to relax.

'Can I get you something to drink, Mr Raker?'

'David,' I said. 'Some tea would be great.'

I followed her into the kitchen and, as we talked politely while the kettle boiled, I spotted a series of photos in a collage on the wall. The one in the centre was of Margaret Conister, her two children and her husband: they were on holiday somewhere, the skies blue, a white wall at one edge of the picture, a palm tree at the other. Her children – Seb, who Margaret had told me on the phone was fifteen, and Katie, who was twenty – were both five or six years younger in the photo; her husband, Paul, who was the same age as his wife, was such a tall man – his upper arms like the spidering limbs of a tree – that his hand rested easily on Seb's shoulder, despite both Margaret and Katie being between them. The other photos were of the same ilk, snapshots of a family's life, of kids growing up, of holidays. There was one from Paul and Margaret's wedding day; one of the kids in school uniforms; another of Paul in the garden. I pointed to the picture in the centre.

'Where was that taken?' I asked.

'Oh,' she said. 'Spain. Marbella.' Her eyes lingered on the picture. 'We had a couple of weeks in a villa down there. It belonged to Paul's old boss.' She paused, a flicker in her expression. 'Beautiful place. We felt like we were royalty for a fortnight.'

It took a moment for her to tear her gaze away.

'After you called me yesterday, I did a little digging around,' I said to her, 'and I was surprised to find that there wasn't much reported in the media about Paul. Not the details of his disappearance, anyway. I guess it just . . . it struck me as a little odd.'

Margaret nodded. 'Odd, because of what happened to him?'

'Right.'

This time, she just shrugged. 'I think people had a hard time believing what we were telling them. And, after a while, I think they believed we might be making it up.'

That was the impression I'd got from the stories in the media as well, and it was definitely the reaction that people had had on Internet forums, true-crime websites and social media threads: whatever had taken place in this house that night, three months ago, couldn't possibly have happened the way Margaret or her kids had described it.

Margaret turned to the photograph again.

'I don't necessarily blame them,' she said quietly, caught somewhere between talking to me, to herself, and to the ghost that was her husband's image. 'I mean, it sounds outlandish, even to my ears. But I swear to you, that was what happened.' She glanced at me and there were tears in her eyes. 'The night he went missing, Paul went upstairs just after eight to take his blood-pressure pill, the same as he did every night.'

I nodded, indicating for her to continue. She'd told me the rest over the phone already, but I wanted to hear it again.

'I heard the floorboards creak in the bedroom,' she said, her words starting to break up, 'and then the squeak of his bedside drawer being opened and shut. That was where his pills were. It always made that same squeak. He'd been meaning to fix it for years.' She stopped, wiped her eyes. 'And then, after that, nothing.'

'He never came back down again?'

'No.' She shook her head. 'He went upstairs – and he just vanished.'

3

I'd glimpsed Katie, Margaret's daughter, in the living room, and as we moved through to the conservatory, Margaret introduced us. Katie looked like her dad – tall, a little awkward, her features plainer than her mother's – and she was quiet and polite. She was twenty years old, so her mobile phone was glued to her hand, but when we started talking, she spoke like someone much older. That could happen sometimes when a parent went missing: kids were forced to grow up faster when they realized the only place you found a genuine happy ending was on Netflix.

'We read about some of your cases,' Katie said to me as she sat, tucking her legs under herself. She was wearing a black T-shirt with Robert De Niro's face on it and a quote underneath: *You talkin' to me?* 'That one up in Yorkshire sounded bad.'

She didn't have to say anything else.

The case she was referring to was the one I'd worked three years ago, where a whole village had vanished. An ex-detective called Joline Kader and I had almost died at the hands of a killer we'd never seen coming. I'd escaped with minor injuries, unlike Jo – who'd spent weeks in hospital recovering from hers – but the trauma continued to hang on, even all this time later: I was still waking up in the night, drenched in sweat, the ordeal playing out behind my eyes.

'What happened to you must have been terrible,' Margaret said.

'It was,' I replied, looking between them.

What else was there to say?

And then I thought of my dad again. *Ghosts are fear, and heartache, and regret.* I flipped my notebook open and went to a fresh page. 'So, Mrs Conister, I –'

'Maggie,' she said.

'Maggie. Paul disappeared on the 8th of April, right?'

'Yes. Just after the Easter weekend.'

'And you said he went upstairs that night at around 8 p.m.?'

She nodded. 'Yes, that's right.'

'What were you doing before that?'

'Just watching TV.'

'And where were you, Katie?'

'I was at my friend's house.'

I asked for the name of the friend and their address, just so I could check it off. I'd already put in a request with one of my contacts for a copy of the missing persons report, but a lot of this information was in the public domain anyway: Paul going upstairs; Maggie staying downstairs; Katie at a friend's house; their son, Seb, in his room, with headphones on, playing *Call of Duty* online with some school friends. In the newspapers, he'd been quoted as saying, 'I didn't hear a thing. I didn't even know Dad was upstairs.' Internet logs and interviews with his friends confirmed as much.

'And Seb was playing videogames, right?'

'Yes,' Katie replied.

I turned to Maggie again: 'So Paul comes upstairs. You said you heard some of the floorboards creaking, and then him opening and closing the drawer. After that?'

'It just went quiet.'

'Immediately?'

'The drawer was the last thing I heard.'

'Even above the sound of the TV?'

'I'd paused the TV. But even if I hadn't, the drawer's very loud. Like I say, Paul had been meaning to fix it.'

'But no sound of movement once the drawer was closed?'

'Nothing I remember,' she said.

'I believe you told the police that all the windows were still shut?'

'Yes. It was April, but it was cold that night.'

'Were they locked?'

'With a key? No. I know you told me you'd like to go up and look for yourself,' she said, gesturing towards the stairs, 'and when you do, you'll see why it would have been impossible for him to climb out of a window and then lock it from the outside.'

I'd noticed already that all the windows were new – uPVC with chrome handles – and there was no way to secure the windows in place unless you were on the inside of the house. If he'd used a window to exit the home, all he'd have been able to do was push it back against the frame. It would have been obvious what he'd done.

That night, none of the windows had been opened.

'Weird question,' I said, 'but did you check his pill tray?'

'Yes. He'd taken his pill.'

'What was he on?'

'Five milligrams of amlodipine.'

I noted it down. 'Any chance the pills could have been tampered with?'

She looked at me, as if confused by the question. It wouldn't have explained how or why he disappeared, but it might have provided a block upon which to build.

'No,' she replied. 'Why?'

'I'm just looking for angles,' I admitted.

'The pills were all in a sealed silver tray. If they'd been tampered with, there would have been damage to the foil.

But I don't know . . . I'm not sure I ever thought to check. I do know the police said he'd taken his pill that night, so you could ask them?'

I could, but I wasn't going to. I had a long, complicated history with the Met and I highly suspected that – even if I got lucky and found a cop who was initially receptive to me – I wouldn't get anywhere fast. The search for Paul Conister was three months old and had already hit a wall, and even a receptive cop would quickly tire of me sniffing around a case they'd come up short on. And, in truth, whether Paul had taken his pill that night or not felt like background noise. Because even if the pill *had* somehow been switched it would presumably have been done in order to disable him – or, worse, kill him. And if that was the case, Paul would have been right there on the bedroom floor.

'Are there any other exits upstairs?' I asked.

Maggie shook her head.

'No escape routes in the loft?'

'No, nothing like that. And, anyway, if he'd got up into the loft, I would have known. We've got a ladder that opens out and it makes this loud rattle when it does.'

'What about the front door?' I asked. 'Was that locked?'

'Yes. We always lock it after it gets dark.'

'The same with the conservatory doors?'

'Yes.'

'So no one could have got in?'

'Absolutely not.'

But could someone have got out?

'There were no keys missing?'

She frowned. 'For the doors?'

'I'm wondering whether it might have been possible for Paul to have, say, taken a key off his keyring, exited the house – and then locked up again from the outside.'

But Maggie had already started shaking her head.

'No,' she said. 'No keys missing.'

Although that didn't necessarily mean he might not have had one cut in the days beforehand, so I said, 'So you don't think it's possible that he might have just walked out?'

'Why would he do that?'

'I don't know. I'm just thinking aloud.'

'I would have heard the conservatory doors opening, and the front door . . .' She came to a halt. 'I guess it's possible he could have walked out, but I'm one hundred per cent certain that I would have heard something. The front door is old. It makes this soft creaking noise when you open and close it.'

Maggie took me to the front door. It had barely swung a couple of inches out on its hinges when it started making a long, low moan.

All these fixtures and fittings, all the noises they made, and after Paul took his pill she didn't hear a thing.

'So how long did you wait before going to check on him?'

Maggie paused, clearly trying to be as accurate as possible. 'I don't know. I told the police it was maybe ten minutes, but it could have been longer. We were in the middle of an ad break in this programme on Channel 4 about diets, so I paused it when he went to take his pill, and just grabbed my phone and started answering some emails.' She stopped again, her skin a little greyer, her eyes downcast. What if she hadn't got lost in answering emails? What if she hadn't waited ten minutes, or fifteen, or twenty?

Would it have made any difference?

'And when you went upstairs?' I said.

'I checked our bedroom first, but the light was off. Then I went to the ensuite and he wasn't there, so I looked in Katie's room and then knocked on the door of Seb's. Like we said just now, he hadn't seen Paul; he hadn't even heard him come up. Paul wasn't in the main bathroom, so I went back downstairs and checked the kitchen and the office . . .'

But he wasn't in those either.

'I went back upstairs.' She took a long breath. 'I don't know if I was in full panic mode by then, but I definitely remember being confused. Paul was a lovely man, a wonderful father, but he wasn't the type of guy to play practical jokes, so I knew he wasn't going to be hiding under the bed. I checked anyway – I checked *everywhere* – and that was when I started to test the windows, to see if any of them had been opened. I couldn't imagine why they would be, why he might have used them, but they were all just like I told you: secure, the handles down. They hadn't been opened. There was no sign of . . .' She trailed off.

I finished writing and looked up at Maggie. She was staring at Katie. Katie was staring back at her. They were both on the verge of tears and had a look in their eyes that I'd seen over and over: a powerful mixture of confusion and disbelief.

'There was no sign of Dad anywhere,' Katie said, finishing off the sentence for her mother. They both started to cry. 'It was like he just went up in a puff of smoke.'

4

I gave them both a few minutes to recover their composure and headed upstairs.

At the top of the steps, there were two rooms on the right and two on the left. On the far left was the main bedroom, where Paul and Maggie had slept; next to that was Katie's room; the family bathroom was just off to my right, and the door to Seb's room was beyond that. Directly above me was the loft hatch: I reached up, pulled the lever on the hatch and a metal ladder slid down.

I climbed up.

It was warm, airless, the heat of the day trapped inside. Flicking on a light switch mounted to one of the struts, I saw that the attic ran the length of the house but that only about a third of it had been boarded over. Most of it was being used for storage, the boxes gathering dust. Just as Maggie had described, there was no skylight and no way out. So could Paul have used it as a temporary hiding place? Why would he even do that? Why would he want his wife to think he'd disappeared? As I looked around, I figured the theory was possible – there was certainly enough room up here – but I couldn't see the motivation for doing so yet. I needed to find out more about Paul, about the marriage, about him as a father and a husband, and once I returned to the living room, I'd try to drill down into that detail. But, even if I *did* manage to zero in on a reason for him to come up here, to hide, wait for a point at which he could exit the house unseen, it didn't explain why Maggie hadn't heard the ladder. I'd noted the harsh, metallic rattle it had made as I'd opened it out. I'd noted too that there was no way to lock the hatch from inside the attic.

He hadn't come up here.

I climbed back down and closed the hatch, then went into Paul and Maggie's bedroom. It was a good size with a pretty bay window that looked out across a series of rooftops towards Wimbledon Common. There were wardrobes against one wall, a dressing table next to the window, and the door to the ensuite in the corner. I opened up the wardrobes and found Paul's clothes: a couple of suits, some trousers, some shirts, name-brand sweaters. Below, lined up, were four pairs of his shoes. They sat on a big box and, when I flipped the lid up, I could see more of Paul's clothes packed away inside. Three months in, it was clear Maggie hadn't wanted to consign any of her husband's belongings to storage yet. That wasn't unusual. If anything, in missing persons, it was more unusual when families got rid of things quickly.

I went through the wardrobe, checked the dressing table and then tried the drawers in the bedside tables. One didn't make any noise at all; one caught on its runner and gave out an irritated squeak. This was the one Paul's pills had been in. They were still in there now, along with piles of junk. I sifted through the junk first, found nothing, and then opened up the box of pills. It contained a half-used tray: one row gone, the other still waiting to be taken.

I put them back and walked over to the ensuite. The units were modern, full of clean lines. A bath was on my right and a shower beyond that, its glass door folded back and, in a basket next to the toilet, were a series of crossword books. I picked a couple out: some were almost entirely full, others newer and had barely been started; a pen with *Tarrington Motors* printed on it had been clipped to one of the pages.

That was where Paul had worked: a used-car dealership with showrooms all across the south-east, including the main branch in Croydon, where Paul had been employed as the sales director. I'd pulled finances for the Conisters through an old source I'd used as a journalist, and while they weren't rolling in money, they were doing pretty well: Paul was making £62,100 a year, plus bonuses; Maggie was on £38,983 as Head of English at a school in Putney; they had savings, a few, decent-sized investments, no debt, no suspicious activity in their bank accounts, and they'd been able to afford a £750,000 house in Wimbledon. There were bigger houses on their road, and there were better-paying jobs in their fields of work, but whatever had happened to Paul Conister, I didn't think it was to do with money.

I took some pictures of the ensuite and the main bedroom on my phone and then moved along the hallway to Katie's room. It was untidy, drawers still open, a few clothes spilling out, and her bed was unmade. At any other time, going through the underwear drawer of a twenty-year-old would have felt completely inappropriate, but this was just work: it was a black-and-white search for evidence, minutiae, any small clue I could use in my search for Paul Conister. When I was done with her chest of drawers and her wardrobe, I went to a series of canvases stacked against the wall, in the corner of the room. Katie was studying at the Slade School of Fine Art, and I could see why.

I dropped to my haunches.

She used oils and specialized in portraits. I didn't recognize most of the people she'd painted, but I recognized her father: he was right at the back of the pile, half turned to her, a smile on his face. It was clearly him: with what amounted to little more than a few brushstrokes, she'd brilliantly captured his slightly uneven nose, his thinning hairline, the stubble that was in evidence in all the photographs I'd seen of him, and the way it was darkest around the wheel of his chin. She had talent, that much was obvious, but perhaps that talent felt more like a curse now. I was willing to bet that it was the reason her father was buried at the back of the pile: she'd painted him so perfectly, it hurt her to look at it.

Again, I took photographs and then finished up in Seb's room: it too was a mess, but the mess was mostly centred on his desk, where there were videogame boxes, a television, a headset, an Xbox and a controller.

I went back through the rooms again, examining the windows, and saw that all of them – as Maggie had already told me – would have been impossible to lock from the outside. The main bedroom, as well as Katie's, looked out over the back garden, and directly beneath the sills was the conservatory. It went from one edge of the house to the other and, through the glass roof, I could see Katie on her phone, in the same seat as before. Maggie had moved outside, into the sun-dappled garden, and was cutting the heads off dead flowers. I watched them for a while, and then returned my thoughts to the conservatory: Paul must have got out somehow, but if he'd exited out of either the main bedroom or Katie's, he'd have landed on the conservatory. Would it have been strong enough to take his weight? Probably, but if he went that way, he would have dropped down into the garden, and – given that the living room and conservatory were joined, and that the TV was in the living room – Maggie would surely have seen him at some point. It was early April when he disappeared, so the garden would have been dark by eight thirty, but I still felt sure Maggie would have clocked the movement out there, even if she'd been engrossed in answering emails.

Unless he waited until she came looking for him.

That would have given him the opportunity he needed,

because while she was on the stairs, she'd have had no view of the garden or the conservatory, and he could have made a break for it then. But even if he had, it still didn't explain how he had re-secured the window from the outside.

I moved back out to the landing.

Seb's room was the only one that looked out over the front of the house: on the other side of his window was a slanted roof, which was much more accessible than the conservatory, and from there it was only a small drop on to the pillared porch, and perhaps another ten to twelve feet on to the driveway. As I studied this other route out, I realized that, if I was willing to believe that Paul's escape – for whatever reason – had happened here, it meant he'd made it out of the house that night by creeping *behind* his son without Seb ever noticing he was there.

I glanced at the desk.

At the games, the headset.

All of it was tucked away in the corner, and when Seb was seated and facing the monitor, absorbed in *Call of Duty*, his back faced the door and most of the window.

That made the idea conceivable, just about.

But, again, it didn't explain how the window was secure when Maggie had come up to look for Paul – unless I was willing to believe something much more troubling.

That Paul really *had* come out this way.

And his son had helped cover it up.

5

'Did Paul ever have any run-ins with anyone?'

I was back downstairs, in the heat of the conservatory. The sun had skittered behind clouds but it was still warm; while I'd been upstairs, someone had brought in a fan and now it was doing rotations, back and forth.

'No.' Maggie shook her head. 'Paul was quiet, understated, but he was fun. Like I said earlier, he wasn't the type to play big, elaborate practical jokes, and he wasn't the type of man who would ever choose to be front and centre of the action, but he had a great sense of humour.' She looked at Katie. 'Didn't he, Kay?'

A smile traced Katie's lips. 'It depends if you like dad jokes.'

But it was said with affection.

'He was just a really kind person,' she added.

'How did he find working in sales?'

Maggie could see where I was heading. 'You mean, you can't be kind and gentle if you're a salesman?' It was her turn to smile. 'I know, it seems an alien concept to me too, but Paul seemed to manage it. He started out at a showroom down in Leatherhead but he hated it there. They sold these rusted-out old bangers and he had to stand on the forecourt and pretend they were brilliant. That always made him uncomfortable. That was part of the reason he went for the job at Tarrington. Paul told me that, within the second-hand car industry, they'd always had a good reputation – honest, no sales crap, no hard selling, you know the sort of stuff.'

'And from there he worked his way up?'

'He was a good salesman – a successful one, I mean – *because* he didn't bother with the usual rubbish. People warmed to him and they trusted him not to screw them over. That was what got him the numbers, and eventually got him promotions.'

'So no run-ins with anyone at work?'

'No.'

'He didn't mention any difficult customers?'

'No, nothing like that.'

'Would he have done, do you think?'

She nodded. 'Definitely. Even as the kids got older, we've always had the rule that we sit down to dinner together, as a four. Dinner is where we tend to thrash things out, get things off our chests. Of course, we talk about lots of other things as well, but Paul would leave his work at the dinner table if he could, even if he'd had a bad day. He hated bringing his work home. Once we'd eaten, we'd just settle down in front of the box, or maybe he'd help the kids with their home-work, or he'd go upstairs and play *Fifa* with Seb – he was terrible at it, but he made himself learn the basics because he said it would only be a few years before both the kids had left home.' She paused, a tremor passing through her throat, be-cause her new reality had come into focus: eventually, the kids were still going to leave home.

And now it would only be her left behind.

I gave her a moment, watched her wipe her eyes again, waited as Katie brought a box of tissues over, then said, 'What about a social life? Did he go out with mates?'

'A little here and there,' Maggie said.

'He didn't have lots of friends?'

'No, it wasn't that. There was a whole crowd of them that grew up going to Fulham games at Craven Cottage, so he'd meet up with them and go along to home games on a Saturday. He'd meet up with a few of the guys at other times too, although a lot of them started their families later than us, so they're a bit more tied down. He'd have work events, the occasional dinner – he wasn't *a*social at all. What I meant was that he generally preferred quiet nights in. He liked to read as well. The dream for him was a holiday with the kids somewhere nice and hot where he could sit in the shade at the pool, with a big beer and a good book.'

I changed direction. 'When was the last time the police were in touch?'

Maggie took a long breath, as if the answer hurt, and then Katie said, 'Mum is too nice to say, so I'll say it for her: it feels like they've totally forgotten about us. In fact, they probably have. The last call we had from anyone was – what, Mum? May?'

Maggie nodded. 'Late May, yeah.'

Over six weeks ago.

'What did they say?' I asked.

'Nothing,' Maggie continued. 'They just told us they were still looking for Paul – but it felt like a lie and that's clearly what it was, because we've heard absolutely nothing since.' She stopped, obviously trying to control her frustration. 'Look, I know they have a tough job, but I honestly believe that part of the problem we've had with them is trying to convince them that it actually happened how we said it did. I mean, I called them about an hour after Paul went upstairs. That's how seriously *I* was taking it.'

'You only waited an hour?'

'Yes. I *knew* something was up. I mean, I've been proven right, haven't I? But I just knew. Paul disappearing like that. It wasn't normal. So that's why I called the police so soon after – and initially they were really good about it. In fact, they sent someone around straight away. I remember thinking that was one tiny crumb of comfort, because it meant they were taking it as seriously as we were – as we needed them to. But then, when this guy, this detective, started asking us questions, I could see it changing. He just looked at Katie and me like we were insane.'

I turned to Katie. 'You came home from your friend's?'

'As soon as Mum called me.'

'I remember saying to him,' Maggie went on, '"This is what happened – Paul went upstairs and he disappeared," and the guy was just, like, "I'm sure he did." I think, because it seems so bizarre and unlikely to them, they've basically written it off as some minor domestic thing. Like he got pissed off with us all and just walked out.'

'You said this guy was a detective?'

'Yes.'

'What was his name?'

'Uh, Fox,' Maggie said. 'Darren Fox.'

I wrote down his name. I didn't plan on calling him – not unless I had no other choice – but it was useful to build a trail from the night Paul vanished. I'd noted Fox's name down for another reason too: it was highly unusual for the Met to send *anyone* out in circumstances like this, especially after only a few hours. Usually, they'd ask the family to come to the station and fill in the missing persons report there. In fact, off the top of my head, I struggled to recall a single time I'd ever heard of this happening, and I'd definitely never heard of a detective being asked to do the initial form-filling, unless the victim happened to be especially high profile. The donkey work was always done by uniforms, then, if alarm bells started ringing, that was when it got kicked up the chain. I circled Darren Fox's name and said to Maggie, 'This detective – had you ever met him before? Ever heard Paul talk of him?'

'Paul? Why would he be talking about a policeman?'

'I don't know,' I admitted. 'Again, I'm just thinking aloud here.'

Maggie shook her head. 'No. Never.'

'Okay. And Paul left his mobile phone behind, is that right?'

Maggie nodded. 'Yes.'

'He didn't take anything – an iPad, a laptop?'

'No.'

'What about Seb?' I asked. 'He definitely didn't hear anything?'

'No,' Maggie said again.

'He didn't hear his dad out on the landing?'

Or actually in his bedroom.

'No, he was playing his game,' Maggie said.

'He's at school today, I guess?'

'Yeah. He finishes at three thirty, but he's got football from four until six. Did you want to speak to him? I'd be happy to bring him to you. You're only in Ealing, right?'

'Do you think he'd maybe have ten minutes after school?'

She shrugged. 'I'm sure he would. It's a school football match, so all he'll be doing is hanging around there until it starts. I can text him and ask him to meet you.'

'Great.'

'At the front of the school?'

'Wherever suits him.'

'I know he'll want to help you,' Maggie said.

I just nodded. *I guess we'll see.*

6

Seb Conister was every inch the fifteen-year-old boy: he followed a wave of other kids out of the school gates, one shirt tail out, his tie loosened, his shoes frilled with mud. On his back was a plain blue rucksack with graffiti – in what looked like white Tippex – all over it. He stopped, looking for me, and when I raised a hand, he trudged over, his dark fringe falling in front of his eyes.

'Hi, Seb. I'm David.'

I held out a hand to him and he shook it, tentatively.

'Where's the best place for us to talk?'

He glanced over his shoulder, to the crowds pouring out of the entrance, but I didn't see anything suspicious in it: not only was it likely to be embarrassing for him to have an adult waiting outside, especially in his fourth year of senior school, he was probably also keen to avoid questions among his peers about why. Maggie had told me that Seb had taken his father's disappearance hard, that he'd been bullied about it at school as well, and my being here could exacerbate both of those things.

There was a teachers' car park at the side of the school with a low wall circling it. I suggested we move there, where he was unlikely to be seen by any of his mates, and where he could still keep an eye on the football pitches.

'Thanks for talking to me, Seb,' I said.

He shrugged. 'Mum said I had to.' He looked up at me from under his fringe. 'I've got football at four.'

'I know. I won't make you late, I promise.' He glanced

from me to the football pitches as if he didn't believe me. I asked, 'Has your mum told you much about me?'

'She said you find people.'

'That's right. People like your dad.'

'Are you as useless as the police?'

'I wouldn't be standing here if I thought I was.'

'So they've just given up?'

'I don't know,' I said. 'I hope not.'

'But they have.'

'I think they've hit a dead end.'

'And you're going to find Dad, are you?'

'I hope so.'

He just shook his head.

'You don't think I can?' I asked him.

'I don't know. But it's a bit fucking late now.'

He looked up at me again. He acted like he didn't care about me taking on his father's case, or wasn't affected by the failure of the Met to find Paul, but he did. It was laced to the anger in his words. He was a kid who was hurting, who'd been hurt repeatedly since April, and he didn't know how to handle it. I thought again about the idea that he had some knowledge of his father's disappearance, that he may somehow have been involved, and – here, now – it suddenly felt less credible. He didn't seem like a boy who was harbouring a secret. He seemed like a boy who was grieving.

'Your mum said you didn't hear anything that night?'

He shook his head.

'You had headphones on?'

'Head*set*.'

'Headset,' I corrected myself. 'When did you realize something was up?'

'I don't know. When Mum came in, I guess.'

'Your dad hadn't been into your room before that?'

31

He looked at me like I was trying to trick him. 'No,' he said. 'Of course he didn't come into my room.'

I changed tack. 'Were you and your dad close?'

He shrugged again and this time I waited him out. When I didn't ask a follow-up question, his eyes shifted to me and he seemed so young for a second: a kid, scared and confused, wanting to hit out at someone, anyone, at any*thing*, but not exactly certain why.

'He was my dad,' he said softly.

I didn't say anything.

'I don't know if we were close or not.' He shrugged yet again: it was a defence mechanism, a way to cope. 'We had arguments about all sorts of shit – mostly about how much time I spent playing games – but, you know . . .' He halted.

He was my dad. I loved him.

'When was the last time you saw him?'

'At dinner.'

'So you finished dinner and then went upstairs?'

'I had to wash up. Mum and Dad always make us do chores.'

'Where did your dad go while you were washing up?'

He opened his hands out. *I don't know.*

I didn't blame him for not remembering: not only was I asking him to go back in his life three months, but what his dad and his mum were doing in the minutes and hours after dinner that night wouldn't have seemed remotely important at the time. It was just routine, and we look least closely at the people we know best.

'Can you remember what your dad was like in the weeks before he disappeared?' I got out my notebook and flipped to a page I'd filled with the answers Maggie and Katie had given me to the same question. *He just seemed normal,* Katie had said. *He was just Paul,* Maggie had added afterwards. *He never changed. Every day he was just solid. Dependable. He never pan-icked about anything, hardly ever lost his temper. He would always see clearly.* I'd underlined that last part, because somehow it seemed important: was he seeing clearly the night he went missing? Was that why he vanished so suddenly? What could have been the catalyst?

'He was normal,' Seb answered, echoing his sister.

'He didn't seem quieter? Angrier? More emotional?'

He shook his head.

'You don't remember him saying anything to you?'

'Like what?'

'Like maybe he was worried about something?'

'No.' Stark, definitive.

From a building at the edge of the football pitches, boys started to emerge. Seb noticed them and scooped his bag off the floor. It wasn't zipped all the way up and I could see an orange kit inside.

'I've got to go,' he said. He got down off the wall.

'If you think of anything,' I said, 'here's my number.'

I handed him a business card.

He took it, studied it for a moment and then glanced at me. This time, there was something different about him. I couldn't put my finger on what, but it passed across his face like a change of light, and – even though he already had his bag over his shoulder, and even though he knew he was going to be late for his football match – he didn't move. In-stead, he gently rocked from foot to foot, as if uncertain.

'Is everything okay, Seb?'

'I saw someone,' he said.

'What do you mean?'

'The night Dad went missing.'

I took a step closer. 'Who did you see?'

'I don't know,' he said, his voice trailing off. He'd been

33

staring at the floor, but now he looked up. 'It was before Dad went missing. I was in my bedroom, waiting for my friends to get online, and I looked out and saw a guy outside the house.'

'You didn't know who the guy was?'

'No. It was too dark.'

'You haven't seen him since?'

'No.'

I wondered for a moment whether it had been Darren Fox, the detective who'd come to the house that night, and whether Seb had got his times mixed up. Maybe he'd been mistaken; maybe he'd looked out and seen the man outside the house *after* Paul went missing, not before. But, if it had been, Seb would have recognized the cop as soon as he came inside the house.

'So what was this man doing?'

Seb shrugged. 'Nothing.'

'Just standing there?'

'Yeah. Just standing on the opposite side of the road.'

'Could he have been waiting for someone?'

Seb's eyes shifted again, out to the football field, and his expression dissolved. 'This is why I didn't say anything,' he muttered, 'because he *could* have been waiting for someone.'

'But you don't believe he was?'

'No,' he said, shaking his head.

'What do you think he was doing?'

'I think he was watching our house.'

7

On a normal day, Wimbledon to Ealing should only have taken me forty minutes, but it wasn't a normal day: traffic was backed up all along Gunnersbury Avenue, so it was after five thirty when I finally got home, hot, frustrated, and still thinking about what Seb had told me. I pulled on to the driveway to find the FOR SALE sign had fallen over for the hundredth time: it seemed a pretty accurate metaphor for the entire selling process. I'd had a slew of offers since putting the house on the market back in January, but only one – in March – had come remotely close to the asking price; I'd accepted that, and everything had gone like clockwork until early June when, a week shy of exchanging contracts, the buyer suddenly pulled out.

I righted the FOR SALE sign and headed to the house.

It wasn't that I hated it here – it was the house that my wife, Derryn, and I were going to start a family in, and her memory was still written into every surface – it was just that I'd had a case that had tainted some of those memories. It had tainted them so profoundly I couldn't get past them any more, and selling and starting over again somewhere else – albeit without the woman I loved – felt like the next best option.

On the floor, in the hallway, was a plain, brown A4 envelope. I picked it up. Written on the front was *Raker*. There were no other markings, but I knew what it was even before I ripped it open: a missing persons report, two months of mobile phone statements for Paul Conister, and the same for the landline at the house too.

I showered and changed, grabbed a beer from the fridge and went through to the back deck. Sunlight was cutting across the garden, painting one half of the decking a pale orange. I sat in the shade with my laptop and started with the phones. Both statements – mobile and landline – covered February, March and the days leading up to 8 April, when Paul went missing. I started with the mobile, because that was normally where the bulk of activity was located, but very quickly the search ground to a halt: I pulled my laptop in and cross-checked numbers on the statements with Google searches, and a lot of the calls were work-related. Personal calls tended to be with Maggie, the kids, and the friends Paul attended Fulham matches with, whose contact details Maggie had given me. There were a few question marks – numbers that I couldn't find an immediate match for, and which I would have to chase up – but I was surprised how little there was to get my teeth into. I was less surprised by how little there was on the landline statements: only six outgoing calls were made, all to Maggie's mother. Incoming calls were few and far between too: there had only been five, and four of the numbers were withheld, which probably meant they were sales calls. These days, decent leads in landline statements were virtually non-existent.

I spent thirty minutes on the phone to Maggie, and then another ten talking to a second contact of mine, ticking off the remaining queries I'd been left with.

Inside an hour I was done.

The phones were worthless.

I turned to the missing persons report.

Paul had vanished on the night of Thursday 8 April. The night before he'd been to a Tarrington Motors corporate event at a central London restaurant called Bartinelli's, on the bank of the Thames. I'd been to Bartinelli's before a number of times, so I could picture it clearly in my head. It didn't seem to have any particular relevance to what had happened to Paul – and had certainly never come up in the perfunctory investigation that DS Darren Fox had put together as a result – but I wrote it down as a possible angle to come back to if necessary. Maybe someone there might remember a conversation they'd had with Paul that didn't feel quite right. Maybe one of his colleagues noticed something odd about his behaviour.

Maybe someone had been watching him there.

My eyes drifted to notes I'd made in the car earlier, after talking to Seb. I'd written down what I could recall verbatim – and one line in particular caught my eye.

I think he was watching our house.

Could a man have been watching the house? Or was it just a false lead?

I went back to the missing persons report.

DS Fox had arrived at the house in Wimbledon at ten past ten on the night that Paul disappeared. There were no transcripts of any conversations between Fox and either Maggie or Katie, but that wasn't particularly unusual: transcripts tended not to make it into missing persons reports until the searches had morphed into something else – like a murder. Frustratingly, though, there were very few notes about anything else either.

In fact, the more pages I turned, the more disappointing the report became. Even without direct quotes, it was obvious from Fox's notes that he'd had a hard time believing that Paul had disappeared the way Maggie had described. Katie had been at a friend's house that night, so she was really there as an emotional crutch for her mum, and Fox's report seemed to confirm as much – he didn't write about Katie, or relay whatever she might have contributed. Instead, he focused his attention on Maggie, and her description of Paul's movements after he left her in the living room. What was surprising and disheartening, though, was that – in spite of him obviously having doubts about what Maggie had told him – Fox seemed neither to pursue an alternative explanation for how Paul had vanished into thin air, nor to home in on a possible reason why she might have invented such a complex and elaborate lie. The only thing that became marginally clearer was why a detective sergeant had turned up instead of a uniform in those first hours: in his notes, Fox said he wanted to see the house and talk to Maggie to try and find a simple explanation for what he called 'an impossible act'. He'd made it sound innocent enough on the page, but I was willing to bet it was more cynical than that: he'd probably seen everything that it was possible for a cop to see as a DS, but he wouldn't have seen anything like this. Which meant it wasn't a rank-pulling exercise, wasn't even really professional curiosity – it was purely rubbernecking. In turn, the big question mark was why he'd let the case fizzle out afterwards.

Or maybe he hadn't.

It was over six weeks since they'd last heard from Fox. This would have felt like a lifetime to Maggie, Katie and Seb, but it wasn't long for a cop who probably had at least one or two other cases in his in-tray. You only needed one of those other cases to be a murder for Paul's disappearance to be pushed down the list. Even so, I googled Fox to find out who he was, to see if he might be the sort of man who would forget a victim's family entirely, and I found my answer. In the press reports and statements from victims and their loved ones I found online, he seemed to have a good reputation – a 48-year-old veteran with a solid record of closing big cases. That suggested to me that he hadn't forgotten Paul Conister, he just didn't have the bandwidth to think clearly about his disappearance. I didn't blame Fox necessarily – he was bound to prioritize his cases – but a simple call to Maggie wouldn't have taken him long.

I closed the file and looked at the notes I'd made, zeroing in on one I'd written a few seconds before finishing the read-through: *Why would Maggie make it all up?* I'd thought about it a lot on the drive over to see Seb at school, and then again on the way home, and, while the question needed to be asked, it seemed like the answer was quite simple.

She didn't.

If you were going to lie, if you were involved somehow, why make the lie so confounding? The best lies were almost always the most straightforward. If you wanted to cover your tracks, you wouldn't make up a story about a man disappearing inside his own home. You would spin a yarn about him heading out suddenly, or not coming home one night. And not only that: it didn't feel like she was lying to me. It was entirely possible that she was just really good at it, but I'd spent my career as an investigator sitting across the table from liars and even the best would leave some trace of their deception behind: a brief look that felt like a glitch; an explanation that didn't quite fit – tiny cracks that you could get your nails into and start to pull apart. My sense was that Maggie was telling me the truth, and that meant I had to believe her: Paul went upstairs, then he vanished.

But how?

I thought again about what Seb had said, about there being someone outside the house the night that Paul went missing, and then grabbed my laptop.

Going to Google Maps, I dropped into Street View on Kilgor Terrace, the road on which the Conisters lived. I hadn't thought to look for surveillance cameras, not only because I hadn't spoken to Seb at the time, but because it was very unlikely there would be cameras on that road. Google Maps seemed to confirm as much. I went back and forth, moving from one end to the other, but failed to spot any CCTV.

London was the most watched city in the UK, with Hackney alone having more cameras than Bristol, Birmingham, Stoke and Liverpool combined. But the basic rule of thumb was, the more expensive the area, the spottier the coverage became. Chelsea and Kensington were the least surveilled of any of the boroughs, with a fraction of the cameras found in Hackney, and because Kilgor Terrace, and the area surrounding it, was dominated by expensive housing, my gut told me that coverage would begin further out. That meant main roads, schools, places of work and railway stations.

I spent an hour searching the roads around Kilgor Terrace, working in a series of concentric circles until I'd created an imaginary ring around the Conisters' street: the idea was to map potential routes that someone might take – on foot – after leaving the house, then the first point at which they'd stray into the eyeline of CCTV.

Eventually, I narrowed it down to three cameras: two to the south of the house, a couple of streets away, where there was a row of shops; and then one to the west, where there was a junior school and an adjoining play park. If Seb was right, the man who'd been watching the Conister house that night would have passed one of those cameras, whatever his destination ultimately was – and that gave me a chance of IDing him. There was a potential issue, and that was that Paul had disappeared over three months ago: few places retained recorded footage for more than a month or so.

But I needed to give it a shot.

First thing tomorrow, I had to try and find out who the watcher was.

8

I walked from the station down Wimbledon Hill.

Two streets south of the Conisters' home, I arrived at the row of shops I'd found online. One of the security cameras was at the far end of the shopfronts, where the stores became a residential road; the other was midway along, directly above the entrance to a wine bar. The wine bar was already open – doubling up as a place to get breakfast before 12 p.m. – but it felt like the camera at the far end might be the most useful: the watcher could have gone either south or west from the house, and if he'd gone south, he'd have had no choice but to exit by the shops.

The camera was mounted above a newsagent's, and inside, at the back, I found a guy in his late forties on a stool behind the counter, reading one of the tabloids.

'Morning,' I said to him.

'Morning,' he responded – and when he finally tore his eyes away from a story about a reality TV star in a bikini, he realized I wasn't buying anything. 'Can I help?'

'I'm investigating a disappearance,' I told him, and then left it there. It wasn't technically a lie, but it wasn't the whole truth either: normally it only took the word *investigating* to get people onside, and it was a tactic I'd employed repeatedly. I tried not to think about how deceptive I was being: people automatically assumed I was a cop, and I never dispelled the idea. 'That camera out front. Does that belong to you?'

'Nah,' he said. 'It belongs to the council.'

41

'Is that the same for the one above the wine bar?'

'I don't know, mate, you'd have to ask them.'

But it seemed likely, and when I headed back to the wine bar, I got my answer: it did. Both were council-owned and that immediately made my life more difficult. I wasn't going to be able to waltz in, asking to see footage, without going through the official channels. Even then, I had serious doubts over whether Merton Council would have the footage after all this time.

I headed back to the Conister house – it was all locked up: Maggie was at work and the kids were at school and university – and then followed the road west, along the only other route out of Kilgor Terrace. Before long, I'd arrived at the junior school and the play park. There were actually two CCTV units on the school itself: another was hidden under an overhanging roof on the side.

I made a beeline for the front entrance.

Inside, the corridor split: to my left was the reception area, to the right was a set of secure doors with a card reader next to them. Each door had a glass panel in it and on the other side I could see a group of tiny kids gathered around a teacher.

At reception, one of the staff asked if she could help. Again, I introduced myself as an investigator, and didn't bother correcting her assumption that I was with the Met, but I knew the duplicity could only last so long. The receptionist had got straight on the phone to the head teacher, and I doubted he or she would be so easily swayed. Even if they did happen to have all the video stored somewhere on site, they were unlikely to simply hand it over.

I waited on a sofa, surrounded by photographs of kids being taught by beaming teachers, and about ten minutes later a woman approached from the other side of the secure doors. She was tall, in her late thirties, and as a boy passed her, she said something to him, smiling at him warmly, and that gave me some minor encouragement: if she was sincere, reasonable, sympathetic, I might get somewhere.

'Mr Raker?'

I stood and we shook hands.

'My name's Jessica Aimes. I'm the head teacher here.'

'Thank you for making the time to see me.'

She gestured past me to a door just beyond the reception area. I could see her name on it. 'Please,' she said, and then asked if I'd like something to drink. I told her I'd take a coffee, and she asked the receptionist to bring one through.

Her office was small, the walls covered by shelves full of books and folders. She closed the door behind us and sat down in front of a window with a narrow view of the playground and the play park that sat beyond that.

'How can I help you today?' she asked.

'I work in missing persons,' I said, and passed a business card across the desk to her. 'At the moment, I'm helping a family here in Wimbledon: the husband and father of the family disappeared just after Easter.' I'd deliberately played all the most obvious notes so far: a local family, a husband, a father. I kept going: 'His name's Paul Conister. It's possible that you might have read about him in the local news. His wife, Maggie, is Head of English at St Barnabas in Putney. Her son goes to Heathpark School in Streatham. They just want some closure.'

It was a blunt and deliberate attempt to get her onside, but almost as soon as I'd mentioned the name Paul Conister I could see something change in her face and she started to nod. 'I know the family,' she said. 'Both of the kids used to come here.'

I hadn't known that, but I pretended I did, and I knew – if

43

I played this right – I could use it to my advantage. 'The police have . . .' I trailed off, shaking my head from side to side, as if reticent to criticize them. 'Well, I guess what I'm trying to say is that Maggie and the kids feel like they've been a little forgotten. Which is where I come in. At the moment, I'm trying to track Paul's movements in the weeks before he went missing, and as you've got two cameras on the building, I was hoping I might be able to look at some of your recordings – if they go back that far.'

She didn't reply immediately, so I waited her out.

Eventually, she said, 'Obviously, it goes without saying that we're dealing with potentially sensitive information here: there are privacy issues, for one – parents haven't signed off on a third party being given access to recordings of their children. And I hope you understand, Mr Raker, that there's simply no way I can let you remove any of the recordings from school premises.'

'You still have recordings from April?'

'We work with the council, who own the play park and the community centre on the other side of the boundary, there.' She pointed through the window to the park and a small, boxy building on the far side that must have been the community centre. 'There's been some issues with the community centre – some vandalism, smashed windows, that sort of thing – so they asked whether they could install a second CCTV camera on the side of the school to complement the one they've already got there. I believe they've been advised by their insurers to keep up to six months of recordings on disc because the damage is being done by the same kids, over a period of months.'

So they had half a year of footage.

Now I had to find a way to get a look at it.

'I completely understand,' I said to her, keeping my tone

neutral, controlled, 'and I wouldn't expect you to sign off on anything until you've talked to the relevant people – and Maggie as well, obviously, so that she can assure you that I'm legitim–'

'Don't worry,' she said, cutting me off. 'I know you're legitimate.' A pause; a brief smile. 'I was working at Newcross Secondary School back in 2011.' It took me a couple of seconds to catch up and, by the time I had, she was filling in the blanks for me, anyway: 'When you were looking for Megan Carver.' Megan had been an A-level student who'd vanished in a place called the Dead Tracks.

The search for her had almost destroyed me.

I smiled in return. 'That was a tough case.'

'I can imagine.' She looked at me and then leaned back in her chair. 'Do you really believe that Paul Conister went missing inside his own house?'

'I don't believe Maggie's lying, if that's what you mean.'

'Oh, no – that's not what I meant at all.' She came forward in her chair and, as she did, the receptionist knocked and then entered holding two coffee mugs. She put them down and left again.

'No, I didn't mean that at all,' Aimes repeated. 'I just meant . . .' She frowned. 'I don't know. It just seems so extraordinary and so incredibly sad. I never met Katie – she was already at senior school when I took over here – but I saw Seb in his last year, and I met Maggie a couple of times. She was lovely, and Seb was always a nice kid . . .'

I eyed her.

This was going somewhere.

And that was when I realized, in taking on the case of Megan Carver all those years ago, in bringing her family some closure, in almost dying for the cause I believed in and a girl I would have stopped at nothing to bring home, I'd inadvertently made an impression on someone else entirely. It was a slice of good fortune I could never have foreseen.

But, right now, I would take it.

Jessica Aimes pushed herself back in her seat and stood up.

'Why don't you follow me, Mr Raker?'

9

She led me to a staffroom further along the corridor. It was empty except for one of the receptionists, using a photo-copier. Beyond a series of tables – between a kitchen and some pigeonholes – was what appeared to be a cupboard.

Jessica Aimes unlocked it and stepped back to allow me past: it wasn't a cupboard at all. It was a surveillance suite, albeit on a small scale. There was a desk with a monitor, the screen divided into quarters: three of the quarters were for different feeds – two of them from cameras on the school and the other from one on the community centre – and the fourth was just black. Under the desk was a PC tower, its lights blinking. On a shelf above was a series of DVDs, stored in unmarked cases, with dates written on their spines. They were in chronological order and went back to February.

Aimes pushed the door shut. 'I know it's a very old-fashioned way of archiving files,' she said, and she was right: now that you could store everything in the Cloud, I couldn't remember the last time I'd worked with rewritable DVDs. 'The Department of Education paid for the cameras on the school, but they won't pay for any sort of digital-storage plan for this footage because it's a "non-essential" cost. Go fig-ure. But we can still write off DVDs as expenses, which makes zero sense.' She pointed towards the shelves. 'Anyway, as I mentioned before, there are some ground rules. You can't take anything away – you'll have to watch whatever you need to watch here – and whatever you do in here, it doesn't go any further than this room. Like I said, there are potential privacy issues.'

I nodded. 'I really appreciate this.'

She hovered for a moment.

I'd thought earlier that my work on the Megan Carver case, and Jessica Aimes being a teacher at Megan's school at the time, had just been a slice of good fortune – and it clearly was. But now I realized there was another layer, buried further down.

'My brother Eric,' she said, almost sighing his name into existence, and then she stopped again, as if she didn't know what she was trying to say. 'I've got three brothers. Eric was the youngest. He disappeared when I was eleven – went to the shop to get Mum some milk. They found him in a field next to the motorway a year later.'

My heart swelled for her.

'I'm so sorry,' I said.

She shrugged. 'It was a long time ago, but I remember, when Megan Carver disappeared, it brought it all back. And I remember watching that case closely, and reading about what you did – how far you went to find her – and I don't know . . .' She paused again, shrugged a second time. 'I guess I just wondered what it would have been like if we'd had someone like you looking for Eric. It could have been different.'

I didn't say anything, just watched her.

'I think the work you do, it's important.'

Her gaze lingered on me for a second and then she opened the door to the staffroom and headed out. I watched her go, then turned back to the shelves full of DVDs.

I took out the discs for April.

There were four – one for each week of the month. Paul had gone missing on the night of the 8th, so I took the second disc out of its case, opened the tray in the PC and loaded the DVD. It took a few moments, the tower under the desk whirring mechanically. There was no one in the staffroom – even the receptionist at the photocopier had now finished up – but I pushed the suite door closed anyway.

When the DVD icon appeared on the desktop, I double-clicked on it and saw there were seven further folders inside: one for every day of that week. The 8th had been a Thursday. I clicked on that folder and found a single MP4 file inside.

The footage started at 12 a.m. on the morning of the 8th and was in the same quarter-screen format as the live feed. The camera – on the front of the school – that had the best view of the road that the watcher had potentially emerged from was in the bottom left. A security light was permanently on at the side of the school and that was both a plus and a minus: it cast a pool-like glow across the pavements beyond the school gates, making it easier to see people walking past, but it was also in a lower resolution than the other two feeds, perhaps because it was an older camera. I remembered Jessica Aimes saying that the camera under the overhanging roof, to the side of the building, had been added later on, after the vandalism had become a more regular fixture at the community centre.

As I let the video tick on, I double-checked my notes: Maggie had said Paul went upstairs to get his blood-pressure pill at the first ad break in an 8 p.m. programme they'd been watching, so that probably meant between 8.15 and 8.20; when I'd asked Seb what time he saw the man outside the house, he was less certain, but it was before Maggie came upstairs to look for Paul – so, in all probability, that meant sometime between 7 p.m. and 8 p.m. In turn, that suggested the man had come into the road, at the earliest, around 6.30 p.m., and left, at the latest, around 8.30 p.m.

Probably.

It hit me again how big a punt this was: I was assuming Seb wasn't mistaken; I was hoping the man had entered and exited Kilgor Terrace from this end and not the end near the shops and the wine bar; and I was hoping, if he had, there would be some way of identifying him on film.

Trying not to feel discouraged, I kept moving the footage on until I got to 6 p.m., when I slowed it down to 2x speed. People passed, a few even entered Kilgor Terrace, but all of them were in either pairs or groups, or had kids with them. After a while, I heard a bell outside the suite and then voices in the staffroom. It was lunch. I kept going, shuffling in closer once the timecode in the corner got to 7 p.m. Onscreen, night had crept in.

At 7.47 p.m., a man appeared.

He was alone.

And he was heading into the Conisters' road.

I hit Pause, rewound a couple of seconds, then inched the video forward, frame by frame, using the cursor. He was in shot for a fraction less than six seconds, but it was enough: as he rounded the corner, into Kilgor Terrace, he passed under a street lamp. He'd already half turned by then, following the line of the street, so his profile was side on – and difficult to make out – but I could see what he was wearing.

Dark trousers. Dark boots.

A green raincoat.

The raincoat had some sort of logo on it.

I leaned in even closer to the monitor, trying to make it out. The logo was white and seemed to be vaguely shaped like a cross, or perhaps something like a pitchfork. I ran the footage on in real time, wondering if it might be clearer in motion, but the man vanished out of sight, into Kilgor Terrace, and I was no closer to any kind of answer.

From there, I let the footage continue rolling, dialling it up to 2x speed, to see when the man re-emerged from the road – but he didn't. By the time the day's video ended, at 11:59:59, he still hadn't reappeared. The reason seemed pretty clear.

He'd exited out the south side, by the newsagent's.

That meant I had a six-second look at him, so I rewound the footage all the way back to when he'd first come into shot and started playing it again. After the third or fourth time, I got out my phone and recorded the segment, then watched it back again. I took a shot of him – paused at the best angle I had – and fired it off to Maggie, Katie and Seb separately, asking if they recognized him.

As I waited for their responses, I ejected the DVD, returned it to its case and slotted the case back on to the shelf. Emerging into the staffroom and locking the door behind me, I noticed a few teachers looking up, but most were barely interested in me. Out in the corridor, I headed to Jessica Aimes's office. The door was open and she was on a call.

She beckoned me in and I sat down and watched the video I'd recorded of the footage on my phone. When I got to the best angle of the man, I paused it, then pinch-zoomed in on him: it didn't do much more than blur detail that I was already struggling to make out, but when I shifted back to the logo on his jacket, I decided it wasn't a pitchfork, probably not a tool of any kind: it looked much more like a cross.

My phone pinged as Maggie replied.

Katie and Seb followed soon after.

No one recognized him.

Maggie asked who he was, and then so too did Katie, but I stopped short of an explanation for now. This was a vague, perhaps futile line of enquiry, a search for a man who may or may not have had something to do with Paul going missing.

Until I had a firmer idea of his relevance, I wasn't going to start floating unproven theories.

'Any luck?'

I looked up. Jessica Aimes had finished her call.

'I'm not sure. Maybe.' I handed her the keys to the video suite. 'But, like I said, I'm really appreciative of you letting me see the footage you've –' I stopped.

'Mr Raker?'

I still had the image of the man up on my phone.

And the logo on his jacket.

'Mr Raker?'

'Sorry,' I said, 'just give me a sec.'

I swiped away the video, went to the browser and did a Google search for Tarrington Motors, Paul Conister's former place of work. The home page was slick, rows of cars scrolling left to right, a horizontal menu below it and a designed header.

I've found it.

The word *Tarrington* in the header had been shaped vaguely like a vehicle, the *T* like the spoiler on the back of a sports car.

It wasn't a white cross on the watcher's jacket.

It was the *T* of the Tarrington Motors logo.

10

Paul Conister's former place of work was just south of Croydon on a dreary trading estate. Most of the units belonged to much smaller businesses and were tucked away in a series of maze-like lanes, but Tarrington Motors was right out front, on the road.

Its fleet of used cars were lined up in three vast rows at the side of a flashy, glass-fronted showroom and, while the rest of the industrial estate appeared to have already descended into a pre-weekend slumber, the showroom and its forecourt were both packed. Even before I'd pulled into a parking space, I'd counted eight customers outside, all with salesmen, and there were at least ten or eleven others seated inside.

On the way down, I'd called Maggie again to ask her to take another look at the photograph of the man. I didn't direct her to the logo on his jacket, and she didn't pick up on it. Once again she told me that she didn't know who he was. The picture quality was poor, and so while I didn't blame her for not being able to ID the man, I was a little more surprised she didn't even clock the spoiler-shaped *T* of *Tarrington* on the coat. Paul had worked for the company for almost fifteen years before he disappeared: she must have seen that unusual *T* frequently over that period, even if she'd only taken it in unconsciously.

'Did you have much to do with the people Paul worked with?' I'd asked her as I'd driven down.

'Not really. Why do you ask?'

'I'm just trying to explore all the angles.'

A pause on the line. 'Is this something to do with Tarrington?'

'No,' I'd lied. 'I'm just ticking boxes here.'

That had seemed to satisfy her. 'To be honest, I didn't really know a lot of the people he worked with all that well. I went to his Christmas do a few times, but while everyone was really nice, you know how these things can be for partners. It was the same when Paul used to come to my school functions. It's a lot of polite conversation as everyone tries to involve you, and then people get on to office gossip and all you're really doing is sitting there, pretending you know who's being talked about, and laughing and smiling at the right moments. Quite a few years back, we both made a mutual decision to go to our work do's alone – it was a lot less complicated that way.'

That certainly explained why she might not have recognized the man, and as I parked outside the showroom, switched off the engine and grabbed my phone, a two-second Google search showed me why she might not have recognized the logo: Tarrington had had a rebrand at the start of April to coincide with the opening of a brand-new showroom in Sevenoaks. Only days later, Paul disappeared.

I headed inside. In the foyer was a wall full of pictures: the entire team at this main branch of Tarrington Motors, their names below. I got out my phone and took some photos, counting twenty-nine employees in all. Of course, it was possible that the man in the jacket worked for one of the other branches, somewhere else in the south-east; it was also possible that he didn't work for the company at all and had simply acquired the jacket for another reason. Maybe Tarrington had given them out to customers when they relaunched their logo, or he was a family member of someone who worked here. For now, I decided not to worry. Until I was certain that none of the people on the wall was the man I'd seen, this remained my best lead.

'Can I help you, sir?'

I turned to find a smartly dressed woman in her early twenties standing at my shoulder. On the lapel of her jacket was a name badge: CARLY WOLSTENE – SALES.

I handed her my card.

'Hi, Carly. My name's David Raker. I'm a missing persons investigator looking into the disappearance of Paul Conister.' I paused, watching her reaction. She clearly knew the name, her mouth forming an *O*, but I got the sense that she hadn't had many interactions with Paul, maybe because she'd joined not long before he went missing.

'I'd only just started working here then,' she confirmed.

'Okay.'

'But obviously it was terrible, especially for his family.' She seemed concerned that she'd come across as uncaring. 'I don't know how they've coped.'

'Is your manager around?'

'Yes,' she said. 'Follow me.'

She led me between a series of desks, towards a glass-fronted office in the far corner. On the door there were two nameplates: one said MANAGER, the other was blank. Inside, two desks faced one another, and as Carly led me in, I could see the second desk was unused and piled high with files.

A man looked up from the occupied desk.

'This is Leon,' Carly said. 'Leon, this man is an investigator. He's looking into what happened to Paul.' She glanced at me and frowned. 'Sorry, I forgot your name.'

'It's just there on the business card,' I said, pointing to her hands.

Suddenly, she seemed flustered.

'Thanks, Carly,' the manager said, as he pushed back on

his chair and came around the desk. 'Leon Hayes.' He held out his hand and we shook, and Carly headed back to her desk on the floor. I watched her go: when she got to her seat, she seemed to realize she'd just taken my card with her, and stared at it for a moment – 'You're looking into what happened to Paul?' Hayes was saying – and then, briefly, glanced towards me.

Our eyes met and she looked away again, and as she did I had the strangest sense we'd met before. Had we? Or was it my mind playing tricks?

'You're looking into Paul?' Hayes repeated.

'Yes,' I said, returning my attention to him. 'Maggie just wants some answers, so she's asked me to look into his disappearance again. It's what I do for a living. I find people.'

He glanced at the card I'd handed him. 'Okay,' he said, and wheeled a chair out from under the spare desk. 'Can I get you a drink?' I told him I was fine, and he slid back in under his desk.

'Was this where Paul worked?'

'You mean this office?' Hayes nodded. 'Right there,' he added, gesturing to the empty desk. 'Paul was my number two. We ran the whole business – all the Tarrington showrooms – from this room.' It could have sounded arrogant, but it didn't come across that way: it sounded wistful, if anything, and I got the impression that Leon Hayes and Paul were close, and Paul was missed.

Maybe it was the reason the desk was still empty.

I grabbed my notebook and went straight to a list of names that Maggie and Katie had given me of friends, colleagues, the crowd Paul had gone to Fulham matches with. Leon Hayes was on the list. So were a couple of others I'd seen on the wall out front. But because Maggie didn't come to work functions with Paul, or hadn't for a long time, she

56

hadn't got to see him mixing socially at Tarrington. That made people like Hayes important.

'It sounds like you miss Paul,' I said.

Hayes nodded. 'He was a good bloke.'

'Did you see each other socially?'

'Sometimes,' he said, 'although I wouldn't exactly call Paul a party animal. He liked to get home to his family and I didn't blame him for that. We work hard here, sales can be stressful: some people, especially the younger guys out there on the floor, they like to let off steam at the pub; others, the elder statesmen like Paul and me, we just like to get home, put our feet up and watch the box in the evenings.'

'Did the police ever come and talk to you?'

'Once,' he said, 'just after he went missing.'

'A Detective Sergeant Fox?'

'That sounds about right, yeah.'

'But you haven't heard from him since?'

'No. Nothing.'

I flipped to a fresh page in my notebook.

'Paul was just a nice guy, you know?' Hayes was saying. 'No bullshit with him. Customers liked him because they knew he wasn't playing them. I mean, basically the first thing we try to do when a customer comes through the door is re-assure them that we're not some stereotype of a car salesman – you know, just a bunch of wide boys who are going to bend the truth and promise the Earth until they get that signature on the dotted line. Paul was instrumental in creating that culture.'

He leaned back in his chair and began to swivel gently from left to right, his expression a little downcast. 'I've been trying to recruit another sales director since April,' he said softly, and then looked at me. 'That tells you all you need to know.'

'How did Paul seem to you in those last weeks?'

'Just normal. Not happier, or upset. Not quieter, or louder. He didn't seem any different. He was just . . .' His silence filled the gap: *He was just Paul.* 'What happened was a shock to everyone.'

'How did you find out he was missing?'

'When he didn't turn up for work, I gave him a call. It was unusual for him to do that – when he was sick, he would always phone in; when he needed to take a few hours off and work them another time, he'd always let me know. I trusted Paul not to take the piss. If he needed to leave an hour or two early, he'd come in an hour or two early the next day. That day, though, he never called in, so at ten, eleven – something like that – I tried calling his mobile. It just went to voicemail.'

I'd seen the call from Hayes on Paul's mobile phone statement.

'And what about after that?'

'I think I called him again at lunch, and then again in the afternoon, and when he didn't pick up, I remember feeling a bit pissed off – and I think a bit worried too. Like I said, it was totally out of character for Paul not to answer his phone like that.'

I knew from the statements that Hayes had made one more call to Paul later on that afternoon, which had finally been picked up by Maggie, and that too worked with the timeline: on the morning of the 9th, she went to the police station in Wimbledon, at DS Fox's invitation, with Katie, to see if they could fill in any more blanks, and then they spent a lot of their day there, only returning to the house at around 4 p.m. The call Hayes made to Maggie lasted about a minute, then, the next morning, Fox turned up at Tarrington Motors and spoke to Hayes, as well as some of the other staff.

I reached into my jacket pocket and removed a printout of the man in the CCTV footage. Before leaving the school and driving down here, I'd made a copy of the picture and then cropped out a lot of the surrounding scenery and zoomed in closer. I wanted people to focus not on where the man might be, but on who he was.

I handed Hayes the picture.

'Do you recognize that man?'

The zoom had blurred a lot of the finer detail, but there was enough to work with: the *T* of the Tarrington Motors logo was visible, and while the man's features may have become less defined the closer in I'd gone, the picture showed that he was tall – maybe somewhere between five-eleven and six-two, judging by the height of a nearby car – with a slim, possibly athletic build, and black or dark brown hair that appeared to be in a side parting. It was harder to put an age on him, but his build and his hairstyle – especially the way it seemed to be styled at the front – suggested to me he was in his twenties or thirties.

'No,' Hayes said. 'I don't recognize him.'

'He doesn't look like an employee here?'

He shook his head. 'I can see why you're asking. That's one of our jackets he's wearing, right? It's possible he works at one of our other branches, but I doubt it. I could name almost all of the people we employ because they have to come for their interviews here, and I'm always part of the interview process.' He stopped again, seeming to think of something. 'There's a way to check. All our photos are on our intranet.'

Hayes handed me back the photo and brought his keyboard towards him. I got up and went around the desk, and then watched as he went to the company intranet and clicked on a section marked 'Staff List'. Seventy-two names. Using a filter at the top, he deselected all female employees. That left a list of forty-one men.

He clicked on a view option so that the men turned from names in a list to a waterfall of photos, and started to cycle through them. 'Tell me if you want me to stop,' he said, but although there were a few men who bore a resemblance to the man in the CCTV footage, none of them looked a match. We went through them a second time, but by the end I still had no name. The man wore a Tarrington jacket, but didn't work here.

'What about former employees?' I asked.

Hayes looked at the image I'd given him and then shook his head. 'I'm pretty certain I haven't ever seen this guy before.'

I glanced out at the floor, frustrated.

As I did, my gaze landed on Carly Wolstene.

She was on the phone, half turned away from me, so I couldn't see what she was saying. But she was still holding my business card, still looking at it.

Eventually, she slipped it into her pocket.

I parked across the street from Tarrington Motors and waited.

At 7 p.m., Carly exited the forecourt in a red Ford. It was still light, the sun shining, so I let her get ahead of me before pulling out of the road. It wasn't long before she'd drifted back into view; she was following the dual carriageway north, in the direction of Streatham. That made sense: in the hour I'd spent waiting for her to finish work, I'd gathered what I could about her, including her home address, a top-floor, two-bedroom flat in Wandsworth. According to Land Registry records, she'd taken out a mortgage on it in 2019 – and I'd found out her brother, Miles, rented the second room.

She had Facebook, LinkedIn and Instagram profiles, but Instagram was the only one I'd been able to access. There were seventy-six photographs on there, going back to 2016. She wasn't a prolific poster, but every photo told a fraction more of her story. A few pictures showed her hugging the same man, albeit surrounded by groups of other friends, and I assumed that had been a boyfriend. The man stopped appearing in shots around 2019, pointing towards a break-up. After that it was shots of Carly with friends, on holidays in places like Spain and Greece, and a few of her with her brother and her father – the mother didn't appear to be around – and of the flat and changes she'd made to it. As I looked through them, I again felt like I recognized her, even though I had no idea where from. It was the rationale behind following her: maybe the reason she felt so familiar to me was also the reason she couldn't look me in the eye at the showroom, the reason she'd kept my business card.

Or maybe all of it meant nothing. She was a 21-year-old woman, basically still a kid: she wouldn't have had experience of investigators turning up, out of the blue, asking questions about a missing man. That could easily have made her nervous, or interested, or both.

Her house was south of Wandsworth Cemetery, in a long, leafy road with oak trees all the way down. Most of the houses were semi-detached and, as I turned into the street, I deliberately kept my distance, watching her Ford slow down next to a slash of kerb three-quarters of the way down. I pulled in myself, behind a row of other cars, and watched as she got out, locked her car and walked up the drive of a plain-looking house with a yellow-brick arch over the porch and skylights in the roof.

She let herself in.

I grabbed my phone and headed down on foot, walking right past the house to start with and only taking a cursory glance at it. At the end of the street, I turned right. I'd double-checked satellite images on my phone and saw that there was an alley running along the back of the properties, separating each garden from those of the houses that faced into the next street over. The alleyway was quiet and shadowed: that suited me fine. I headed down, using the wooden fences as cover, and stopped a couple of houses from Carly's where a neighbour had a long, low, trellised fence.

It gave me a clear view of her house.

I watched the top floor. It had two windows, although one was a bathroom and had frosted glass. I could see some bookshelves in the room next to it, a poster of a female model on the wall, and stacks of what looked like PlayStation boxes. It was possible it was Carly's – but somehow it felt more likely that this was her brother's room.

I headed back around to the front.

As I was rounding the corner, into the road, I stopped: Carly was coming down the driveway again, car key in hand. She'd changed and was carrying a laptop bag. Once she was back inside her car, she made a call. It didn't last long – thirty seconds, maybe less – then she started up the engine and began coming in my direction. I took a couple of steps back, using the boundary wall to hide me from view. Once she was past, I watched her all the way down to the end of the road.

She was heading north, towards the city.

I waited fifteen minutes, just in case she was only running errands. I doubted she was – why take her laptop if she was? – and then returned to the house. Under the porch, I pushed the button for Carly's flat.

No one responded.

I looked over my shoulder, out to the street, searching for windows that might overlook Carly's front door. It was really only the property directly opposite I had to worry about, and there were no lights on in there and no car in the driveway. I eyed the homes on either side of me too: someone was in next door – I could hear a TV on – but, even if they looked out of a window, there was no clear view of Carly's door.

I buzzed the downstairs flat, and then again a second time.

No one was home in either property.

I took out my lock picks.

Checking over my shoulder again, I leaned into the door and started working on the lock. It was a simple cylinder de-sign. It always amazed me how often the main doors on converted flats were this basic. I didn't know if it was just negligence, naivety or some psychological thing, a snow-blindness based on the fact that, in order to access the flats inside, you needed to go through two doors, not one. But two doors weren't twice as good as one if you could pop the lock on the main door inside a minute – and that was exactly what I did.

I checked the road one last time.

And then I slipped inside.

The hallway had a thin, grey carpet and two mail trays on a bleached sideboard. If there had been mail for Carly, she'd already collected it. Beyond was the downstairs flat, its door marked with a brass *1*. To my right was a staircase with a door marked *2* immediately at the top. I headed up and set to work on the lock.

It took me slightly longer – but not much.

I let the door swing back, into the flat. It opened on to a lounge-diner. On the right was the kitchen, through an arch; on the left was Carly's bedroom. At the back was a bathroom and the brother's room.

I moved inside, pushed the door closed and checked the street to make sure Carly hadn't returned. It was just before nine and the light was starting to dwindle. I had to be careful it didn't mask someone's approach.

Starting with Carly's bedroom, I worked as fast as I could. I wasn't sure what I was looking for, still wasn't certain that I hadn't got this whole thing wrong, and as I went through her wardrobes and drawers and found nothing, the doubts began to kick in again. I searched the bathroom, then the living room and the kitchen, and then checked the street again. The sun was gone. It was almost dark.

What the hell am I doing?

I headed back into the living room and looked around. On the wall closest to me was a series of photo frames, a collage of shots of Carly and some of the people in her life. I stepped up to it, studying her face, and again I was struck by the strong sense that I'd seen her before somewhere. But from where? Could it have been on a previous case? That was the only possibility I could think of.

I searched the flat again, trying to figure out why I couldn't shift the idea we'd crossed paths, and then I very quickly went around for a third time, taking shots of the rooms. Every picture was coated in grey, the entire flat in a half-light now. I didn't want to use the flash and attract attention from anyone on the street, so while the photos weren't perfect, they were good enough as a reminder.

And then I stopped.

Something caught my attention in the brother's room.

I hadn't noticed it to start with and it wasn't visible in the shot I'd taken, but as I'd backed away from his bedroom, I'd been able to see further under the bed – and now I realized there was something weird under there, in the corner, by the rear legs.

A square of differently coloured carpet.

I hurried back to the bedroom, shifted the bed away from the wall and got in behind it. There were two separate imprints in the carpet from where the legs had pressed against the floor. It seemed to suggest that the bed had been moved fairly recently and it hadn't been placed back in the same position as before.

I bent down.

The carpet in the rest of the flat was a flint grey, but the square was lighter. Almost the same colour, but not quite.

I picked up the square.

Underneath was an almost identical area of underlay.

Under that were floorboards, two of which were loose. I pulled one up and set it against the wall and then the one next to it. To start with, it was hard to make out what was hidden in the darkness – but then I could see the edges of a metal lockbox.

I lifted it out.

With the picks, it was easy enough to get into, and after I felt the latch turn, I raised the lid. Inside was a thin pile of headed paper and corresponding business cards.

It definitely wasn't what I'd been expecting.

I removed them.

On the letterheads was a name: ROBBIE AVERY BUILDING SERVICES. The cards were a match too: the same address, the same email contact details, the same website. They were both for the same business, and they looked legitimate.

So what was Miles Wolstene doing with them?

And why hide them like this?

I took a letterhead and a business card, pocketed them both, still trying to work out what was going on with Carly's brother, and if it might involve her – and, just as I'd put everything back and returned to the living room, I heard a vehicle pulling up.

Carly was outside.

And she was already locking her car.

13

There was no time to get downstairs without being seen. Panicked, I looked around the flat, trying to come up with a plan. I heard Carly setting the alarm, saw the double orange flash of the car locking, then the crunch of gravel as she headed up the driveway.

I glanced in at her brother's room again.

The window.

Hurrying through, I looked out at the back garden. It was a straight drop, no roof: maybe fifteen feet down, maybe even more. If I landed awkwardly, or too hard, I might be limping away, or crawling on my belly, or I might not be capable of leaving at all. Pressing up against the glass, I looked left and right, searching for a drainpipe.

It was on the right.

I heard Carly opening the front door.

Popping the catch on the sash window, I manoeuvred it upward, as quietly as I could. It was difficult. The house was built in the 1930s and the windows were all originals: time had made the runners gummy. They jammed and rocked and, as they neared the apex of their opening, made a squeal, like the cry of an animal.

A second earlier, there had been footsteps on the stairs.

Now they'd stopped.

She's heard me.

I didn't have time to worry about it. It was dark now, the garden black, but as I put a leg out of the window, I could see lights on next door and all along the terrace.

Carly had started moving again.

I shuffled around, so my backside was facing out, put my other knee up, on to the windowsill, and then dangled my left leg out, to where the drainpipe was. It had metal notches all the way down, securing the plastic to the render. As soon as my toe found one, I pressed my right knee into the sill and, with one hand and one foot on the drainpipe, and the rest of me on the sill, started to slide the window back into place.

I heard keys in the front door.

Punching the flat of my hand to the bottom of the window frame in order to get it the rest of the way down, it jammed back into place with a thump as the door to the flat opened. I didn't see Carly walk in: I was already on the drainpipe, feeling it straining to take my weight. I dropped down to the next notch.

And then I dropped the rest of the way to the ground. I landed hard. Shuffling into the darkness, under one of the windows of the ground-floor flat, I looked up and saw Carly come to the glass. My heart was beating hard, a fierce drumbeat in my ears. She didn't seem to notice that the catch on the window was still undone but her eyes stayed on what she could see of the garden, as if she sensed something was up.

For a moment, I realized how comical this might have been at any other time: a man escaping a house using a drainpipe. It was like a scene from a seventies sex comedy.

But it didn't feel comical now.

I'd almost got caught breaking into someone's house. I'd found nothing in the flat to tie Carly to the disappearance of Paul Conister. But I'd found something that felt odd: a box full of letterheads and business cards hidden under some floorboards.

Carly pulled the curtains across and I made my move, following the darkest part of the garden to a gate at the rear fence. The whole time I was still thinking about what I'd found under Miles Wolstene's bed.

Why was he hiding something like that?

And could it have anything to do with Paul?

It seemed a huge stretch, not least because I hadn't even found a connection between *Carly* and Paul, let alone between Paul and her brother – but as soon as I got back to the car, I grabbed my phone and put in a Google search for Robbie Avery Building Services.

It was an immediate dead end.

The URL of the website just brought up an error page. When I put the street address into Google – the business was apparently operating out of a road in Balham – I found out there was no street with that name anywhere in London. When I sent a test email, it bounced back; when I called the landline, I hit a recorded message that said the number was dead. Finally, I went to Companies House and searched there.

There was no Robbie Avery Building Services.

There never had been.

The business had never existed.

PART TWO

The Jump

14

On the drive home, I thought about Miles Wolstene, the fake business, whether he could have been the man in the CCTV footage wearing the Tarrington Motors jacket – given to him, presumably, by Carly – and then decided to call an old contact of mine.

Ewan Tasker was in his early seventies now, but for most of his career he'd worked in the NCIS, a precursor to the National Crime Agency, and then, afterwards, in the Met as a consultant. Back when I'd been a journalist, our relationship had started out as the purest form of quid pro quo: I tapped him up for database searches or for background checks; he fed me stories that he wanted put out into the public domain. We'd long since become good friends, though, and in fact I was due to meet him and his wife for a drink in a couple of days, at their favourite pub near Hampstead Heath.

'Raker,' he said when he answered, 'you're not cancelling on me, are you?'

'Would I do that to you, Task?'

'It depends on what kind of shit you've landed yourself in this time,' he replied. Tasker had seen the full force of some of my cases, and the impact they'd had on me.

'Sorry to call so late,' I said.

'It's not even 10 p.m. I've got plenty more UK Gold to go yet.'

Ahead of me, traffic began to slow.

'Would you have a second to check something for me?'

'A database search?' Tasker replied.

'Only if you've got time.'

'Yeah, I can check it remotely. Give me a sec.'

I heard him moving between rooms and heading to his office. As a consultant, the Met had given him login credentials for the Police National Computer, as well as the Police National Database, which held 'softer' intelligence – stuff like allegations about someone that didn't result in an arrest, or concerns passed on by social services or schools. The government was in the process of combining the two into the newly renamed Law Enforcement Data Service – but as with anything driven by the government, it was lagging behind deadline.

'Okay,' Tasker said, 'what's the name?'

'It's two, actually. The first is Carly Wolstene.'

I spelled it out for him.

I heard him tapping a keyboard and then, after a pause, he said, 'Carly Maria Wolstene. Born 4 January 2000. Do you want the address listed here?'

I told him I did and it was the address I'd already been to.

'Apart from that,' he said, 'there's nothing. She's clean.'

I tried to think whether that made things better or worse: if she was clean, it supported the residual worry I'd had all along that this was a blind alley, a lead based on little more than her pocketing my business card; on the other hand, if she had no record, it didn't necessarily discount her involvement in something or mean she was innocent – it just meant that she'd never been caught. I moved things on with Tasker and said to him, 'Okay, the second person has the same surname. He's her brother.'

'First name?'

'Miles.'

Again, there was a brief pause as Tasker entered the name. 'All right, this is a bit more promising.'

I felt a surge of anticipation.

'Miles Avery Wolstene, born –'

'Avery?'

'Yeah. Why, is that significant?'

Robbie Avery Building Services.

'It might be,' I said to Task. 'What else is there?'

'Born 17 October 1997. No actual recordable offences – no arrests, nothing in the way of cautions, reprimands or warnings – but there *is* something in the PND.'

'What is it?'

'A suspicion more than anything.' I heard Task tap a couple of buttons. 'Four months ago, his father died in Canary Wharf. He was head of HR for the AS City Bank group. Middle of March, this guy jumped off the roof of their building and landed on the glass roof of a restaurant about forty floors down. The whole family – including your Miles Wolstene – told the cops that the suicide came out of nowhere.'

'What was the name of the father?'

'Robert Wolstene. He was fifty-three.'

Robert.

Or Robbie.

'You said the "whole family" felt the suicide came out of nowhere?'

'That's what it says here.'

'So who does that refer to?'

'Both the kids, obviously, plus it looks like Robert Wolstene had two older brothers. They basically said the same thing.'

'No mother on the scene?'

'Says here she died when Miles and Carly were in their early teens.'

That explained why Carly's mother hadn't made it into any of the pictures that she'd posted on Instagram. I was more interested in the timings, though: Wolstene jumped off a roof in March – and then Paul disappeared less than a month later. Did it mean anything if one died and another vanished within four weeks of each other?

'Anything suspicious about the mother's death?' I asked.

'She killed herself in their garage. Carbon monoxide poisoning.'

'And forensics backed that up?'

'Yes. Apparently, she was a manic depressive, so something like that had been on the cards for a while. That's what it says down here, anyway. But I guess your brain – at this point – is fixating on the fact that Mum and Dad both took their own lives.'

It was an obvious thing to zero in on.

'We looked into that too,' Tasker said.

'"We" now, is it?'

He laughed. 'The royal "we". Yeah, detectives searched for possible links, but there didn't seem to be any. Her death was only a matter of time according to Robert Wolstene and her side of the family. But *his* death hadn't been expected at all.'

I saw a layby up ahead and pulled into it. Grabbing my notebook, I wrote down what Tasker had told me. 'So you said there was suspicion about Robert's suicide?'

'No, he jumped all right, and he left a note behind at home to tell his kids that he loved them. Hold on, there's a copy of it here.' He paused for a moment. '"To my wonderful children, just know that I will always love you." It wasn't the actual death that was suspicious, it was more that the cops don't seem to have believed that Miles was being a hundred per cent honest with them. Nothing specific – more a general air of distrust.'

'Was it something he said – or didn't?'

'Hard to say because there's no transcripts, but in the notes here it looks like they felt he was holding back on them. As in, maybe his father's suicide *hadn't* come out of the blue.'

I tried to bring it all back to Paul Conister.

What if Miles Wolstene was the man outside the house that night? It was a big stretch, based on no actual, provable evidence. All I knew about him so far was that he might be a liar: he'd created letterheads and business cards for a fake company, and the cops thought he might have lied to them, or held back, about his father's suicide. From photographs I'd seen of him, he was the right build and age profile for the watcher in the CCTV footage, and he would have had access to a Tarrington Motors jacket through Carly. But if it *was* him, could he really be the man responsible for Paul's disappearance? Why target Paul in the first place? Did he blame Paul for his father's suicide?

I looked at the names in my notebook and realized how little I still had, and how thin the case was. At the top I'd written *Paul Conister*. Lines were coming off to *Carly and Miles Wolstene*, and to *Robbie Avery Building Services*. I added *Robert Wolstene* under the names of his kids and put question marks next to all of them. But there was no direct line between Paul Conister and Robert Wolstene. The only line I could draw was from Paul to Carly, and only because they worked at the same place.

'Anything else on this Robert Wolstene guy?' I asked.

'No record, if that's what you mean.'

'You said he worked for AS City Bank?'

'Yeah, he'd been there since 2006.'

Idly, I circled his name, my mind still turning over.

'According to the background we did on him, Wolstene was also on the board at Fulham.'

That stopped me. 'As in, the football club?'

'Yeah. He was a non-executive director.'

The same club Paul supported.

I put the notebook down, thanked Tasker for his help, and then dialled Maggie Conister's number. She picked up straight away. It sounded like she was driving.

'Are you okay to talk?'

'Absolutely,' she said. 'I'm just on my way back from the gym.'

I flicked back a few pages and was now looking down at the list of names that Maggie had given me of the friends Paul had gone to see Fulham with at weekends.

Wolstene wasn't on it.

'Have you ever heard of a Robert Wolstene?' I asked.

'Wolstene?' she repeated.

I spelled it out for her.

'Oh, wait, he was one of the guys at the football, wasn't he?'

'You mean, one of the guys Paul went with?'

'No, not exactly. Robert Wolstene was high up in HR in some banking firm. I think he died a few months back, actually. I remember Paul telling me something about it. Anyway, Robert was on the board of Fulham for a long time, I think, and a while ago – this must have been a year ago, maybe more; I mean, it could have been much more – I remember he started talking to Paul about sponsorship.'

'As in, shirt sponsorship?'

'I think so. I just remember they met at some social function somewhere and then they got together quite a few times after that to talk about Tarrington possibly sponsoring the club. It didn't happen in the end. Paul said it was way too expensive.'

'You said "guys" earlier.'

'I'm sorry?'

'You said, Robert was "one of the *guys* at the football" just

78

a minute ago. So, do you mean Robert started hanging around with the friends Paul went to games with?'

'No. Robert's crowd were a separate lot. The blokes that Paul used to go to the games with were *much* older friends – they all went to university together. No, they had nothing to do with Robert. What I meant is, Robert had his *own* group of mates, they just happened to be Fulham supporters too – and I remember Paul met up with *them* a few times.'

'Do you know the names of any of Robert's friends?'

'No, sorry. I never met them. I never even met Robert himself, not face to face. He called the house a few times and I picked up, because I remember we spoke on the phone, but I never met him or the friends.'

I thought about the incoming calls I'd seen on the Conister's landline statements: there had only been five, and four of the numbers were withheld. I'd assumed they'd all been sales calls. But maybe they'd been Wolstene.

I tried to work out whether that mattered or not.

'I think there were three of them, though.'

'Three of them?'

'Robert's group of friends at Fulham. The ones that he introduced Paul to. For some reason, I've got the number three stuck in my head. I think Paul must have said there were three of them – plus Robert – at some stage, otherwise I don't know why I'd remember it.'

It was vague, but I made a note of it anyway.

'What about Robert Wolstene's kids? Do you ever remember meeting them?'

A confused pause. 'No. Why?'

'I was just wondering.'

She was quiet for a moment. I felt uncomfortable at shutting her down and keeping information back from her, but I needed to know where I was being led first. Maggie asked,

'Does Robert Wolstene have something to do with Paul disappearing?'

'Wolstene died before Paul went missing,' I said.

'Yes, of course,' she replied.

But it was obvious what she was thinking.

That wasn't the question she'd asked.

15

I got up early, showered, and then sat at the breakfast bar in the kitchen. I'd put all the pictures I'd taken – at the Conisters, of the CCTV video I'd watched at the school, and of the rooms of Carly Wolstene's flat – on to my laptop, and as the sun poured in through the front windows, I slowly started cycling through them.

I had a video and some stills from the surveillance footage of the unidentified man, and – after rewatching the film and again not being able to tell for certain if it was Miles Wolstene or not – I switched to the stills. They were no less clear, just frozen versions of the individual frames I'd cycled through in the footage, but I could zoom in and manipulate them a little easier. One particular split second focused my attention: it was just as the man rounded the corner, into Kilgor Terrace. For a brief moment, he was caught on the edges of a pool of light, formed by one of the nearby street lamps.

Only one side of his face was visible.

Even that was blurred: the further in I got, the more the image pixelated; the further out I went, the clearer it became – but the angle of his head, the way his face mostly pointed away from the camera lens, made it look a lot like Miles Wolstene.

I returned to the shots I'd taken inside the Conisters' and Wolstenes' homes, looking for things I might have missed, particularly things that might in some way connect the two families. The only thread I had tethering them together at the moment was the fact that Paul Conister and Robert Wolstene had known each other – had, according to Maggie, become quite friendly – in the months after Robert Wolstene had tried to pitch a possible sponsorship deal for Fulham FC to Paul. What happened between them after that?

Was it the reason Wolstene killed himself?

Was it the reason Paul eventually disappeared?

It didn't fit perfectly, given that, at the time of Paul going missing, Robert Wolstene had already been dead for nearly a month, but I couldn't discount the idea entirely. I also couldn't discount the idea that Miles Wolstene was somehow involved in both cases, and possibly in at least one death: his father's, and maybe Paul's too – because three months on from him vanishing, and with no sign of him since, it was a distinct possibility that Paul was deceased. Add the fact that Miles could easily be the man in the CCTV footage, and that his sister had worked with Paul at Tarrington Motors, and the questions were building.

There was something else that continued to bother me too: why I felt like I'd met Carly Wolstene before. I'd tried to tell myself that she must only *look* like someone I'd known or met, because I couldn't think where in my life I might have come into contact with her before. I'd compiled backgrounds on her and her brother, on their father as well, and not only did none of it ring any alarm bells – it did, genuinely, appear as if Robert Wolstene's suicide had come out of nowhere – I also couldn't see where their lives and mine may have intersected.

That meant I needed to keep looking.

Miles Wolstene was the assistant manager of a restaurant just off Leicester Square. I arrived at the house in Wandsworth early, to ensure I was there before either he or his sister had left for work. I parked in the next street along, and when I got back to their road, Miles was already on his way out. He didn't have a car and probably wouldn't have used one anyway: getting into the centre of London was easier on the train, even on a Saturday morning.

He walked ahead of me, headphones on, totally oblivious to what was around him. Outside the station, he paused momentarily to check his phone and then went from Wandsworth Town into Waterloo, getting the Northern Line from there. I followed him the whole way, keeping my distance, unsure exactly what I expected to find out. Once he arrived at work, he would be gone for the day, and that would make this whole tail worthless – but, more than anything, I just wanted to get an idea of who he was, how he looked, his behaviour and his routines.

It was obvious Carly and he were related. In the photographs I'd seen of them on Carly's Instagram page, I knew they shared the same green eyes, and had similarities around the nose and jaw too. He was good-looking like his sister, and both had the same build.

Nothing happened between Wandsworth and Waterloo, but as soon as we arrived at the Tube, on the northbound platform, something changed: he made for a specific carriage right at the end, despite four others being closer. As I followed him, slipping into the next carriage down from him, I watched him find a seat, swing his bag around to his front and fish out a copy of a book about cinema in the 1940s and '50s. I wouldn't have made anything of the fact that he'd grabbed a book, or gone to the end carriage, if I hadn't seen what came next: as the train slid out of the station, his eyes shifted from the pages of the book to a woman sitting opposite him. She was a petite blonde, strikingly pretty, and was reading a biography of the film director Robert Hosterlitz.

I knew Hosterlitz's work, and knew that his most lauded films, including seven-time Oscar winner *The Eyes of the Night*, were made between 1949 and 1953.

Miles had chosen his own book deliberately.

The woman must have sensed she was being watched, by both of us, because she looked up from the biography, first at Miles – who smiled at her – and then in my direction. I'd already turned away by then, my eyes on the darkness of the windows as we carved through the earth. But I kept my gaze on her reflection as she returned her attention to Miles. Instantly, he started instigating a conversation with her, gesturing to her book and then to his, and – for the first time – I felt a flutter of disquiet: to know what the woman would be reading, or at least the *type* of book she'd be reading, to know which carriage she'd be sitting in, that she'd be here on a Saturday – it would surely have required a period of reconnaissance.

It meant he'd seen the woman before.

He'd noticed her, and he'd watched her. He'd taken note of what she read, where she sat, what days she worked. None of that made him guilty of anything in the eyes of the law – not yet – but it painted a picture of who he was, and it was a picture way clearer than anything I'd had of him until now. Because he may or may not have been the man in the CCTV footage; the fake business cards and headed paper he'd hidden may or may not have mattered; getting close to the woman, bringing out a book he knew she would respond to – it could just have been an innocent way to initiate a conversation with her. Or perhaps there was nothing innocent here. Perhaps all of these acts mattered.

Perhaps Miles Wolstene was a fraud, or a liar.

Or something much worse.

16

I followed Miles Wolstene to the restaurant he worked at, a high-end Italian place just behind the National Portrait Gallery, and then watched him through the windows. The manager must have been off because it looked like Miles was in charge for the day: he spent the first ten minutes pointing waiting staff to different tables, and then another twenty writing out the day's specials on a chalkboard. Just before 11.30 a.m., he finally opened the doors. The restaurant didn't close again until 11 p.m., so even if he wasn't doing the entire shift, it didn't seem likely he'd be going anywhere for a while.

I headed all the way down to Charing Cross and jumped on the Tube again, switching lines at Waterloo. At Canary Wharf, I headed south across Bank Street, in the direction of the AS City Bank building. Four months before, Robert Wolstene had plummeted forty floors and landed on the glass roof of the restaurant next door.

It was another hot day, the sun contained and trapped by the concrete and steel, its light winking in every window. The weekend and blue skies had brought a different kind of crowd: tourists gawking at the skyscrapers, locals sunbathing in Jubilee Park, a few workers – casually dressed, their weekday suits cast off – moving in and out of buildings doing overtime. As I entered the restaurant's foyer, I was immediately blasted by cold from the air-conditioning vents either side of me. It was obvious why they were running full tilt already: without them, the temperature under the spider-webbed glass ceiling, even this early, would have been unbearable.

The trajectory of Wolstene's fall was easy enough to map. Looking up through the glass, I could see the rear of the AS City Bank building, and the angled kink at its flank. In order to land where he did, on the back arc of the restaurant roof, Wolstene would have had to have jumped from the south side of the tower. As I looked around the restaurant, which was starting to fill up for lunch, it became easier to imagine how horrific a sight it must have been for the patrons who were eating here that day. I'd found newspaper articles online in which witnesses had recalled the horror of it – calling it 'terrifying' and 'harrowing' and 'one of the worst things I've ever seen' – but, afterwards, and again now as I looked up at the roof for a second time, all I could think about was Miles and Carly Wolstene. What would their reactions have been like that day when the police came to tell them the news about their father? Ewan Tasker had been right about something the previous night when I'd called him: in the investigation the Met had put together on Robert Wolstene's suicide – which Task had now sent over to me – there was the definite sense that the cops felt Miles had left something out: some small but crucial detail.

The question was, what did that have to do with Paul?

I headed out of the restaurant again, back towards the Tube station, and then joined a queue for coffee on Reuters Plaza. As I waited, I grabbed my phone and went to the file Tasker had sent me, swiping through the PDF until I got to the section that contained the witness statements. There were ten from people who had been eating in the restaurant at the time Robert Wolstene landed on the roof, but it wasn't those I was interested in. I was much more interested in the statements the cops had taken from people who worked alongside Wolstene at the financial firm.

I'd been through them once, very quickly, before leaving

86

home that morning, but now – coffee in hand – I found a bench in Jubilee Park and started reading them more carefully. The vast majority veered towards the same basic conclusion: the person being interviewed didn't have any idea why Wolstene would jump to his death and had seen no indication, in the weeks beforehand, that he was depressed or contemplating taking his own life. In fact, quite a number of them suggested that Robert Wolstene was incredibly social, even extroverted, and would often entertain co-workers with stories about the things he'd been up to, or the gossip he'd heard. Again, that seemed to play into the idea of his suicide being a real bolt from the blue.

There was one interview that gave me pause, though.

Guy Miertans had worked in the same team as Wolstene, was originally from Belgium but had been in London for almost eight years, and had sat next to Wolstene for five of those. He said the two of them had got to know each other pretty well, without it necessarily becoming a proper friendship. He repeated much of what I'd seen already about Wolstene – the gregarious nature of his personality, how the suicide had come out of nowhere – but then, below the last lines of his statement, one of the cops who'd been a part of the investigation had written a note at the bottom of the page.

It said: *Mira Ibragimova.*

Under that was an address and a mobile phone number.

I moved forward in the file and then went back to the start, trying to find mention of the same person, but there was nothing, so I googled her. This time I got a few hits, including a Facebook profile; other pages below were entirely in Cyrillic. The Facebook profile *was* for a Mira Ibragimova, though, and there was a photograph of her – she was pretty, dark-haired, in her late twenties or early thirties. Otherwise, all I could see was her 'Current Home City and Town' listing – London – because her privacy settings were preventing other information from being on public view.

Returning to the search, I took a quick look at some of the pages in Cyrillic using Google Translate. Most, even translated, seemed unrelated to Mira Ibragimova, and only came up in a search because they included one of her names, so inside a few minutes I was back to where I started: with a name and a number at the bottom of a police investigation – and no idea how she could relate to Paul Conister.

Maybe because she doesn't.

If Mira Ibragimova was relevant to any of this, it was because she was somehow pertinent to the suicide of Robert Wolstene, not to the disappearance of Paul almost a month later. I'd been through Paul's life exhaustively the night he vanished, his phone calls and activity before that, his work, his friends, and the name Mira Ibragimova hadn't come up once.

Again, I wondered if any of this mattered, and then looked up from my phone, across Bank Street, to the restaurant. *Well, I've come this far.* The only outstanding line of enquiry here was the name Mira Ibragimova: the suicide of Robert Wolstene appeared pretty unequivocal, even if the cops felt Miles had been holding back on them, and nothing else directly linked Paul Conister to any of this.

Maybe Mira Ibragimova did.

I dialled her number. It rang three times and then hit voicemail: 'Hello, this is Mira,' a soft, heavily accented voice said. 'Sorry I've missed your call. Please leave me a message.' The line sounded a sharp beep, but I hung up.

I looked at her address.

She lived in a flat towards the southern end of the Isle of Dogs, close to the Greenwich Foot Tunnel. That was barely thirty minutes' walk from where I was now.

I decided to take a chance on her being home.

17

The flat was in a four-storey building overlooking Island Gardens.

I buzzed Mira Ibragimova's third-floor flat.

As I waited, I went to my phone and dug out the file on Wolstene's suicide, rechecking it for any other mention of Ibragimova that I might have missed. But the only page on which her details appeared was at the bottom of the interview with Guy Miertans, Robert Wolstene's co-worker.

The pages of the PDF were scans of the physical file, which was why the handwritten notes were visible. I much preferred this version: the investigation on the database was, in theory, supposed to mirror the physical one exactly – and, in fact, in most ways, supersede it – but a lot of cops, especially older ones, still preferred to work on paper first. I understood why: paper helped you see more clearly, and especially to find the tethers between apparently unconnected people and events. The fact that Ibragimova's name had been added to the bottom of the interview with Guy Miertans suggested that one of the investigators had found a link to her, had maybe even spoken to her, but it had ultimately led nowhere.

'Yes?'

I looked up.

A woman was leaning out of a third-floor window.

'Mira?'

'Yes? Can I help you?'

'My name's David Raker,' I said.

It was hard to see her clearly: half her face was hidden behind the open window and the glass was reflecting wisps of cloud in the sky. I took a small step to my left to get a better view of her.

'I'm an investigator,' I said.

She didn't react.

'I was hoping to talk to you.'

'About what?'

'Robert Wolstene.' This time there was a flicker of something in her face, but she was trying hard not to show it. 'I really would appreciate a few minutes of your –'

She pulled the window shut.

Well, that's a good start, I thought, and glanced across to the park. There were a few people looking over, obviously having caught the tail end of the conversation. I stepped away from the door, thinking about where I went next, about the expression on Mira Ibragimova's face when I'd mentioned Wolstene's name. I had her number, so I could call her, try to talk her around, but that relied on her actually picking up.

The door buzzed.

I looked at it, surprised, and when I moved inside and went to the stairs, peering up through the spiral of the stairwell, I could see Mira looking down at me, her dark hair cascading past her face.

'Okay,' she said simply, and disappeared back inside.

I took the stairs two at a time. She'd left her door open, and a block of sunlight was pouring out, into the corridor, exposing every blister on the wall and blemish on the carpet. Her flat was different, though, small but clean and very modern, a total contrast to the communal hallway. She was running a fan on a side table next to a couple of smart grey sofas, and another on the worktop of a neat, black and brushed-chrome kitchen; on the right was a bedroom, its pastel curtains billowing as the wind passed through an open window.

I pushed the door shut and, when I turned, saw that she had stopped behind one of the kitchen worktops, as if she wanted a solid object between us. I smiled at her, trying to reassure her that I didn't pose any threat – but it made me wonder what might make her feel so on edge.

'Thank you for speaking to me,' I said to her.

'This is about Robert?'

'Yes. Well, partly about him.'

This time, she frowned.

'I'm trying to find a man called Paul Conister.' I paused, waiting to see if she responded to the name, but there was no movement in her eyes, no shift in her expression like last time. 'Paul and Robert knew each other, so I've been looking into Robert a little bit – and, in the investigation into his suicide, your name is listed.'

'I worked at ASCB with Robert.'

She still seemed nervous.

'Could we maybe sit?' I asked.

'Oh.' She gestured to the sofas. 'Yes.'

She came out from behind the worktop for the first time, and I saw that she was wearing a pair of cropped leggings, and a thin, long-sleeved white top with a floral pattern on a single breast pocket; just sneaking out from under her left sleeve was the tail of a tattoo in deep red.

'Would you like something to drink?'

'Something cold would be lovely,' I responded.

'I have some iced tea.'

'That sounds great.'

For the first time, the hint of a smile flitted at the corners of her lips, though it was more polite than warm, and while she prepared the drinks, I looked at a photograph on the wall

91

of her as a girl, wedged between a couple who – judging by their physical similarity to her – must have been her parents. Next to that was a second, almost identical shot of her and her father, his arm around her shoulders; he was darker than her mother, more bronzed, and Mira had inherited his skin colour.

She brought over our drinks.

'Are those your parents?' I asked.

She glanced at the pictures. 'Yes.'

'Are they here in London with you?'

'No,' she said. 'I came here by myself.'

She spoke excellent, heavily accented English, her words precise and correct. It was clear that she didn't want to talk about her parents, that there was a story there that she didn't have the desire to delve into. I slid a photograph of Paul Conister across a low table towards her.

'As I mentioned, I'm an investigator. I find people.'

'When they disappear?'

'Exactly. I'm looking for him at the moment.' I gestured to the picture of Paul.

She picked up the photo. It was a shot that Maggie had given me of Paul on a hike in the Derbyshire Dales, the view beautiful and rugged behind him. He had one foot up on a stile, seemingly amused about something that had happened off-camera.

'Do you recognize him?' I asked.

She shook her head. 'No.'

I took the picture back from her and said, 'The reason I'm asking about Paul is because he went missing just after Easter and no one's seen him since. So I'm trying to look at the people he might have had contact with, even a couple of years back, to see if anyone might be able to help me under-stand where he went. And one of those people is Robert

Wolstene, because I'm told that Paul and Robert got quite friendly.'

'I wouldn't know,' Mira said.

'I understand. I just need to find out more about Robert, and your name was listed in the police investigation that looked into his suicide. I understand that he was head of HR?'

She nodded. 'Yes.'

'And you worked in HR too?'

'Sort of,' she said. 'I didn't work directly in human resources, more alongside them. I helped develop a new database, which we pushed out across the whole UK business.' She shrugged. 'It's very boring, but it's specialist. It was how I got my visa. I did a similar job in Ukraine.'

'That's where you're from?'

'No, not originally. I moved there when I was eighteen.'

'From where?'

'Turkmenistan.'

I looked from her to the photograph of her father. I didn't know much about Turkmenistan, but I knew it was repressive: a police state on the Caspian Sea run by an autocrat, most of its people impoverished, its media a propaganda tool and any hint of opposition crushed. I remembered reading about how, in 2018, the Turkmen government had started trying to prevent people under forty from leaving the country entirely because so many of them were trying to get out. Mira had arrived in London before that, because she'd been here long before Robert Wolstene died, but it did make me wonder whether there was a story buried beneath her history somewhere: whenever she looked at the photos of her parents, her expression changed subtly. Sadness maybe. Or pain.

'So you worked in the same office as Robert?'

'Yes,' Mira said. 'I sat opposite him.'

93

'You said that was why the police talked to you?'

'They came in a couple of days after he died and asked us all questions about Robert.'

'What sort of questions?'

'You know, if he seemed depressed, upset, that sort of thing.'

'How many people are in your department?'

'There are ten people in HR and two of us on the database side of things. They asked us questions individually and as a group. It wasn't just me that they spoke to.'

That was true: they'd spoken to Guy Miertans, whose statement I had read, but if anyone else in HR had been interviewed, their statements hadn't been added to the case file, presumably because they hadn't provided anything of any real interest. So why had Mira's name, address and mobile number been added? What made them want to remember her?

'So Robert's suicide came completely out of nowhere?' I asked.

'I don't think any of us expected it.'

'How many times did you speak to the police?'

'Just once.'

'Just that one time they came into the office?'

'Yes,' she said.

'It's just, I'm trying to figure out why the police would have come to your office and spoken to all twelve of you – but only included a statement from Guy Miertans.'

'Guy was Robert's – how do you say?'

'Right-hand man?'

'Yes. Like, his deputy.'

That explained why Guy Miertans's statement was included: it was a kind of umbrella account for the whole department; how everyone in HR had felt at the time.

So why had the cops included Mira's details as well?

94

'Did you ever meet Robert's kids?'

'His kids?' She seemed thrown by the question. 'No, never.'

'You were never introduced to Miles or Carly?'

'No.' There was frustration in her voice now.

'Why would the cops include your name in the file?' I said to her gently.

'They talked to everyone there.'

'But didn't include anyone else's name.'

'I don't know, then.'

'Are you sure?'

She frowned. 'What do you mean?'

'I'm not accusing you of anything. All I want is the truth.'

'I'm telling you the truth.'

'Okay.'

'I *am*.'

'Okay. I believe you.'

'I just . . . I don't . . . I don't know what you're . . .' She trailed off, suddenly unable to hold my gaze. Her head dropped.

'Mira?'

She didn't look up. Her fingers were linked together on her lap, her palms up, her nails painted a faint pink. As she moved her hands against one another, the sleeves of her top rode up again, and for a second time I glimpsed the tattoo on her wrist.

'Mira, it's okay.'

'I don't know anything,' she said quietly.

Except this time it felt like she was lying.

'Mira, you're not in any trouble.'

'I don't know anything,' she repeated.

'I mean it. I'm not with the police. Anything you tell me won't go further than this room, I can absolutely promise you.'

This time, she didn't respond.

'Mira, I promise you, you're not –'

She said something, almost inaudibly.

'What was that?'

She said it again, her head still down.

I leaned forward. 'Mira,' I said quietly, 'I can't hear you.'

'I don't want to go back,' she said.

I didn't say anything, just watched her.

Finally, slowly, she looked up. Tears were running down her cheeks in a series of stained paths that snaked towards her mouth. She didn't wipe them away, didn't even attempt to. She just said, 'I don't want to.'

'Go back?' I said. 'You mean, go back to Turkmenistan?'

'Yes.'

'I thought you had a visa?'

'I do.'

'Then I don't think that's going to happen.'

'He said he would make sure it did.'

I frowned. 'Who? Robert Wolstene?'

She nodded, almost imperceptibly. 'He said he'd get me deported.'

'Why?'

She wiped her eyes.

'Why would Robert threaten to get you deported?'

'Because I knew who he was.'

'Who he was?'

'Who he *really* was.' She squeezed her eyes shut. 'A monster.'

18

She studied me for a moment, as if deciding whether she could trust me.

'Mira, it's okay.'

And then, still not saying anything, she moved her arm to her lap, palm facing up. From under her sleeve, the tattoo crept out again.

Except now I realized it wasn't a tattoo at all.

It was a scar.

Something heavy settled in the pit of my stomach.

A monster.

'What did he do to you?' I asked her. I tried to keep my voice small, benign, but her expression was so stark and frightened, it hurt to even look at her. Whatever she'd buried began to ripple out across her face. 'It's okay, Mira,' I said to her again, but it was a reassurance that was months too late. Wolstene's damage was already done.

It was still being done, even now.

'He . . .' She stopped, swallowed.

I studied her arm again.

'He hurt me.'

The scar looked like it had been made with a knife.

'It started off . . .' It seemed like she wasn't going to be able to form the words, but then she took a breath, her eyes returning to me, and there was a flash of steel in her face; the kind of strength that an eighteen-year-old would have had to have shown to flee the country of her birth. 'It began with small things,' she said. 'I would catch him looking at me in the office, or – when something needed doing – he would sit next to me, but too close. He would stare at my legs or my breasts. I'd worked with men like that before. I mean, I came from a country where men did and said whatever the hell they wanted to. I hoped it would be better once I got to the UK but it's not. It's the same. The men here, they all behave the same way.'

She looked away for a second and, when her gaze came back to me, I could barely meet it. *I'm not one of those men*, I wanted to say to her, because I really, truly believed – *knew* – that I wasn't. But any denial would have been meaningless, in fact little more than an insult: her belief had been trampled, her trust had been shattered. She didn't want to hear another man try to tell her that he was different from the others.

'We had a Christmas party,' she said, and then stopped.

It wasn't hard to imagine where this was going.

'He'd been making comments for weeks, especially when it was just the two of us in the office alone. He kept telling me I had a "spectacular body".' She brought her legs up to her stomach, as if trying to shrink herself. 'To start with, I just . . .' She waved her arm around, searching for the right word. 'I just tried to brush it off.'

'What sort of thing did you say?'

She shrugged. '"Thank you" to start with, because I thought he just wanted me to take it as a, you know . . . as a . . .' *Compliment*. Her English was still exemplary, easily as good as a native speaker, but as she became more upset, she was starting to lose sight of individual words. 'After a while, I said to him, "You shouldn't be saying things like that," and when he *still* didn't take the hint, I told him I didn't like it and I wanted him to stop.' She reached over to a side table and took out a tissue. 'He didn't like that. It upset him.'

'Upset him how?'

'It made him angry.'

'Did anyone else see this?'

'The anger?' she said. 'No. It was always when we were alone.'

'And it came to a head at the party?'

'*Before* the party,' she said, and fell silent. This was it. This was the night she didn't want to go back to. 'We all got changed at the office. I worked for another thirty minutes after everyone else stopped, so I wasn't quite ready, and told them I'd meet them in the bar of the hotel the party was in. It was only across the footbridge, on Marsh Wall. Five minutes' walk from our office, maybe not even that.'

For a moment, the flat was quiet again.

Just the whirr of the fans.

The hum of people in the park.

'I thought the office was empty, but it wasn't. He was still there.' She looked at me, her eyes shimmering. 'I came out of the toilet and he grabbed me. I didn't know what was going on to start with. He was just . . .' Images were flashing in her head. I couldn't see them but I knew they were there. 'He was just so strong. He had me up against a wall before I even knew what had happened. I couldn't fight back. He was crushing my face against the wall, I had an arm trapped under me. I tried to grab him with my hand, to get hold of his hair – but then he . . . then he . . .' She started crying.

'Take your time, Mira.'

But, in this moment, words were worthless.

'He tore my dress,' she said. 'He ripped it all here.' She traced a line with her finger, from knee to hip. 'Then he . . .' A beat. 'He started trying to pull my legs apart . . .' A second beat. 'He got my underwear down but I managed to fight him off, and I kicked him. I just kicked whatever part of him was nearest – it was more like a, you know, a jab. I had stilettos on. I jabbed with the heel, you know?' She mimicked the movement. 'I caught him high up, at the top of his thigh, and it hurt him, because he started swearing at me and there was blood on his trousers. I screamed at him. I told him I was going to go to the police and tell them everything, and that was when he said he'd get my visa taken away.' She ground to a halt again, blinking a couple of times; a fresh tear trail snaked down the side of her face. 'He said, if I did, he would deny everything and tell the police that I was lying, that I was doing it to protect myself, because my visa had been obtained illegally and he'd found out. He'd tell them I'd lied during the application process, that I didn't have the skills I claimed to have and that the visa shouldn't have been granted. He'd tell them that he'd found out and was about to tell management at ASCB, and that was why I'd started making up lies about him.'

Basically, he'd played on her worst fear.

Being sent home.

'I can't go back to Turkmenistan,' she said, her voice quiet, her eyes skirting to the picture of her father. 'If I go back . . .' She shook her head. 'If I go back, I'm dead.'

'Why?'

'My father was a journalist. He worked on a radio station, broadcasting in Turkmen. It was banned by the government, but they kept on broadcasting in secret until one of the people that worked there informed on my father. After that, he . . .' She paused. 'He got taken away and we never saw him again. I was sixteen. At seventeen, they took my mother away too, because they said she was communicating with anti-government organizations in Russia. She wasn't, she'd just made a phone call to my uncle in Volgograd. The last thing she said to me was that I needed to get out before they came for me too.' She started to cry again. 'They dragged her out of the door. I can see it like it was yesterday. They dragged her out and left me alone. I was just a child.'

She dabbed at her eyes with a fresh tissue and then pulled her legs out from under her again. I thought she was about to get up, to get herself another drink, but instead she glanced at me uncertainly, as if doubts about me were playing on her, even now. But then she shuffled her sleeve all the way up.

Now I could see the wound clearly.

It had scarred over, but it was still fierce, a worm of pink and red that seemed to zig-zag from her wrist all the way up to the crease in her elbow. It didn't take me long to realize something even worse.

There wasn't one wound.

There were at least ten of them.

'He did that to you?' I asked.

'It was always how he kept me still. He would cut me once and then threaten to do it again if I moved.'

Two sentences that seemed to suck the light out of the room. And just as I was trying to process the terrible suffering Mira Ibragimova had endured – not just in London: at home, where her parents had been ripped from her when she was still just a kid – she reached down to the hem of her leggings and began to pull them both up.

There were more cuts on her legs.

'Why didn't you tell the police what he did?'

'I was scared,' she said, and that must have been why the police had written her name down. They'd seen a tiny flash of something in the chat they'd had with her. Maybe they hadn't thought she was scared. Maybe they'd thought she was lying. But that was why her name was in Wolstene's file.

'I understand you were frightened,' I said, 'but by the time the police came to talk to you, Wolstene was already dead.'

'I didn't want to go home.'

She started to cry again.

'I didn't want anyone to look at me closely,' she sobbed. 'I didn't want anyone to look at my work history, or my visa, or anything about me. I didn't want them to investigate me in case there *was* something, some tiny thing that the government had accidentally overlooked when they'd given me my visa. I can't go home. I *can't.*' She stopped, glanced at me. 'I just want to forget,' she muttered. 'I just want to be normal.'

Except things were never going to be normal.

And Mira would never forget.

19

I got the train back to Leicester Square and then headed to the restaurant where Miles Wolstene was working. The whole way I was thinking about Mira, about all that she'd revealed, the anger burning a hole in my chest. I'd promised her that nothing she told me would go further than the room – it was most of the reason she'd agreed to trust me – but now I couldn't think of anything worse than keeping her suffering a secret.

If I stayed silent, she would never get justice.

If I told someone, I betrayed her.

As I hurried down Charing Cross Road, I tried once again to draw lines back to the disappearance of Paul Conister, and this time I found a potential tether. What if Miles *was* the man that Seb had seen waiting outside the house on the night Paul had vanished – and, increasingly, I was becoming certain that he was – and the reason he was there that night, the reason he targeted Paul, was because Paul had discovered Wolstene's secret? I didn't know how Paul would have found out – how he first started to suspect; how he knew for sure – but the repercussions seemed pretty clear. In fact, if Paul had found out what Wolstene had done to Mira – maybe to other women as well – it explained all sorts of things. Why Wolstene might commit suicide, apparently out of the blue: because Paul had threatened to expose him. Why Miles had gone to the Conister house that night: for revenge. Why the cops had felt like Miles had been holding something back about his father's death: because he was. And why Carly had been so panicky the day I'd driven down to the car dealership: because, just like her brother, she knew what had happened to Paul, and had helped to instigate his disappearance.

But what was Miles and Carly's motive? The heinous nature of Robert Wolstene's crimes couldn't be laid at their door. The absolute darkness of his past, the lies he told, the apparently flawless reputation he'd managed to promote and maintain while he was alive, shouldn't have mattered to them – or, at least, it shouldn't have mattered enough for them to have abducted Paul in order to preserve the silence. It wasn't like there was some family business they had to protect, a public-facing company that could face financial ruin if the truth got out: Miles worked in a restaurant and Carly worked in a car showroom. They weren't protecting their mother either, because she'd died when they were kids. I thought again about whether the mother's suicide could be related to this somehow, but let it go for now. I needed to concentrate on Robert, on his kids, on what I knew.

There *was* the small possibility they were actually a part of what Wolstene had been doing while it was going on, helping him, perhaps even joining in, but that seemed incredibly unlikely to me. Much as I'd seen duplicity in Miles's behaviour towards the woman on the Tube earlier – an ability to plan, to disguise his intentions, a patience, a fraudulence – Mira hadn't mentioned anyone else being involved while the attacks were going on, and this type of crime was so rarely committed by families. It was almost always a solitary affair, perpetrated by a single person, normally a man.

Almost always.

So if not Miles, what about Paul?

I thought about the idea, distasteful as it was to me, that Paul might have been involved, that he was the same as Wolstene. But something about it didn't fit. Sexual predators were skilled at hiding in plain sight, that much was true – Wolstene being the perfect example – but, given what I'd heard about Paul, and more importantly what I'd found out myself, it just didn't sit right in my gut.

When I finally got back to the restaurant, it was still busy. I could see waiting staff milling around tables at the front, close to the glass, and more at the back – on the other side of a bar – pouring drinks. There was no sign of Miles Wolstene, which didn't mean he wasn't there: at the back there was a red door clearly marked OFFICE.

I waited. Ten minutes passed. Twenty.

After thirty minutes, with no sign of him, I headed inside, keeping my eyes on the office door. It was marginally ajar and now – closer in – I realized something.

No one was in there.

I moved towards the doors to the kitchen. A waiter stopped me.

'Can I help you, sir?' He looked pissed off.

'I'm looking for Miles,' I said.

'He's not here.'

His name badge said RYAN.

'So where can I find him, Ryan?'

'May I ask who you are?'

'My name's David Raker. I'm an investigator.' I watched his expression drop. 'I need to speak to Miles urgently.'

'Uh, well, he's gone home.'

'Already?'

'He said he was feeling sick.'

'Sick?'

'A migraine.'

My mind was already skipping ahead. 'Listen, Ryan,' I said, leaning into the guy: he was young, and that played to my advantage because he already looked scared. 'I need my being here to remain between us, okay? Miles isn't in any trouble, but it's really important that you don't contact him until I've had a chance to speak to him.'

'Okay,' Ryan said.

'Thank you. I appreciate it.'

I headed out and hurried to the Tube again, jumping on the Northern Line. At Clapham, I switched stations, from North to High Street, then took the Overground one stop to Wandsworth Road. From there, I retraced my footsteps from the day before, ending up at Miles and Carly Wolstene's flat.

Neither of them was home.

Carly's car wasn't on the driveway and, when I buzzed the flat, no one answered. I did a circuit of the house, checking Miles's bedroom at the back, but there was no sign of him in there. To be certain, I buzzed the flat again, watching the front windows, waiting for signs of anyone peering out to see who was at the door.

Grabbing my mobile, I dialled Carly at work.

'Tarrington Motors.'

It was a man.

'Is Carly around?'

'No, sir, I'm afraid she's had to go home ill.'

'Oh, I'm sorry to hear that. Is she okay?'

'Uh, yeah, I think so. A migraine. Can I ask who's call—'

I hung up.

Two people, same story.

And then, in my hand, my phone started to vibrate.

I looked down and saw that it was Maggie Conister's number. I hit Answer, my eyes going back to the house, still thinking about where Miles and Carly might have gone – and why they'd have faked being ill in order to get away from their jobs early.

Did they realize I was following them?

'David?'

I instantly tuned back in. 'Hey, Maggie.'

It sounded like she was crying.

'Is everything okay?'

'No,' Maggie sobbed.

'What's the matter?'

'It's Katie.'

I paused. 'What about her?'

'She didn't come home last night.'

20

Maggie was waiting for me at the front door.

I followed her inside. Seb was in the living room, on the edge of one of the sofas. He glanced up and nodded at me. He looked scared. They both did. I could feel it in the room, and I could see it: Seb wasn't remotely interested in his mobile phone, which was next to him on a side table, buzzing as new messages flashed up; Maggie was sobbing, pretty much unable to speak, but managed to point me towards the other sofa. As I did, a breeze washed in from the sun-drenched garden, through the open conservatory doors, and the mechanical buzz of a lawnmower carried in, a sound of normality passing from outside to in.

'What happened with Katie?' I asked.

Maggie swallowed, wiped her nose with a tissue. 'I don't . . .' She paused. 'I don't know exactly. She texted me yesterday afternoon and said a group of them were going to one of the other girl's houses to work on a project. She said she would text me again to let me know what time she was leaving. She doesn't have to – I mean, she's twenty years old; if she was going to university in any other part of the country, she wouldn't be living at home, so I'd never know where she was – but she does it out of courtesy. She knows I worry about her getting the Tube home alone late at night.' Maggie's chin quivered as she tried to halt a fresh wave of tears. 'It got to about ten thirty and I hadn't heard from her, so I texted her and told her I was going up to bed – I suppose what I was really doing was trying to force a reply, just so I could get a rough idea of when she would be home – but she never responded. That's unusual.'

'She always responds?'

'Always, yes.'

'So you got no reply from her at all?'

'Not to that one.'

'Do you mean you sent her a follow-up text?'

Maggie nodded. 'At midnight, yes.'

'What did she say?'

'She said she was going to stay over at her friend's.'

'Was that normal?'

'It happens. Like I say, she's twenty.'

'Okay, so what did she say in the second text?'

Maggie handed me her phone and I read Katie's reply.

> Relax. Everything's fine, Mum. I'll speak to you in the morning. Stop stressing!

'Did you phone her?'

'No. I didn't want to. I didn't want her to feel . . .' She stopped.

Like a kid again, like I didn't trust her. She didn't want to be the parent who the child ended up hating because all she did, even at twenty years of age, was baby her.

This whole thing felt like a huge overreaction – although, in light of everything that had happened to the Conisters, I could understand Maggie's response: Katie may have been an adult, a university student, but Maggie's kids were the next line of defence in a family that had been broken beyond recognition already. She was paranoid about losing them, just like she'd lost Paul. And yet, while I understood Maggie's desire to have her children under her own roof, all the time, especially after everything they'd been through, Katie could do whatever she wanted now. Maggie's time for telling her

109

daughter she had a curfew, or requesting a text when she left a friend's, was over. As a parent, all she could do was offer a hand; she couldn't force her daughter to take it. And, in truth, nothing in the message seemed particularly troubling. She'd gone to a friend's house after lectures, she'd stayed on, she'd even replied to her mum eventually.

'Have you heard from her today?' I asked.

I could already see from the phone that Katie hadn't texted.

'No,' Maggie said.

'Look, I understand you're concerned, but I don't see anything here to –'

'Katie's not like this.'

I took a breath, trying to think of the best response.

'Sometimes kids Katie's age can do things without –'

'Katie's not like other twenty-year-olds. This isn't how she is. She doesn't text me like this, with vague details about what she's up to. She wouldn't ignore me.' She paused, searching my face for something she could grab hold of: a recognition that, having spent a couple of days sifting through Paul's life, *their* life, I understood her family, their new dynamic, the way they'd fused together as a unit in the months since Paul had gone missing. 'This is why I didn't call the police. You know what happened to us, you know how they didn't believe me. I can't go to them and have them look at me that way again; it's why I called *you*. But now I can see that you don't believe me either.'

'I believe you.'

'You don't believe something is wrong.'

I looked at the text again.

'Something's wrong,' Seb said.

It was the first time he'd spoken.

I glanced at him.

'Mum's right,' he continued. 'Katie wouldn't do this.'

'And that's not how she signs off texts,' Maggie added.

I stopped, looked at the phone again.

'That text she sent me last night. That's not how she signs them off. Ever since Paul disappeared, the three of us, we've texted more, talked more, don't like being away from each other as much. She never signs off texts without a kiss, ever. A lot of the time, she'll fill the end of them with emojis too. Kisses, hearts, heart eyes, all of that stuff.' She paused, looking over at Seb. 'She does it to Seb too, doesn't she, son?'

He nodded. 'It's really annoying.'

I looked at the text again.

And then I understood what Maggie was telling me.

'That's not her,' she sobbed. 'That text's not from my Katie.'

2 1

I asked Maggie if she'd contacted any of Katie's friends and she said she'd spoken to some of them but hadn't been able to get in touch with them all so far. I told her to keep trying – just in case she was wrong about the text *not* being from Katie, and Katie had in fact stayed over with a mate after all – then hurried upstairs to Katie's bedroom. The whole time I was thinking about Miles and Carly Wolstene, their possible role in this, and why they might do something as extreme as kidnap Katie – if that was even what had happened. I'd asked Maggie the day before if she'd ever met Robert Wolstene's kids and she'd said no – but though the pieces didn't fit together perfectly, especially in terms of timings, it was just too convenient that Katie was suddenly unaccounted for on the same day that both the Wolstene kids had faked migraines to get out of work.

In Katie's bedroom, I started going through her wardrobes again; I went through books she'd left piled up on her desk, looking for slips of paper that might have been left inside, notes, clues, anything I'd missed first time around. When I was done, I dropped to my haunches and started going back through the canvases on the floor. I'd got halfway through when I heard Maggie on the stairs.

She appeared in the doorway. 'No,' she said. She looked like she was about to cry again. 'No one's seen her. I've called as many of her friends as I know. She could have gone to other friends, I suppose, ones I'm not familiar with, but I . . . I just . . .' She couldn't even finish her sentence.

I thought again about what Maggie had told me before I'd come upstairs – *That text's not from my Katie* – and then we headed back downstairs to the kitchen, where she'd left her phone. I rechecked the last message she'd received from her daughter, and then kept going, scrolling back to the previous days. Maggie was right: the text she'd got yesterday didn't match Katie's style. She used a lot of shortcuts, she abbreviated long words, she overloaded the ends of her texts with emojis. Her last text had none of those things. I looked up, trying to keep my expression neutral, even though I could feel a low-level alarm starting to build, and said, 'You remember I asked you yesterday whether you'd ever met either of Robert Wolstene's children?'

'Yes,' she said, quickly, hopefully. 'Yes, I remember.'

'Did Paul ever meet them?'

'No, not as far as I'm aware.'

I looked out at the back garden, bathed in sun; I could see Seb in the living room on his phone now, greyed by the same worry that was making his mother so desperate. I tried to figure out what exactly I should share with Maggie about Miles and Carly Wolstene, not because I wanted to keep information back from her – there seemed little point in doing that any more, especially because the search for Paul was starting to balloon – but because I wasn't exactly certain of how the Wolstenes and Katie were linked. If Miles and Carly *were* the ones who had sent that text to Maggie, pretending to be Katie, why? Why make Katie a target in the first place and not Maggie or Seb? They all had pretty much exactly the same idea of where Paul had gone, and that was *no* idea. Or, at least, that was what I'd believed.

Could Katie have been lying to me?

I looked at Maggie. 'Did Paul ever say he had concerns about Robert?'

'Concerns? Like what?'

It was vague and I didn't blame her for not understanding what I was trying to get at. Delving into the awfulness of what Wolstene had done to Mira didn't seem to serve a point, though, not at the moment, so I tried to loop back around to the central question: what had Miles Wolstene done to Paul? And what had happened to Katie?

'What was Paul's reaction to Wolstene's death? Did he seem shocked? Did he ever mention it to you?'

'He mentioned it, yes.'

'Were they still friendly at that stage? Was that the case all the way up to Robert's death?'

Maggie closed her eyes, trying to think.

And then they snapped open again.

'Wait a second,' she said, 'wait a second.' Her fingers massaged her forehead. 'There *was* something. This was back when Robert died. I read about his funeral arrangements in one of the news stories about him, and I remember mentioning them to Paul. I mean, I *expected* us to go because they'd known each other through Fulham, and Paul was friends with a lot of Robert's friends too. So I think I said something like, "What time do you want to leave?", something along those lines.'

'You mean, leave for the funeral?'

'Exactly, yeah.'

'And what did Paul say?'

'He said he wasn't going to be able to make it.'

'But Robert was his friend.'

She nodded. 'I thought it was strange too, so I asked him again later on, and he repeated the same thing: he had something on at work so he couldn't make the funeral. Tarrington were always pretty good when it came to stuff like that – funerals, hospital appointments, things to do with the kids – so

I was surprised he didn't try to organize the time off.' She paused, staring into space, obviously trying to force more memories to the surface. But there wasn't anything else: 'Honestly, I didn't really think about it again after that and haven't thought about it since. He certainly never talked about them falling out.'

Or what he'd found out about Wolstene.

More and more, it felt like that was where we were heading: Paul and Robert had become friends, but then Paul had found out something about Robert – maybe even glimpsed the entire shape of the secret Wolstene was harbouring.

That was why he didn't want to go to the funeral.

And then another thought struck me: could Paul have had something to do with Robert's death? Could Robert have been pushed? I dismissed it, because Robert had been captured on CCTV going to the roof of the ASCB building alone the day he jumped. But then I circled back around to it: what if it *was* true and Miles and Carly found out? Could revenge be the reason they targeted Paul after all?

Where would Katie fit into that?

I glanced at Maggie, then at the wall behind her, trying to align my thoughts – and my gaze snagged on the photos I'd seen a couple of days before. At its centre was the one of the Conisters in Marbella, taken five or six years ago. Around it were others, all of which I'd already looked at: more of the four of them, the kids at various ages, shots of Paul and Maggie that went all the way back to their wedding day, trips they'd been on as a family, things they'd done to the house . . .

I stopped.

Things they'd done to the house.

'Just give me a sec,' I said.

Moving past Maggie, I leaned in closer to a photo at the bottom of the cluster: it showed a low wall being built in the garden around the patio area. Paul was in the middle of the shot, smiling for the camera and holding up a mug in a *cheers* gesture, his sweatshirt covered with mud, sweat and what looked like wet cement.

'Did you take this?'

Maggie looked at the picture.

'Yes,' she said. 'That was when we did the garden.'

But Paul wasn't alone in the shot.

At the very edge of the frame was half a face: an eye, part of the nose, a mouth, also smiling. Like Paul, the person was in a dirtied sweatshirt, was also holding a coffee mug, and had his visible foot resting on the horizontal angle of a shovel blade, as if he'd just paused to pose for the camera. I remembered studying the photo the first time I was here. But not closely enough, I now realized, because I'd missed this man.

'Who's that?' I asked, pointing to him.

Maggie leaned in further.

'Oh, he helped us put the wall around the patio.'

I studied what I could see of the man's face.

'He was recommended to us,' she added.

'So he was – what? – a landscape gardener?'

'No, he just did the wall. We did the rest.'

'So a builder?'

'Yes,' she nodded. 'His name was Robbie Avery.'

22

'That's not his name,' I said.

Maggie looked at me, uncertainly.

'That's Robert Wolstene's son, Miles.'

Her eyes flicked back to the picture.

'Paul didn't know him by that name?' I asked her.

'No,' she said, shaking her head. 'No, his name's Robbie Avery. He came around to our house before the work ever started and gave us a quote on the job. Look . . .' She broke off and went to a sideboard, searching around inside. 'I've got his quote here somewhere.' She took out some paperwork, some pens, what looked like a diary. Inside the diary was a folded piece of paper. 'This is the quote he gave us.'

It was on the headed notepaper I'd found at the flat and there was a business card stapled to the corner. *Robbie Avery Building Services.* There would have been no reason for the Conisters to have considered it fake. I set the quote aside and said to Maggie, 'He was recommended?'

She was still gazing at the photo of Paul, her husband smiling broadly as he laid the wall around the patio. I looked again at the edge of the picture: had Miles deliberately positioned himself there? Or had he intended not to be in the photo at all?

'Who was he recommended by, Maggie?'

'He came door to door. He had this whole binder full of reviews, all these phone numbers of people he'd done work for. We thought it was unusual – a builder coming door to door like that – but he was so engaging, and seemed so convincing.'

'He had phone numbers?'

'Yes. He said we could call them for references.'

'Did you or Paul call any of them?'

'I think Paul did.'

'Have you got a list of those numbers?'

'I, uh, I don't know if we kept them.' She started to go through the paperwork again. 'Wait, here we are . . .'

It was a list of five numbers, with a description of the work Robbie Avery had apparently undertaken for each. I grabbed my phone and started dialling them one by one. The first just rang and rang, as did the second. Three and four went to a BT-standard voicemail message. Only the last, attributed to a customer called Judy Flint, got a response: '*Hello. I'm really sorry that I can't get to the phone right now, but if you leave a message after the tone I'll get back to you as soon as I can. Thanks.*'

I hung up, recognizing the voice immediately.

It was Carly Wolstene.

'Did Paul speak to this one?' I asked, pointing to Judy Flint's details.

Maggie shook her head. 'I can't remember. I think so. I don't know. It was five or six months ago. He spoke to *someone*, and whoever it was, he said they seemed really impressed by the work that Robbie had done for them. He was cheaper than some of the other quotes we got too. Much cheaper. That was why we went with him. And when he came, and Paul helped him out with a few things, like mixing the cement, he knocked even more money off the final bill. He just seemed like a really nice bloke.'

'These numbers are fake,' I said.

Maggie frowned. 'What?'

'They were set up by Miles and Carly Wolstene to make it

look like Miles was who he said he was – this builder, Robbie Avery.' I paused, watching Maggie's face dissolve, and then let the rest of it come together in my head: Paul would have gone through the list of names Miles provided, and he would have hit either unanswered calls or voicemails until he got to Judy Flint, just like I'd done. Flint, he *definitely* would have got through to, and she would have gone on to tell him how great Robbie Avery was, and that she'd have no hesitation in recommending him. Avery's cheap quote was the cherry on the top. But it was all a lie: the number must have been for a phone the Wolstenes bought.

So why build such an elaborate deception?

Had Miles just wanted to take a closer look at the Conisters, their routines, who they were and how they behaved? Was this how his revenge plot began? Why pretend to be a builder and go to all the trouble of giving them a quote and then actually *doing* the work? I'd never seen anything like it before. Normally, when a killer zeroed in on potential victims, they did it via reconnaissance, background checks, even equipment like bugs.

I turned to Maggie again: 'So all of this was in February?'

'I, uh . . .' She shook her head. 'I don't . . .'

But I knew it was. The date was on the quote.

February was the month before Wolstene jumped. Something else seemed clear too: Paul definitely *hadn't* met Miles, which was what Maggie herself had said, because if he had, he would have recognized him the minute he turned up on their doorstep, posing as Robbie Avery.

'What about other work?'

She frowned. 'Other work?'

'Did this guy do anything else to the house?'

'Yes,' she said. 'Yes, we got him back again.'

'When?'

'A few weeks later . . .' She faded out, memories replaying, her intelligence getting ahead of her emotion now. She was starting to see how things were fitting together.

'Around the time Paul went missing?'

'Yes,' she said. She glanced at the ceiling. 'We'd been wanting to redo our bathroom for ever, and Robbie had made such a good job of the wall, and been so lovely, we thought –'

'He redid your bathroom?'

'Yes,' she said again. 'He remodelled the whole thing.'

23

We both rushed upstairs to the ensuite, taking in the bathroom.

'Have you got any pictures of how it was before?'

Maggie nodded and headed back to the kitchen.

I moved inside, looking around at the same things I'd seen a couple of days before. What caught my attention this time were the tiles around the bath to my right, and all along the wall on that side. They seemed newer than the ones in the rest of the room.

The new tiling came about halfway up the wall. I tapped my knuckles just above the apex of the tiles: it was plaster-board. All the other walls in the ensuite – in fact, the walls throughout the entirety of the house – were either cement or stone.

Like the tiles, the wall itself was new as well.

I moved back into the bedroom just as Maggie arrived. She handed me a picture of the bedroom and ensuite as it had been, and I could see that I was right: in the refurbish-ment, the size of the ensuite had been reduced in order to create more space in the bedroom. Before that, there had been a much bigger bath, an alcove built around it, and the cavity wall had been narrower.

'When did work start on this?' I asked Maggie.

'Three or four weeks before Paul went missing.'

'Was this his suggestion?' I asked, showing her the photo-graph and then the newly tiled wall. 'To bring the wall of the bathroom in, I mean. Did he suggest that?'

'You mean, Robbie?'

I looked at her. He wasn't Robbie, but I didn't blame her for finding it hard to adjust. More interesting to me was the fact that Miles clearly wasn't a complete fraud: he knew the work, he knew how to carry it out, he'd done a good job in the garden and up here. It made me wonder why he wasn't *actually* doing this sort of thing for a living. Why work in a restaurant?

'So was it his suggestion?' I pressed.

'Yes,' Maggie responded. 'He said bringing the wall in would give us a lot more space in the bedroom. I mean, it allowed us to get that,' she added, and pointed to an antique dressing table in the bedroom, sitting in part of the space the bathroom had once taken up.

I looked at the photo, and then thought of what Maggie had just told me: that Miles had started the rebuild only three or four weeks before Paul disappeared. I said to Maggie, 'What happened after Paul went missing? Did Miles come back here right away – the day after – and just carry on?'

'No,' she said. 'We were going crazy here.'

'So when did he return?'

She grimaced. 'I don't know.'

'I need you to try and think if you can.'

'A couple of weeks later maybe.' She paused. 'At the time, I was losing my mind about Paul, about where he'd gone and what had happened to him. We all were. Robbie had almost finished the job. He called a couple of times to ask when I wanted him to come back and complete it, and I just said I'd let him know. Eventually . . .' She halted again. 'Eventually, I think it was Katie who called him.'

'Katie arranged for him to come back?'

'I think so.' She squeezed her eyes shut. 'It all seems so long ago, and I never thought for one second that it would even matter. But, yes, I think Katie said she would take care of things for me – not just that, but lots of other stuff too. Day-to-day stuff. She was so good in those first few weeks. So strong for us.'

I remembered Katie on the day I'd first come to the house, the way she'd been there to support her mum, the way they'd cried together as they'd described what had happened to Paul, and I remembered thinking that she'd spoken like someone more mature than a twenty-year-old. I even recalled my thought at the time: *Kids were forced to grow up faster when they realized that the only place you found a genuine happy ending was on Netflix.*

'What do you mean, "day-to-day stuff"?' I asked Maggie.

'I'm sorry?'

'You said Katie took care of "day-to-day stuff"?'

'I don't know. Just life, I guess. Shopping. Driving Seb to football matches. I was in pieces. I was calling the police every five seconds trying to find out what they were doing about looking for Paul, and it was like I was screaming into a hurricane. They just kept fobbing me off the whole time . . .' She trailed off. 'I should have handled it in a better way than I did. It shouldn't have been down to Katie to hold things together.'

'You said Miles was almost done with the refurb but not quite. What else did he have to do?'

'Some painting, some grouting around the bath. Tiny things. Most of the big stuff had been done by then.'

I looked at the wall.

'Have you got any other pictures of the refurb?' I asked her. 'I'm looking for some you might have taken midway through, as he started moving the wall.'

'I'm not sure. I might have some on my phone.'

I watched her go and then hurried through to Katie's

room again. Something didn't feel right: why would Maggie go completely to pieces over Paul's disappearance and Katie stay strong? People were different, loss hit everyone in different ways at different times, and I'd seen Katie cry the day I'd come to the house – and it was totally genuine – so it wasn't as if she'd shown no emotion at all. But it struck me as strange that Katie had held it together so well early on, and even stranger that she could think so matter-of-factly about something as perfunctory as a bathroom renovation.

I looked around her room. Had I missed something?

'Is everything okay?' Maggie was standing in the doorway, holding out her mobile phone to me. I told her everything was fine and then studied the shot she had onscreen. 'This is the only one I've got, I'm afraid.'

It was of the bathroom, the bath dragged to one side; the wall had been knocked out between the bathroom and bedroom. There was nothing else to see.

I handed her back the phone and then returned to the bathroom, running a hand along the wall again. It seemed sturdy. But I couldn't shift the idea that the rebuild had been used to hide something, that this was how Paul had vanished that night. I checked the building work again: the tiles were all grouted; the bath had been secured to the tiles with sealant, its panels fixed to the walls. If something was hidden behind the tub, there was no way to get at it. And why would you hide something you could never get at?

Unless you didn't want to get at it.

Unless that was the whole point.

I looked at Maggie, considering for a second the idea that Paul's body might be behind the bath – but then instantly dismissed it. Even forgetting for a moment that the smell would have been horrendous, Maggie had said the work on the rebuild had been completed *before* Paul went missing. Apart from some painting and a little grouting, there had been nothing else to do. That meant that – in order to get Paul's body into the cavity wall – Miles would have had to *undo* a lot of the work he'd already done up to that point; and even if Paul had engineered his own disappearance and Miles had nothing to do with it, he would have had to do the same. And both of those ideas raised even more questions, like how did Miles get into the house that night without Maggie hearing him? I looked at the bath again, and then leaned forward, running a hand along the tiles, the sealant, the grouting, the wall, searching for hints of anything. And then I got to the taps.

The hot felt fine.

But something was wrong with the cold.

It felt slightly looser, shifted fractionally as I rotated the tap on and off. 'David?' I heard Maggie say behind me as I dropped to my haunches and looked at it more closely. It wasn't very loose – in fact, the difference between the two taps was marginal – but there was a slight movement to the left and right as if a screw had begun to detach somewhere underneath. I tried lifting it towards me. Nothing happened.

And then I pushed down on it.

This time, something clicked.

It took a couple of seconds for me to realize what had changed and then I saw: beside me, almost unnoticed at my thigh, the side of the bath had come towards me. I leaned away from it, got my fingers around the edges of the panel and pulled. The whole thing swung out, like a horizontal door on a hinge.

'What the hell is that?' Maggie asked, stepping closer.

'I think it's a hiding place,' I said.

24

The moving panel was so well disguised – its edges hidden by subtle, hooded ridges – that I hadn't once suspected it might come out, despite having examined the bath twice already. But now, on my knees, my phone out and the light function on, I pulled it as far as it would come – about sixty degrees on a ninety-degree axis – and then shuffled forward until my ducked head was under the rim of the bath.

Directly inside, in the top right-hand corner of the interior, was a catch. It had been fixed to the underside of the cold tap. I shone the torch further inside, under the U-shaped dip of the tub itself, and saw that the space went all the way back into the cavity wall.

At this end of the dip, there was room to crawl past.

Not much, but enough.

I got down on to my belly and dragged myself through. I wasn't as tall as Paul, but I was wider, and – as I hauled my body past the dip – I could feel the buckles in my belt snagging on something, could feel old pieces of tile gathering under me, dust in my throat. I heard Maggie say something behind me, but her voice was dulled by the bath and by the walls, so I simply concentrated on shining the light ahead of me.

I stopped three-quarters of the way in.

The space under and around the bath led directly into the area between the bathroom and main bedroom wall. The whole thing was like a reverse L-shape.

There was nothing in here now.

But something had been.

Not a person, although this could still have been where Paul disappeared that night, but boxes or containers of some kind. There was dust everywhere, settled on the floor like a vast carpet of grey lint – but at the back, the covering was much thinner.

And those thinner coverings were all rectangular.

There were three.

On my belly, I went to my phone, switched to Camera and took some pictures of them, and then used the torch to double-check the spaces around me again, making sure I hadn't missed anything. If I'd been hoping for evidence of someone having lain here for a time, I didn't see it: that didn't mean Paul hadn't been here – in fact, it seemed like the only way he could have disappeared like he had – but there was nothing to confirm that. No footprints in the dust. No swish to suggest that a person had entered or exited. No indication of when, after Paul had crawled into here, he'd left again.

But why?

Why hole up in here? Why create the hiding place at all? Was it a decision driven by Paul? Or was it one instigated by Miles, with Paul just a victim?

Or were Paul and Miles working together?

Even if they were, how did Miles get into the house?

How did Maggie not hear him?

I wriggled back out again, thinking about the boxes or containers that had been in here. Could they explain why Paul had gone missing that night? It didn't feel like a stretch: you only hid things as well as this if you didn't want them found.

'Did you see anything?' Maggie asked as I finally got up, on to my feet. She'd got a towel for me, had filled the basin with water so I could wash my face, and as I tried to wipe myself down, I explained to her about the box-shaped impressions I'd seen in the dust on the floor.

'Did Paul ever store stuff in containers like that?'

'Maybe in the loft.'

After I was done cleaning myself, I went to the loft, dropped the ladder and headed up. Maggie was right: there were plenty of boxes, but as I went through them, using the torch to search, I found nothing of note. These boxes weren't the ones that had been hidden under the bath, I was certain.

And then my attention was captured by something else entirely: when I got to the bottom of the ladder, I glanced in at Katie's room, and my eye was drawn to the stack of canvases Katie had painted. Somewhere in the pile was the portrait that she'd done of her father. I couldn't see it from where I was.

But I could see one of the others.

It was poking out from the middle of the pile.

I rushed over, dropped to my knees and levered it out. It was a side profile of a woman with dark hair, her face a series of mauve strokes. I hadn't twigged the first couple of times I'd checked the canvases, because there was an abstract quality to this painting, but now I could see the resemblance. Now, finally, I realized why I'd felt like I'd known Carly Wolstene, despite never having met her before.

Because Katie had painted her.

25

I stared at the portrait of Carly Wolstene on the floor, trying to figure out what was going on – and then, a second later, Maggie's mobile started humming in her hands.

'Oh, it's Katie,' she said, her voice shaking. 'Oh, thank you God, thank you.' She answered. 'Katie?' There was a brief period of silence and then a response that I could hear in the quiet of the house: *Hi, Mum.* 'Where have you *been*?'

Sorry I didn't call, Katie replied.

I glanced at the portrait of Carly Wolstene again.

Something was badly off here.

'Where the hell have you been?' Maggie said.

A group of us went out and we got a little drunk.

'I was worried *sick* about you.'

I know. I'm sorry, Mum.

'Why didn't you text me back this morning?'

Like I said, it was stupid. I got drunk. I'm so embarrassed, Mum, I'm really sorry to have worried you. She said something else I didn't pick up. *Are you okay?*

'No, I'm not okay, honey. I'm pretty *far* from okay.'

I closed my eyes, listening to Katie's responses.

'I lay awake all night worrying about you,' Maggie went on. 'I've been crying constantly. You can't just pull crap like this, Katie.'

I know.

She wasn't arguing with her mum, wasn't annoyed with her, which struck me as odd: she was twenty, and crashing at a friend's house should have meant nothing.

Why wasn't she telling Maggie to calm down?

To stop being so controlling?

'You know how things are, Kay,' Maggie said.

I know, Mum.

'We're not like this.'

I know.

'I even called David because I was so worr–'

David's there?

'Yeah.' Maggie looked at me, embarrassed now by the seemingly ordinary way in which this whole thing had concluded. 'We were trying to figure out where you were all day. Didn't you stop for one minute and think to yourself th–'

Can I talk to David?

Maggie frowned. 'What?'

I need to talk to David, Mum.

'What are you talking about?'

Put him on the line.

Maggie glanced at me.

Please, Mum, just put him on the line.

Maggie let the phone drop away from her ear and just held it there in her hands, staring at it, confused. 'She wants to talk to you.'

I took the phone.

'Katie?'

'David.' A pause. 'Hi.'

'Your mum's been worried about you.'

'I know.'

'We all have.'

'I know.'

Another pause.

'What's going on here, Katie?'

'Nothing, I just . . .'

She faded out and, for the first time, I heard something in

the background of the call. It sounded like the faint crackle of wind in the mouthpiece. She was outside.

'Where are you, Katie?'

She didn't respond.

'I saw the painting you did of Carly,' I said.

Maggie glanced at the portraits.

But again there was no reply from Katie.

'Do you know where Miles and Carly are?'

I heard the faintest sound of her breath catching and then the line lost some of its clarity for a moment. Had she covered over the mouthpiece? A few seconds later, she came back on the line and said, 'There are some things you need to know, David.'

'I think you're right.'

'Can you meet me?'

'Right now?'

'Yes.'

I glanced at Maggie. 'Where do you want us to meet you?'

'No, not us,' Katie said. 'Don't bring Mum.'

Again, wind hissed like static on the line.

'Just come alone.'

PART THREE
The Line

26

I parked on the fringes of Sydenham Hill Wood.

It was a zigzag of forest just south of Dulwich, and although I didn't know it that well, I'd read up on it before I'd left Maggie's, so I knew enough. It was eleven hectares of trees and trails, and the site of the old Nunhead to Crystal Palace railway line. The line had ceased to exist in the 1950s, after the palace burned down and passenger numbers dwindled, but a hint of it remained: it was possible to follow the trackbed where the old railway line had once been, all the way through the woods to a disused tunnel, secured behind a gate, that was now home to protected bats. Just before the tunnel's entrance, on its left, was an old branch line. This was much less visited because it had been closed off to the public since 1954: a high fence ran across the path the line once followed, and carried on into the trees on either side, eventually disappearing out of sight. I had no idea how far the fence ran, but I knew it hadn't stopped people gaining access to the path on the other side. There were still the remnants of houses along it somewhere, all of them destroyed by fire, all of them long since collapsed into half-walls and memories; in the pictures I'd seen, they'd been reclaimed by nature, their shapes obscured or concealed by the density of the woods in that part. That made them the hangout of choice for drug addicts, the homeless and teenagers on a dare.

And Katie Conister.

Her choice of meeting place gave me pause, not just because I couldn't explain it to Maggie, or explain why Katie wanted to meet me here alone. It wasn't even that this place was secluded – as secluded as a place in London could be, at least – or that Katie had hung up on me when I'd tried to press her on what was going on. Instead, the woods put a hitch in my stride because, in the pictures I'd seen of it online, it bore an uncanny resemblance to the place that had existed behind the farm I'd grown up on. The place, at seventeen, where I'd rediscovered the old Montgomery house with my dad, and he'd first revealed its history to me. It was like two moments in time had become bound and, as I thought of that, I thought of what Dad had said to me, years later, when he'd asked me if I believed in ghosts.

They aren't things that go bump in the night, son.

As I moved from the road, through the gate and in under the thick canopy of the woods, I could hear my father's voice, as clear as if he were walking alongside me.

They're things you can't let go of.

They're fear, and heartache, and regret.

Which of those would I find here?

I reached the old branch line after about ten minutes. The fence meant to keep people out was chain-link, frilled with rust, its top slightly rounded where people had hauled themselves up and over the top. Huge signs saying KEEP OUT!, PRIVATE and TRESPASSERS WILL BE PROSECUTED had been attached all the way down, but a lot of them had been rinsed pale over time and others had been vandalized.

I looked around, checking no one was close by, and then scaled the fence. At the top, I could see through a gap in the trees, down the old track, towards the first of the ruined buildings. It was about two hundred metres further along and looked like it might once have been a station house: it was built on what appeared to be a platform, and although the platform was overrun with vines and grass, a sign speared upward, partly broken, with SYDENHAM SOUTH written on it.

I landed on the other side.

The ground beneath my feet was hard, the forest floor cracked and split by the long spell of dry weather. Even so, it was cooler beneath the canopy and, as I started along the trail, I felt goosebumps scatter up my arms. I shrugged them off, but then they came again, and the further along the trail I got, the quieter and more shadowed my surroundings became. Katie hadn't given me an exact meeting place, just told me to meet her on the branch line, so as I arrived at the old station house, I stopped and called out for her. There was no response, only the sound of a soft breeze in the trees.

The station house had been boarded up once, but at some point the roof had caved in, and now one of the doors had been forced open and some of the boards in the front windows had been deliberately broken. Weeds crawled out from inside, like fingers reaching for the sky. There was the faint smell of vinegar in the air too, which I guessed was heroin. I got up on to the platform and looked inside one of the glassless windows: there was cooking equipment on the floor, beer cans, old food wrappers, blankets, clothes.

Suddenly, my phone shattered the hush of the woods.

I grabbed it from my pocket, looking at the screen, wondering if it might be Katie again. It wasn't her mobile phone number; it wasn't a mobile phone number at all. It was a landline: a payphone in north Wales, 250 miles away. I could picture the payphone, I could see the village it was in, and I knew exactly who it was.

But Colm Healy would have to wait for now.

I killed the call. And then: a noise.

I pocketed my phone, looking towards the track, and then got down from the platform and started following the old line again. I passed a second building and then a third, both little more than foundations: a square of walls, and the sub-sections within them that must have once been rooms. Beyond, I could see the trail curved to the left and the elevation dropped marginally. In reality I'd only come about a quarter of a mile, but it felt as if I'd walked much further than that. I knew for a fact that there were main roads less than half a mile away, but I couldn't hear any of them. There was still just the wind and the sound of birdsong.

So what was the noise I'd heard?

I moved on, further along the trail, passing three more houses – these dotted in a clump, roofless, windowless and hollowed out by a mix of branches, weeds and vandals. Then I heard the same noise again, ahead of me. It was hard to judge from where, but it was more obvious what it was now: stones scattering underfoot.

Someone was moving around.

'Katie?'

Ahead of me now, its mirror image sitting on the opposite side of the path, was the remains of a footbridge. The horizontal crossing itself was gone but the staircases on either side of what was once the track were still standing, enclosed within two identical wooden structures. I knew instantly I'd reached the meeting place.

The door to the stairs on the right was open.

'Katie?'

I heard the same scratch of footsteps.

And then, out of the darkness of the staircase, a shape began to emerge. I saw her face before anything else, her

eyes on me. She looked washed out, as if she'd been crying. When I'd seen her at the house, she'd looked older
than her years.

Now she looked like a child.

'Hello, David,' Katie said.

27

'Are you okay?' I asked her.

She nodded.

'You're not hurt?'

She shifted from one foot to the other, as if she didn't know what the right answer was. I looked her over, searching for injuries, for evidence that she might be wounded, but there was nothing that I could see. She wore a black vest-style top with a pattern on the breast, a pair of three-quarter-length jeans and dirty white trainers; on her exposed arms, her neck, her face, what I could see of her legs, she was unblemished.

No cuts. No bruises.

'What's going on, Katie?'

Her eyes dropped to the floor.

'Katie?'

I glanced out into the woods again, looking for anybody watching – specifically, two people. It felt like Katie had been contained somehow, not only frightened about being here, but frightened of saying the wrong thing. So were Miles and Carly close? Had they told her exactly what to say and do?

My eyes went to the staircase behind Katie.

'Are you going to tell me what's going on or not?'

As I took a step closer, her eyes snapped to my feet – to the distance between us – like she was telling me not to come any further.

I held up a hand.

'You asked me here, remember.'

She nodded again. 'I know.'

'So *are* you going to tell me what's going on?'

She blinked a couple of times and something glinted in her eyes. *Tears.* Again, I searched the blackness of the staircase behind her for any sign of Miles and Carly. It didn't look like they were in there, although it was impossible to be sure. They could have been further up the staircase, deeper into the dark – or somewhere else entirely.

'Are you alone, Katie?'

She looked at me, and again something played across her face, I just couldn't figure out what. It definitely seemed like she was inhibited somehow, and it made me even more certain that Miles and Carly were somewhere close by, watching us. I glanced behind me, in the direction I'd come, and saw the path of the old line was still empty. I scanned the woodland on either side of me for places where they could seek cover – trees, hollows, old walls. It didn't appear as if anyone was hiding in those places.

Which meant it was the staircase or it was nothing.

'It's okay,' I said to her.

She shook her head.

'Everything's okay.'

Her head went down again.

'Why don't you just tell me what's going on?'

She sniffed, wiped at her cheeks, and then – when she finally looked up again – I could see more tears in her eyes. Worse than that was the fear: it clung to every part of her face, the corners of her mouth, the angle of her jaw, the colour of her skin.

I took a step closer to her.

'Katie . . .'

She didn't react.

'Your mum's really worried about you,' I said.

'I know.'

'She just wants you home.'

'I know.'

'Whatever's going on, we can sort it ou–'

But then I stopped.

There was movement beyond her, within the staircase, and gradually – like a pair of spectres emerging from the dark – Miles and Carly finally fell in behind Katie.

I looked at all three of them.

'There's something I need to show you,' Katie said.

28

Katie could hardly look at me.

Neither could Carly.

Their eyes skittered between where I was standing and the ground under their feet, as if they didn't want me to recognize something in their faces.

Miles was more steadfast, though: he stared me down for a while, like he was sizing me up, and then, slowly, he started to move across the path of the old line, towards the other staircase.

He glanced at me, double-checking I hadn't shifted position, and, with a sudden show of force, began levering away the wood panels that made up the exterior of the left staircase. It took a lot of work, his teeth gritted, the strength of his arms evident beneath the sleeves of a sweat-stained T-shirt. I hadn't seen it when I'd followed him because he'd been wearing a thin jacket, hadn't even seen it in the photo Maggie had on her wall, but Miles was brawny, the type of man who could really hurt you if he wanted to. So was that why Katie and Carly were so quiet? Were they scared of him?

I noticed something else too.

The nails in the wooden panels.

As Miles pulled them away from the structure, it was obvious they weren't the originals. The nails should have been black, speckled with rust, weakened by over sixty years of neglect and incapable of presenting any challenge to Miles's strength – but instead they were silver, almost entirely unsullied by time, and it took Miles a profound effort to prise them away from the staircase. It was possible the new nails had been put in by the council, or a woodland trust, or whoever it was that looked after the old branch line.

But I didn't think so.

'Did you put those nails in, Miles?'

He looked across at me.

'*Did* you?'

I took a step towards them all. He didn't answer.

'What's going on?' I said once again.

Miles glanced at Carly and Katie and then back at me.

'Stay there,' he said.

'All I want is the truth.'

Miles smirked. 'The truth?'

He pulled another board away. He'd taken off three of them now, in a space to the side of the staircase. I could see the profile of the steps inside, could smell rotten timber and stale urine. He glanced at me again, checking I hadn't tried to inch closer. As he did I said to Katie, 'This is ridiculous. Just tell me what's going on.'

Miles stopped to look at her.

Carly glanced at her brother, as if she knew exactly what he was thinking, and then she said, 'Just carry on with what you're doing. Katie knows how to handle this.'

He frowned at her.

'Trust me, Miles,' Carly said, sharply.

Miles let out a hiss, a sound of utter disbelief: 'Trust? What, you trust *him*?' He eyed me. 'You trust *this* guy? How do you know he's not exactly like the rest of them?'

'He's not,' Katie said, her gaze on me.

The rest of them.

'Why did you ask me here?' I said to Katie, but it could have been to all three of them because it seemed absolutely certain now – if I'd ever had any doubts once I'd seen the painting of Carly in Katie's room – that the three of them were in it together.

Whatever *it* was.

'Where's your dad?' I asked her.

Something fluttered across her face.

'Katie?'

'Why couldn't you just leave us alone?' Miles said.

I looked at him.

'Everything was fine until you showed up.'

'I showed up because Katie's mum asked me to.'

Miles and Katie glanced at each other, and I could see Maggie's decision in asking me to search for Paul had created conflict here. For Miles, it was the sole reason we'd arrived at this point. For Katie, hiring me was something that she hadn't been able to dissuade her mum from doing, and, from there, this whole thing had spiralled beyond her control. It made me wonder what exactly was coming next.

What they were hiding.

Where all of this led.

Miles wrested another panel away from the staircase. And then he stopped, sidestepped away from the structure, as if he was now deferring to Carly and Katie, and then the two women looked at each other, a message clearly passing between them. I wondered how much of this thing they'd rehearsed.

Katie pointed to the gap Miles had created. 'Okay,' she said, slight, sombre, 'you can go inside.'

I didn't move, just looked between them and the staircase.

'Why would I go in there?'

'You need to understand what happened,' Katie replied.

'"What happened"?'

She nodded. 'With Dad.'

Her eyes met mine. They flashed under the pale yellow

sunlight that escaped through the canopy, and as she stared to her right, to the narrow, dark space that Miles had opened up, my heart sank.

I could see it written in her face.

I knew what was inside the staircase.

29

None of them moved, even as Katie cried.

'Is your dad dead?' I asked her.

'You don't understand,' she sobbed.

'Did you kill him?'

Wind murmured through the trees.

'Did you kill him, Katie?'

'We did what had to be done.'

She glanced at me and then away, unable to hold my gaze, and my heart sank even further. So it was true: Paul was dead – and his own daughter was responsible.

'You did what had to be done?' I asked. 'What does that mean?'

'You don't understand,' she said again.

'Then help me understand.'

She looked up from her hands, to Carly and then to Miles. There was no give in him at all, virtually no reaction to anything I'd said, and I became more certain than ever that, whatever had happened to Paul, why ever it had been done, Miles had been front and centre. Even as Carly stepped forward and said to me, 'I think you should look inside,' there was no doubt in my mind that Miles had carried out whatever their plan had been. The women were there, they may even have formulated and instigated the entire lead-up to the night Paul went missing – but Miles was the one who did it.

He pulled the trigger.

He wielded the knife.

He'd brought Paul's body to this tomb.

'Katie?' I repeated. 'Why did you kill your dad?'

'I think you should look inside,' Carly said again.

'This isn't a game any more, Carly.'

'It's *never* been a game,' she responded coldly.

'So why not give me an answer?'

'We will,' she said. 'Just look inside first.'

I moved forward, keeping enough distance between me and the three of them that I could react if need be. But it wasn't a trap – or, at least, this part wasn't. They made space for me as I got closer, backed away, their feet scuffing on the compact ground.

I peered inside the staircase.

Immediately, I could smell human decay. It had faded, been superseded by the tangy stench of rot, but it was still ingrained, even three months after Paul had vanished.

He was in here.

I looked up the steps.

The staircase had been protected somewhat inside the structure, so while the exterior panelling had been battered by wind, rain and time, the interior was dusty, full of cobwebs, the wooden steps blistered and pale. But they would hold. I knew it even without setting a foot on them: all the way up, they were marked by muddy prints, an outline of a shoe – the same shoe – in a repeated pattern. Some of the footprints were older, the mud dried and crumbly; others were newer, dark brown and more defined.

Someone had repeatedly been inside.

I was betting it was Miles.

Right at the top I made out a landing area, where the footbridge would once have been connected. I couldn't see much more than that: it was swathed in an oily black.

I glanced over my shoulder at Katie.

She'd recovered her composure slightly, was looking at me, and it made me wonder why she'd asked me here. Was it a confession? Or could it actually be a trap?

'So this is where his body is?'

'Just look inside,' Carly repeated.

I ignored her. 'Why would you kill him, Katie?'

'We did what had to be done,' she said for a second time.

'What does that even mean?'

'It means he got what he deserved,' Miles said.

I studied him, his sister, then Katie.

'He got what he deserved?'

I frowned, looking from her, to Miles, to Carly. And then my memories spooled back to Mira, to all the suffering she'd endured at the hands of Robert Wolstene, and as the smell of decay drifted out of the stairs, everything seemed to rush me at once.

Finally, I could see what had bound the three of them together.

Miles. Carly. Katie.

Their fathers were both monsters.

30

I thought I'd known who Paul Conister was. I'd dug into his life and found nothing even remotely concerning. Save for the night that he disappeared, his life had been unremarkable and prosaic, with no alarm bells anywhere, so, in my gut, I'd felt sure he wasn't the same as Robert Wolstene. How had I been so wrong?

How had my instincts been so off?

'Paul hurt people?' I said to Katie, almost needing to hear myself saying it in order to make it real. She looked at me, over to the others. 'Did he . . . did he hurt you?'

Her eyes came to me.

'Just look inside,' Katie said, echoing Carly. *'Please.'*

I got inside the structure and placed a foot on the first step. It felt soft but not broken. As I glanced out, into the woods, the three of them stared back at me through the gap. Even Miles seemed unsure, perhaps worried about how much I already knew and how much I was about to find out. I studied Katie, her face flushed from the tears, and thought of Paul, of his friendship with Robert Wolstene, of how – if what Katie was saying was true – the men had been so similar. Fathers. Husbands.

Rapists.

The word barely seemed to fit with what I knew about Paul. Perhaps, in some part of me that I could see more clearly now, a thread had been left dangling after talking to Mira, a connection I couldn't quite make – or wasn't willing to – between Robert Wolstene and Paul. It wasn't that I ever believed for one second that they might be tethered to one another in this way, that they might share this kind of bond, it was more that I could never quite figure out the reason why Miles and Carly, especially Miles, seemed to be targeting the Conisters. The connection had never been clear, and it had become even muddier after what Maggie had told me about Paul, and how he didn't bother to go to Wolstene's funeral. Had that decision been made, not because he'd found out who Wolstene truly was, as I'd suspected for a time, but because – when Wolstene jumped to his death – Paul knew it would invite questions? Had he realized it would bring investigators, and if the cops connected the dots from Wolstene to Paul, it would deliver the police into Paul's life too?

I moved further up the staircase, the whole structure creaking around me, and, as I did, I heard Miles say something to the others that I couldn't pick up. One of the women replied, and then they were silent again. As I climbed, as it got darker around me, I thought again of Robert Wolstene, of the jump he'd made from the top of the ASCB building, and how his suicide – according to pretty much everyone the cops had talked to – came out of nowhere. Maybe whatever awaited me in here explained why.

The staircase spiralled once and, as I came around the last arc of its turn, the landing area I'd seen from the bottom emerged, bigger and wider than it seemed from below. It was like a room. A lot of it – in fact, most of it – was still concealed in the shadows, so I had to go to my phone and select the torch. Holding it up, the light washed into the black.

My blood froze.

Close to me, I could see a pair of feet.

I glanced back down the stairs, heard the three of them talking about something – perhaps even arguing; it was hard to tell now – and then turned to the room again, to the feet

I'd seen. Except I quickly realized it wasn't feet, but a pair of boots.

They were empty.

To the right of the room, I could see the former entrance to the footbridge, now completely bricked up. When the light landed on it, I spotted a series of steel hooks, all of them embedded in the brick about halfway up and placed three feet apart. I felt a flutter of disquiet: from each hook, a thick chain snaked off into the darkness.

There were four separate chains.

And they were all attached to something.

Or someone.

I followed the lines of the chains from the wall further into the blackness.

To start with, because the range of the torch was so limited, I couldn't quite figure out what I was looking at. The old structure was grimy, the dark wood panelling inside withered and addled by age, making it hard to properly decipher any shape in front of it.

But I could see enough.

One of the chains closest to me led off to the right, into an alcove, and stopped at an ankle. The chain was padlocked in place. Another went left and was connected to a wrist, padlocked again, the fingers of an upturned hand, like a spider on its back, facing the roof of the structure. The third chain also went left and looped around a thin waist, clothes gathered above and below it, the space in between revealing blanched skin, bruising, cuts. Again, a padlock had been used to secure the chain in place and make it impossible to free. The fourth chain crawled off into the dark – to the left again, but beyond the range of the other two – and from where I was, my light couldn't find its end.

I took a couple more steps forward.

As I did, I thought of something Maggie had told me about Paul's relationship with Robert Wolstene, and the friends of Robert's that he'd become associated with – not the university pals that Paul had been going to Fulham matches with for decades, but a new set of acquaintances, established after Robert had approached Paul, and Tarrington Motors, about sponsorship: *Robert had his own group of mates, and I remember that Paul met up with them a few times.* I looked around the room, right and then left, at the chains, at the body parts they were attached to. The ankle, wrist and waist: they belonged to different people.

I think there were three of them, Maggie had said.

Three friends. Three chains.

Three different bodies.

It wasn't just Paul Conister in here.

The nearest body, to my right, in the alcove, was the one with the chain at its ankle. I used the torch to light up the space properly, to free it from the intensity of the shadows, and I was able to confirm it as a man: the top of his chest was partially visible, the T-shirt he was wearing torn at the neck, revealing the hair dotted along the line of his sternum. He had a faded pair of jeans on, and a single shoe; the other was about a yard from him, mud caked to the underside. I couldn't see much of his face but what I could see stirred something in me: had I met him before somewhere? I tried to get a better view of his pale features, his eyes, mouth, and then pushed the light out – to my left – into the back of the room.

I saw the wrist and then the glimpse of someone's waist.

They belonged to a second and third man.

I didn't recognize either of the other two, but all three *had* to be Robert Wolstene's friends; they had to be part of the group that Wolstene had introduced Paul to. The second and third men were both on their bellies, one facing me, one looking away, the eyes of the one facing me still squeezed shut as if he'd suffered in his last moments. The other I couldn't see as much of, but I could see the side of a heavily stubbled face streaked with dirt and blood. The forefinger on his right hand seemed broken. I looked quickly, but couldn't see the injuries that had killed them. I didn't see a knife wound, a bullet hole, any evidence of choking. There was hardly even bruising.

My gaze switched to the fourth chain, trying to see where it ended and who it was attached to. But as I slowly began following its path, into what remained of the interior, something flickered at the back of my mind, and I instinctively stopped.

There were no fatal injuries on the bodies I'd already found.

And if they were dead, why weren't they decaying?

Suddenly, the one to my right moved.

Shit, they're still alive.

The movement came out of nowhere, a jolt of electricity that seemed to travel the entire body length of the prone figure in the alcove. He moaned, and then again, the noise indistinct and feeble – and then he was quiet, as if the power had been cut.

I shone my torch at the others.

It was clear now: the slow, shattered movement in their chests; the faint sound of their breathing.

I shifted my attention to the very back of the room, to the part of the structure that my light didn't yet reach. As I slowly began to move, following the path of the fourth chain, I pictured Paul in the photos I'd seen at his home. I thought of how his manager at Tarrington had described him. I remembered the love Maggie had for him, written into everything she'd told me, and prepared myself for what was coming: not the Paul I'd been told about, not even the Paul I'd seen in portraits.

Someone else.

Someone much worse.

My torch caught the edge of a pair of feet, socks on them,

the bottoms covered in earth and dust. The body beyond it appeared to be sitting up, slumped to one side slightly, one arm out – palm facing up – the bent wrist supporting some of his weight. The other arm was behind him, chained and padlocked, caught between his backside and the wall. He was wearing a white dress shirt, one of the tails out, and a pair of black trousers. A tie had long since been discarded and lay on the floor.

I moved the torch to Paul's face.

His head was down, nose pointing to the floor, but I could see him look towards me, see his eyes swivel upward into the top of his skull. As they did, his hair, matted to his scalp by grease and dirt, fell forward over his face. His skin was as pallid as sour milk. His breathing sounded like an old engine. He'd been in here for over three months, but it could have been way longer. He was almost catatonic.

But then he started raising his head.

He moved it slowly, like an animal waking from hibernation, and then his eyes – struggling to focus – must have found the vague shape of me again at the edges of the torchlight, because he stopped, blinked, and made a low moan.

By then, I'd already stopped breathing.

I hadn't seen it when his head was down, couldn't make out the familiar profile of his nose and jaw, the contours of his face, because they were disguised from view.

But I saw everything clearly now.

It can't be . . .

This wasn't Paul.

It was Robert Wolstene.

32

I stared at Wolstene, completely thrown, trying to remember what I'd read about his suicide in the police report. Had I been so focused on trying to seek out his connection to Paul that I'd missed something in the details of his death? Why hadn't the authorities realized it wasn't Wolstene on that roof but someone else? He moaned again in front of me, shifting against the wall and bringing me back into the moment.

He got what he deserved.

That's what Miles had said outside.

But he hadn't meant Paul.

'David?'

I moved back to the stairs. Katie was peering up at me, her face painted white by the sunlight. She was struggling to see me against the shadows, her eyes flicking from one side to the other. I glanced at Wolstene, at the other three men on the floor of the room – chained to hooks on the walls like animals – and then started down the stairs.

As soon as she saw me coming, she reversed out.

At the bottom, I emerged into daylight again, the fresh air a relief after the heat of the staircase. The three of them – Katie, Miles, Carly – had fanned out into a semicircle and were watching me closely, eyes narrowed, waiting to see what my reaction was. I looked between them and then back to the structure, the smell of mould and sweat and decay on the wind.

Before saying anything, I went to my phone.

'What are you doing?' Miles said.

I didn't answer, just went to my email.

'Don't.'

I looked up.

Miles had a gun pointed at me.

I eyed him. 'What the hell are you doing, Miles?'

'What does it look like?'

'You're going to shoot me?'

'If that's what it comes to.'

The two women were glancing between the two of us. Katie especially looked distraught. She was a child again, a child complicit in the imprisonment of four men.

'I need to check something,' I said.

'Check what?' Miles responded from the other side of the gun. I watched him, saw how steady he was with the weapon in his grip. 'You're calling the cops,' he said.

'No, I'm not.'

'Then what are you doing?'

'I want to see how you did it,' I said, and in my email I found the message that Ewan Tasker had sent me, with the file on Robert Wolstene's suicide attached, and looked across at the three of them. Carly and Katie were both still. Miles had stepped closer, his head cocked to one side, as if he was still trying to figure me out – who I was and what made me tick.

'What the hell does that mean?' he asked.

He jabbed the gun at me.

'Who was that on the roof, Miles?' I looked at my phone, at the file on Robert Wolstene's suicide, and started swiping through the initial pages. 'Who fell from the top of the ASCB building if it wasn't your father?' I stopped at the page I needed and skim-read the forensic report, seeing exactly the same things as last time: Wolstene – or whoever really hit that roof – weighed about fourteen stone, which meant he'd travelled at about sixty-five metres per second, and the fall from the roof of the ASCB building to the roof of the restaurant below had taken less than three seconds. At that speed, the aftermath was absolutely devastating: the top of his spine had fractured, which transected the aorta carrying blood out of the heart, killing him almost instantly; he'd landed on his head, the impact so hard, the brain had almost exited the front of the skull; all his major organs were fatally damaged, and there was so much trauma beneath the skin, to the bones and muscles, that his body appeared as if it had bypassed rigor mortis entirely, the legs and arms like jelly, the torso as malleable as a damp blanket.

Because of the way he'd landed, his face had almost concertinaed, breaking his teeth and displacing his jaw, making it impossible to identify him from the photographs that Miles and Carly had provided of Robert Wolstene. DNA tests were never carried out to confirm it was Wolstene, because as soon as the cops discounted the idea that he may have been pushed – CCTV footage from inside the ASCB building had shown him going to the roof alone, and no one else arriving either before or after him – the case ceased to be anything other than a box-ticking exercise. Wolstene's wallet was found in his trousers. His ASCB ID was still on a lanyard around his broken neck. And in the inside pocket of the coat that he'd been wearing was Wolstene's mobile phone. For the investigating officer, most likely overworked, almost certainly overrun by other, far more important, complex cases, that had been enough.

My gaze went back to the line about the surveillance footage that had shown Wolstene on his way up to the roof, and I realized it either *had* been Wolstene in the video, on his way up there for whatever reason, or the footage had been replaced. I looked up at Miles. 'So, did you ask me here just so you could stick a gun in my face?'

'What are you doing?' He gestured to my phone.

'I was reminding myself about your father's death.' I glanced at the door to the staircase: a black maw stared back at me. 'Or rather, the death of whoever replaced him.'

'Miles, put the gun down,' Carly said.

'We can't trust him.'

'I think it's a bit late for that now.'

Miles seemed to understand instantly. He'd got hold of a gun. He was pointing it at me. He, Carly and Katie had just shown me the extent of their secrets, the four lives hidden away in a broken staircase, half a mile along an old railway line. They'd trusted me enough to show me, whatever the endgame ultimately was; now there was no going back. They'd either brought me here to tell me everything – or they'd brought me here to kill me.

And I didn't believe that they wanted me dead.

'Why don't you just tell me what's going on?' I said.

They all looked at each other, Carly's eyes boring into her brother's until, with almost a slump of the shoulders, he dropped the gun to his side.

'Where's Paul?' I asked Katie.

And then I realized something.

They were all staring beyond me now, to a spot over my shoulder, where the trees met the staircase. I spun on my heel, trying to see what had got their attention.

But I didn't have to look very hard.

'Hello, David,' Paul Conister said.

33

Slowly, he edged around the side of the staircase. It looked like he'd emerged from the spot in the trees that was thickest, where he had most likely been watching everything unfold. He stared at me for a moment, almost apologetically, his mouth flattened into a line, and then, finally, after a few more steps, stopped a couple of feet short of me.

'I'm sorry it had to come to this,' he said.

He was softly spoken, his voice – his entire manner – completely unassuming, just as Maggie had said, as I'd come to expect myself until the revelation that he may have been a rapist like Robert Wolstene – or, perhaps, something even worse. But, as I looked from him to the three people behind me, as I saw an awareness pass between them, I started to realize that he wasn't like Wolstene at all. He was exactly the man my gut had told me he was – the father, the husband, the co-worker who everyone loved – except for a single aberration: he'd helped keep four men prisoner.

'You probably have a lot of questions.'

I studied him without replying, searching for signs of distress, for bruises on his body, cuts, wounds, torn clothing or sallow skin, anything that might suggest the past three months had been a struggle for him – but there was nothing. He was dressed in a pair of jeans and a plain red T-shirt. His skin was lightly tanned and unblemished.

He was healthy.

'What the hell's going on?' I said.

He nodded, as if expecting the question, and then looked

beyond me to Miles, Carly and Katie. 'Is that place further down still vacant?' he asked them, gesturing over his shoulder.

'Yes,' Miles said.

'Okay.' Paul turned to me again. 'Follow me.'

'And why would I do that?'

'Because you want answers.'

'And – what? – you just expect me to leave these four men here?' I pointed at the stairs, at the entrance Miles had created. 'They're dying in there. They need help.'

He nodded again, but this time it was more contemplative, a slight furrow on his face, as if he was trying to figure out the best response. He ran a hand through his thinning hair, the sun a painted blob on his scalp.

'Do you know who Robert Wolstene is?'

'That doesn't mean we should leave him here.'

'But you know.' He studied me. 'You know what he did to the women he met, the women he worked with. Those other men in there, they were exactly the same. They were animals. They were a pack. You can't even begin to imagine the suffering they inflicted upon their victims. You think you know everything about him, David, but you don't. You just don't.'

'If that's true, the police should be dealing –'

'It's too late for the police,' he said calmly, steadily. 'It's far too late for them. We gave up on the police helping us months ago. The police are part of the problem.'

'What does that mean?'

'Exactly what I say.'

'You told them about Wolstene?'

He paused for a moment. 'Why don't we talk about this?'

'I thought we *were* talking.'

'Somewhere else, I mean.'

I looked beyond him, along the path of the old line, wondering what exactly awaited me there. He'd talked about a place further down – did he mean another broken property? My gaze came back to him and, as it did, I started to realize something: I'd spent days searching for this man, had made him the biggest priority in my life, had sunk hours into the hunt – and now I'd found him, I didn't trust him.

'This isn't a trap,' he said, as if seeing where my thoughts lay.

'Then why do we have to go anywhere?'

He looked at the staircase. 'I don't like it here.'

'You made it what it is.'

'True.'

As I watched him, I was struck again by how tall he was – six-three, maybe even six-four – his long arms at his sides. He wasn't physically intimidating, despite his height, but there was something about him, something that made me cautious – and afraid.

'I just want to help you understand,' he said.

'Understand what exactly?'

I heard the snap of a twig behind me and turned: Miles had broken away from Katie and Carly and was aiming the gun directly at my face.

I looked at Paul.

'I want you to understand why we did what we did.'

34

They walked me further along the line until, out of the trees, another old building emerged, less ruined than some of the others. Half a roof covered one side of it, and although the windows had long since gone, there was a door still attached – open, and squeaking softly on its hinges – and a wall around what must once have been a front garden. A rust-eaten gate lay on the floor, red and crumbling.

Paul scanned the woods briefly, presumably searching for addicts who'd made it on to the line, the homeless, trespassers, then he turned to Miles and said, 'Okay, Miles, I think we can lose the gun now.' Miles didn't seem to like it, but he did as he was asked and dropped the weapon to his side. I watched as Katie and Carly caught up with us, pausing next to the wall. 'Go back and close everything up,' Paul said to Miles.

The four men were about to be entombed again.

Miles headed back the way we'd come.

There was an old, makeshift bench outside the house, built from moss-speckled bricks and pieces of broken masonry. Paul looked at his daughter, at Carly, and then asked them if they wanted to sit. He was gentle with them, his words soft, soothing, a smile on his face as he addressed them. It felt absolutely genuine, his actions those of someone who cared for them deeply, especially his daughter, and somewhere at the back of my head, a light went on, a stark understanding of what was about to come.

'It's hard to know where to start,' he said, watching as the two women sat down. He turned to me, his eyes searching my face, and it felt like he'd somehow managed to claw his way inside my head and see exactly what I was thinking. It was impossible not to see the fierceness of his intelligence, the way it flickered like a fire, incapable of being put out; that part of him hadn't come alive in the photos I'd seen of him, but it was clear as day now. Miles had taken the gun with him, back to the staircase, but I got the sense Paul had never needed it in the first place. He was totally in control of where we were heading.

'You've got a daughter, haven't you, David?'

He was standing on the other side of the wall, inside the boundaries of the old house, basically inviting me to just turn around and walk away if I wanted to.

'Annabel, right?'

I pictured my daughter. She was thirty-three and lived in south Devon. I hadn't spoken to her for a couple of days – not since taking up the search for Paul Conister – but the image of her on my laptop during our last conversation was easy to visualize.

I looked at Paul and then at Katie.

She was staring at her father and seemed like she might be about to cry again. Carly had a hand on her knee and had already started. Paul glanced at them, took a breath, and – when his eyes settled on me again – pain was written all over his face.

'I read about Annabel,' he said. 'I know you try and keep your private life away from the media, which I understand, but there are a few things you can find online about her. I'm sure you know that.' He glanced at Katie again. 'We do what we can to protect the ones that we love. You went to the ends of the earth for Annabel, literally as I understand it, and I'd do the same for Katie. I would do the same for Seb. I would do absolutely anything – *anything* – in a heartbeat to make sure they were safe. And if I thought others like them were being hurt, I would do the same for them as well.'

He meant Carly.

He meant Miles.

If I'd had any doubts before, I didn't any more. This hadn't begun with Mira Ibragimova. It hadn't begun with the many other, nameless women that Wolstene and the three men in the staircase had attacked. It had begun with someone much closer to home.

I swallowed. 'Katie was a victim.'

Paul nodded.

'Of Wolstene?'

'Yes,' Paul said simply.

I looked at the two women. They'd been diminished somehow: no longer women, just girls.

'Like I told you,' Paul said, 'those men were animals.'

Katie started to break down completely, her face buried in Carly's shoulder. Back along the line, I could see a glimpse of Miles in the trees, putting the panels back into place.

'Robert got in touch with me about sponsorship,' Paul said, the wind moving the branches above us, the sun turning one side of his face white, like enamel. 'You know all this already, I'm sure. Me and a few friends had paid for a box at the football for our play-off semi-final last year. We normally sat in the stands, but this was a one-off, a big match, a chance to get promoted, so we decided to treat ourselves. At half-time, Robert came in and started introducing himself, and the two of us got talking. I liked him.' Paul paused, hindsight giving him a new perspective on that statement. 'Anyway, like I say, when he found out who I worked for, and saw how successful Tarrington was, he got in touch, asking about a possible sponsorship.'

He looked at Katie and Carly.

'The match was in May and we kept in touch over the summer; in August, I met him for dinner for the first time. Him and three of his friends.' Paul regarded the woods behind me for a moment, the trees, the staircase, the secrets inside it. 'We all went for a curry. They were nice guys too. They seemed pretty ordinary, down to earth. One of them, Lee, worked for a BMW dealership in Richmond, so we immediately had something in common; another, Kevin, did something clever with computers. The third guy . . .' He faded out, his attention switching to his daughter. 'You wanted to know earlier why I didn't go to the police when I found out what was going on. Well, Darren – in there – was why.'

Darren.

'Darren Fox,' I said softly.

Paul nodded.

That was why I recognized the face inside the footbridge. He was the detective who'd worked Paul's disappearance, who'd let the case fizzle out, who'd turned up at Maggie's house only hours after she'd called the police. It was why Maggie didn't see a uniform that night and wasn't asked to come to the station straight away, even though that was the protocol in missing persons cases: Fox wanted to see the house for himself. He needed to know where Paul was. It wasn't a search for answers, it was a hunt.

The police are part of the problem.

'Darren could make things go away,' Paul said, 'and that was exactly what he did.' For the first time, he started to become emotional, his words slightly stilted, his Adam's apple shifting up and down like a piston. 'We met up a few times – *quite* a few times, actually – and on each occasion, I started to like them even more, but I also started to catch just a glimpse of something. At the time, I couldn't have described to you

what it was, I just had the sense that there was something –
some mutual understanding between them – that they shared,
that I wasn't privy to . . .' He ground to a halt and shifted
from one foot to the other, looking at his daughter. 'But then
Katie came home and said she was interested in capturing
the workplace as part of some visual study they were doing
at art school, and she was imagining skyscrapers and views
out across London from high up, and I just . . . I just thought
that it would be . . .' He stopped.

'It's not your fault, Dad,' Katie said.

He gave her a small smile, an apology for all that had followed. Tears flashed in his eyes. 'My baby,' he said faintly, and
wiped them away. 'Katie, she loves her art so much. She's so
talented, she's doing so well. I mean, you must have seen it for
yourself at the house. She said you mentioned on the phone
that you saw the painting she did of Carly, that it must have
been one of the ways that you connected the two of them.'
He turned to his daughter again. 'She painted that after I went
missing. It was a mistake on her part, because that painting
turned out to be a way for you to find me, David, but I don't
blame her for not thinking about it at the time. I don't blame
either of them. These two' – he gestured towards the two
women – 'they're kids. They should be out there in the world,
doing things that people their age are doing, not worrying
every second of every day about whether they might be
caught in a lie. The paintings she did were a way for Katie to
escape, a way for her to do something she loved.'

They studied each other.

'Robert said she could come to ASCB,' Paul said distantly,
'that they'd set her up with a desk on one of the top floors
and let her paint. His only stipulation was that – when she
was done – she let them hang her best picture in the office
somewhere.'

'It's not your fault, Dad,' Katie said again.

'I thought he was being so nice to her.'

'*Dad.*'

But either Paul wasn't listening or he didn't agree. 'I thought, at the time, that Robert organized it so quickly because we were friends and he wanted to help me. But it wasn't that at all. He'd met Katie once when she came to pick me up from a dinner, and I'd showed him, showed all of them, photos of her, because I was so proud of her.'

He swallowed, sniffed.

'That was the reason he offered to help her.'

A chill seemed to settle around us.

'He knew that building,' Paul went on. 'He knew the layout back to front. He knew the hours people kept, he knew where all the cameras were, knew how to hide.'

That echoed exactly what Mira had said.

'I thought I was doing something good by sending her there,' Paul muttered, his words choppy, hard to even hear. 'But all I did was send my daughter to the devil.'

35

Paul looked at Katie. 'How many times was it?'

'Dad,' she said, shaking her head. 'Stop.'

'How many times?'

Her eyes moved between me and her father.

'Three,' she replied.

'Three times he attacked her inside the space of the week she was there,' Paul said, 'and I never even got a whiff of it. Nothing. Not a hint. She came home, same as always, and she went to her room, and Maggie and I, we just put it down to her being a normal kid. Then, she came to us on the Thursday night – her fourth day of having to go to that place – and said she didn't feel well, and wasn't sure she could go in for her last day. But we . . .' He stopped, closed his eyes, shook his head. 'We made her go in. I said to her, "You just need to get through one more day." All I was thinking about at the time was what Robert had done for me. I thought, "I don't want to let him down, not after he organized this so quickly." Katie said she really didn't feel well, and even Maggie said to me, "Maybe she shouldn't go in." But I made her. I forced her to go . . .'

For a moment, I was unable to look at Paul, at the weight of the guilt he was carrying, or at Katie, whose suffering mirrored everything I'd had described to me already by Mira. Next to her, there was something similar in Carly's expression, hurt and anguish, humiliation and anger, but of a different kind. Somehow, I didn't think she'd been subjected to the same things as Katie – but she was here for a reason.

Her dad had infected her life too.

'I overheard them talking one night,' Carly said, speaking for what felt like the first time in hours. I looked at her, Paul did too, and I could see this for what it was: a story that the four of them – Paul, Katie, Carly and Miles – had been over and over; a tragedy in which all knew their parts. 'Dad and Lee and Kevin and that Darren guy. I heard them all. I think Darren, the policeman, he might have been the worst of them.' Something flickered in her face. 'I was supposed to be staying at a friend's, but she started feeling ill, so I came home early. Miles was out with his mates at the pub, so Dad had invited the three of them round. I got in and heard them talking about Katie.'

The two women joined hands.

'Dad was describing what had happened. Everything. Every little detail. He'd threatened her, promised her that – if she told anyone – he knew people who would hurt her, hurt Paul, and Maggie, and Seb. I listened to him tell the others about what he did to her, about how she started crying when he told her what would happen to her parents if she ever breathed a word.' Carly looked up the track, towards her brother. Miles was returning now, the panels back in place, the men reconsigned to the shadows. 'Those four, they don't look so frightening in there,' she said quietly, eyes shifting to the staircase. 'You can't imagine them being the men we're describing. But they are. Believe me, they are. After I heard them that night, I told Miles, and we started looking into who our father *really* was. We went looking for his secrets, for the things he'd never told us, and that was when we found out the truth about our mum.'

'You're saying he killed her?'

She nodded. 'He made it look like a suicide. Buried in the loft, we found some correspondence he'd had with Darren

Fox at the time. Little things, hints that built into a bigger picture. If there were question marks, Fox made them go away. I mean, Mum was depressed – for most of our lives up to that point, she was on medication; she'd have these huge swings – but she wouldn't have killed herself like that. There was no way she'd have stuck a nozzle in the car, run the engine and smoked herself out. We became ninety-nine per cent sure he did it, Miles and me, and then – when we finally brought him here – when we pushed him about it, that was when he told us he had. He said he'd killed her because she found out about him, about him and his group of psychopaths. And you know the worst bit? Mum died when we were in our *teens*. That means – until we stopped him – Dad had been doing this for at least a decade.'

It was hard to process the fact that she was talking about her own father, that the man who was supposed to have been her protector, the ultimate bulwark in her life, the person she could trust above all others, had done something so heinous. And not only that: he'd covered the entire thing up and, afterwards, hadn't changed his behaviour one iota. Perhaps, after his wife, he hadn't *physically* killed anyone else – but psychologically it wasn't far off. What he'd done to Katie, to Mira – what he and his friends like Darren Fox had done to others – had destroyed a part of those women for good.

I looked at Carly, trying to clear my head, and said to her, 'So after you heard your dad and his friends talking that night you got home early, you contacted Katie?'

She nodded. 'I found her number, and I called her. I pretended I was with an art gallery and that I wanted to speak to her about exhibiting her work, because I knew that she would never come if I told her what I *really* wanted to talk about.' Carly watched as Miles stopped at the wall. 'I wanted Katie to know that she wasn't alone.'

I turned to Paul. 'So how did you find out?'

'I just started noticing a change in Katie,' he said. 'She was painting a little less, she didn't seem as engaged. She'd spend more time in her room. Maggie tried to talk to her because – again, naively – we thought it might be an age thing. She was only just out of her teens at the time. But I don't know . . .' He faded out and turned to his daughter, and I could see that same perception in his eyes, his intellect working intricately, like the gears and wheels of a watch. 'One day, when Maggie was out, we were alone in the house and I asked Katie if everything was okay. I told her nothing she could do, or feel, or think, would ever change how much we loved her, and then I left her and went downstairs to make some coffee, and a couple of minutes later, she just walked into the kitchen.' He looked at me. 'She was crying her eyes out. More than crying: she was absolutely inconsolable. I'd never seen her like that – not ever.'

From somewhere, there was the far-off drone of a plane.

'I'd been angry before,' Paul said, 'but never like that. It was the kind of anger that I couldn't control. I was trembling. I wanted to break something. That day when Katie told me the truth, the days after when she introduced me to Carly, and Carly told me all about who her father really was . . . All the other women he'd hurt, that his friends had hurt. The texts she'd found on his phone, or emails she'd got into and read. The Internet searches he'd forgotten to wipe . . .' Paul stopped, breathing harder. 'The anger, it was like a tremor deep in my bones. I couldn't stop it. I just wanted to hurt them.'

I looked back along the line, to the staircase. 'So this was how you hurt them,' I said. It wasn't a question, it was a statement of fact: these men weren't being hurt with one devastating blow – not a gunshot, not a knife in the chest, not a pill or a noose – they were being hurt incrementally, slowly, broken down piece by piece until, eventually, there would be nothing left. This was the ultimate act of revenge.

'Who was the man who jumped from that roof?' I asked.

'He ran a website.' *A website.* I could imagine what kind: the sort that Robert Wolstene and his friends would find mirror images of themselves on. Paul glanced at Miles. 'That was when Carly suggested bringing Miles in. He's not a builder, he's not really in the restaurant business – those are all just ways to blur the image of what we did, to hide us from view and build barriers between us and the authorities if they started looking closer. No, what Miles is good at, what he's *really* good at, is technology. He tracked this guy down and started talking to him, pretending to be Robert. He per-suaded him to meet at the ASCB building, said he had something to show him that he wouldn't want to miss, and – when he got there – I met him in the lobby and told him I was Robert. By that time, Robert was already gone.' He meant Robert was already a prisoner inside the darkness of the staircase. 'We took him on the Tuesday and called him in sick, then on the Thursday we used his access card to get to the roof – and, when that piece of shit from the website turned his back, well . . .'

'You pushed him?'

'Absolutely, I did.' He looked at me, not a mote of regret in his face. 'After that, Miles went into the ASCB system and replaced the footage of me on the stairs, of the guy from the website following me up there, with an archived video of Robert going up to the roof to join one of his work col-leagues for a smoke, taken three weeks before.'

'Did he even look like Robert?' I asked, thinking of what I'd read in the file about Wolstene's suicide, of how investi-gators didn't pick up on the fact that the two men weren't the same person. Even with injuries, it should have been obvious eventually.

'He was about the same age, the same weight and height.'

'But there must have still been anomalies.'

'That was where Darren Fox came in,' Paul replied.

'What do you mean?'

'I mean, two things happened when he thought Robert Wolstene jumped off that building. One, he started keeping a close eye on the investigation, because Fox had to make absolutely sure that *nothing* came up in Wolstene's life that could tie him to anything criminal – and if he *did* find something, we knew it would be a fair bet that he'd do what he always did and make it all go away. In turn, that would play into our favour because it would dilute the efficacy of the case as a whole, *if* there were ever any suspicions that it wasn't a suicide. But, of course, there weren't: Wolstene's death was ruled a suicide early on. We got away with that part, and so did Fox. The second thing was kind of tied into that, though, because – even though Wolstene's death was ruled a suicide and closed within weeks – we *knew* that Fox would think otherwise. They'd known each other for a long time and, if Wolstene was so racked with guilt over the terrible things he was doing, he would have jumped years ago. So we figured, rightly, that Fox would start fixating on the idea Wolstene was pushed.'

'Which would eventually bring him to you.'

'Correct. So we laid a trail of breadcrumbs for him, just in case.'

All the way into their trap.

I looked back at the staircase.

This trap.

Paul broke out into a smile. 'You're smart, David, so we knew you were getting close. Miles said he suspected you might even have been inside his flat, which is why him and Carly called in sick today, so we could all meet here and work out our plan of attack. The whole time you've been looking for me, you've been applying pressure, whether unwittingly or not. I mean, Katie came to see me yesterday at the hotel I've been staying in down in Sussex – under a false name, of course – which is why she wasn't at home last night. I thought she'd arranged it with Maggie. But she forgot, and I forgot to remind her. So Maggie started panicking, and then we both started panicking, and we sent those texts to Maggie to explain what was going on – only, we left out one crucial part. The kisses. The emojis. After all this time, most of that stuff I feel like I've got a handle on. I feel like, in most respects, we've pulled this whole thing off perfectly. But, even now, when the pressure kicks in, the panic hits – and as we've seen you drift in and out of view over the past few days, as we've watched you get closer, believe me, the panic has got real.'

'Is that why you disappeared in the first place? Panic?'

'Yes,' he said simply. 'We'd been planning this for a while, the four of us. Like I said, I felt strongly that we had it all worked out. We'd taken all the necessary steps.'

'Was that what the building work was for?'

Paul frowned.

'The bathroom,' I said. 'Your little hiding place.'

His mouth dropped open a little and then he nodded, as if he'd almost forgotten all of that himself. '"Robbie Avery",' he said, his voice low, his eyes on the ground now, going back over the decisions they'd all made together. 'Miles wasn't a builder, but he knew more than enough. Before he got into computers, he trained as a bricklayer. Did you know that? I think that's one of the reasons Miles is hard to get a handle on: he's done a lot of things, been a lot of things, and when you're planning the sort of stuff we were planning, that

176

diversity actually becomes very useful.' He looked at Miles and smiled at him. 'Anyway, yes, the building work was all part of the plan. The garden wall was to convince Maggie that Miles was the right workman to do the bathroom, which she'd wanted refurbished for a while. And the "hiding place", as you call it: that was just an insurance policy, in case Plan A didn't come off.'

An insurance policy.

He was talking about the boxes I'd seen evidence of in there.

'What was the insurance policy?'

'Paperwork linking the four men – Wolstene, Darren Fox, Kevin, Lee – to some of their crimes. We'd done our research, David. We'd put these men in the same places as some of their victims – and, of course, we had Katie's testimony, and what Carly had overheard. We hid it in there for emergency use only: if we didn't manage to get them here, to this place, to their prison, if they got to one of us first and took that person out of the picture, the others knew to go to the house to get those boxes.'

But the plan worked.

The men were all in their prison.

That was why the boxes weren't under the bath any more.

'But I don't understand,' I said. 'If it all worked, why disappear?'

'It *did* work – but there was one complication. We'd got Wolstene here, we'd got Kevin and Lee. I mean, those two definitely weren't the brains of the operation: it was so preposterously easy to pick them off. We just lured them to places based on conversations we were having with them online, posing as other people. I'd like to say that they were jumpy after Robert's "death", that they were careful, but they weren't: they were still led by their desires, by their natures.

So it was easy to get to those two, easier to manoeuvre them to where we needed them to be. Miles's gun . . .' He stopped, gestured towards Miles. 'It's not even real. But it's real enough when the person you're pointing it at thinks you'll fire it.' He stopped, sighed. 'But DS Fox, he was different.'

'And he was the reason you had to disappear.'

'Yes.'

'He was the complication.'

'Yes,' he said again, quietly.

He took a long breath then, his hand on the wall. Behind him, the women were very quiet, their faces less tearful, almost opaque, as if the time for showing emotion had passed. Across from him, Miles just watched us silently, his expression inscrutable. But it was absolutely clear: we were here.

We'd finally arrived at the end.

The night Paul Conister vanished.

36

'I got Carly that job at Tarrington a week before I went "missing",' Paul said, and I remembered her telling me, when I'd turned up there, that she hadn't worked there long. 'I had no ulterior motive, I just wanted her to get a start somewhere, get a job where the people actually cared about her. She hadn't had much of that in her life – except for Miles. They haven't had anyone to care for them for a very long time.' He looked at them in the same way he had looked at Katie. 'But, in the end, she was the one that repaid the favour. Somehow – and I still don't know how – Darren Fox had caught my scent. I don't think he knew that I was the one who pushed Wolstene, but he knew I was involved somehow. And the day I went missing, as I was driving home, Carly called me from the office and said that Fox had been in. He told her he was just checking up on her and Miles, seeing how they were doing after their father's suicide – but he kept asking about me as well.' He stared off, into the trees, for a second. 'Did Seb see him?' Paul asked. 'Did he see Miles that night?'

I nodded. 'Yes.'

'I thought so. Miles said he thought he got spotted.'

'What were you doing at the house?' I asked Miles.

'I got that call from Carly,' Paul said, answering for him, 'and I got home, and I tried to act normal. Maggie said Katie was at a friend's house, so that was good – that was one less thing to worry about – but I'd done my research on Fox by then, knew an awful lot about the type of man he was, and there was no way he was going to leave it at a quick visit to the showroom. If he didn't find me there, he'd come and find me at home. Like I say, he had the scent. He was an animal. Admittedly, I didn't think he would come to my house *that night* – but I knew he had me in his sights. He was going to make me go away. I was just another problem he'd have to dispose of.'

'But *you* were hunting *him*, weren't you?'

'We were. But we weren't ready to strike. We'd literally put *months* of planning into Wolstene's suicide, and even with the other two, simpler though they were, it took us weeks to man-oeuvre them into place. With Fox, we'd have to be even more careful. He was a policeman, a detective. Detectives who go missing raise *massive* red flags – so, when those flags finally went up, we had to make sure we were totally insulated.'

'So, that night, you weren't in a position to take care of him?'

'No,' Paul said. 'Not then. Not by a long shot.'

'But he could take care of you?'

'I don't think he was putting the same level of thought into coming after me – and how he would do it and cover it up – as *I* was putting into going after him. But, still, I maybe thought I had a couple of days before he launched his attack, a week at most before whatever offensive he was planning. But I didn't. I went upstairs to take my pill that night and I'd left my phone up there, charging. I had a second phone too, which no one else but these three knew about, and whenever I went up to take my pill, I'd always check the second one – and on it was a message from Miles. It said that Fox was already outside the house. He'd parked at the end of the street. He was waiting. Miles had been keeping an eye on Fox for me, shadowing him, part of the reconnaissance we were doing on him – that was why Miles was outside our house that night. He told me I had to do something, that Fox had a mask in the car with him. Worse, Miles told me that he thought he'd glimpsed Fox with a gun.'

'You really think he was coming to kill you?'

'One hundred per cent.'

'With Maggie and Seb in the house?'

'Do you really think he would give a shit about something like that? This was a *rapist*, David. This was a rapist with a history of violence. He was coming for me, no question. This wasn't a man who was going to sit there and try to persuade me not to make public all the terrible things he'd done. If he murdered me, I wasn't a problem. If he wore a mask, Maggie would never be able to ID him. It was really very simple.'

'So you hid under the bath?'

He nodded. 'I crawled into that wall cavity, and I pulled the panel shut, and I stayed there for fifteen hours.' He sucked in a long breath. 'Fifteen *hours*, I lay there stock-still, barely breathing. I heard Fox come to the house that night under the pretence of giving a damn what had happened to me. He must have heard about me on the airwaves at the Met, I suppose. I heard him talking to Maggie, heard her telling him what had gone on, and I could *hear* he didn't believe her, didn't believe it could have happened like she said it did; it was in his voice, his contempt for her. He thought she was mixed-up and panicked. I mean, Maggie sounded way too emotional, too confused, even to me, and *I* knew she was telling the truth. To him, it must have sounded ridiculous. And because there was no evidence to back Maggie up, no evidence of a hiding place anywhere in the house – I heard him trying windows, doors, opening and closing the conservatory – he just figured I'd exited the home without her noticing. I think he genuinely thought Maggie was off her rocker.'

'I'm sure she appreciated you making her look like that.'

'I did it to protect her.'

I couldn't help reacting, my expression showing my disgust.

'You don't believe me? This was about protecting my *family*. I mean, why else would I have been hiding out in a hotel on the M23 for three months, using a fake name, working cash in hand as a bloody delivery driver? Why else would I choose to only see my daughter once a week, and not see my son or my wife *at all*?'

'So why are you still doing it? Why are you still hiding?'

'I'm not any more.'

I frowned.

A half-smile formed. 'Oh, you didn't see, David?'

'See what?'

'Darren Fox took a two-week holiday and didn't come back.'

'What?'

'He was supposed to be back in the office three days ago – but no one has seen him. He didn't come in. He has no girlfriend, no family, so I think he was only reported missing yesterday by the people he works with. It's all so strange.'

'You took him before he went on holiday?'

Paul nodded. 'Like I say, months of planning.'

That was why, when I'd googled Darren Fox, I'd found no mention of him being reported missing: the story hadn't made it to the press yet. He went on holiday two weeks ago and failed to return. Except he never *went* on holiday: before he got the chance, he was added to the staircase. The final piece of the jigsaw. The last man.

Paul Conister's grand plan, fulfilled.

'The dust has settled now,' he said.

'What does that mean?'

'It means I was going to give it a month after Darren went

missing, but I don't think that's necessary. The police will find no leads. There will be no trail leading back to me.' He smiled at Katie, a look of genuine affection. 'So now I'm ready to go home.'

'And how are you going to do that?'

'You mean, how am I going to explain my absence?'

'No,' I said. 'I don't care how you explain this to Maggie. What I mean is, I can't let you just reappear and carry on like nothing ever happened. What those men did to Katie, to all the others, it makes me sick to my stomach. I hate what they are as much as you do, believe me. But you can't just leave them to die in this place.'

'Why not?'

'It's not right. You might think it is, but it's not.'

'So what are you saying?'

'I'm saying, if you don't call the cops, I will.'

I expected some reaction from him, but instead he didn't move. None of them did. It was almost like they'd been expecting me to say something like that. I looked towards the others and they simply stared back. When I turned back to Paul, he just smiled again, but it wasn't destructive, or malicious, or unkind. In fact, it was totally the opposite.

It was like he pitied me.

'We don't want to hurt good people, David,' he said softly, almost respectfully. 'It's why we decided to let you come here. It's why we've been completely honest with you about everything. Even the pond life that we've got tied up in there, people who barely deserve the oxygen they're breathing, we haven't physically injured. Not with knives or guns, anyway. We feed them occasionally. We let them drink. The point of the exercise is for them to suffer, slowly, and eventually to wither away and die. But we don't inflict violence upon them.' He pushed himself away from the wall and moved back in my direction, over the old, fallen gate and on to the line. 'But if you're not with us, David, you're against us, and the same plans we enacted on them, we'll enact on you.'

I smiled at him.

'Is something funny?' he asked.

'You think this is the first time I've been threatened?'

'No, I don't. But the difference is, I imagine when people threaten you, they don't actually think about the best way to get at you. But I have. *We* have. We've been thinking about it from the second that Maggie picked up the phone and called you.'

I eyed him.

'We've put something in your house.'

My heart dropped. 'In my house?'

'It belongs to Darren Fox. We've hidden it somewhere. In fact, it's hidden so well that, in all likelihood, you'll never find it. I mean' – he pointed behind me, towards the staircase – 'we've become pretty good at hiding things. It's a personal item, something that was very important to Darren, something very specific to him that people will associate with him, and you should know something else too: it's got your fingerprints on it; it has your DNA on it as well. We got both of those off a cup you drank from when you went to see Maggie.'

I looked at Katie.

'I'm sorry,' she said, and the strangest thing was, it sounded like she genuinely meant it. A moment later, unable to hold my gaze, she looked down at the floor, and Carly glanced out at the trees as Miles took a couple of steps closer to me. Of all of them, he was the most comfortable with this. In Paul, he seemed to have found a man much kinder and more loving than his father – but, in his own way, just as ruthless.

'How do I know this isn't another lie?' I said.

'You don't. But do you think I'm making it up?'

We looked at each other.

No, I thought, *I don't.*

'So,' Paul went on, taking a small step forward, 'you can let the police know about all of this. But when you do, they'll get an anonymous call about an item in your house. And given that it has your DNA on it, and given that I hear the Met *despise* you and have been looking to bring you down for years, I figure that – even when you try to tell them it was me – they won't believe you. Not with the reputation you have there. Not with all the cold cases of theirs you've taken on down the years, and solved off your own back, making them look incompetent in the process. I think they'll be desperate to put you in handcuffs.'

I stood there, speechless.

Because he was right.

The Met loathed me.

He backed away, the light dappling his skin, and gestured for the others to follow him. 'Again, David, I'm so sorry to have to threaten you like this, but I hope you understand why.'

Katie, and then Carly, and then Miles, joined him.

'In the end,' he said, 'family is everything.'

37

I searched my house from top to bottom. I worked methodically through each room, pulling up carpets and floorboards, even yanking old Victorian ventilation grates off the walls to look for hiding places that I knew weren't likely to have been used. I turned over earth along the lawn, picked apart the rock garden that Derryn had put together in her last months, and then got under the decking at the rear of the house that hadn't been touched for a decade. I went up into the roof and pulled up insulation, loosened boards so I could search underneath, and found nothing. There were no items that I didn't recognize, and nothing that I could identify as belonging to someone that wasn't me.

By rights, that should have exposed Paul as a liar.

And yet I still couldn't shake the idea that this wasn't a lie, that somewhere in my life he'd buried a bomb and the second that I picked up the phone to the cops, it would go off in my face. I'd spent so many years searching for people, and just as many years facing down the terrible secrets they could carry and the extraordinary lengths they'd go to, to protect themselves – and the one thing it had taught me was how to detect a liar. And, as much as it pained me to admit it, Paul Conister wasn't a liar. He may have lied to get what he wanted and to carry out his plan, but he hadn't told a lie to me.

The bomb was real.

I just had to choose whether to set it off.

*

Early the next morning, I returned to the woods, got over the fence and followed the old railway line back to the foot-bridge. It was a much cooler day, the skies greyer, the spaces under the canopy less defined. It was breezier too, the trees moving the whole time, branches bowing, leaves twisting. As I levered off the boards with a claw hammer, I kept seeing movements in front of me, over my shoulder, out of the corner of my eye, shadowy flickers that seemed like people passing in and out of view. Every time I stopped and looked around, there was never anyone there.

Once I'd got enough of the panelling off, I climbed through the gap, switched on a torch and watched its beam arrow up the stairs, towards the darkness of the room at the top. Even before I'd taken the first step, I could sense something had changed: I could smell disinfectant in the air, sharp and caustic, and there were patterns and whorls in the wood, from where water had been poured down the steps and dried. By the time I got to the top, it was obvious what I was going to find here.

Nothing.

All four men had been moved.

When I arrived at the Conisters' house an hour later, I was already behind the curve: I could hear voices inside, laughter, excitement, glimpsed shapes through the living-room windows that I knew were Maggie, Katie and Seb, and – hugging them – Paul.

'David,' Maggie said as soon as she saw me, 'he's home!'

I forced a smile, tried to make it look genuine, and then followed Maggie into the house. As I got to the living room, I saw them all, rain hitting the glass roof of the conservatory behind them, three pairs of eyes fixed on me: Seb, elated that his father was home, completely unaware of the truth; then

Paul and Katie, the smiles on their faces not quite reaching their eyes.

'This is David,' Maggie said. 'This is who I was telling you about.'

Paul broke from his kids and came over, hand out. I looked at Maggie, could see the absolute joy in her face, and realized that there was no way I could ruin it here. So I took Paul's hand, squeezed it so hard I saw him flinch, and said, 'What a surprise.'

Paul's smile dropped away for a second, out of Maggie's line of sight, and then – when he opened himself up again, allowing her to see him – the smile was back, as if it had never left in the first place. 'I know,' he said to us all. 'It all happened so fast.'

'What happened so fast?'

'I had an accident,' he said.

'Yeah?' I looked between him and Katie, and then across to Maggie. She was watching him, had apparently already heard this story and, crucially, seemed to have bought it. 'What sort of accident did you have?' I asked him, trying to sound neutral.

'The night I "disappeared" ' – he even made the air quotes with his fingers – 'I just had this episode. I can't explain it. I went upstairs and it was like everything went blank. Completely blank. I stood there in the bedroom and had no idea how I'd got there, or even where I was.' He paused, looking between us all but especially at Maggie. 'I was saying to Mags, it was so scary.' He was talking to me now. 'I just went downstairs and walked out the front door.'

'I wonder why Maggie didn't hear you?' I said innocently.

'Oh, you mean the squeaky door?' he responded immediately, as if he knew exactly what I was going to come at him with. 'I'd oiled it the day before.'

I looked at Maggie.

It was ridiculous, but she'd been blinded by his return.

'I felt like I had to escape the house,' he went on, 'because I didn't know this place and it was crushing me, you know? I was struggling to even breathe.'

I could see exactly where this was going.

He was going to pretend he'd gone into a fugue state.

I'd worked a case once where a man woke up with no recollection of his name or who he was. For a time, the authorities had pursued the idea that he might have entered a fugue state, a dissociative condition where the sufferer was, for a period of days, or months, or years, unable to recall anything about themselves or their life. It normally righted itself and those lost memories came back, and for Paul Conister, it was the perfect disguise to put on as he walked through the door after three months.

'So what happened to you after that?' I asked.

'I don't really remember,' he said, his expression pained, the words so convincing I thought again about the item he'd claimed to have hidden in my house: I still didn't believe that he'd lied to me the day before at the railway line, about everything he'd done, about the item, but it was more obvious than ever that he could lie when he needed to, and do it with absolute conviction. Maggie and Seb couldn't take their eyes off him. Even Katie seemed to have forgotten that she was in on it. They all just watched, enraptured.

'You don't remember where you've been for three months?' I asked, and – just for a moment – the spell was broken, and Maggie looked at me. But it wasn't with a sense that I'd hit on something. It wasn't that she was starting to doubt the reason he'd given her for suddenly recalling who he was and walking through the front door. Not being able to remember how he'd survived the last three months, or why no police officer, or doctor, or anyone in the media had ever come into contact with him and raised the alarm, didn't seem to be the issues that bothered her.

It was, instead, the way I'd spoken to him.

The look she gave me was disappointment, even anger. She didn't like the way that I was talking to her husband, didn't like the way that I seemed to be belittling his suffering, the confusion and pain he'd had to endure during his fictional fugue state. The shield had come down, and that was when I realized just how skilful Paul was, and how quietly manipulative he was when it counted: he'd created a story that would hold up to no scrutiny whatsoever, but his family loved him so much it didn't even matter.

None of them needed me any more.

Not my questions, not my suspicions.

I was a ghost, already forgotten.

PART FOUR
Man

38

On a muggy morning in the middle of September – two months after Paul Conister reappeared out of nowhere, spinning the story about a fugue state – I got back from a run and found a car parked on my drive and a woman I didn't know at my front door.

'Can I help you?' I asked, moving around her car. On the passenger seat there were a couple of files, both in opaque plastic folders with identical logos on them.

The logo looked vaguely familiar.

'Mr Raker?' she asked. She was in her forties, her blonde hair curly and blowing around in the wind. She held out her hand. 'Hi, my name's Dr Garrison.'

I got to my front steps and we shook.

'Sorry for turning up out of the blue like this,' she said. 'I'm a psychiatrist over at St Augustine's Hospital. Uh, I guess you know us.'

That was an understatement, and she clearly knew it.

St Augustine's was a psychiatric hospital in east London, built on the edge of the Thames, that I'd encountered in a previous case: the same case that eventually became the reason I'd put my house on the market; whose dark, writhing trail had tried to challenge everything I knew about Derryn, my wife, the woman I'd loved. I'd ended up at St Augustine's looking for answers, and my memories of that place – and what had happened there – still hurt deeply. I was tempted to tell Garrison to leave.

I didn't want to go back in time.

But, in the end, my curiosity got the better of me.

'How can I help you, Dr Garrison?'

'I wanted to talk to you about one of your cases –'

'No,' I said, closing her down instantly. 'I'm not talking about that.'

'I'm sorry?'

'I'm not talking about what happened at your hospital.'

'Oh, no, sorry, you misunderstand me. It's . . .' Garrison paused. 'It's not to do with what happened to you at St Augustine's. It's to do with one of your older cases.'

I frowned. 'Really?'

'Yes.' She gestured to my front door. 'Maybe we could talk inside?'

Two days later, I was down in Devon visiting Annabel, the two of us out on a beach that my parents used to take me to growing up, when my mobile phone started buzzing. It was a London number, one I still had logged, months later.

Maggie.

I pushed Answer.

'David?' Maggie said softly as, close to me, waves lapped against the shore. I told Annabel to give me a moment and moved up the beach, leaving her and her dog, Bear, by the water. I watched her as she threw a ball across the shingle and Bear went after it – streamlined as a bullet – catching it in his jaws before it even hit the beach.

'Are you okay, Maggie?'

'Yes.'

But she didn't continue.

'Why are you calling?' I asked her, my tone – on the surface – as neutral as it had been that last day at her house. But she was smart, switched on, and, just like at the house, she could see what lay beneath. *I'm done with your case*, it said.

'I think you may have been right.'

I paused. 'Right about what?'

'The last time we saw you, at the house, there was something in your voice. I could sense it.' She took a long, deep breath, her exhalation so hard I could hear it, even above the waves. 'I don't know, I guess I just . . .' A beat. 'When Paul walked through the door that day, that was all that mattered. I was overwhelmed by it. The sense of relief, it was just dizzying. I'd wanted him back for months, I had missed him so much every day; there were evenings when he was gone when I would just cry all night. So when he returned . . .' She sighed again. 'That day, the suspicion I could hear in your voice – even though I *know* you were trying to disguise it – I didn't want to hear it. And I think it's maybe because, deep down, I was suspicious myself.'

I didn't respond; just waited her out.

'Do you think he'd been in a fugue state?' she asked.

I thought about my answer for a moment, thought even longer about how conflicted the case had left me. The four men that Paul and the others had imprisoned in that staircase were beasts, profoundly evil, and I couldn't in all honesty pretend that I'd spent a single second worrying about their suffering and whether they were still breathing. But, even so, there was a system, legally and morally, that I tried to uphold, structures that needed to be followed in order to maintain a semblance of order, and Paul Conister had ignored all of it. If I believed, even for one second, that he was bullshitting about having something on me, some piece of evidence that might cost me my freedom, I would have gone straight to the cops, much as the Met distrusted me. But I hadn't because I *did* believe him, and because I believed him – and because everyone else in his life did too – I'd had no choice but to remain silent.

'I don't know,' I said to Maggie. 'Do you believe him?'

It was obvious she didn't, or at best was having doubts, but I let her respond first anyway, watching as Bear brought the ball back to Annabel. As I studied them, heat shimmering off the beach in the midday sun, my thoughts spun back to the conversation I'd had with Dr Garrison at the house, to what had happened at St Augustine's Hospital two years before that, to Derryn, to the case I'd worked where all I ever believed about my wife had been challenged. In the middle of it, when I'd started to become completely overwhelmed – when I'd even, despite how much I'd loved my wife, suspected Derryn of lying to me – it was like drowning. I couldn't get my head above water.

And I knew that was what Maggie would be feeling.

Except, in her case, the person she loved *had* lied.

'I don't think he's telling me the truth,' she said finally.

'Why not?'

'I don't know,' she said again. 'It just doesn't add up.'

'So what are you going to do about it?'

'I'm not sure.' She paused. 'Can you help me?'

'No,' I said. 'Not this time.'

Silence.

After a while, I could hear her crying.

'Don't call me again, Maggie, okay?'

'Okay,' she sobbed.

'And one other thing.'

She sniffed, her breath crackling down the line.

Sow the seed and then hang up.

'You're right,' I said. 'He's not telling the truth.'

39

The day of my father's funeral, I read out a poem, written in 1949, called 'Man' by Karl-Heinz Güsen. Before I found it at the back of the attic, the day after Dad died, buried in the middle of one of the old English textbooks I'd left behind after I moved to London, I'd only heard it read aloud once, when I was six: Dad read it at his own father's funeral.

In all the years I spent working with words, first at school, then at university, then finally as a journalist, I never once thought about that poem, even in the times when I would remember my grandad, my dad's father. But then, alone in that attic – Derryn downstairs in my father's old kitchen, emptying out the cupboards of a house Dad would never come back to – I picked up that textbook, and I read that poem, and I realized it was everything that my Dad had tried to explain to me in his last days. It was all that I would come to learn about hurt and misery, about the terrible crimes of Robert Wolstene and Darren Fox and others like them. It was all I would come to learn about men like Paul Conister – and the ghosts of loss, and grief, and pain.

> We are what we leave behind,
> and what we leave behind we are.
> In a life to come, that better life,
> there will be no regret,
> there will be no heartache,
> there will be only good,
> and there will be only love.

But we have to wait.
For our three score and ten,
we have no choice but to wait.

Until God calls us, we are just
ghosts,
vessels,
prisoners,
because this life is not the better life.

Man will make sure of that.

CASE #2
Bags

They'd called Gerry Stein lots of names down the years.

One of the guys he'd worked with on the Northern Line had spent a few months referring to him as 'Gerry Can', not just on account of it sounding like a container you could store fuel in, but because Gerry was the kind of guy who tended to help others when he could. 'Gerry Christmas' was another – because he loved the festive period – and he'd also heard one of the younger guys refer to him as 'Stein Kampf'. Gerry had no idea if that one had stuck, if it only got used in whispers behind his back, but he knew where it had come from, and why: he'd had to bollock the kid one night because he'd borrowed Gerry's torch and then couldn't remember where he'd left it. And judging by that nickname, and the way he always glared at Gerry whenever they passed each other in the stations, the kid had clearly taken it personally.

Mostly, though, Gerry tended to get called 'Johnny', as in Johnny Cash. It had been going on for so long now that a lot of the people he worked with didn't even know that wasn't his real name; he suspected even his boss thought his actual name was Johnny. The irony was, Gerry didn't look anything like Johnny Cash, and he certainly didn't know much of the guy's music, it was just that he happened to do the thing Johnny Cash sang about in one of his most famous songs.

In fact, Gerry had been doing it for twenty-five years.

Every night, between one and five, he took to the tunnels of the Underground, armed with a radio, a torch and a comfortable pair of shoes, and he walked the line.

He'd walked most of them during his quarter of a century as a patrolman – the Northern, the Central, the District, the Jubilee – but he liked the Circle Line the best. The stations were close to one another and mostly subsurface or above ground, unlike the deep-level lines on the Northern, Jubilee and Central. With those ones, you were surrounded by dark and silence most of the time, with little or no respite from it; on the Circle, you got to see the stars in the sky occasionally and hear the hum of the street.

What he also liked about the Circle was that it brought him into contact every week with his best mate, Stevie O'Keefe. Stevie was a patrolman on the Jubilee Line. They'd grown up together in Dagenham, had lived on the same street, been to the same school, and had both been offered jobs on the Tube within six months of each other. They'd started out as ticket inspectors but when the bosses asked for patrolmen, people who were prepared to check the lines when the live rails were off, when commuters were asleep at home and tourists were tucked up in their hotel rooms, the two of them had looked at each other and decided to give it a shot.

Gerry had never married, but at the time he took the job he had a young daughter, Kerry, who'd been the one good thing to come out of the short, ugly relationship he'd had with her mother, Mandy. He'd only got to see Kerry at weekends for most of the years his daughter had been growing up, but it was different these days: Kerry was now married herself, with two boys, and, in theory at least, Gerry got to see her whenever he wanted. Stevie, on the other hand, had always been part of a tight family unit, but when he and Gerry took the jobs as patrolmen, Stevie's boy was already a teenager, so relatively self-sufficient, and his wife was working as a nurse, clocking all sorts of irregular hours. That meant Stevie had never been drawn to the normal nine-to-five routine. And, in turn, it was why, all these years on, the two of them – both sixty, both greyer than they would have liked, weightier too – were still marching out a route through London's hidden world, and ensuring their paths crossed twice a week at Westminster, where the Circle and Jubilee connected.

Of course, the bosses didn't know about their meetings, and probably wouldn't have been too chuffed to find out either, but Gerry didn't care. He spent an hour with Stevie on Tuesdays and Thursdays, and if the suits didn't like it . . . well, good luck finding a replacement. He smiled at the thought of that, wondering how exactly they would advertise the role if they really did get rid of him. *Do you like to work in pitch-black? Do you like minimal interaction with other human beings? Do you like rats? Do you like the burning stench of brake fluid? Then we've got the job for you!* 'Don't forget the fluffers,' Gerry said quietly to himself, except of course there weren't many of them left any more. It was mostly just machines these days. 'Fluffers' was the name given to the people who used to wipe down the walls of the tunnels at night, getting rid of all the gunk – the hair and skin – that was matted to the brickwork. Back in the day, a lot of them were West Indian women, and he often used to stop and chat to them. They were always fun. He thought of them frequently when he passed through a tunnel and heard the buzz of a machine and the trickle of running water.

Emerging from the dark and into the half-light of Westminster Tube station, Gerry got up on to the platform, via the access stairs, and headed for the exit. On a Tuesday, like tonight, he met Stevie in the Circle and District Line concourse, part of the vast cathedral of concrete and stainless steel, of criss-crossing pillars and brushed-chrome escalators, at the heart of the station. None of the escalators worked after hours, so the two men would have to use them like a regular staircase, Gerry returning the favour on a Thursday and going down to meet Stevie at the equivalent concourse on the Jubilee Line. Normally, they'd be able to hear each other before they saw one another, their heavy footsteps ringing on the escalators in the silence of the station.

As Gerry got to the concourse, he could see that Stevie hadn't arrived yet, so he found a pillar to lean against and waited. Night lighting was on, pale cream bulbs doing little to eradicate the great pockets of darkness that existed in the hall at night. It seemed to make the place bigger somehow, more intimidating, the complete lack of sound and movement adding to the effect. Sometimes, in his more sombre moments, it put him in mind of a tomb. He'd eventually come to appreciate the quiet, because London could get pretty bloody noisy, but the lack of transit, the stillness, that was different. Gerry found comfort in feeling people move past him in the street. He liked seeing cars on the roads and planes in the sky. Maybe it came from having no one waiting for him at home, but he liked knowing he wasn't alone out there. In here, though, that was exactly what he was, and he'd never got used to it, not entirely.

Earlier in the week, the station had been busy. There had been men in high-vis jackets strapped to the pillars above him, working on the escalators, repairing broken lights. Torches were looped around their heads and music was playing somewhere on tinny radios. It felt less lonely then. Now there was no one, no music, no voices, no footsteps echoing through the emptiness of the station. It was so quiet he could hear the soft wrinkle of his trousers. He could hear his bones clicking.

He thought again about how this place was like a tomb.

He loved the history of the city, used to read about it all the time. He used to tell Stevie how the Tube was built on plague pits, how it was just rivers of bone, streams of decayed marrow and minerals. He'd told him how the authorities had once wanted to build a station at Muswell Hill, but could never finish it because there were simply too many bodies in the way. At the height of the Great Plague, seven thousand people were dying every week. *This city is just one big grave*, he thought, checking the time.

Tap tap. A noise.

Gerry turned around, the soles of his boots squeaking against the polished floor, and looked back in the direction he'd come. The walkway ran for about twenty feet, then angled off along a short tunnel to the platform somewhere out of sight.

'Stevie?' he said.

When he got no response, he flicked on his torch and shone it out into the space between him and the tunnel entrance. He didn't really need his torch – the concourse had just about enough light of its own – but it was a natural reaction to spending so much time on the lines. As he swept the torch around him, moving it left to right, and especially as he shone it upward into the fifty-foot-high chasm above his head, he realized – not for the first time – how much space there was in Westminster station.

How many corners the light could never hope to reach.

How much pure, undiluted darkness.

He glanced back up the dead escalators that took passengers higher, towards the ticket hall, and then pushed off the pillar and directed his torch in the opposite direction, the glow winking in the stairs as they descended to the Jubilee concourse.

'Stevie?'

Nothing.

Then: *tap tap.*

Tap.

Tap.

What the hell *was* that? It sounded like it was coming from the next level down, from the Jubilee Line: up from the direction Stevie was supposed to be coming from.

Gerry checked his watch.

Three fifty.

You're officially bloody late, Stevie.

'Steve?' he said, his voice less certain than he would have liked. He cleared his throat. 'Steve, is that you?' He sounded more confident this time. If Stevie was pissing around down there, he'd know that Gerry wasn't amused because he only ever called him Steve when he was narked off about something. But, when there was no response, Gerry's stomach started to clench, as if his body had skipped ahead of him somehow and was sending out a warning message.

Tap.

Gerry headed for the escalators.

At the bottom, he swept the torch from side to side, trying to light up corners of the concourse he couldn't see into, or that weren't illuminated by the night lights. The phrase *the silence is deafening* had never meant much to Gerry, but it meant something now. He'd never worried about being down here, cloaked in the kind of darkness most people would never experience in their lives, but that was also starting to get to him too. He wasn't even sure why. He heard tons of noises on his nightly walks – all sorts of creaks and moans – yet there was something about this.

Something that didn't feel right.

'Stevie?'

Tap tap.

It sounded like it was coming from the actual line itself, on the platform. At the bottom of the escalators, Gerry took a step along the concourse, gingerly at first and then – as reason took over – more confidently. *You've been walking these stations for twenty-five years. Get a bloody grip on yourself.* He headed towards the platform. A few seconds later, he was emerging on to the eastbound line.

The deepest part of the station.

Transparent screens had been erected all the way along, which – during the day – would slide back once the train was in the station. They were closed now and, beyond them, it was hard to make out the line without the help of a torch. The far tunnel, at the opposite end to where Gerry was now, was black, like an infected wound. Shadows were everywhere, on the ceiling, on the floor, in the pockets and grooves of the platform. Gerry swung the torch from left to right, and then stepped up to the screen.

That was when he saw it.

A black holdall, sitting under a bench, right at the end of the platform. It was closed, the metal zip *tap-tap-tapping* against the bench in a faint breeze.

Gerry let out a breath.

'Shit a brick,' he said quietly and broke into a smile.

Lost property.

Bloody lost property.

Almost on cue, on the other side of the screen doors – at the far end of the platform from where Gerry was – he saw torchlight carving out of the blackness of the tunnel. He turned all the way around and, a few moments later, Stevie appeared. As soon as he saw Gerry, he broke into a smile, picking up his pace.

'Sorry, Johnny,' Stevie said.

His voice was muffled by the screen doors.

'Maintenance at Green Park. Bunch of prats over there asking me a load of stupid bloody questions.' Stevie rolled his eyes and started coming up the steps on to the platform. 'Makes you pine for better days,' he went on, coming out of the other side of the screens, making his way down. 'Used to be that contractors and cleaners actually spoke English. You know what one of them said when I said "hello" to him?'

Gerry smiled. 'What?'

'Nothing. He just stared at me.'

Stevie did a comical death stare, and then added zombie arms to the act and they both started laughing. He was carrying a backpack and had started to unzip it.

'Got Colombian coffee tonight, Johnny.'

'Nice.'

For a long time, Gerry had been the one who had brought the coffee – just a simple flask of instant – but recently, Stevie had started getting into all sorts of different blends and types, and so the roles had reversed.

'It was actually the missus that suggested this one,' Stevie went on. 'She drank it at some get-together she had with her *book club*.' He rolled his eyes again, but it was with affection: Stevie absolutely doted on his wife, and on his boy too, who was some kind of computer whizz. He was big on family generally, in fact, and sometimes Gerry would feel a little jealous. It wasn't like Stevie rubbed it in, but sometimes when they got together, Stevie would get carried away and spend their hour together just talking about his wife, or his son, or his mother, or the advice that his dad used to give him growing up. Gerry would find himself over-compensating when that happened, and he'd start inventing stories about Kerry, about how close they were and how much of each other they saw, when in fact he didn't see his daughter anywhere near as much as he wanted. One reason was Mandy, her mother, who was an absolute bitch from hell and had mounted a sustained campaign against Gerry, bad-mouthing him in front of Kerry so often that, after a while, some of the shit had started to stick. Another was that Gerry found it hard to connect with his grandkids. He didn't know what to say to four-year-olds. He didn't know how to interact with them, and they made so much damn noise. One time, a few months back, he was at Kerry's house and overheard her husband, Zack, telling her that Gerry was a bit weird around the children.

Gerry hadn't been back since.

Tap.

Tap.

Stevie looked up from the backpack. 'What was that?'

Gerry directed a thumb towards the holdall.

'Some prat left his bag here.'

Stevie made an *of course they did* expression. During their time, they'd found all sorts of things on and off the lines: money, files, photos, dead animals, even false teeth. People dropped things when they boarded. They dropped things through carriage windows during the summer. They left things on platforms, on concourses, in toilets; the two men had found things jammed into escalators. It happened at every station, all across London.

'We just booked a holiday,' Stevie said.

'Yeah?' Gerry replied. 'Where to?'

'Mallorca.'

'Lucky you.'

'Yeah, can't wait, Johnny. Me and the missus were saying last night, it's going to be so nice just to be on a sunlounger somewhere, next to a swimming pool, a beer in one hand and a bonus one in the other, with no responsibilities other than making sure you top up the suncream. I can't wait to get away with the O'Keefe tribe. We're so lucky that we all get on so well. I mean, some families go away and all they do is . . .'

Here we go again, Gerry thought, checking his watch and tuning Stevie out.

'Johnny?'

'Yeah?'

'Are you all right?'

Gerry frowned. 'Yeah, of course. Why?'

'I couldn't get any response from you.'

Gerry's frown deepened. He was unsure what Stevie was talking about: it had literally been a matter of seconds since Stevie had started talking about how well him and his family got on – what response was Gerry supposed to have shown in such a short period? But then Gerry checked his watch again and he was startled by what he saw there.

Four minutes had passed.

He'd completely lost all sense of time.

'You sure you're all right?' Stevie asked.

'Yeah,' Gerry said, but he felt uncertain all of a sudden. And though the rest of the hour with Stevie was much better, and Stevie didn't bog the conversation down with constant talk of his family – instead, they talked about football, about the uselessness of politicians, and about craft beer, which they had a passion for – when Gerry left, and moved back into the darkness of the tunnels, he felt like something had happened to him. He felt like a piece of himself had fallen out of place. The sensation stuck with him for a day, but then it began to fade and, by the time he met Stevie again two nights later, it was like nothing had ever happened.

'Did I ever tell you I love the Polish?'

Gerry watched Stevie pour the coffee.

They were back on the platform at Westminster, the Tube station silent as a graveyard around them. Gerry had brought some sandwiches for them both tonight and had set them out, on top of a blanket, on one of the platform benches.

Gerry smiled. 'Why's that then?'

'Well, they've employed a couple of Polish people down at Waterloo and one of them is an absolute beauty.' Stevie whistled and then winked at Gerry. 'She's got legs all the way up to her ears, and her boobs . . .' He stopped again and shook his head, like her boobs were one of the greatest things he'd ever witnessed in his life. 'She speaks bloody good English too, better than you and me. Name's Katerina. Kat. I'm in love.'

Stevie started laughing, and then so did Gerry. It was unusual to hear Stevie talk about a woman who wasn't his wife, even if he was clearly being light-hearted. It reminded Gerry of their younger days, when they were both single. They used to go to a nightclub in Whitechapel in the 1970s called The Orange. It was an absolute dive but the women were always incredible; that place just drew them in like a magnet. Stevie was always far more confident than Gerry when it came to that kind of thing, which had slightly gnawed at Gerry when they were that age: often, Gerry would end up with the fat friend and Stevie would bag the beauty, but they were at The Orange so often that Gerry would still end up with his fair share of lookers.

Just never as many as Stevie.

All of that came to an end once Stevie met his wife, though. Him and Gerry stopped going out as often and Stevie stopped talking about other women, even in passing. Gerry had no wingman any more. That was why it was so funny hearing him talk about the Polish girl. It was like the Stevie of old. It was the Stevie he wished for.

'So how old is this Kat?' Gerry asked.

'Much too young for us, Johnny.'

'Maybe for you, but I'm a single man.' Gerry gave Stevie a cheesy grin.

Stevie burst out laughing again. 'Look, Johnny, you're my best mate and all that,' he said, 'but you ain't bagging a woman like her at this point. Those days are over, my friend. You're about thirty years too old and your dinger has got way too many cobwebs on it.' He held out one of the coffees to Gerry. 'Anyway, you'd need about two hundred Viagras to keep up with a woman like that.'

Gerry took the coffee.

For some reason, he felt annoyed by what Stevie had said. It wasn't that he'd said anything that wasn't true: Gerry *was* far too old for a woman like that, and even in his prime, beautiful women had never been drawn to him. It was more that it felt like a deliberate insult: in an impossible scenario where a stunning woman might be interested, it wouldn't be Stevie's dinger that had cobwebs on it, because he had his wife at home; and it wouldn't be Stevie who would need dick pills to keep himself hard, because *obviously* he was still getting plenty at home. Gerry tried to let it go, knowing that in the grand scheme of things it didn't matter, but the irritation hung on, bubbling away, making his coffee taste sour.

'This is Ethiopian,' Stevie said, holding up the plastic mug he'd detached from the flask. 'Did you know they produce 384,000 metric tons of Arabica in their fields each year?'

Gerry tried to swallow down his ire.

'No,' he said.

'Their coffee industry accounts for ten per cent of their GDP.'

Gerry nodded.

'Anyway, that's just the kind of useless crap I remember.'

Gerry just nodded again.

'What do you think of it?' Stevie asked him.

'It's nice,' he lied. It tasted like shit, but Gerry wasn't sure if it was the coffee itself or the bitterness he felt. *Get over it. It was a joke. What's the matter with you?* 'Was this another recommendation from the wife's book club?' Gerry asked. Stevie looked at him. The question had come out hard, as gnarled as the bitterness that lingered in Gerry's gut. 'Sorry,' he said, frowning, suddenly conscious of himself and the way he'd spoken to his best and oldest friend. 'Sorry. I didn't mean it to sound . . .' He stopped.

Stevie tilted his head slightly. 'Are you sure you're okay, Gerry?'

Gerry, not Johnny.

This was serious.

'Yeah, I'm fine. Why?'

'You just don't seem yourself lately.'

'I'm fine,' Gerry said again, and tried to think of a way to alter the direction of the conversation. For some reason then he thought of the Body Snatcher, a psychopath who'd stalked the Tube nine years ago. What the hell had Gerry thought of him for? What could possibly make him think of that psycho all of a sudden? Had he heard someone talking about the Snatcher? Had he read about him somewhere? He looked across at Stevie, who was still staring at him, still trying to work out what was up with him, and he said, 'Do you remember the Snatcher?'

Stevie frowned. 'Yeah, of course. He's pretty hard to forget.'

Gerry nodded, agreeing, but then, again, couldn't think of why, after all this time, he would start remembering the Body Snatcher and what he'd done.

'I've no idea why I just thought of him,' Gerry started, 'I just –'

Tap tap.

Gerry's attention immediately shifted. He put the coffee down and pushed himself off the bench where he'd laid out the sandwiches that he'd made.

'Johnny?'

He looked along the platform.

Tap tap.

The same noise as the last time he was here.

'You hear that?' Gerry replied, and started moving towards the sound. He wriggled the torch away from his belt, flicked it on and shone it at the far end.

That was when he saw it.

The holdall.

It was still there.

Tap tap.

'Didn't we take this to Lost Property last time?' he asked Stevie.

'Take what?'

'That,' he said, pointing to the holdall.

'Last time?' Stevie asked.

'The other night, when we met.'

No response from Stevie this time.

Gerry glanced back at him. 'Stevie?'

The two of them looked at each other and, on Stevie's face, Gerry could see a real expression of concern now – as if Gerry was losing it right here on the platform.

'This was here the other night,' Gerry said.

'Okay,' Stevie responded. 'I guess I forgot.'

Gerry looked at him again. Was he just trying to placate him?

'So what's in it?' Stevie asked.

'What's in what?'

'The holdall,' Stevie replied.

Gerry stared at it. Had he looked inside when they found it the other night? If he had, he couldn't recall what he'd found. *I definitely took the bag to Lost Property.*

Didn't I?

'There could be gold bullion inside,' Stevie said.

Gerry smiled at him. 'Or sweaty gym shorts.'

Stevie laughed. 'Or sweaty gym shorts.'

Gerry left Stevie to pour them more coffee and headed down to the end of the platform. The holdall had been left beside the bench, half underneath it. There were no identifying tags on it or a luggage label. It was just a standard polyester sports bag.

Getting on to his haunches, Gerry slid the holdall towards him, pinched the zip between his thumb and forefinger and started to open it. It jammed at first, and – when he looked closer – he could see some sort of gluey gunk in the teeth of the zip.

'This tastes so good,' Stevie said.

Gerry looked back at him. 'This thing's rank.'

'Why?'

'The zip. It's all . . .' He looked at the gunk.

'It's all what?'

'I don't know. Something's stuck to it.'

Applying a little force, the teeth finally began shifting, peeling open. Gerry pushed the zip all the way from one end of the holdall to the other, pulling the bag apart on both sides in order to make sure it definitely wasn't bullion.

The thought made him smile again – but it wasn't gold bullion. In fact, it took Gerry a few moments to actually figure out what it was. None of this really made sense.

'What's in it?' Stevie asked from behind him.

'I don't know,' Gerry replied, still trying to work it out. 'I can't quite –' He stopped.

'Johnny?'

Wait, Gerry thought. *Wait, what is that?*

'Johnny, don't keep me in suspense.'

And then it hit him, hard as concrete.

'Shit!'

Gerry stumbled back from the holdall, collapsing on to his backside, and scrambled further away on his hands. Behind him he could hear Stevie asking, 'What? What is it? What is it, Johnny?' But when Gerry went to speak, his throat closed up.

He heard Stevie coming towards him.

'Gerry? What is it?'

It's the worst thing I've ever seen.

'Gerry?'

It's fucking horrible.

'Gerry, what's going on?'

'Police,' Gerry croaked. 'We need to call the police.'

Gerry looked around the room.

It was small, the walls a bland cream, the door blue, its paint peeling from the corners. There was a grey ridge around the middle of the room – what Gerry knew the coppers referred to as a 'crash bar' – which they would push in an emergency if a suspect started getting violent. On the table in front of him was a plastic coffee cup, empty now, and the remains of a sandwich that a uniformed officer had bought for him from a garage close to the station. He'd eaten the first half hours ago, and had to basically force even that little down. He still felt nauseous, hollowed out.

And angry.

Why did he feel angry?

He looked down at the sandwich again, a slab of processed cheese escaping from between two slices of limp brown bread, the ham so pathetically thin it was almost transparent. Maybe it was because, although he didn't feel like he was hungry, he actually was. *It's just I don't want to have to eat this shit*, he thought.

There it was again.

The anger.

He closed his eyes and shook his head, as if he could get rid of his rage through a brief, violent movement, and when he opened his eyes, he began to retreat, back to the platform at Westminster, to the holdall he'd found, to what was inside it.

Suddenly, he didn't feel angry any more.

He felt scared.

His emotions were all over the place.

Get a grip, Gerry.

A couple of minutes later, the door finally opened and a woman entered. Gerry hadn't seen her before. She wasn't one of the coppers who'd come to the Tube station after Stevie called the police, and he didn't think she was one of the people who'd been out front, or who'd brought him here, to this room, in order to give them a statement.

She looked like she was in her early forties and was dressed in a grey skirt-suit and cream blouse. He thought that per- haps he'd made a mistake and that he did know her after all, because when she sat down opposite him, she smiled at him and said, 'Hello, Johnny,' and her tone, and the way she'd used his nickname – not his given name – gave her greeting an air of familiarity.

'I'm Emma,' she said.

Emma.

No surname, no job title.

Gerry frowned. 'What's going on?'

She seemed confused by the question and looked down at the file she'd put on the table between them. Paper – tons of it – crept out from under the file's brown cover. There was a label on it too, although Gerry couldn't read it from where he was. Emma placed her hand flat on the file and moved it slightly back in her direction.

'How are you feeling, Johnny?' Emma asked.

Gerry frowned again. 'Have we met?'

She looked at him, her head fractionally tilted, as if the answer wasn't certain. After a moment, she reset herself, sitting up straight, and said, 'Would you rather I called you "Gerry"? Or "Gerald"?' She shrugged. 'I assumed you'd prefer "Johnny".'

'"Johnny" is what my friends call me.'

Which, actually, wasn't technically true – but Gerry didn't bother attempting to correct himself. There was something about this woman that he didn't like – or, more accurately, couldn't entirely trust – so letting her use his nickname didn't feel right.

'Okay,' Emma said. 'I understand.'

'Understand what?'

'No nicknames.'

Gerry looked from her to the door. There was a small, rectangular window in it, the glass reinforced, thin black wires spidering from one edge to the other. Beyond, the corridor was dark and, when Gerry glanced at his watch, he saw why. It was 9 p.m.

'How long have I been here?' he asked.

'Yes, I'm sorry about that,' Emma replied.

He tried to remember what time he'd been brought in. 4 a.m.? 5 a.m.? And now it was nine at night. He looked at Emma again, waited for her to say something else, but she didn't. She hardly even moved, her hand still flat to the file,

218

her blue eyes fixed on him, like she knew exactly what he was thinking: where the hell had the time gone?

'Why don't we start at the beginning, Gerry?'

'The beginning?'

'Yes,' she said, same soft tone.

'What do you mean, "the beginning"?'

'Why don't you tell me about the backpack?'

'Backpack? No, it was a sports holdall.'

Emma didn't say anything.

'Anyway, it doesn't matter,' he said – he was just glad they were getting on to something more certain – 'point is, I got to Westminster station at around three forty-five, and then walked through to the escalators that take you down to the Jubilee. I walked in there because I knew my friend Stevie was going to be waiting there for me, and –'

'Let's start with the backpack, Gerry.'

He paused. 'What?'

'Let's start with the backpack.'

Gerry leaned away from her. 'What the hell are you on about?' he said, hearing the anger and frustration in his voice. 'You asked me about the holdall that –'

'I thought we agreed to go back to the beginning.'

'We did.'

'Then we need to start with the backpack, don't we?'

He frowned yet again. It felt like it had become a permanent fixture, a feature written into his expression like a scar. What the hell was this woman talking about?

'It was a holdall,' he said, 'not a bloody backpack.'

'This morning it was a holdall, Gerry, but if we're going back to the beginning, we have to start with the backpack.' She stopped, eyeing him; he looked back, totally at sea. He had no idea what she was saying to him. 'You know that's where we start.'

He shook his head. 'What the fuck is this?'

Emma flipped back the cover of the file. On top, paper-clipped to a piece of card, were some photographs. She levered off the paper clip, pocketed it, and then turned the photographs around so that Gerry could see them. There were four of them in all.

She spread them out.

Four faces.

A man in his fifties.

A woman about the same age.

A kid in his early twenties.

A woman in her eighties.

'Do you recognize these people, Gerry?'

He didn't, but the photographs were nice. The people all looked happy, were smiling, even laughing in the case of the kid. At the edges of two of them, he could see that, in the original shot, there must have been someone else, shoulder to shoulder with the person in the picture – perhaps a family member – but now they'd been cropped out.

'You recognize these people, Gerry?' Emma repeated.

He looked at them all.

Four faces.

They *did* seem vaguely familiar now she'd asked the question, just like Emma seemed familiar when she'd first entered. He looked at her, then back to the pictures.

'It's great that you found a holdall this morning,' she said. 'That's really great, Gerry. It's progress. It means we're continuing to head in the direction we need to go.'

He looked up at her again.

Something was different.

It was the room. It had changed somehow. Like a light being switched on, it had altered around him: there was no crash bar any more, no blue door. The room was still the same size, but it was set into the corner of another, much larger room. As he looked out, through the doorless entrance, Gerry could see other people, all in white.

What the hell was going on?

Emma put a finger to the first photograph.

It was the woman.

'This is Sandra, Gerry. Do you remember her?'

He shook his head.

'This is Brian,' she said, pointing to the kid.

'I don't know them,' Gerry responded.

'Do you know her?' She gestured to the woman in her eighties.

'No,' he said.

'That's Eleanor. Do you remember her?'

'*No*. What's going on?'

He ripped his eyes away and looked past Emma again. There was a television on in the other, bigger room; he could see two men at a nearby table, just staring into space.

'Concentrate if you can, Gerry.'

He turned back to Emma.

Her blue eyes were still fixed on him. 'You've found two bags for us over the last seven months, Gerry – the backpack, in February, then the camera case ten weeks ago, at the end of June – and both times you've found a bag, it's been very helpful.'

'I've only found *one* bag,' he said. 'The holdall.'

'No, you've found two. The holdall is the third.'

'I don't understand.'

'Every time you've described finding a bag – every time you've described what you found *inside* that particular bag – you've been able to give us a name and a map.'

'A map? What are you *talking* about?'

'A map to a location.'

'*What* location?'

'The location of a body.'

Gerry just stared at her.

'Every time you find a bag, we give the families some closure.'

'Closure?'

'They get to bury their loved one.'

He looked out into the room again and then back to Emma and, this time, he saw she was wearing a name badge. He wasn't quite sure how he'd missed it before.

DR E GARRISON.

'You're a doctor?' he asked.

'Yes,' she replied. 'I'm *your* doctor, Gerry.'

He didn't get it, didn't understand.

'Do you know where you are?' Emma asked.

'I'm at a . . .' He stopped.

This isn't a police station.

'I'm in a . . .' He paused. 'Hospital.'

'Yes. That's right, Gerry. You're at a hospital called St Augustine's.'

'No,' he said.

'Yes.'

He felt another spear of anger. 'What the hell *is* this?'

'That's why it's important for us to go back to the beginning,' Emma said, as Gerry dropped his head and looked at his hands, uncertain now what was real and what was imagined. 'It's better if we go back through the bags we've already seen inside of first – because that seems to help you see things more clearly when we get to the new one.'

'I don't want to talk about this.'

'It's important that we do.'

'I don't even know who these people *are*.'

Emma paused. 'I think you do, Gerry.'

He shook his head.

'I think you do.'

He shook his head again. '*No.*'

'They're all members of the same family.'

He shot her a look. 'What?'

'Every bag represents someone you've hurt.'

'*What?*'

'When you imagine finding a bag, you seem to be able to recall the location in which you left one of these people.' Emma stopped, shuffling forward in her chair. 'So I need you to go all the way back, to remember the two previous bags, so that when we get to this new bag – this holdall – you can see clearly whose body parts are inside.'

Gerry looked at the four faces spread out in front of him, and then at the card folder, at some of the paperwork that had started to slip away from the doctor's file.

On one sheath, he saw nine words.

Handwritten.

Talk to David Raker. Is GS a Snatcher copycat?

'Gerry?'

A Snatcher copycat?

GS. That was him. His initials.

He dragged his eyes away from the words.

'Gerry, look at me.'

'What's going . . . I don't . . .'

He ground to a halt, glancing at Emma.

'This is important,' she said, almost whispering it to him. 'And, who knows, if we keep going, we may even get to that place where you said you wanted to end up.'

He grimaced. 'What place?'

She pushed the fourth photo towards him.

The man in his fifties.

'These photos are a few years old now, Gerry, but they

223

were all members of the same family. They all lived together. And on the last occasion we talked, you told me this man was where you *really* wanted to end up. The location of *his* body: that was the place you really wanted to remember.'

Gerry stared at the face of the man.

I know you, he thought.

'But we're not there yet. You've managed to remember where you buried both Sandra and Brian, and in the holdall you visualized last night, you said you found Eleanor and a map of where she is. So I need you to describe Eleanor's map to me.'

Gerry couldn't stop staring at the man in the photo.

Because now he knew why he recognized him.

'After that, we can move on to him.'

She tapped a finger on the photo as Gerry thought, *You're my friend.*

My best friend.

'We can move on to where you buried Stevie O'Keefe.'

CASE #3
The Red Woman

PART ONE
The Girlfriend

Now

It's the middle of September.

Healy steps off the trawler and on to the wooden slats of the jetty, and then begins hauling the ice boxes from the boat across to the quay. There are three of them on the boat, each dressed in identical bibs and braces, their T-shirts soaked through with a mix of sweat and seawater. It's baking hot, the sun a searing white disc in a cloudless sky, an entire swathe of coast almost paralysed by its power: the day's so still it's like the Earth has stopped spinning on its axis; the only thing that seems to move are the three men and the sea itself, slapping against the hull of the boat.

They load the catch into the back of a van that belongs to the skipper, a guy in his forties with cherry-red cheeks and a fading Liverpool football shirt, and then the skipper and the second fisherman — his scrawny, acne-faced son — tell Healy to be at the jetty again at five the next morning. 'Don't be late, got it?' the son says to Healy, his father out of earshot at the front of the van. 'We're not waiting around.'

Healy just looks at him.

'Did you hear what I said?'

The kid's all puffed up and red in the face.

'I said we're not —'

Healy takes a sudden step towards the son, and the teenager backs up, almost stumbling into the rear doors of the vehicle. The kid likes having someone to boss around, someone lower down the ladder than he is, and most of the time Healy just lets him have his fun. He can't afford to make a big deal out of it because he doesn't need anyone asking questions. But today it's too hot, the air too thick, and Healy's had enough of the kid's shite for one day. Healy glares at him, the kid

229

swallowing nervously, and then his father calls him to the front of the van and the kid hurries away, looking over his shoulder at Healy. Healy just watches him, watches both of them get into the van, and a minute later they've driven off.

Boots clopping against the road, Healy leaves the village — a tiny gathering of old cottages, a pub, a butcher's and a corner shop, right on the edge of the coast — and begins the climb back up to where he's staying. It's an old fisherman's cottage, but more isolated than the rest, half concealed by trees at the top of a ridge. He only passes one other house on the way, a small cottage — like his — set back from the road, belonging to a woman he's barely said a word to in the entire time he's been here. She's coming around the side of her house as he looks up, a cat following in her wake. He half smiles but doesn't make eye contact, then ups his pace. A few seconds and he's out of sight.

Sweat's running down his face by the time he reaches the entrance to his house, an easy-to-miss, nondescript gate that sits right on one of the bends in the lane as it snakes up further into the hills. The approach to the house, even the house itself, reminds him of a place he lived in before, the last time he was trying to stay off the radar. That had been down in south Devon. He'd worked on a trawler there too for a time, until things had got complicated and people had come asking questions about who he was and where he'd come from, and he'd had to drop everything and run. It took time — months of moving around between cheap hotel rooms and even cheaper hostels — but, eventually, things started to settle down again and the questions stopped coming, and that was how he eventually ended up here: a very different part of the country, far away from south Devon, but the same type of existence. He's a fisherman again, working for a father and son who pay cash in hand and don't probe him on his history or the things in his life he's buried deep.

The sight of his reflection in the windows of the house brings him back into the moment, and he watches as his image takes shape in the glass: tall and skinny, but not as sickly thin as he once was; bald by choice, his hair shaved so close there's only the vaguest hint of its original *colour; a thick, dense beard — unruly, unrefined, crawling all the way to the bottom of his throat — that he's allowed to consume his entire jaw and neck. He keeps no pictures here of the person he was before this, before Devon, before he started working on trawlers, before he ran in the opposite direction the second people asked difficult questions. He keeps no pictures of that person, but he remembers him well. He remembers the thick thatch of red hair he used to have. He remembers all the weight he carried. He remembers all the anger he had.*

He remembers everything he gave up.

He remembers being a cop.

Thirteen Years Ago

'Boss, can I ask you something?'

Healy looked up from his desk.

Detective Constable Rosa Naughton was standing beside him, a file in her hands. It was opened at an interview transcript. He looked at the report he'd spent the entire morning trying – and failing – to write, and then at his computer screen, frozen on a spreadsheet he didn't understand and couldn't be bothered to read, and came to the conclusion that anything Naughton had, however tedious, had to be better than this.

He wheeled his chair out. 'Why not?'

'I don't want to waste your time with this.'

'You're not wasting my time, Rosa. *This* is wasting my time,' he said, and pointed accusingly at the spreadsheet. 'If I wanted to spend my days looking at shite like this, I'd have been an accountant. So, what excitement have you got for me?'

Naughton smiled, laying the file down in front of Healy and then dropped to her knees next to his desk. She couldn't have been more than five-four or five-five, maybe ten stone, but there wasn't an ounce of fat on her. You could see the muscle through her clothes, the tautness of her skin above her roll-neck sweater, in her cheeks, around her eyes. He'd heard some of the blokes talking about her in the toilets one time, saying that she was into bodybuilding, that she'd bulk up and then starve herself for competitions. One of them said he saw photographs of her online, her skin bronzed with spray-tan. It wasn't Healy's idea of a good time, but he admired her dedication.

He'd thought at first that the men in the toilets felt the same way, that they were discussing her because they admired her, but then they began describing what they imagined she'd look like naked, and what they'd do to her if they had the chance. One of them said she had so much muscle that, if she rode him, she'd probably break his pelvis and snap his cock in half. They'd all started laughing at that – like a pack of hyenas – and they only stopped when Healy flushed the toilet and came out of the cubicle. He was going to rip them a new arsehole – but one of the men turned out to be Healy's DCI.

Healy looked at Naughton's file.

'Thomas Coventry,' she said. 'You remember him?'

'No.'

Naughton flipped the file back to the opening page, where the photograph of a well-built man in his fifties looked out – shaved head, beard, piercing blue eyes. He was in a suit, smiling for the camera, a wedding party in the background of the shot.

'Ringing any bells?' Naughton asked.

Healy looked at the guy some more.

'Not really,' he said.

'Six months ago, this guy's girlfriend reported him missing. He went out to work one morning and never came home again.' She paused for a second and flipped forward a few pages. 'A missing persons report got filed downstairs by the girlfriend and then eventually wound its way up to me, and so I started looking into it. Long story short, this Coventry guy was a wannabe gangster – mostly just low-level shit like stolen goods – but he also happened to be in a ton of debt. He owed a bunch of loan sharks half a million or thereabouts. So, point is, the idea of him leaving home and making a break for it, then holing up somewhere no one would ever find him again . . . well, let's just say it wasn't beyond the realms of possibility. In fact, although I didn't have any evidence to prove it, I thought that was exactly what had happened at the time.'

'Okay. So?'

'So, anyway, in my downtime, I've got into this routine of returning to some of the older cases that I never put to bed. Don't worry,' she said quickly, holding up a hand, 'I'm not neglecting anything. I guess this is' – she gestured to the file, to the photograph of Coventry – 'well, this is, for want of a better word, what I do for fun.'

'Most normal people play golf or go to yoga.' But Healy was smiling at her, a smile that she returned. He liked Naughton, and not just for her work ethic. She reminded him of a girl he'd gone to school with back in Dublin. Kathleen. She'd been fierce and intense, and built like a battering ram, but she had a smile she kept back, for rare occasions, that would light an entire room. As a teenager, he'd had a thing for Kathleen, and although he didn't feel the same way about Naughton – and couldn't afford to: he was her boss; she was in her twenties and he was creeping towards his mid forties, married, with three kids – he always felt bad about what he'd heard in the toilets that day, and worse about not coming to her defence.

'Anyway,' Naughton continued, returning Healy to the conversation, 'this Coventry guy, he had no family left. Mother and father both deceased, no brothers or sisters, no cousins. He was married, but they'd been separated for a year when he vanished. It was just this girlfriend of his, and . . . I don't know . . . I don't know how to explain it, but there was just something about her that didn't quite sit right with me. She just set my Spidey sense tingling. I could never put my

234

finger on it, and when I started following the money and seeing who Coventry was in debt to, I guess I just forgot about her.'

'But now you've changed your mind?'

Naughton rocked her head from side to side, flattening her lips. 'I don't know about changed my mind, because, whichever way you shake it, Thomas Coventry owed a shitload of money to some pretty shady people. But I pulled the file out yesterday and started going through it and I came across this girlfriend – her name was Marie Havendish – and I thought, "Why not drop her a line?" Last time I tried to speak to her was a courtesy call about four months ago. I didn't have anything specific to give her, I just thought I'd check in. Anyway, she wasn't home back then, and – again – I sort of forgot about the case, forgot to try her after that. Until yesterday when I dug the file out and I tried calling her *again*, just to reassure her that she hadn't been forgotten.'

'Did she appreciate the call?'

'That's the thing. I can't find her.'

'Can't get through to her?'

'No,' Naughton said, shaking her head. 'Not can't get through to her – can't actually locate her. At all. The phone number she gave me is now dead. I get a bounce-back from her email. She was some kind of a . . .' Naughton paused, waving her hand around in front of her face as she searched for the word. 'Like a historian. She wrote about the Second World War and all of that. Point being, she had a website with her photograph on it and all the information about the books she wrote and talks she gave.'

'That's gone too?'

'It's a dead URL now.'

Healy leaned back in his chair, catching a glimpse of his reflection in the PC monitor. He was overweight, his shirt straining at the belly, his chin sitting inside a tyre of flesh at his throat. He'd started to grow a beard in an effort to disguise it, but Gemma, his wife, kept joking that he looked like an Irish Father Christmas. The comment pissed him off, but he'd been forced to laugh along with her because the kids had found it inexplicably funny and he didn't want them to think he couldn't take a ribbing. The best thing he could do for himself was get on a treadmill and cut back on the coffee and the overtime runs to the chip shop, but it was hard when he had cases coming out of his ears, staff to look after and a billion reports to fill out. There weren't enough hours in the day for any of that, and he didn't have the willpower to eat salad.

He turned his attention back to Naughton. 'How long were Coventry and this girlfriend going out?'

'Five or six months.'

'And you said she's an author, right?'

'Right.'

Healy nodded, his eyes dropping to the file again, to the picture of Thomas Coventry. 'If she's an author, you must be able to find her books somewhere online.'

Naughton shook her head again.

'No books?' he said.

'No books.'

'So she lied about being an author?'

'Well, put it this way: I haven't found any author with the name Marie Havendish online. So there's that. But the reason I mentioned Coventry not having any family is because there's no one to confirm that this woman was even a part of this guy's life. She never met his parents or his siblings or his cousins, because – at the time he vanished – he never had any.'

'He must have had friends.'

She flipped through to an interview transcript.

'This is an interview with Coventry's friend Gregory Ritter. The two of them had known each other for years. Decades. I didn't like Ritter – he was a rat-faced little scroat – but him and Coventry were like this.' She crossed the first two fingers of her right hand. 'He wanted to know where Coventry had got to, just as much as the rest of us did. Maybe more, since Coventry and him were supposed to be "business partners" and the day before Coventry got up and disappeared, he kindly cleared out their bank account.'

'Coventry took all the money him and Ritter had?'

'All of it. Almost twenty grand.'

Healy whistled. 'Nice. Any CCTV of Coventry at the bank?'

'No, it was all done electronically.'

'From where?'

'From Coventry's place.'

'So where was the money routed to?'

'A bank in the Empress Islands.'

Healy smiled, but there was no humour in it. So many investigations fell through the cracks because of moments like this: trails that went immediately cold, doors that were impossible to open, people quietly doing small things that obscured bigger, more terrible acts. He tapped a finger on the file and said, 'So Coventry empties twenty grand out of his and his business partner's account, wires it to a tax haven in the south Atlantic where no one will be able to get access to it, then vanishes into thin air?'

'That's pretty much the sum total of it.'

'I can see why this has got its hooks into you, Rosa.'

She smiled. 'His friend, Ritter, had a vested interest in finding Coventry, but he also knew him better than anyone. So, if anyone was likely to have met Coventry's girlfriend – this so-called author "Marie Havendish" – it was Ritter, agreed?'

'Agreed.'

'Read this bit.'

Healy grabbed his glasses from his desk. Naughton had directed him towards a transcript from an interview that Naughton had done with Gregory Ritter, two days after Thomas Coventry had gone missing. She'd used a highlighter pen to show Healy exactly the section she wanted him to read, but he decided to start a bit further back.

NAUGHTON: Were you and Mr Coventry getting on?

RITTER: We always got on. That's what I can't understand. Why would Tommy steal all our money? It don't make any sense.

NAUGHTON: He owed about half a million pounds to a series of potentially very dangerous people. That's a lot of money, Mr Ritter. If he didn't have any way of paying that back, then trying to disappear like this actually makes a lot of sense.

RITTER: Tommy ain't like that.

NAUGHTON: What do you mean?

RITTER: I mean, he don't run from a debt.

NAUGHTON: Half a mill's a hell of a debt.

RITTER: He don't run from a debt, all right?

NAUGHTON: Okay. Okay. So where is he then?

RITTER: Someone got to him.

NAUGHTON: 'Got to him'?

RITTER: You know what I mean.

NAUGHTON: Are you suggesting someone killed him?

RITTER: Look, the two of us, we run a pretty tight ship. Me, I'm good with numbers. But when Tommy goes out on his own, he ain't so good. He gets careless. He's got himself into some right old fixes. Like you said yourself, away from our business, he personally owes a lot of money to a lot of different people, and some of those people ain't gonna take it lying down. The fact Tommy don't run from his debts, it means he's easy to find. So, yeah, it's possible.

NAUGHTON: It's possible someone killed him?

RITTER: Like I said.

NAUGHTON: So who?

RITTER: You're the bloody copper, not me.

NAUGHTON: Do you think you're in danger?

RITTER: Me? No. I ain't in debt to anyone.

NAUGHTON: What about Thomas's girlfriend?

RITTER: What girlfriend?

NAUGHTON: His girlfriend, Marie Havendish.

RITTER: Who? He don't have no girlfriend.

NAUGHTON: Marie reported him missing.

RITTER: What? What are you talking about?

NAUGHTON: Marie Havendish, his girlfriend. She came in and filed a missing persons report two days ago.

RITTER: Never heard of her.

Healy looked across at Naughton. 'You didn't think it was weird that his business partner and best mate hadn't ever heard of a girlfriend he'd been dating for six months?'

'Now it does, yeah.' Naughton paused, grimacing. 'Now it *definitely* does, but not then. Back then, her landline worked, her email, I was looking at her website every day. I interviewed her a couple of times – here and at her house. She lived up in Tottenham. She said they'd been seeing each other five, six months but it had only got serious the last couple, so that was the reason she hadn't had the chance to meet up with friends like Ritter. I couldn't find a reason not to believe her. All of it tallied up.'

Healy flipped back to the beginning, to the photograph of Thomas Coventry, looking at his face, his address in Barking, his personal details, known relationships.

'What about this ex-wife of Coventry's?'

Naughton shook her head. 'Nothing doing. Like I said, they'd been separated a year. They hadn't divorced yet, but the paperwork was in the process of being sorted. I called her up, just to dot the i's . . . uh . . .' She reached over for the file and found the page she wanted. 'Cara Coben. She confirmed it. Said she and Coventry hadn't seen each other for over nine months, and that they only ever spoke through a solicitor because – and I'm paraphrasing here – Coventry was an angry piece of shit. At best she was wary of him, at worst scared. I spoke to the solicitor and she pretty much backed up everything that Coben had told me.'

'So that just leaves Marie Havendish.'

'Right. The girlfriend.'

'You think she got rid of Coventry, took the money and disappeared?'

'I think it's worth exploring.'

'So what are you proposing?'

She took a breath, as if gathering herself.

'I just need a day or two on this, Boss. There's something here, I can feel it in my bones. Give me forty-eight hours, and if nothing comes of it, I'll just forget it all.'

Healy glanced at his monitor, at the spreadsheet that needed filling out and then at his desk. The Coventry file was covering up the reports he was supposed to be writing. In his in-tray was even more paperwork. Forms to fill. Things to sign off.

He looked at Naughton, then at Marie Havendish.

'Is this the only photograph you have of her?'

'Yes,' Naughton said. 'It's from the website she set up.'

Healy eyed Havendish. She was a timid-looking woman in her late thirties with long, mousy hair that was becoming wiry as it started to grey, dull brown eyes and a small, pale mole next to her nose. She wasn't unattractive, though. In fact, the more Healy stared at her, the more he realized it was the opposite and he started to wonder if she might be wearing a disguise: not literally, but in the unkempt hair she'd allowed to grey and grow long, in her demure expression, and in the slight tilt of her head – her eyes looking up from under her brow – as if embarrassed at being on camera.

'So is that a yes?' Naughton pushed, half smiling.

'Forty-eight hours, okay? No more.'

'Thanks, Boss. I owe you.'

'I know. Just don't reward me with chocolate.'

He patted his belly for effect and then watched her stand, her grey trouser-suit tight against the lines of her body. Was this what happened when she started to bulk up? Was she building up to some sort of competition? He'd never asked her what she did away from the office, what she enjoyed, TV she watched, how she filled her downtime. He didn't know if she lived alone, or with someone else, or with a whole bunch of people. He didn't know if she was straight or gay or somewhere in between. He never asked because he was her boss, and she was fifteen years younger than him, and he was always scared that it would come across as inappropriate. But then she scooped the file off the desk and started to head back across the office to her booth at the far end of the room, and he found himself swivelling on his chair and calling her back.

'Rosa, wait a sec.'

She stopped. 'You haven't changed your mind already, have you?'

He looked at the file in her hands and thought of

everything she'd told him – about the disappearance of Thomas Coventry, about the girlfriend who didn't seem to exist. 'This case,' Healy said to her, and glanced at the spreadsheet again, at the reports that needed writing. 'How do you feel about an old man tagging along for the ride?'

Now

At the door, Healy lets himself in, locking it behind him, a habit he's developed since he's been here, just in case. He showers and changes, and then collapses on to one of the sofas in the cool of the living room. The cottage is old, its bones moaning in the heat, but he's slowly got used to its sounds over the time that he's been here: to the soft tick of the grandfather clock on the wall, to the clunk and gurgle of the central heating, to the whistle of the wind as it escapes through the paint-peeled windows that no longer fit their frames properly. When he first arrived, he thought he'd go mad, confined to this small, bleak sliver of coast on the Irish Sea, miles from anywhere. But instead the opposite has happened: a part of him has come to like it.

Often, there are moments when he pines for his sons: he'd grown apart from them at the end, but he still loves them deeply, and not speaking to them, not seeing them, not watching them get older, hurts. He missed Liam's graduation; he'll never meet Ciaran's fiancée; he'll never see either of them getting married, or get to hold his grandchildren in his arms. But as much as those things tug at him, as much as he mourns the loss of them, he never doubts that he's made the right decision. He was no use to his boys. He was no use to his wife either. He was just an angry drunk, an obsessive, a man who'd made a series of terrible decisions – and would keep on making them. It's better that they believe he's six feet under the earth in a Hertfordshire cemetery. It's better for them, better for him, better for everyone that the world now believes him dead. That way, what was once his family can at least remember him with some fondness, because he can no longer screw up their lives.

Marcus Savage is the name that he's been using here. That's what it says on his fake passport. It's the only ID document Healy has: there, under his mattress, just in case he needs to make another quick getaway. He doesn't have a driving licence or credit cards. He doesn't have a car and only ever takes public transport. He has no Internet in the house and uses no mobile phone. He's renting from an old couple in Bangor, but someone else pays them rent on his behalf. The same person pays the electricity bill, and gas and water too, and Healy just repays him the money he owes him – in cash – when they meet up every quarter. It's in both their interests that no one looks too deeply into who Marcus Savage really is, or how he ended up in this house and this village. Because behind that name is Healy, and behind Healy are the things in his past that need to stay hidden. The man Healy was, his life before this, his former career, his lapses, his choices, they're all buried in that cemetery – and the world needs to believe that's all there is left of him now: just bones, and memories, and a headstone. Except, of course, two people know that Healy is alive and well.

One is Healy himself.

The other is David Raker.

Thirteen Years Ago

On the way out to Barking, Healy read through the file on Thomas Coventry's disappearance. A couple of times he asked Naughton questions, but mostly he just soaked it up. He didn't blame her for overlooking the girlfriend; even as he leafed through the investigation with the benefit of hindsight, he didn't see many red flags.

A couple of Marie Havendish's answers could, perhaps, have been termed elusive, but it would have been harder to see them as questionable at the time. He already knew what had happened when Rosa had tried to get back in touch with Havendish. He already knew Havendish had abandoned her landline, her email, her website and her history, both as a writer and as a person. That gave Healy an advantage. What was obvious was that something was going on, and it was down to Naughton's inability to let the case die that they were even in a position to try and find out what.

Once he had finished reading, he snapped the file shut and looked out of the passenger window, watching the streets of the city pass in a blur of phone shops, takeaways and low-rent furniture stores. A while later, he caught a glimpse of himself in the wing mirror and didn't much like what looked back, his face bloated, his expression heavy, the whites of his eyes bloodshot. He had bags under both of them, smeared beneath his lashes like lines of dark paint, and the irony was, none of it was down to proper police work. The way he looked wasn't the result of late nights in an interview room, trying to drag a confession out of some arsehole who wouldn't fold. It wasn't solving crimes. It wasn't trying to make some sort of difference. It was forms and spreadsheets. It was sitting in front of a computer until there was no one left in the office, and filling in columns on a document. He hated it. He'd taken the promotion for the money – but money didn't matter when you never had any time to spend it.

'You all right, Boss?'

Healy tuned back in. 'Yeah, just thinking.'

'About Havendish?'

He glanced at Naughton. She had her hands on the wheel of the Volvo and a pair of aviator sunglasses on, which made it hard to get a handle on her. He returned his gaze to the streets. It was late January and freezing cold, but the sky was empty of cloud and a pale sun winked beyond the rooftops of east London.

'Yeah,' he lied. 'Just thinking about what her story is.'

They reached the house a couple of minutes later. It was a pebble-dashed mid-terrace with two bay windows top and bottom and a door with peeling white paint. The street was long and tightly packed, cars parked on one side, old telephone poles on the other, wires fanning out to surrounding houses like the spokes on a wheel. The birds that hadn't flown south for winter were perched up there, and there were two kids who probably should have been at school playing football at the end of the road.

Naughton found a parking spot a little further on, and then they walked back while she fished around in the evidence packet for the keys. At the house, she let them both in.

Inside, it was musty.

There was a kitchen ahead of them, a living room off to the right and a staircase to the left. Sunlight carved across the garden and into the kitchen, highlighting a damp patch on the wall and fading lino. Dust swirled in the hallway.

246

Healy made his way into the living room, a space full of expensive furniture that didn't feel like it belonged in the house. There was a TV too big for the room, shelves packed with DVDs, CDs and LPs, and a lot of paintings – what Healy supposed was termed 'modern art' – all of which, to his eye, looked like the same pretentious shite.

In his time, he'd been to a lot of homes like this.

It was the home of the middle-aged crook still swimming upstream in his fifties, still trying to crack the big one that was going to make him his millions and let him retire to Spain. But the trouble with people like Thomas Coventry was that they were never vicious enough to make it really big, so they either got banged up or killed. Or neither, in which case, this was what happened: they filled their shitty homes with stuff they thought spoke of how successful they were, how cultured they'd become off the back of it. It was a very particular mix of narcissism and tastelessness.

'I'm going to look upstairs,' Naughton said.

After she was gone, Healy moved to the shelves, running a finger along the spines of Coventry's albums. He didn't display much taste here either, but at least his taste in music was better than his taste in DVDs, which seemed to extend to straight-to-video mockney crime thrillers and live stand-up from racist comedians.

Halfway down the room was a sideboard.

Healy started going through its drawers. It was a mess of old papers and pens, utility bills, receipts, table mats, miscellaneous junk. He didn't find much worth stopping for and walked to the back of the living room, where a set of patio doors looked on to a small, drab garden, hemmed in by six-foot walls. It was like a prison yard. The lawn was brown, the grass still packed tight from the morning frost; the beds were full of rusted leaves; and cheap plastic furniture had toppled over in the wind, rain pooling inside the upturned grooves of the chair legs.

As he headed into the kitchen, he heard Naughton moving around above him, the floorboards creaking. He flicked a switch and a long strip light hummed into life, revealing old-fashioned pine cabinets and white work surfaces long since marked with food and drink stains. Again, Coventry had spent his money not on the kitchen itself, but on equipment to fill it with – an expensive coffee machine, a rack of Japanese knives, a microwave with so many buttons it looked like a NASA computer.

Healy heard Naughton coming downstairs again.

'See anything?' she asked as she approached from the hallway.

He shook his head. 'No.'

'There's nothing upstairs either.' She stopped in the doorway and scanned the kitchen worktops. 'It's hard to tell for sure, but I don't think anyone's been back here.'

Healy looked out at the back garden. 'Just remind me again what happened on the day he disappeared.'

Naughton pulled out her notebook. 'Coventry left for work at about 8 a.m.' She stopped, shrugged. 'I mean, this is all according to the so-called "girlfriend", so it's up for debate, but Havendish said she left at the same time, because she wanted to get to the library. She said she was going there to do research and only returned to the house the next day, when Coventry had gone a full twenty-four hours without responding to her calls.'

'She didn't have a key for this place?'

'No. She said it was because they'd only been dating seriously for a short time. He hadn't offered her one; she hadn't asked.'

Healy nodded. 'Did she ever say how they met?'

'In a coffee shop in Beckton.'

'Beckton? She lived up in Tottenham, didn't she?'

'Yeah.'

'So what was she doing down in Beckton?'

'She said she'd gone there for research.'

'Sounds like "research" is a popular pastime.'

'That's what I thought at the time,' Naughton said. 'So I pulled some camera footage from around the library and out at the café they met at in Beckton, and there was nothing screwy going on. Havendish was at the library and they were at the café.'

'So she was telling the truth.'

'About that, yeah.'

Healy rubbed his fingers together, a habit he'd developed during his latest attempt to give up smoking. Reaching into his pocket, he took out a pack of nicotine gum and shook a piece loose. It was becoming clearer than ever why Naughton hadn't seen anything to trouble her about Havendish when she originally worked the case.

Popping the gum in, Healy walked back through to the living room, looking at the same pieces of furniture as before. He opened the drawers of the sideboard again. In one of them, there were photographs of Coventry: with what must have been his parents; with a group of men at an England football game; by himself in a pub garden holding up a pint. There were none of him with Marie Havendish, but there was one of him with his ex.

'What was the name of his ex-wife again?' Healy asked.

'Cara Coben.'

'You said you talked to her?'

'Yeah.'

'What did she say about him?'

'She just said he was incapable of behaving like an adult,

that he could be nasty, and that she'd wanted the divorce to be as straightforward as it could be. But Coventry made that impossible, which is why they were doing all the mediation through a solicitor.'

'Did you ask her about Havendish?'

'Not directly, because at the time it didn't seem relevant. But I spoke to her in general terms about him having a new girlfriend, and she didn't seem very surprised.'

'Why's that?'

'She said he was cheating on her for most of their marriage.'

Healy put the photograph back into the drawer, but there was so much stuffed inside already that it slid off the top. It floated to the floor and came to rest under the sideboard. When Naughton bent down to pick it up for him, she immediately paused: something had caught her attention under the sideboard.

'You all right?' Healy asked her.

'Yeah,' Naughton said, but she was distracted now. Dropping on to her knees, she peered beneath the unit. Healy backed away a little bit, trying to see what had got her attention. The carpet looked dusty down there, like it had never seen a vacuum cleaner in the entire time it had been laid. Rosa angled her shoulder, pushing it closer towards the floor, so that she could more easily get her hand under. Healy moved again, coming around to her side, watching. She slid her arm even further.

'Rosa?' Healy said. 'What is it?'

But then, finally, she had hold of it.

She brought it out, pinched between thumb and forefinger, and held it up for Healy to see. He moved closer, frowning. 'Is that what I think it is?'

She got to her feet, and then – with her spare hand – went to the pocket of her trousers for an evidence bag.

'Yeah,' she replied, 'it's exactly what you think it is.'

Naughton sealed the bag.

'So what's a shattered front tooth doing on Coventry's carpet?' Healy asked.

Now

After the sun goes down, Healy heads back to the village.

It's the middle of the week, so, although there are a few people in the pub, it's pretty quiet. The shops are all shut for the night, and in the homes overlooking the beach, all the curtains are drawn.

He heads for the phone box.

It's a tattered relic from the 1990s, one of its panes spiderwebbed with cracks, old graffiti carved into it, outside and in. Despite how old it is, it takes credit cards, but Healy doesn't have one of those, so he drops a fifty-pence piece into the slot and dials a mobile phone number. He knows it off by heart.

It connects.

As it rings, he looks out along the front, over the seawall where the water is calm. Sometimes, during the day, when it's absolutely clear, he can see all the way to Ireland, although the hint of it on the horizon is only ever vague. Healy likes the idea of it being there, though, even if it's only an obscure grey streak: once upon a time, Ireland was his home, his birthplace, where he went to school, and there's something weirdly comforting about being this close to his childhood.

'Hello?'

A voice on the end of the line.

'How are you doing, Raker?' Healy says.

Thirteen Years Ago

Rain lashed the North Circular as Healy and Naughton headed in the direction of Tottenham. Traffic was heavy, but the stop-start nature of the journey gave them a chance to discuss what they'd found at Thomas Coventry's house.

'Maybe the tooth came out accidentally,' Naughton said.

'You mean, he tripped over and knocked it on something?'

'It's possible.'

Healy looked at the evidence bag he was holding. The tooth was chipped along the top, in a jagged forty-five-degree line, and there was blood on the enamel.

'It's possible,' he said, but when he glanced at Rosa for a second time, he could see that she was thinking the same thing: given who Coventry was, how much of Gregory Ritter's money he'd taken, and how much he owed people who were much more dangerous than his friend, tripping over a bulge in the carpet seemed unlikely.

'So it got punched out,' Naughton said softly. 'Or ripped out.'

'Ideally, we'd get a forensic team in there,' Healy replied, but they both knew that would never get signed off without concrete evidence that Coventry had come to harm, especially because the case had been dormant for six months. 'There could be blood in that house, but we'd never know without a blue light.' Even if the house had been scrubbed down, there might still be proof of it on the walls, the furniture, the doors. Except all of that was irrelevant for now. They weren't going to get a forensic team.

Not with what they had.

'Do we know who's renting this place now?' Healy asked.

He meant the place they were headed to, where Marie Havendish – or, at least, the woman who had used that name – had lived for almost half a year.

'It's between tenants,' Naughton said.

'Some good luck. Who'd have thought it?'

She smiled. 'The landlord's going to meet us there.'

'Good.'

Healy looked at her, sensing something else was up. 'You okay, Rosa?'

She shrugged. 'Maybe if I hadn't missed the tooth the first time –'

Healy held up a hand.

'It's true, though, Boss.'

'It was a small fragment of tooth, under a sideboard, half disguised by carpet. Anyone could have missed it. And, anyway, we don't know if it's even relevant. Much as we both *suspect* it means something, there's just as much chance that it doesn't . . .'

Naughton smiled at him again, but differently, as if she appreciated the fact he was softening the blow. For some reason, it reminded Healy of his daughter, Leanne. She was impossible to talk to most of the time – always spoiling for a fight, always defensive – but occasionally Healy would get through. He'd crack the shell and see inside the teenager to the little girl she'd once been. And those moments were the ones he always grasped the hardest because she wasn't on the attack, wasn't ignoring him; those moments were when she relented and let him parent, and just silently said, *Thank you, Dad*.

'You okay, Boss?' It was Naughton's turn to ask the question now.

'Fine,' he said, forcing a smile. 'Just thinking.'

They were quiet for a while.

'I hear you do bodybuilding,' Healy said eventually.

Naughton burst out laughing.

'What?' he asked.

'Where did that come from?'

'I don't know. Just making conversation.'

He felt embarrassed now, diminished by her response.

'I do,' she said.

He just nodded.

'I'm about to start bulking up, actually,' she continued, clearly aware that she'd made him feel uncomfortable. 'That means I'm going to have to put the deep-fried Mars bars on the backburner. It's okay, though. I get to eat lots of steak and protein pancakes.'

He looked at her. 'Must be hard.'

'What?'

'Bulking up and dropping weight all the time.'

'It's not all the time. I do two competitions a year, one in May, one in October. Either side of that I just look like this.' She paused for a second, focusing on the road ahead: they were coming off the North Circular, into Tottenham. Once she took the exit, she glanced at him again. 'I like it, but I know not everyone in the office is a fan. For the record, though, I seriously doubt I could snap a pelvis or break a dick in half.'

Healy looked at her.

'I overhear what people say about me.'

He didn't know how to respond.

'It's okay, Boss. There are worse insults.'

'I'm sorry you had to hear that, Rosa.'

'Why, were you the one who said those things?'

She was smiling, but he could tell the answer mattered.

'No,' he said.

I just stood there and said nothing while others did.

'Then you're not on my kill list,' she joked.

But it wasn't a joke. Not to her.

And, because of his own inaction, not to Healy either.

The landlord was a grey-haired man in his sixties called Ray-nold Yintley, but he told Healy and Naughton to call him Ray. He met them at the front of the house, a small mid-terrace, east of the High Road, which Marie Havendish had lived in for six months. She'd been a tenant here from February to July the previous year, then a new tenant had moved in for six months after that and had, according to Yintley, only just moved out. When Healy looked at the tiny paved front garden, he could see some potted cacti with a note: *Please don't get rid of these!*

'They've still got a few things to pick up,' Yintley mumbled, as if a row of seven or eight miniature cacti were some huge problem. 'Supposed to be yesterday, but they had some issue with their kids.' He rolled his eyes at Naughton, and then at Healy as well.

Naughton gave Healy a sideways glance.

This guy sounds fun.

Yintley opened up for them.

'Did you have much to do with Marie Havendish, Ray?' Healy asked as he and Naughton looked along the hall. The house was narrow but it went back a long way.

'No,' Yintley said. 'Never had a problem with her rent, never had a complaint from her about anything. She phoned me once because the oven packed up, but then I called someone out, got it fixed, and didn't hear from her again until she moved out.'

'A good tenant, then?' Naughton asked.

'As good as any.'

'Do you do your letting through an agency?'

'No,' he said to Naughton, 'they're a bunch of bloody crooks. Like I'm going to give up fifteen per cent of the money to some arsehole in a suit. No, I do it all myself. I advertise on the Internet and in the local paper, and I never have a problem getting people in.'

Naughton glanced at Healy and he saw that they were in tune again: if Yintley had gone through a lettings agency, there may have been some sort of paper trail, and a paper trail may have led them somewhere else. As it was, they were busy staring at another dead end: Naughton had already checked in with Yintley on the phone, when she'd been setting up this visit, and Yintley didn't retain records of previous tenants.

'What would be the point of that?' he'd said to her.

It was possible a paper trail wouldn't have led anywhere, anyway – Havendish had proved already, just by the mere fact that Healy and Naughton were scratching around at a rented house she hadn't lived in for six months, that she was very careful – but it would have been good to have the option. As it was, they had nothing so far.

Nothing but a broken tooth.

'You told DC Naughton on the phone that Ms Havendish paid you her rent in cash every month,' Healy said to Yintley. 'Any particular reason she would do that?'

Yintley frowned. 'What do you mean?'

'I mean, most people would just do it electronically.'

They stared at each other.

The insinuation could have been that Yintley preferred cash because then he didn't have to declare the rent. But

Healy wasn't asking the question because he cared that the taxman had lost out. He was asking because Naughton had told him in the car that – when she'd done some ringing around – she'd found out Marie Havendish had never opened a bank account. As in, no one with that name, who was registered to this address, had ever put as much as a penny into a bank. And *that* meant that whatever cash Havendish was using for rent – and her rent at this place was £805 per month; so £4,830 for the six months, plus whatever she needed for bills and food – she was keeping in the house, close to her. The twenty grand wasn't withdrawn from the business account belonging to Thomas Coventry and Gregory Ritter until *after* Marie Havendish's six months were almost up here, so she wasn't paying the rent from that, *if* – as was looking increasingly likely – she was the one that took the men's money. Instead, she was paying the rent – thousands of pounds' worth of rent – from money she already had on her. That meant, back then, she'd had another source of revenue. They just had to figure out what it was.

'Ray?' Healy asked, prompting him.

'I don't know what you want me to say,' Yintley responded, shrugging. 'Rent was paid in cash. It didn't bother me, as long as she paid. Anyway, it was her idea . . .'

And there it was. *Her idea.*

They weren't any further forward, but they were building a clearer picture of who this woman was: her identity was fake, her career was fictitious, the email she'd used was temporary, as was the mobile phone number she'd provided. She had no NI number and no bank account, so she had no job, paid no taxes, contributed nothing at all to any organization or structure. But she had money on her. And with enough of that, there were certain things – like paying your rent in cash, so you left no digital trail – that you could organize. You just had to take your time, do your research and find someone who didn't go through a lettings agency, who wasn't all that good at paperwork, and who wouldn't ask questions. A man exactly like Raynold Yintley.

'What did you make of her when you met her?' Naughton asked Yintley, who still had a frown on his face. It was there to start with because he'd been confused. But now it was because he was starting to understand.

'Is she in some kind of trouble?' he asked.

Naughton shut him down straight away. 'No,' she said. 'We just need to get in contact with her.'

He looked between them.

'Ray?' Naughton prompted. 'What did you make of her?'

He opened out his hands. 'I don't know.'

Healy and Naughton waited.

'She just seemed normal,' he said quietly, but Healy could see his brain humming. He was trying to work out if finding Marie Havendish was the *only* reason the police had come to a house she'd rented, asking questions about her. 'She was a nice-looking girl.'

Still they waited.

'She had this red coat she always wore.'

Healy, frustrated, glanced at Naughton. *A red coat?*

Naughton smiled, despite herself. *Stop the presses.*

'Like I said to you already,' Yintley went on, 'she was a good tenant. But when I came to the house that time, to talk to her about the oven, I did have to tell her off.'

Healy snapped back into focus.

'Tell her off?' Naughton asked. 'About what?'

'She'd put this oil drum in the garden,' Yintley said.

Healy glanced at Naughton for a second time. But this time it wasn't out of frustration. As a shot of adrenalin charged through his veins, he said, 'An oil drum?'

'Yeah, one of the neighbours called me about it.'

'To say what?'

Yintley shrugged. 'They were pissed off.'

'Yeah, but about *what*, Ray?'

'The smoke,' he said. 'She was always burning stuff.'

Now

Their routine is always the same.

Once a week, Healy will call Raker from the phone box in the village, Raker will immediately call him back, and then Raker will drive up to see Healy every three months. And, during their phone calls, Raker will always ask the same things. How are you doing? What have you been up to? Has anyone been asking questions?

Is anyone acting suspiciously?

Healy has been living in the village since April 2019. In a month's time, he will have been here two and a half years, and there have never been any issues. No one has been acting suspiciously and no one is asking any questions.

But Raker still sticks to the same routine.

Healy understands why, but it gets annoying. Raker is pretty much his sole contact with the outside world, or at least the world that Healy existed in before he faked his death, and going over the same old shite every week and giving the same answers to the same questions every seven days uses up valuable time on the call. Tonight, though, they're finished with the checks, so Healy asks, 'You been busy?'

As he asks the question, laughter erupts from the pub at the other end of the village. There's some men out front at one of the tables. The air is still warm, despite the darkness, and it's incredibly still: a Welsh flag, on the pub roof, has fallen limp.

'Yes,' Raker replies. 'I finally finished up something today.'

'Come on, then, let's have it,' Healy says.

He likes hearing all the details because it transports him. For a time, on the calls, Healy isn't here any more, in this place, this hideaway; he's not in this pretend life where he spends his days up to his elbows in fish guts. In his head, he's back at the Met. He's a cop again. His mind is ticking over as Raker describes the missing persons case he's completed, and he's thinking about what he'd have done in the same situation; he's putting himself in Raker's place and making those choices.

It's like a charge of electricity.

'Wait,' Healy says, 'so this guy disappears —'

'Inside his own house, yeah.'

'What?' Healy frowns. 'How?'

'He was watching TV with his wife one night, he leaves her on the sofa to go upstairs and take some medication — and then he just completely vanishes.'

'What do you mean, "vanishes"?'

'I mean, he vanishes. Never comes back downstairs.'

'Are you serious?'

'One hundred per cent.'

'And this is the first I'm hearing about it?'

'After it was done, I just didn't want to talk about it for a while.'

The men at the pub are laughing again. Healy looks at them: one of them, on the end of the table, is looking back. The phone booth is in the shadows of the houses, so it's unlikely the man can see Healy from where he is. He's probably just registered movement. Just to be sure, though, Healy turns around so that his face is obscured.

'So did you find him?' he asks Raker.

'I don't know if I found him or he found me.'

'What does that mean?'

Raker tells him about his search for a guy called Paul Conister, about how his wife, Maggie, was the one who instigated the search, and then, afterwards, he says to Healy, 'Maggie called me this morning. This case happened back in July — that's when I found Paul — but Maggie called me out of the blue this morning, after two months, and said she didn't know if she could trust Paul any more. The thing is, she's right not to trust him. I'm just not sure now if I should have been the one to tell her.'

'You did the right thing.'

'You would have told her?'

'That her husband was a fucking fraud? Absolutely.'

'What if he really has got something on me?'

Healy pauses. 'Even if he has, you couldn't stay silent.'

'Yeah, well, I've done it before.'

Healy looks out to the darkness of the sea.

The village.

The life of anonymity they've built for him here.

'This isn't the same,' he says, although he's not sure if he really believes that, so he doesn't say anything else because he can hear in Raker's voice that he's troubled by the case, troubled by his part in it, and still needs time to process it all. In a way, though they're very different, Healy and Raker are also very similar: Healy used to linger on cases, even after they were done, wondering not about the major events of an investigation but all the minor ones. Often, it was those minor decisions – those seemingly trivial leads that accumulated over time, becoming one homogenous mass – that dictated your direction of travel: it either helped you break through and get the answers, or the entire thing folded like a deck of cards.

As he thinks of that, he thinks of Rosa Naughton.

He's been thinking about her a lot lately.

In January, it'll be the anniversary of when it happened.

Thirteen Years Ago

Healy and Naughton moved across the garden.

It was small and unimpressive, hemmed in by grey concrete breezeblocks. There was a two-tiered patio area with some empty flowerbeds on the second level, and then the lawn itself was on a third level, up another short flight of stone steps. In a back corner, on a bed of old patio slabs, was a charred, blackened square with a blistered oil drum sitting on it. Its lid was on.

Neither of them spoke as they approached the oil drum. Above them, it was all cloud, dark as granite and pregnant with the threat of rain. It had been at least six months since Marie Havendish had burned anything here, so the chances of them finding evidence of any kind was small – but they needed the weather to hold, just in case.

Naughton had brought some gloves with her: she handed a spare set to Healy, which he snapped on, and then – after removing the lid – crouched in one corner, using a pen to shift dirt and debris around on the floor. Healy moved to the other side of the drum, concentrating on the drum itself to start with: the insides were speckled with rust and still stank of gasoline. As Healy leaned over the edge, at the bottom he could see a lump of milky plastic – melted beyond recognition – and a lot of ash. Otherwise, the drum was empty.

With far more effort than Naughton had shown, he eased down on to his haunches and, with a pen of his own, started to sift through the flecks of detritus that the oil drum had spat out, and which still remained on the ground all this time later.

Mostly, what he found was too hard to identify. The last six months, with all the weather that autumn and winter would have brought, had scattered and destroyed most of what might have been here. Occasional lumps of black, twisted debris shifted as Healy moved the nib of his pen through the dusty silt, but – like the plastic he'd found inside the drum – it was either too misshapen to identify or it fell apart the moment he touched it.

He hauled himself to his feet and watched Naughton work for a moment, thinking about the tooth they'd found at Thomas Coventry's place. Was it likely that Marie Havendish had brought Coventry here and burned his body in the oil drum? Healy knew that both he and Rosa had been thinking it as they'd approached, but – seeing the drum for himself and digging through what remained here – Healy was less certain now. It was possible Havendish had cleaned the entire drum out afterwards, but burning a body would have been messy, difficult, risky, especially out in the open – and would also have left a parade of evidence.

Bodies didn't just turn to ash in a fire.

Even in something as efficient as a crematorium, parts of the skeleton survived. It wasn't the flames that turned it to ash, it was the cremulator they used afterwards that ground the remains to a fine dust. So, after a body was burned in an oil drum, there would be plenty of it left behind: so much that Havendish would probably have been out here for hours afterwards, and that made it just as big a risk as getting the body out to the oil drum in the first place. As well as that, the stench would have been horrendous, and her neighbours had complained to Raynold Yintley about the smoke, not the smell. If a body had been burning, they would definitely have smelled it.

'If Havendish killed Coventry,' Healy said, 'it wasn't here.'

Naughton looked up. 'She could have killed him somewhere else.' The inference being that Havendish had just used the drum for disposal. But Healy could see Rosa was playing devil's advocate: like him, she didn't believe the body had been cremated here.

'So what was she using the drum for?' Healy said.

Naughton stood, shrugged. 'Evidence.'

Healy nodded. That made more sense. Paper, weapons, clothes, plastic, those things could all be burned or melted down. Most would eventually disappear entirely, and those that didn't – like the plastic – wouldn't be recognizable any longer, as Healy had seen himself in the drum already. Perhaps, with the full weight of a forensic team behind them, they might have got somewhere, but they didn't have that and weren't likely to. If Healy went back to his DCI and asked for manpower and some techs, he'd probably get laughed out of the room. Because, when it came down to it, this case, if it was even that, only had two things going for it.

A woman with a fake identity.

And half a tooth.

'I might go and check the house,' Naughton said.

'Okay.'

He watched Naughton go, then turned his attention back to the oil drum. As he did, his phone started buzzing in his pocket. He took it out and looked at the caller.

Gemma.

He watched his wife's name flashing, wondering if he should pick up or just let it go to voicemail. They'd had a blistering row the previous night because Healy had promised to be home for dinner but didn't get back until ten thirty.

266

When he'd got up this morning, Gemma had already left for work, Ciaran and Liam were on their way out, and Leanne had basically ignored him at breakfast when he'd tried to talk to her.

'Why are you ignoring me, Lee?' he'd asked her.

She'd just shaken her head.

'I can't do anything about it if I don't know what I've done.'

This time, she'd looked up. 'Seriously, Dad?'

'What?'

'You're never home.'

'I couldn't help it last night –'

'I'm not talking about last night. I'm talking about *every* night.'

Healy had grimaced. 'It's not every night.'

'Whatever.'

'You kids are everything to me, you know that.'

Leanne had looked up at him again. 'You're never fucking *home*, Dad.'

'Hey, watch your language.'

She'd almost laughed at him.

'That's not true, anyway,' he'd said, feeling the anger rising in him. He'd paused deliberately for a second, tried to stave it off and push it down; it wasn't the time to be losing his rag. He had to stay calm to prove his point. 'I know I'm late sometimes, but this job . . . The hours can be hard. But that's not true. Even when I have to stay a little later at the office, I always come home. You can't say that I'm not home, Lee, that's –'

'I'm not talking about you *physically* being here.'

He'd just stared at her.

'You might be here in person, Dad, but you're never home.'

Before he'd had the chance to respond, Leanne had grabbed her toast off her plate and stormed out the front door. That was when Healy noticed the boys were still there, watching, bags slung over their shoulders: Ciaran was eighteen months older than Leanne, in his first year of university, but Leanne was always the one that spoke for him when it came to things like this. Liam was two years younger than his sister and worshipped the ground she walked on, so it was obvious which side of the fence he was on. His sons had lingered there in the doorway for a moment, two pairs of eyes fixing him with a look every bit as angry and disappointed as their sister's.

And then, without a word, they'd all left.

Healy returned to the present just as the phone stopped buzzing. He watched it for a moment, wondering whether to call Gemma back, but then the handset hummed again and he saw that she'd left him a voicemail. It wasn't going to be an apology – neither of them were good at that – so it would be something which made his life more complicated. He looked at the oil drum, and then to the house that Marie Havendish had lived in, where he could see Naughton – nothing more than a shadow – in the living room.

I'll deal with whatever it is later.

He pocketed the phone.

And then something caught his eye.

It was on the outside of the oil drum, almost fused to it, and it was hidden: a ridge around the circumference, at the top, had kept it protected. It must have fluttered up and out of a fire at some point, and then stuck to the side: it was paper, or maybe card, but it had a glossy surface. When the gloss had melted, it had acted like an adhesive, binding it to the drum's metal.

Healy leaned in and peeled it away.

It was about an inch high by an inch and a half long and looked like it was once part of a leaflet or a poster. It took him a couple of seconds to decide which way up it was supposed to go – and then he noticed the writing at the bottom.

He headed back around to the front of the house.

'Ray, can I ask you something?'

Yintley was on the front wall, smoking. He shrugged in response.

'The tenant you had in here *after* Marie Havendish,' Healy said, the scrap of paper pinched between his fingers, 'do you know if *they* ever set fires in that drum?'

'No way.'

'Definitely not?'

'After I told Marie that time to stop burning shit out the back, I said to the guy there and the old woman on this side' – he pointed to the houses that flanked his – 'that if anyone else did the same thing in the future, they were to call me right away.'

'And they didn't call?'

He shook his head. 'No more fires.'

Healy studied the scrap of paper again.

'Nothing in there,' Naughton said from behind him, reappearing out of a door at the side of the house. She seemed despondent but also embarrassed: she was regretting bringing this case out of cold storage, but more than that, she was regretting the fact that Healy had come along to personally witness a total dead end.

'Cheer up, Rosa,' Healy said.

She frowned. 'Why, have you got something?'

He handed her the scrap of paper. 'I guess we're about to find out.'

*

269

The building was in Hackney, on the south-west corner of Victoria Park, an ugly slab of brutalist design. Above the main doors were the words PARKLAND COMMUNITY CENTRE, but some of the letters were missing, the shadows of where they'd been still evident on the brickwork. Someone had spray-painted extra letters into the gaps so that, from a distance, it read ARSELAND.

Naughton parked the Volvo out front and then Healy led the way to the main entrance. It was locked. Through a window to the side, he could see a long corridor, rather like a school, with doors on either side and sickly green linoleum on the floor.

Healy knocked on the glass.

As they waited, he glanced at Naughton. She had the scrap of paper between her thumb and forefinger and was turning it gently back and forth, deep in thought.

After thirty seconds, someone appeared from a door at the end of the corridor and shuffled down towards the main entrance. Healy assumed this was Marjorie. On the way down from Tottenham, Rosa had called the community centre and talked to a woman with that name. She was in her seventies, had a mop of grey, frizzy hair, and was swamped in a maroon cardigan that was about three sizes too big for her.

She unlocked the door and opened it a crack.

'Marjorie?' Naughton asked.

She looked between them. 'Are you the police?'

Rosa got out her warrant card and held it up for her to see, before introducing Healy, who did the same. He noted how Marjorie didn't fully open the door until she'd taken a good long look at both warrant cards and checked that the photos matched. That was a good sign: it suggested someone who wouldn't easily be fooled.

Someone who took note of things.

She let them both in, locked up behind them, then led them back along the corridor. The place smelled of disinfectant, and when they got to the room at the end, they were suddenly in a hall with a stage at one end, which also smelled strongly, but of boiled food. On the right was a kitchen with a serving hatch. On the left were doors that opened on to a small, high-walled children's play area.

'Do you want a cuppa?' Marjorie asked.

'I'm fine, thank you,' Healy said.

Marjorie looked at Naughton.

'I'm good,' she said in response.

'Well, I hope you won't mind if I make myself one.'

On the drive down, Naughton had suggested Healy lead the questioning, as he'd been the one to find the scrap of paper, so, as the kettle boiled, he got down to business: 'As DC Naughton said on the phone, we're looking into the disappearance of a lady called Marie Havendish. Earlier, you said you didn't recognize the name?'

Marjorie shook her head. 'No.'

'That's okay. Instead, what you might be able to help us with is this.' He nodded to Naughton, who handed Marjorie the scrap of paper. 'As you can see, the address here is for this community centre.'

Marjorie took the piece of paper, studying it.

There wasn't much to see on it, but there was enough: *Parkland Community Centre, Roman View Road, Hackn–*. The rest was missing, but it was obvious they were at the right place.

The line above was even more interesting.

Sober in Hackney Supp–.

Again it had been cut off, but it wasn't hard to imagine what the leaflet had been advertising: a support group for alcoholics. Raynold Yintley seemed certain that the tenant he'd had *after* Marie Havendish hadn't burned anything in the oil drum, and while it was possible he was wrong, for the sake of pursuing a lead, Healy was willing to go with the idea that the leaflet had been destroyed during Marie Havendish's time at the house. The question was, why bother burning it? She could have torn it up and dumped it in the bin and it would have had the same result.

Except it wouldn't.

Not quite.

If she tore it up, there would be fragments of it left behind. If she burned it in the intense heat of an oil drum, it would disintegrate into ash in a matter of seconds.

Or, at least, that was the theory.

As Healy watched Marjorie with the scrap of paper, he painted a picture in his head: a shred of leaflet catching a breath of wind and then fluttering upward in the oil drum; and what happened next – the gloss on its surface liquefying, acting like a glue, the scrap brushing the heated steel exterior of the drum and fusing to it. Maybe Marie Havendish saw it and didn't think it mattered. More likely, she never even noticed it.

'So what's the verdict then, Marjorie?'

She looked up at Healy.

'Does any of what's on there ring a bell?'

'What part of Ireland are you from, sweetheart?' she asked in return.

He eyed her. He needed her onside, so he said, 'Dublin.'

'I love the Irish accent. I used to have a boyfriend from Galway, back when my jugs were like hers' – she pointed at Rosa – 'and my arse wasn't heading south.'

'You're still rocking it, though, Marjorie,' Healy said.

She laughed.

'So what can you tell me about that?' he added, gesturing to the piece of paper.

'Yeah, this is our address,' she responded, handing the scrap back to him. 'That looks like one of them posters they had up in here for the AA meetings.'

'Is this group still running here?'

She shook her head. 'No.'

'How come?'

'They merged with another group in Bethnal Green a while back. They hold their meetings down there.' She paused, frowned. 'Just off Brick Lane, I think.'

'Any idea who ran the group here?'

'I wouldn't have thought so.'

'You "wouldn't have thought so"?'

'Well, it was Alcoholics *Anonymous*. It's kind of the point.'

Healy couldn't tell if she was being humorous or obtuse, but he kind of liked Marjorie already: she was quick-witted and sharp-tongued, but she looked sweet and harmless – and she used it to her advantage. Healy said to her, 'So someone came in here, booked the hall and never had to provide contact details or even a first name?'

She tilted her head slightly.

'As we Irish say, Marjorie: that's shite.'

She laughed again, and when Healy glanced at Naughton, she also had a trace of a smile on her lips. It was clear what she was saying to him.

You've got an admirer.

'Someone must have at least given you a first name?' he said, pushing.

'Well, let's see,' Marjorie said, and asked them to follow her, back out of the hall, to her office. It was small, with one high window that let in only the bare minimum of light. On a day like this, depressed by grey skies, she had to switch on a lamp to find her way around the desk.

She woke a computer from its slumber.

'I'm not very good with these things,' she said, 'but I'm sure we had a list of names on here somewhere.' As she started searching, Healy glanced at Naughton again. The smile he'd seen on her face back in the hall was gone, and now she looked concerned – that this wasn't going to go anywhere, that this whole thing was a waste of time instigated by her, and that, in the end, she would be blamed for it all.

Subtly, Healy held up a hand to her.

Relax. Everything's fine.

'Here we go,' Marjorie said. She pointed at the monitor. 'Not a full name.'

'Anything you've got will do.'

'It's a first name and a surname initial.'

'Like I say, anything you've got.'

'Okay,' Marjorie said, reading off the screen. 'I don't have a phone number or address or anything, but the contact name for that support group was a "Cara C".'

Healy and Naughton met each other's gaze.

Cara C.

Cara Coben.

Thomas Coventry's ex-wife.

Now

He's still thinking about Rosa Naughton.

The case they worked together.

The way it twisted. The way it turned deadly.

It had been a minor decision by Healy, a throwaway, spur-of-the-moment choice to join her in her search for Marie Havendish. If she'd never gone back to that case, if she'd never come to his desk that day, if he'd turned her request down and not let her re-examine the evidence, Healy would never have asked if she minded him tagging along. And he never would have helped lead her to where they ended up.

To Cara Coben's house.

To what happened after they got there.

'Does the name Gerry Stein ring any bells with you?' Raker asks.

Healy tunes back in. 'Who?'

'Gerry Stein?'

'No. Should it?'

'He worked as a patrolman on the Tube.'

This time, Healy makes the connection: it's not the name that sparks off his recollection, though — he still doesn't remember a Gerry Stein — but he now knows where this conversation is going. It feels like a lifetime ago that all of that happened, but it's only nine years: Raker had been looking into the disappearance of a man called Samuel Wren, who'd vanished after getting on to a Tube train as part of his morning commute; Healy had been part of a task force trying to find a psychopath the media had labelled the 'Body Snatcher'. Eventually, their paths had crossed. By the end of it, Raker had almost lost his life, and Healy had been fired from the Met.

That case was the seed of the reason Healy was here.

'Did we meet him?' Healy asks.

'Not him, no, but a friend of his, Stevie O'Keefe. Stevie was the guy who took us down on to the line at Westminster that time.' Raker pauses, and in the quiet they both remember that night: they'd been looking for clues, working separate cases but ones connected by the same events. And they'd found something down there, on the line at Westminster, that neither of them were likely to forget. 'Okay,' Healy says, 'so what's the story with this Gerry Stein guy, then? Why you dredging all that stuff up?'

'It's not me doing the dredging, it's a doctor.'

'A doctor?'

'Her name's Emma Garrison. She turned up at my house a couple of days ago. We talked, she told me a little, but she wants me to go to the hospital tomorrow for the rest of it.'

'The rest of it?'

'A fuller explanation, I guess.'

'What hospital is this?'

Raker pauses for a moment. 'St Augustine's.'

'Shit, really?'

'I know. I don't want to go there, but I want to hear what she has to say. This Gerry Stein guy has been there since February – he killed O'Keefe and his family.'

'Seriously? Weren't him and O'Keefe mates?'

'Very best mates.'

'So what happened – Stein just flipped one day?'

'I guess I'll find out tomorrow.'

Healy thinks of that case again, the hunt for the Body Snatcher, and how it completely destroyed his life. It was four years after his and Naughton's search for Thomas Coventry – but, with the benefit of distance, he can see now that the cracks were already showing, even before Rosa came to his desk with that case. His marriage was crumbling. His relationship with his kids was breaking down. His decision-making – at home, at work – was off. Four years later, all of those things came *together, like the wires of a bomb, and went off in his face. Before that, on the case with Rosa, at home with Gemma and the kids, he never saw things as clearly.*

As he remembers the Coventry case, he closes his eyes.

It barely seems possible that so much time has passed.

His memories are painful. In fact, it hurts him just to recreate images of it in his head, to be reminded of what happened after he and Rosa went to see Cara Coben. Not Coben herself, not the interview they did with her, but what came after.

More laughter from the pub drifts across the stillness of the evening.

'Healy?' Raker says. 'You there?'

'Yeah,' he says, and then stops.

He's still thinking about Rosa Naughton.

'Listen, Raker,' he says. 'I need you to do something for me.'

'Okay.'

He can hear the wariness in Raker's voice, and he knows Raker's immediate thought will be: 'What's he going to ask me to do and how will it have the potential to hurt us?' Healy understands, but what he's going to ask is important, and the one thing he knows about Raker, above all else, is that, like Healy himself, he's grieved.

He's grieved deeply and been broken.

He'll understand, even if he doesn't like it.

'It's a good few weeks away yet,' Healy starts, 'so you've got time to figure out a story for why you're there, if anyone questions you.' He stops, knowing Raker wants to ask the obvious question first: what's the 'there' that Healy is talking about? But he doesn't. He just stays on the line, patiently, silently, waiting to see where this is heading. 'Next month, I'll need you to buy some flowers.'

He pictures Rosa inside Cara Coben's living room.

'I'll need you to put them on a grave for me.'

PART TWO
The Ex-Wife

Thirteen Years Ago

Cara Coben lived in Canning Town, midway along a cul-de-sac of identical yellow-bricked terraced houses. On the drive down, Healy and Naughton had stopped to grab some lunch and, as they ate their pre-packaged sandwiches and drank their takeaway coffee, rain hitting their parked car in a relentless salvo, they laid out what they had.

'So, first, we've got Thomas Coventry,' Naughton said. 'He disappears and then his business account is cleaned out to the tune of twenty grand. There's nothing at his house *except* for a piece of broken tooth – which may or may not be relevant to this.'

'It is,' Healy said through a mouthful of sandwich.

'We can't prove it.'

'No, we can't, but we will. What else?'

'Marie Havendish: the woman Coventry was seeing for six months, who now appears not to exist at all, anywhere, ever. Whatever her real name and identity, she rented a house in Tottenham for the same period of time she dated Coventry, and the rental on that house came to an end' – sandwich propped between her lips, she flipped through the pages of her notebook – 'six days after Coventry vanishes into the ether.'

'A piece of timing that is far too coincidental.'

'*Far* too coincidental,' Naughton echoed.

'And then there's mystery-guest number three.'

'Cara Coben.' Naughton paused again and turned back in her notebook to the information she'd added right at the start of the case, when she'd spoken to Coben. 'I don't have much on her, I'll be honest. Forty-two, pissed off with her ex-husband, in the middle of divorcing him. I wonder, legally, how she was set at the point that our guy disappeared. What I mean is, they haven't divorced – so what then?'

'You mean, does she inherit his estate if he dies?'

Naughton shrugged. 'It's worth looking into.'

'Make some calls, find out. If that *is* the case, it begs the question as to why she hasn't done something with Coventry's house. Why leave it there, empty, collecting dust, when she could put it on the market, or rent it out and make some money?'

'Maybe she's just being cautious.'

'It's possible.'

'It's only been six months since Coventry disappeared: if she sold the place off the bat, it might look suspicious. If it sits there for a while, no one looks twice at her.'

'Or she could be innocent in all of this.'

Naughton nodded. 'She could be.'

But they both acknowledged the same thing.

Even if she was, something was off.

Healy knocked twice on Cara Coben's front door while Naughton stayed in the car, making a call to Coben's solicitor. To his left was a bay window. He took a step back so he could see in. Light reflected off the glass, despite the rain, but he could see enough: part of a sofa, a jumper draped over one of the arms; a coffee table with an open laptop on it; some papers next to that, a mobile phone, a mug, an empty plate.

She was home.

He knocked again, harder, and glanced at Naughton. She was speaking but, when their gaze met, she rolled her eyes at him. Healy suspected she wasn't getting much joy out of Coben's solicitor, which wasn't surprising: the solicitor wouldn't be under any obligation to tell them anything until Naughton came back with a warrant.

Movement beyond the door.

Healy watched as a shape formed in the door's single frosted-glass panel, and then, right on cue, he heard Naughton getting out of the car.

'Nothing?' Healy said, keeping his eyes on the door.

'We'll need a warrant,' Naughton confirmed as she fell into line next to him, her attention fixed on the same shape in the glass. They could see a distorted version of a face now: enough to make an identification. 'Looks like her,' Naughton whispered.

Cara Coben opened the door.

She was an attractive woman, with a short black bob and high, sculpted cheekbones. Healy wondered for a moment if she'd had work done, because the lines of her face seemed almost unnaturally perfect, but when she spoke, it was with no restriction, no sense anything on her had been carved, filled or moved.

'Ms Coben?' Healy asked.

'Yes.' She looked between them. 'Can I help you?'

He showed her his warrant card.

'I'm Detective Inspector Healy, this is DC Naughton. We were wondering if it might be possible to speak to you, perhaps inside.' He gestured to the rain, which was still falling in a fine drizzle. 'It's not such a great day to be out here.'

'What's this about?'

She didn't seem fierce exactly, and her response wasn't aggressive, but she had a definite hardness, a barrier, built close to the surface. *Perhaps that's what happens when you spend three miserable years married to a prick like Thomas Coventry.*

'It's about your ex-husband.'

Her expression changed, although it was hard to say into what. Healy studied her and didn't know if she was surprised at the mention of Coventry – or panicked.

'Have you found him?' she asked.

'No, ma'am. Maybe it's better if we talk inside.'

She didn't concede any ground for a moment, just looked between them both, but then she retreated, pulling the door the whole way back, and invited them inside.

They moved through to the living room.

'Did you want something to drink?' Coben asked.

'A cuppa would be great, thank you.'

She asked how they took it, snapped the lid of her laptop shut, then vanished into the kitchen. Once she was gone, Healy took a sidestep closer to Naughton and said quietly, 'This is your show. You know this case the best. You ask the questions.'

'Thanks, Boss.'

He saw a flicker of relief in Naughton's face. She was a tough cop, a good cop, but even strong personalities like Rosa Naughton sometimes had doubts. And, as she and Healy had been chasing leads today, following fractional clues to a destination they couldn't see, and didn't even know if it was possible to reach, those doubts had begun to feel overwhelming. But they were edging closer to something here – both of them could feel it – and, as Coben returned to the living room, Healy could see Rosa physically change: her shoulders rose a little, her chest puffed out, she looked more confident. It gave him a brief frisson of pleasure to witness and in his head he saw Leanne again: not the closed seventeen-year-old who'd sat at the breakfast table that morning but the much younger girl who he could always find a way to comfort.

Coben put two mugs of tea down on to the coffee table and perched on the edge of one of the sofas. Naughton sat on the other. Healy remained standing for a moment, looking across the living room to the patio doors: beyond the back of the garden, on the other side of the boundary fence, was an art deco swimming pool, long since closed down. He could see its main, red-brick tower, with three long, vertical windows embedded in it, the letters of its name – CANNING TOWN PUBLIC BATHS – punctured and broken at the apex of the glass. The canopy, reaching out above the entrance and partly collapsed, still had *We're Open Today!* printed on it, even though it must have been at least a decade since that was true. The whole thing was cordoned off behind ten-foot barricades.

'As DI Healy said,' Naughton started, bringing Healy back to the room, 'we're looking into the disappearance of your ex-husband, Thomas Coventry. I spoke to you six months ago, when this case first landed on my desk, and now I'd just like –'

'Why now?'

Naughton paused, looking at Coben.

'Why look for him now?' Coben repeated. 'I mean, he's been missing six months already and you couldn't find him back in July, so why bother looking for him again?'

'You wouldn't like to know where he is?'

'I'm curious, sure, but Tom was a total bastard. I hated him. He treated me like shit the entire time we were married. So, yeah, there are days when I wonder what happened – but that's it. I wonder. I don't pine for him and I *definitely* don't want him back. My life's been a hundred times better since he fell off the map.'

'So you wouldn't care if he was dead?'

'*Is* he dead?'

'Well, he's been missing six months.'

Coben paused for a moment, looking between Naughton and Healy, and then her mouth formed an *O*. 'I see what's going on here. You think I had something to do with him going missing, don't you?' She shook her head. 'Believe me, there were a lot of times during our marriage where I gave serious thought to jamming a crowbar into his skull. I'm not going to sit here and pretend it didn't cross my mind. He made me miserable. He hurt me, he taunted me, belittled me. He was an awful human being.'

'Was he physically violent?' Naughton asked.

For the first time, Coben looked less certain of herself, as if she hated the idea of going back. 'Yes,' she said finally, her voice shorn of its confidence. 'He would push me around. I fractured my wrist once when he shoved me out of the door at the back of that house in Barking. I broke my fingers when I tried to shield my face from a punch. He was a violent piece of shit. But the physical stuff, that was really just the side-show: what really got him off was playing with my head. Gaslighting, I guess they call it now.' She was finding her feet again, showing the same assurance they'd been met with when Healy and Naughton had first arrived. 'That was how he pinned me down and kept me in place: not with his hands, but his words.' She gestured to the laptop on the coffee table. 'I work now, just a boring admin job, but I love it. When I was with Tom, he wouldn't let me. He wouldn't let me do anything. I was a prisoner.'

'A literal prisoner?'

'I might as well have been. He locked me in when he was out, and I didn't have any keys to the house. He disconnected the phone and the Internet. I had no mobile. Before I met Tom, I used to work in advertising – I was bloody good at it too – but by the time I finally found the courage to leave him, I'd been unemployed for a year and a half. I'd completely separated myself from my friends and family, to the extent I didn't even *talk* to my mum any more. So was I a prisoner? Absolutely I was.'

As Naughton finished making some notes, Healy looked out at the garden again, at the public baths beyond the back wall. It felt like something had registered with him but he couldn't figure out what. He wandered across the living room to the patio doors and took in the garden again, trying to grasp at a thread he couldn't see. Was it something out there?

He looked at Cara Coben. *Or is it her?*

'You ran an AA group, didn't you?' Naughton asked. 'In the Parkland Community Centre?'

Coben looked surprised, slightly thrown.

'Ms Coben?' Naughton prompted.

'Yes,' Coben said. 'Yes, I ran that group.'

'How come Mr Coventry let you go out and do that?'

'Because we were both recovering alcoholics,' Coben said, 'that's how we met; and because the first year of our marriage, it wasn't as bad. He wasn't the total psycho back then that he'd turned into by the end. When we first got together, believe it or not, he was actually quite sweet. He told me he ran an import-export business and I believed him. That sounds naive now, but he had the gift of the gab; he could talk you into trusting him on anything, so even when I got the sniff of something – that maybe he was into drugs, stolen goods, that sort of thing – he always had some story and it always sounded plausible. So, yeah, we met through an AA group in Beckton. He had a warehouse down that way – so he was always in the area – and I used to live nearby.'

Healy glanced at Naughton and could see, from the notes that she was making, that she'd connected the dots, same as he had: Marie Havendish had told Naughton, in their original interview six months ago, that she'd met Coventry in a coffee shop in Beckton. That was *after* the split with Cara Coben, but if Coventry was always in the area – at his warehouse – it might explain how Havendish knew where to find him.

But not why she'd targeted him.

Turning his back on Coben for a second, disguising what he was doing, Healy got out his phone and sent a quick text to Rosa.

Did you check the warehouse?

Her phone beeped a couple of seconds later. She asked Coben to give her a few moments, checked who the sender was, read the text, then fired off a quick response.

Healy's handset was set to silent so made no sound as her reply came through.

Yes. Found stolen goods but nothing re: disappearance.

'Sorry,' Naughton said. 'Please, continue.'

'There's not much more to say,' Coben went on. 'Long story short, I eventually ended up running the AA group in Hackney, so obviously we both went to that one. Like I said, he was basically fine in that first year of our marriage, so we went on like that for a while, and then it was decided that our group should merge with another small group in Bethnal Green to create something bigger. I went to the first few at the place on Brick Lane but didn't like it as much. I always preferred the group when there was less people, and I liked running it, which I didn't get to do there – plus, Tom had started boozing again by that time, so he didn't give a shit about coming along, or supporting me. In fact, he didn't want me going at all, to that, to anything. When he took up the drink again, that was when it started up – all the shit, the cruelty, the pain he would inflict on me. I stopped going to meetings but I've never touched a drop of alcohol, even when I was in the middle of it all, unable to leave my own house. Tom? He was on it for most of our second year together, and every day for the final twelve months.' She stopped, a little beaten down now. 'People said to me after the split, before that arsehole vanished into thin air, "Why don't you go to the police and tell them what happened? He deserves to be punished for what he did to you" – but I don't want that. I've got some semblance of a life back now, I see my family. I just need to move on – and every day that I don't see Tom's face? Believe me, that's a good day.'

Naughton removed a photograph from her notebook.

'Do you recognize this woman, Cara?'

She slid a picture of Marie Havendish across the table. It was from the file on Thomas Coventry's disappearance, and the only picture they had of Havendish: there had been no photographs of her at Coventry's place, and because she'd had no social media profiles, there were none of her on the web. Naughton had taken this one, six months ago, from the fake website Havendish had set up to support the idea that she was a writer.

Before Coben took the picture of Havendish from Rosa, Healy glanced at the timid-looking woman in the photograph again. The dark, wiry hair, threaded through with grey; the pale mole to the side of her nose; the expression on her face that made it seem as if she was embarrassed about being photographed: all of it apparently an act. The only reason they even knew this *was* the same woman who had come in and reported Thomas Coventry's disappearance – and not just a random portrait dumped on to a fake website for a fake writer – was because Rosa had met Havendish in the flesh.

'No,' Coben said, taking the picture between her fingers.

'You don't recognize her?' Naughton responded.

'No. Who is she?'

'This is the woman your ex-husband dated after you split.'

For the first time, something gave way in Coben's face. She'd been hardened by a terrible marriage to a repellent human being, but some of her ferocity, her anger, started to dissipate as she looked at Havendish. When she finally tore her eyes away from the photo, she glanced at Naughton and then at Healy, holding his gaze, and again he couldn't get a read on her. Was she looking at him because she thought this was some strategy, a game where Healy would wait in the wings silently until Rosa tapped out? Was she expecting some good-cop, bad-cop routine where he would now come at her? He watched Coben, watched as her eyes switched from him to Naughton, then to the living room and out to the patio doors. Or was that it? Was she searching for something outside?

Healy followed her gaze, out to the garden, to the public baths.

When he looked at Coben again, she'd dragged her eyes back to Naughton. 'I'm surprised anyone would have him,' she said finally, and then tossed the picture back on to the coffee table, so that it skidded across the glass top to Naughton. 'That arsehole cheated on me so often that I lost count. It doesn't surprise me he found someone so soon after we split. But it surprises me they stayed together for six months.' She dabbed at an eye.

'Can I ask you a question about his house?' Naughton said.

'His house?'

She nodded. 'Does it belong to you now?'

But Coben was shaking her head. There were tears in her eyes, although it was clear that she was trying her hardest to hold them back. She got up, looked between Naughton and Healy, and then said, 'Can I just go and clean myself up a little first?'

She didn't wait for an answer.

She headed out of the living room and they heard her open and close a door in the hallway, sobbing gently as she went. Healy and Naughton looked at each other. *What do you think?* she asked, the question written plainly across her face. *I don't know*, he responded with a shrug, and then gestured for her to follow him over to the patio doors.

'Do you think she's hiding something?' he said softly.

Naughton frowned. 'Honestly? I don't know.'

'Something's bugging me.'

'About what?'

'About her.'

They scanned the garden but it didn't take long: it was small, the lawn a square of thick green grass, the patio slick with rain, the flowerbeds dotted with pale colours.

Healy's eyes went to the public baths again.

'How do you want to play it from here, Boss? I think we need to –'

But then Healy's phone started buzzing.

'Sorry,' he said, and checked the number.

It was Gemma again.

He remembered the voicemail his wife had left him that he hadn't bothered listening to yet, and then realized it was probably only an hour and a half since she'd called him the first time. That was unusual for Gemma: she generally didn't bother him at work unless it was an absolute emergency; even then, she'd rarely call him twice about it.

He'd missed two texts from her as well.

Answer your phone.

And then:

ANSWER YOUR FUCKING PHONE.

He accepted the call and stepped away from Rosa. 'Gemma?'

'Did you get my messages?'

She sounded pissed off, flustered.

'I haven't had a chance to –'

'Well, maybe for once in your life you should prioritize your actual family over the fucking Met.' She was breathing hard, hissing the words out.

Healy looked at Naughton, suddenly flushed with embarrassment, unsure how much of that she had heard. Stepping even further away and then turning his back, he spat a reply at his wife: 'What the *fuck* is the matter with you, Gem? I'm at work.'

'You're always at work, Colm.'

He felt the fire burning in him.

'Are you *drunk*?' he said to her.

'*What?*'

'I can't be dealing with this now.'

'You think I'm *drunk*?'

He glanced at Naughton. She was pretending not to notice.

'Well, what the hell are you calling me –'

'Of course I'm not *drunk*,' Gemma seethed, cutting him off. 'You want to know what my problem is? You *really* want to know what my problem is, Colm?'

'I haven't got time for this.'

'No, I'm sure you haven't,' Gemma said witheringly. 'But I thought it might be important for you to know – which is why I left a voicemail message two *hours* ago and sent you two separate texts in the meantime – that I'm currently sitting in A&E.'

'What?'

'I'm here waiting *on my own*, because Leanne – that's your *daughter*, just in case you're struggling – is currently on an operating table being sewn back together.'

Healy's stomach dropped. '*What?*'

'She was in a car accident this morning.'

'Are you serious?'

'What do you think?'

'Is she okay?'

'Well, she's in an operating theatre, Colm, so why don't you take a guess?'

'I had no idea. You know I would –'

'I don't know anything any more. That's the point.'

Healy felt stung. The anger still bubbled.

'Look, Gem, you can't blame me –'

'Come or don't come,' Gemma said, 'but I thought you should know.'

She hung up.

Frozen for a moment, Healy just stood there, phone to his ear. *Leanne. Oh shit, Leanne.* He thought of her that morning, remembered the things she'd said to him.

You might be here in person, Dad.

But you're never home.

He pocketed his phone and hurried across to Naughton.

'Is everything all right, Boss?'

'No,' he said. 'It's my daughter.'

Naughton frowned. 'Is she okay?'

'No.' His head was full of static. 'No, she's been in a car accident.'

'Shit. Do you need to go?'

He nodded, looking at Naughton, then out through the door of the living room to the hallway. Cara Coben was still in the downstairs toilet. He thought of her, of how he felt – instinctively – that something was off here, felt a magnetic pull to stay, to get answers, to figure out what was bothering him, and then he thought of Leanne again.

My daughter. My girl.

'I need to go, Rosa.'

And that was when he suddenly recalled something that Coben had said just before she went to the toilet: *It doesn't surprise me he found someone so soon after we split. But it surprises me they stayed together for six months.* Except, they'd never told her how long Coventry and Havendish had dated. She shouldn't have known that.

'Go and get Coben out of that toilet,' he said to Naughton.

'What? Why?'

'Because she knows something –'

Except he never got to finish his sentence.

A split second later, Cara Coben appeared.

But not in the living room.

She emerged like a bullet from the side of the house, sprinting across the lawn, heading for the back gate. Before Healy and Naughton had even had a chance to react, she'd already yanked the gate open and was tearing through, to what lay beyond it.

The place she'd been eyeing before.

The place she hoped to lose them in.

The old public baths.

Now

After the phone call with Raker, Healy makes his way back home. The further up the incline he gets, the darker the night becomes, moving in like a cloak. He's left a light on in the house, and the curtains slightly ajar, so it acts as a kind of beacon. As he passes his neighbour's place, for a second he can see in through one of the front windows: she's watching television, the cat on the sofa next to her. Her living room is small, modern: pale colours, uncluttered, the patio doors open. Through them, Healy glimpses lights in the back garden, only pinpricks from this distance.

Until now, Healy hasn't paid a lot of attention to her – mostly, when they pass each other, she's out front, working in the garden, or walking along the beachfront – and when that happens, he deliberately tries to avoid eye contact with her, because eye contact means conversation. She probably thinks he's unfriendly, or maybe just shy. But this time, as he passes her, able to see her but she unable to see him, he takes a longer look and thinks, from this distance, she appears very attractive: perhaps late forties, early fifties, slim, light hair. In another life, maybe he'd stop and talk to her, find out her name and how long she's lived here. Maybe he'd talk to someone who isn't either Raker or the father and son he spends his days with and actively dislikes.

In another life, but not this life.

In this life, all the people he's ever cared about are gone.

Thirteen Years Ago

They sprinted after Cara Coben.

Before they'd even got to the back door, Naughton was already well ahead of Healy, her reactions quicker, her body stronger. He watched her pass from the house to the garden, bypassing the steps entirely. She landed like a cat and was gone. In contrast, he lumbered out, heavy-footed, already starting to breathe hard. His head was still so full of static he could barely think straight. He thought of Leanne at the breakfast table this morning, what she'd said to him, and then it was like a strobe of images: a wrecked car, the twisted metal, his daughter's face, the blood leaking from her lips, her prone body on the operating table. It knocked him out of his stride completely and he almost stumbled as he reached the back gate, muscles weak, body unresponsive.

For a second he paused, watching Naughton dart between puddles of ice in a narrow back alley, and looked back at the house: it felt like he was getting further away from Leanne, abandoning her, drifting out across a sea he would never return from. *I should go back.* He glanced at Naughton: she had headed right, towards the alley's end, which finished in the looming side wall of the public baths. *I should go with Naughton. It's my job. I'm her boss.* He glanced at the house again, at the open door.

But Leanne's my daughter.

It felt like he was being torn in two.

He had a second to think about all the things that would be thrown at him if he let Naughton go, if something happened to her in there. He watched her squeeze into a gap in the barricades that surrounded the baths – the gap levered open by vandals, its surroundings adorned in graffiti – and then she disappeared out of sight. She could handle herself, he knew that. He could leave her and head to the hospital and she would probably be fine. *Probably*. But if things went bad, if it all went south in there, if this was some kind of plan that Coben had made in advance, Healy would at best find himself suspended, at worst lose his job. Naughton was his responsibility.

But so is Leanne.

Except Leanne had Gemma for now.

Naughton had no one.

He headed after Rosa, running as fast as he could towards the gap. By the time he got there, he was sucking in great lungfuls of air, his head swimming, and he was sweating profusely despite how cold it was. He pushed through the gap in the boards, on to the other side, and found himself in a narrow alleyway between the barricades and the public baths. Boarded windows all the way down. A rusting metal staircase zigzagging up to a top-floor door, which had also been boarded. To his left the alley ended in a pebble-dashed wall. There was no way into or out of the building that way.

To his right, a door was open.

It too had been boarded up but the wood had been prised open some time ago and now it hung off a single hinge. Healy headed towards the black sliver that marked its opening. As he did, he fumbled in his pocket for his phone, struggling to grab hold of it, and even when he did, he couldn't unlock it: his movements were too heavy, too jarring and his skin was slick with sweat. He stopped at the door, stared into the absolute blackness of the interior, and then finally managed to get his mobile open.

He switched on the torch function.

It was weak, a sickly yellow glow. He squeezed through the gap and directed the phone's light out in front of him. A corridor unravelled, its walls peeling, broken tiles on the floor. There were cobwebs everywhere, weeds creeping through. The whole place smelled damp, the ceiling marked with brown rings, the background noise a constant *drip, drip, drip*. An office, padlocked shut, was off to his left. There was a second further down on the right. At the end, the corridor opened out into a much bigger space. To start with, even as he got closer, he wasn't certain what it was. But then, as he passed into it, he realized.

The changing rooms.

'Rosa?' he said gently.

Nothing came back.

He shone the torch from left to right. He had no idea when the baths had shut down, but it must have been decades ago: it wasn't just the slow march of decay that was evident on every surface, but the whole design of the place. There was no male or female designation here: just stalls all the way down, on either side, grubby curtains sitting like shrouds at every one, some hanging off their rings, some covered almost entirely by mould. Most had been pulled all the way across – and that was what Healy was worried about.

They were the perfect hiding place.

'Cara?' he said softly, keeping his eyes on the cubicles ahead of him where the curtains were pulled across. 'Let's talk about this. Whatever's going on, we can talk –'

A click.

He stopped. 'Cara?'

Where had the noise come from? One of the stalls?

He glanced between the rows of cubicles on either side of him, angling his head, angling the torchlight too, trying to see under the curtains for signs of feet. It was too dark, there were too many shadows. And then his mind spun back to the click he'd heard.

Could it have been a gun being cocked?

The thought sent a spark of fear through the centre of his chest and he came to a complete halt. As he did, he heard movement again: the soft crunch of tiles underfoot, an alteration of weight, one foot to another, from somewhere further down.

He switched off the torch.

The second he did, he heard more movement. It was why he'd got rid of the light: it had put him at a disadvantage. Pitch-blackness wasn't much of an advantage either, but it put him in the same position as whoever he could hear in the cubicles.

Especially if they had a gun.

He stepped forward.

He willed himself to see, but it was impossible to make anything out. With his right hand, he pawed at the spaces to the side of him, trying to get a sense of what was immediately surrounding him. His fingers brushed a curtain. He sidestepped closer to it, the curtain wafting and falling back into place. Beyond the tiny whisper of the material settling, he thought he could hear movement again.

He swallowed. The silence was so absolute now, the movement of whoever else was here was like a scream in his ears. Again, he thought about who it could be, about whether they really did have a gun on them, and while he wasn't sure about the gun, there were only really two people who could be making noise here.

And if it was Naughton, she would have responded.

Why didn't she respond?

He forced the answer to the back of his mind and, as he

did, another terrible image of Leanne hit him, hard as a sledgehammer. He saw his daughter rigged up to a hospital bed, tubes everywhere; he heard the soft, repetitive beep of the machine she was attached to. He saw Gemma and Ciaran and Liam, and they were all screaming at him, pointing at him, telling him they didn't want him at the bedside. *You're not here*, they kept saying to him. *You're never really here. You failed us all.*

And then he was back in the baths.

He could hear footsteps.

He froze for a second, then found himself again, stepping back further into the stall behind him, the curtain gathering at his shoulders like a cape. The footsteps were soft and deliberate, coming down the middle of the corridor at a careful pace, about ten, maybe fifteen feet back. It could have been further, it could have been closer. It was hard to be sure in the gloom. After a few seconds, they stopped again and it went quiet.

The silence seemed to go on for ever.

But then, softly: a beep.

Healy's heart almost hit his throat.

The noise was from a digital watch. It had come from a position no more than a foot in front of him. Whoever was there had got within touching distance of him and he hadn't heard a thing. As he thought of that, something strange started to happen.

He could hear someone sniffing.

Healy listened for a moment, trying to work out what the best plan was: stay put or launch himself? And then he heard the sniffing again. Was it just dust in their nose, or a cold, or the way they breathed – or were they sniffing the air? Were they trying to pick up a scent, like an animal? The smell of his deodorant – or his sweat?

It was so weird, so bizarre, it scared him. His heart started beating even faster. Suddenly, he wanted to swallow, his mouth full of the dust that was in the air, but he didn't. He just stood there at the edge of the stall, the curtain around him.

'Are you here?'

Healy stiffened.

A female voice, whispering.

'Are you hiding from me?'

Her words were barely audible. In fact, they were so quiet, if Healy hadn't been beside her, he might not have even heard. He took a couple of small steps back.

'No need to hide.'

He tried to get a handle on the voice. It definitely wasn't Naughton. She spoke with a faint London accent. Cara Coben had a London accent too, but a lot stronger.

'Let's do what you suggested,' the voice said. 'Let's talk.'

And that was when Healy knew for sure.

It wasn't Cara Coben either.

It was someone else entirely.

Now

The next afternoon, after he finishes his day out on the trawler, Healy gets the bus into a town further along the coast. It's slightly bigger than the village he lives in and has a Co-op, a chippy, another pub which he's never been in, and a few other shops which he's also never visited. There's a library too, right at the edge of town, on a village green. It's small but it has a decent selection of books and DVDs, as well as a computer terminal. Once a week, whenever he's picking up food at the Co-op, he goes in and grabs something to read and to watch – and to use the Internet.

He arrives in the town just after five. He always gets here at this time, as all the shops, apart from the Co-op, are closed or about to, and the library is winding down for its last half-hour. This time of day, no one takes out books. He's worked it all out, over the course of the nearly two and a half years that he's been here: the older, retired people come in the morning; the kids come with their parents after the schools kick out at three fifteen; that means after four – and definitely after five – it's quiet.

He enters the library and heads straight for the computer. As he sits, he glances at the two women who work behind the desk at the front. They are both in their fifties, and one of them Healy thinks is gorgeous, but while they've both said a passing hello to him before, they've never had a proper conversation. When, once, the pretty one tried to talk to him, he made up an excuse about running late for an appointment and hurried out. He felt foolish, even though she seemed to buy it; mostly, though, he felt disappointed. Like the neighbour he'd never talked to, he would have liked to have stayed, maybe got to know her a bit – even just a conversation about something mundane and boring.

But all he can ever hear in his head is Raker.

Keep your head down.

Don't take risks.

If anyone asks questions, get out.

Drawing the keyboard towards him, he goes to Google, then to Instagram, and after clicking on the blue LOG IN button in the top bar, he puts in an email address that he created when he first arrived in north Wales, his password – Leanne2011 – and then hits Enter. It takes a couple of seconds, but then the landing page for the Instagram account @MichaelSanderson16386 loads in. According to the profile, Michael Sanderson has 0 posts, 0 followers and is following 30 people.

Healy starts scrolling down the feed.

Twenty-seven of the accounts being followed, he doesn't give a single shit about. They're just filler: one of the Kardashians; a couple of so-called celebrities; some arsehole he saw on a cooking show one night who kept talking about how he's addicted to Instagram; and then the official pages for companies he's got precisely zero interest in. All these people and organizations are just his cover story.

The cover story for the three accounts he does actually care about.

When he gets to the first post that actually matters to him, he stops and stares at the face in the photograph, the eyes, the smile, and he hears Raker in his head once again. And then he looks at the face in the picture, and then the one he finds further down in the second account that matters to him, and then the face in the third account.

I'm sorry, Raker, he thinks.

And then, like every other week when he comes to the library to see what his two sons and his ex-wife are doing, he talks himself into believing it doesn't matter. Michael Sanderson is just a random name he plucked out of a newspaper. The five digits that follow that name, 16386, are just the first numbers Healy could think of.

All of this is perfectly safe, he's made sure of it.

None of this is a risk.

He's been way too careful.

Thirteen Years Ago

As Healy stood there, in the darkness, the woman spoke again.

'Why don't you put your light back on?'

It sounded like she'd gone a little distance past him now – or maybe it was how the blackness, the high ceiling, the stalls, were all bending sounds. He was big, bigger than he should have been, and that gave him a weight advantage. There was no way the woman was going to be as heavy as him, so if he hit her with the full force of his body, he could take her down with him, to the ground. From there, all bets were off.

He could hurt her and subdue her.

She could drop the gun.

Or she could fire it into him.

If she even *had* a gun. He thought about that, let it swill around his head, used it as a focus rather than the thump of his pulse in his ears. He was *assuming* she had a gun – he thought he'd heard a click; that click was the whole reason he'd switched off his light in the first place – but maybe she didn't. If she had a gun, why didn't *she* turn on *her* light? If she had a gun, why would she be worried about hiding? She already had the crucial edge. She'd just have to point the gun at him to be in control.

And where the hell was Naughton?

He pictured her, sprinting across the lawn, heading after Cara Coben. He saw an image of her slipping through the gap, into the narrow alley that led to the baths' entrance. What had happened after that? How was this woman here and not her?

Was Rosa hurt?

Injured?

Was she dead?

Suddenly, the woman sniffed again. The sound was so sudden, and so close to him, that he took a step back and accidentally moved the curtain, still draped across his shoulders. Somewhere above him, curtain rings rattled against a rust-speckled runner. The noise was like a shriek.

He heard a whisper, too quiet to make out.

And then: 'Boss?'

Naughton.

Confused, uncertain what to do, he stood motionless, staring into the impenetrable blackness, willing himself to see Rosa. Nothing looked back. It felt like he was in the deepest, darkest place he'd ever been. He squeezed his eyes shut, trying to hear, trying to pick out minute sounds against the silence, and then he thought again about the gun. If the woman had one, she would surely have fired it at him by now, or she'd have switched on a torch and told him to step out of the cubicle.

Another whisper: 'Boss?'

He swallowed.

'Boss, *please.*'

'Put on your light or I cut her throat.'

The same woman again.

Healy wavered.

'Put on your *light.*'

If she was talking about cutting Naughton's throat, she didn't have a gun. But there was something in the woman's voice that was different now, more threatening.

You can't let Naughton die.

She's your responsibility.

For a second, he thought of Leanne again, of how Gemma

305

and the boys would think – *hope* – that he was on his way to the hospital. How long before they realized that he wasn't? How long before they realized he'd let them down yet again?

He took out his phone.

The second he did, it lit up, casting a ghostly white-blue rinse across the stall he was in and the immediate area beyond it. At the very edge of the light, he saw them.

'Put on your torch,' the woman said.

Healy did as he was asked and then took them in properly.

Naughton was out front, her back arched as if something was being pressed into the base of her spine, a dull blade at her throat. Her eyes were on him – panicked, frightened.

The woman was behind her.

She was half concealed but Healy could see enough. It was Marie Havendish – or, at least, the woman who had taken that name. She looked different from the photograph he and Naughton had of her. In that picture, her hair had been mousy, wiry, tinged with grey; here, it was jet black, straight as a ruler and cut neatly to shoulder-length. The dull brown of her eyes in the picture had gone too: she had obviously been wearing contacts. Now her eyes were blue, both bright as polished marbles, even in the low light. There was a dusting of make-up on her face, mascara, eyeliner. In the photograph she'd been plain, unremarkable, but beneath it all he'd always been certain he could see an attractive woman and had started to wonder if Havendish's unexceptional appearance wasn't some kind of disguise. He now knew for sure that it was. This woman, whoever she was, whatever her real name, was beautiful.

But there was a ruthlessness in her eyes.

And it was so plain, it scared him.

He held up a hand to her. 'Let's calm down.'

'I'm calm,' she said. 'Are you?'

He looked at her, then at Naughton.

'Are you okay?' he said to Rosa.

'She's fine,' the woman replied for her. 'And she'll stay that way, just as long as you don't do anything stupid.' She paused, adjusting her position slightly, the knife at Naughton's neck drifting up and down her throat. The woman was more visible now.

She was wearing a red coat.

As he saw it, he recalled what Ray Yintley had said about Marie Havendish at the rented house – and how he and Rosa had dismissed Yintley's comment as having no value.

She had this red coat she always wore.

Now he understood why Yintley remembered her always wearing it and why it was important: because of its colour and because of its unusual design. It was thin and perfectly tailored, presumably so it wouldn't restrict her movement, and there were four pockets on the front – easy to get at – just above the breasts. Two poppers, two zips. Three were open. The click that Healy had heard must have been one of the poppers, not a gun being cocked, and the knife had come from the zip on the left; on the right, the zip had been opened already but what was in it hadn't been taken out – another knife, just the tip of its bone-coloured handle on show. If she kept knives in her zip pockets, he didn't know for certain what had been taken from the pocket with the popper, but he could guess. As his eyes adjusted to the half-light, he realized that the woman was wearing a pair of very thin, skin-coloured latex gloves. It was clever, cogent and calculated thinking: if things went south and she dropped the knife, she wouldn't leave behind a single print.

It's not a coat, Healy thought, looking at what she was wearing.

It's an armoury.

She pulled Naughton in closer to her, disguising much of the coat again, and then said, 'Are you even listening to me?'

He nodded. 'I'm listening.'

'Don't do anything stupid or your friend dies.'

Healy glanced at Naughton.

'Where's Coben?' he asked the woman.

'Not here.'

'I can see that. So where is she?'

'Gone.'

'Where?'

'*Gone*. You and her' – she meant Naughton – 'just made sure of that.'

'You mean, she's dead?'

'No, I don't mean she's dead. I mean, she's gone. The minute you turned up at Cara's house and started asking your stupid fucking questions again, you made certain of that.' She readjusted the knife. 'Now, here's what you're going to do. Here's how it's going to work.' She drew Naughton even further back into her and, as she did, the blade nicked Rosa's throat. Rosa flinched, sucking in a sharp breath, a speckled graze forming on her skin. 'I'll go this way' – the woman pointed deeper into the darkness of the baths, in the opposite direction to where Healy had come in – 'and you'll stay here for ten minutes. You'll literally time yourself.'

'I can't let you leave,' Healy said. 'You know that.'

'You can do anything you want.'

'If Cara or you are responsible for her husband's disappear–'

'Why would you want to find a piece of shit like Thomas Coventry this badly?' She stared at Healy. 'The search for him was dead. Everyone was happy. No one – maybe apart from his shit-heel business partner – was missing him. He

308

was the type of low-life scumbag that the police should have been *thanking* me for getting rid of.'

Healy studied her. 'So *you* killed him?'

'What do you think?'

'Why?'

'I just told you. He was a piece of shit.'

'There's a lot of pieces of shit out there. Are you going to kill them all?'

'You've got no idea.'

Something cold prickled in Healy's scalp. 'What does that mean?'

The woman tugged at Naughton again, shuffling her a couple of feet further away from Healy: a retreat. When he made a move to follow them, the woman's hand squeezed the grip of the blade and she forced the knife even closer to Rosa's throat. 'I don't think you're listening to me,' she said, eyeing Healy for a moment, her gaze so intense, he had to glance at Naughton just to free himself from it. 'I *will* go this way, and you *will* wait ten minutes. And if you don't, if you decide to come after me, if you try to be a hero, I promise I'll put this knife so deep in her neck, I'll be sawing out her spine.'

Healy swallowed, looked at Naughton.

Naughton looked back.

She was trying to be brave, he could see that, trying to say to Healy, *Do whatever you've got to do to stop this woman,* but if he did, if he made some sudden attempt to get to her, Rosa would die. The woman was probably six inches taller than Naughton, and while she might not have been as strong as her, she was clearly strong enough, and she was smart: he could see it in her eyes. They were what really stopped him. They showed what this woman was truly capable of. He wondered if she had been a soldier once, because she had

309

that kind of focus, that clarity of purpose. She knew exactly where the endgame lay.

'Are you going to tell me who you *really* are?' he asked.

She smirked. 'What do you think?'

'You're not Marie Havendish.'

'No, I'm not.'

'So who are you?'

'I'm no one,' she said, and started backing away again, into the black.

'We will find you,' Healy said impotently, staring off into the shadows as they swallowed first the woman and then Naughton. 'We will never stop looking for you.'

But there was no response this time.

Only silence. Only darkness.

Healy waited seven minutes. He knew his impatience might get Naughton hurt, but – as he watched his clock tick over, the seconds like minutes, the minutes like hours – he knew that, with every moment he lost, the woman was getting further away from him.

He didn't have to go far to find Rosa.

She was just beyond the changing rooms, where they opened up into a corridor. She was unharmed and she was terrified. In the pale glow of the light from his phone, he saw her cheeks were streaked with tears. He pretended not to notice, unsure if she would want him to draw attention to them. As soon as she saw him, as soon as she realized the woman wasn't coming back, she immediately began wiping the tears away, desperately, furiously.

'Are you okay?' he asked her.

She nodded. 'She went that way.'

Naughton pointed along the corridor, further into the gloom of the baths. Healy helped her to her feet and, when it became obvious that she would rather go with him than be left alone again, he told her to get behind him and led them deeper into the building.

They didn't find the woman, but they found her exit.

Before they got to the area that had once housed the baths themselves, they found a door. It had been left slightly ajar and a faint grey light was leaking in. When Healy pushed at it, they found themselves looking along another corridor with another door: this time, the door led outside, because he could see puffy clouds and concrete.

As soon as they were back at Cara Coben's house, Healy phoned through for more bodies and a forensic team, and then he and Naughton searched the place. It was hard to know exactly what they were looking for beyond some clear piece of evidence of what the hell was going on. If Cara Coben was now on the run, presumably with the woman who'd claimed to be Marie Havendish, then there was no indication at the property of what their plans were. Coben's clothes were still in her wardrobes, apparently undisturbed. Her phone was still on a kitchen worktop. Her Citroën was still on the drive, the keys hanging from a peg in the hallway.

Healy's phone buzzed.

Even before he took it out of his pocket, he knew who it would be. It wasn't back-up and it wasn't forensics. It wasn't anything to do with what had just occurred.

It was Gemma.

So I take it you're not coming?

He looked up at Naughton, watching her for a second as she started searching around in the downstairs toilet. She was pretending everything was normal, that she felt fine and was ready to push on and find both Havendish and Coben, but although Healy didn't know her well, he'd found out enough about her today to see the truth.

She was barely holding it together.

There was still blood at her throat.

He sent a text to Gemma.

Stuck in traffic. I'll be there, I promise.

He hit Send, then lingered on the last part of that message – the *I promise* – and wondered if he should have left that out. Promises were things you didn't break.

Barely thirty seconds later, he got his response.

Fuck you, Colm.

His heart plunged. She knew he was lying.

'Boss?' He looked up at Naughton. She was in the doorway of the downstairs toilet, propping the door open with the underside of her heel. 'You need to see this.'

Heavy-legged, he moved across to her.

'What is it?' he asked.

'Look.'

She was pointing to something, just above the door. Healy squeezed into the bathroom and followed her eyeline. To start with, he didn't even know what he was looking at: he thought it might be something to do with the hot water – a thermostat of some sort – because it was small and cream, and there was white plastic trunking coming out of the bottom, which went all the way down the wall, through the skirting board and a space in the lino. But then, with a hand pressed flat to the wall for support, he got up on to his toes and saw that right at the top of the box was a digital readout. Numbers were flashing on it. Just to the left of that was a small yellow button.

'What *is* that?' he asked.

'Can you see what the numbers say?'

Healy got up on to his toes again.

'No,' he said. 'Why?'

'Two thirty-five p.m.'

Healy frowned. 'Okay. So?'

'So that was about the time Cara Coben went and made our cups of tea.'

Healy was still frowning, still trying to work out what Naughton knew that he didn't. But then he looked at the device again, at the time, and everything snapped into focus.

'Shit,' he said quietly.

It was a panic alarm.

Except this one didn't alert the cops.

It alerted the woman calling herself Marie Havendish.

Now

Six days have passed and the weather has completely changed. The hot sun is a distant memory and fierce, violent storms have been tearing down the coast for seventy-two hours straight. Because of that, it's been three days since Healy was last able to go out on the trawler and three days since he earned any money. As he walks down to the phone booth in the village, he tries to figure out how long he can last without work. He has some cash hidden behind a wall panel in the house – it's what he and Raker have set aside for an absolute emergency; a situation where he needs to drop everything and leave immediately – but, without digging into that, he's maybe only got a few weeks' worth of money. That will take him to the middle of October if he's lucky. But not much further.

Tonight, the wind has died down a little but it's still raining hard and, by the time he gets to the payphone, he feels like he's drowning. Water runs off his shaved head, into his beard and down his neck. The anorak he's wearing is basically useless.

He yanks open the door of the phone booth, then draws it closed again. The sound of the rain on the roof and windows is like a drumbeat. Fumbling around in his pocket, he gets out a fifty-pence piece, drops it into the slot and dials Raker's number. As soon as Raker picks up and hears it's Healy, Healy hangs up and Raker calls him back to save him spending any more. They take the first five minutes – as always – to go through the same questions. How are you doing? What have you been up to? Has anyone been asking questions? Is anyone acting suspiciously?

After they're done, Raker says, 'So I went to see that doctor last week.'

'The one from St Augustine's?'

'Yeah. Dr Emma Garrison.'

'And what did she say?'

'She was basically trying to work out if this Gerry Stein guy was inspired by the Snatcher.' Again, Healy thinks of the Snatcher, the psychopath he'd hunted, of how that hunt had been his last case at the Met, of how everything after that had eventually led here. 'That's why Garrison called me,' Raker continues. 'I mean, the murders that Stein committed and the Snatcher case are totally different – but it's weird that Westminster Tube station is connected to both of their crimes.'

'You said Stein killed a family?'

'The family of his best friend, yeah.'

'Not actually in Westminster station, though?'

'No, in their home. And then he wrapped them up in plastic and, one by one, drove them all to different dump sites outside London. That's what Garrison says she's trying to get at: the location of the dump sites. They've got three of them now, but they still don't know where his best friend is. She says Stein has totally erased that entire period of time from his head, as part of some catastrophic meltdown he's had. But he has this thing – this quirk, this visualization, whatever they actually call it in the trade – where he's able to picture himself at Westminster, with this Stevie O'Keefe guy, finding a bag. The bag changes every time, for each of the people he murdered, but in the bag he finds the face of the victim and a map to their location.'

'Are you serious?'

'That's what Garrison says.'

'That's messed up.'

Raker doesn't respond this time.

'I mean, how do you even get like that?'

'In his case,' Raker replies, 'just a build-up of pressure, I guess.'

'What, you're under pressure, so you go and murder an entire family?'

Again, Raker doesn't reply, and for some reason it aggravates Healy.

315

He knows why he's been met with silence and what Raker's saying in choosing not to respond: *you see the world in black and white, Healy – but it's not. It's grey.*

'Whatever,' Healy says.

For a third time, Raker is quiet.

'So this Stein just suddenly flips out, is that it?'

'No,' Raker says, softer now, more circumspect, as if he's guarding against a fight. 'Garrison didn't really go into it, but I did some reading up afterwards: the newspapers said he had – quote – "an undiagnosed mental illness", basically some sort of psychosis, and it had been there, untreated, for years. People he knew said he could become aggressive suddenly or totally uncommunicative. His family reckoned he'd been acting weird for a while, and were worried about him being around his grandkids, and he told Garrison he kept losing chunks of time and seeing things that weren't there. It doesn't match anything we know about the Snatcher – he was always in control and knew exactly what he was doing – so I'm not sure how much there is in this idea of him being inspired by what happened back then. But you know how it is: Garrison's a psychiatrist and they're paid to look at things as closely as possible, for as long as possible, and then they try to find things that aren't there.'

Raker is being facetious – and he's also acting as peacemaker, draw-ing the fire out of Healy before this all descends into an argument – but that last part isn't so far from the truth in Healy's opinion. He hates psychiatrists and psychologists. Maybe it's because they can never give a straight answer to a straight question. Or maybe it's because, deep down, he's frightened about the idea of sitting across from one of them – because he's frightened about what they might find in his head.

Some memories aren't meant to be relived.

Some memories you bury for a reason.

'Anyway,' Raker continues, 'the whole point of this, and what I really wanted to say to you, was that there's already been plenty of coverage of this story in the media, and if Garrison connects the dots publicly to the Snatcher – even if it's in the loosest of ways – there's going to be more. You know the press will lap this up.'

'So?'

'So there's going to be a lot of focus on what happened back then.'

'The Snatcher case?'

'Yeah, once it hits the papers. If Garrison floats even the remote possibility of a connection, it's a story that will sell, believe me.'

'Okay.'

'So it's a risk.'

'A risk?'

'A risk to you, especially. If all this goes off again, it'll mean people sniffing around. I mean, Garrison didn't even realize you were "dead". She's got a list of the people who worked on the Snatcher case and she's going through them one by one. So if she's asking about you, you've got to expect the press to be asking the same sort of questions once this goes public. And, as we both know, we've already had a few problems with hacks sniffing around asking me questions I don't want to answer.'

Raker is talking about a tabloid journalist called Connor McCaskell who had pursued him in the aftermath of his last big case, where a whole village had disappeared in Yorkshire. McCaskell had got close to something big – a hint of the truth about Healy, and his faked death – but Raker had battened down the hatches and managed to stave McCaskell off. He's been quiet ever since, but that's never necessarily a comfort: an animal is always at its most silent before it attacks.

'Okay,' Healy says. 'So what are you saying?'

'I'm saying, is there anything – anything at all – that you can think of, even if it seems completely irrelevant, that could potentially be a problem for us?'

Healy pauses and looks along the seafront.

There's no one outside the pub tonight, not with the rain. But it's not the pub he's looking at, it's the flickering lights beyond it. It's the white dots in the blackness.

It's the next town.

He imagines the library there. The computer he uses.

'No,' he says to Raker. 'We're fine.'

'Are you sure?'

He pictures the Instagram feed he was looking at six days before: he sees the photograph of Ciaran with his fiancée, turning over flower beds in their new home; he sees Liam and his mates, gurning youthfully for the camera, pupils white from the camera flash, on a night out in the city; and then he sees Gemma, posing on a neat patio, in an even neater back garden of a house Healy has never seen and will never get to. Her new partner, taking the shot of her, is reflected in the kitchen windows.

'Healy?'

His focus returns and he's back in the phone booth.

'I'm sure.'

'There's nothing that could be a problem?'

'No.'

'Nothing that could be traced back to us?'

Healy looks at the lights of the town again.

'No,' he says finally. 'Nothing at all.'

Thirteen Years Ago

Within days, it felt like every avenue had been explored in the search for Cara Coben and the woman who'd helped her: Healy and Naughton talked to Coben's friends, her work colleagues and her neighbours, and no one provided any leads on where the women might have gone; they put alerts on Coben's bank account, but her ATM card had been left at the house and the £421.63 in it wasn't touched; forensics went through her laptop in an effort to identify Marie Havendish or find out where she was based, but if the two women had communicated, it wasn't electronically; Naughton had even trawled CCTV footage from that day at the baths, using cameras on surrounding streets, in an effort to trace the route the two women took as they exited the baths. But while she had some initial success and was able to follow them both south-west along Barking Road, she lost them in a side street, close to the junction with the A13. She told Healy that she was almost certain they'd collected a car from the side street and then used the dual carriageway to head east, towards the North Circular, because only a few minutes after they entered the side street, a red Ford Focus pulled out. None of the cameras subsequently gave Rosa a clear view inside the car – the weather had been bad, the rain coming down hard, and the spray off the road obscured the people within the vehicle – and once the Focus got to the North Circular, it disappeared in heavy traffic. But Naughton was convinced it was Havendish and Coben in the car, and Healy agreed, not least because – after a few calls – Naughton discovered the Focus was registered to an Ellie Austin.

Ellie Austin had been dead for seven years.

At the time of her death, she'd been ninety-one.

It was another fake identity and another dead end.

Healy got to Leanne's bedside three hours after Gemma had called him. His daughter had got through the worst by then and the doctors had told his wife that, for now, she was stable and out of the woods. When Healy arrived in the room, the temperature seemed to drop; Leanne was asleep, an oxygen mask on her face, oblivious to it all, for which he was grateful. The rest of them said nothing: Gemma, sitting on a green hospital chair, Leanne's hand in hers; Ciaran beside her, against the wall, taller than Healy now, as if standing guard over his mother; Liam next to him, shaking his head.

Healy stepped further into the room. 'How is she?'

None of them responded. They all looked away from him, at Leanne, Gemma's cheeks flushed with anger. She started stroking Leanne's cheek, clearly trying to calm herself down, her fingers moving in a rhythm, almost in time with the soft hiss of air being pumped through the oxygen mask. Eventually, Ciaran said to his brother, 'Come on, Liam,' and the two boys left.

'I'm sorry,' Healy said to Gemma.

It was like she hadn't even heard him.

'A suspect bolted about a second after you called.'

A sad smile on her face this time, there and gone again.

'It's true,' Healy said.

'I'm sure it is, Colm.'

'Gem, you *know* I would have wanted to be here.'

She glanced at him. 'Okay.'

'Leanne's my daughter, of *course* I wanted to be here.'

'So why weren't you?'

'I just told you.'

'See, I think you've got things slightly mixed up here, Colm.' She was talking in the calm, considered tone of someone deliberately suppressing her rage. And it was worse – she knew it, and he knew it. When they were shouting at each other, it was much easier for Healy to view it as just another argument and move on. When she was like this, it was as if thousands of needles were in his skin.

He walked to the other side of the bed.

'You *think* you wanted to be here,' Gemma said, not looking at him now, her eyes fixed on her daughter's pale face. 'But you didn't. Not really. You tell yourself the same thing all the time. "I *wanted* to be home for dinner. I *wanted* to take the boys out at the weekend, like I promised them repeatedly for a week that I would. I wanted to be there to help Leanne with her homework." You promise yourself a lot, Colm. You're good at making promises. But there's a difference between *saying* you want to do something and actually carrying through and doing it.'

'You seriously think I didn't want to *be* here?' he said through his teeth, trying to keep his voice down. 'She's my daughter. My baby girl. Why would I ever want t–'

'I don't know, Colm. Why would you *ever* do *anything*?'

Some of her control was slipping.

'What does that even mean?' he said.

She just looked at him, saying nothing. Like Healy, she was in her early forties, but she wore it much better. In fact, weirdly, his first thought after he'd arrived was how good she looked, her dark hair parted to one side and hanging in a ponytail against the other shoulder, her eyes a deep green in the low, pallid light of the hospital room.

'I'm sorry,' he said again.

'"I'm sorry",' she echoed, her voice tight.

She had an Irish accent like him – they were both from Dublin, although they'd met in London – but it was usually softer than his, less pronounced, modified more by their twenty years in England. Except for when she was angry: then it changed, retreated somehow, and Healy would hear the girl from Ballymun that he'd fallen in love with.

'I just . . .' He paused. 'I just couldn't . . .'

'I just couldn't get away,' Gemma said, mirroring his words again. She shook her head. 'That's just the thing, though, Colm, isn't it? You never *can* get away. This job, it's completely and utterly consumed your life.'

He shook his head. 'It hasn't,' he countered.

'It's the most important thing you have.'

'Don't talk shite, Gem.'

'Liam played for the county on Tuesday.'

Healy frowned. 'What?'

'Liam played football for the county on Tuesday, in Watford. That means he's one of the eleven best boys in the county in his age group, Colm – a *huge* achievement for him, which the five of us actually *talked about* at the weekend, believe it or not – and the last thing you said to me *and* him was that you'd go up there and watch him.'

Something curdled in Healy's stomach.

'You said you'd watch him and bring him back.'

He didn't know what to say; couldn't think fast enough.

'Instead, I get a call from the coach telling me that no one has come to pick our son up and that he's the only kid left there. So, because I can't get you on the phone at work – because you *never* answer your fucking phone at work – I have to drive all the way over to Watford to pick him up at ten o'clock at night. And after I get home, and his brother and sister have gone to sleep, I pass Liam's room and see that he's still awake, and I ask him what the matter is, and he asks me, "Why didn't Dad come tonight?" And do you know what I said?'

Healy swallowed, barely able to meet his wife's eyes.

'I said, "I don't know, sweetheart. I don't know why your dad didn't come and watch you tonight. I don't know why he just forgot. I don't know anything about him any more." And then, when I was in bed afterwards, so angry with you I couldn't drop off, I thought to myself, "I'm not going to say anything, and we'll see whether he even realizes." And here we are, Colm. You never even realized you missed it. I mean, I can see you've been trying over the last month or so, that since I raised this same shite with you the *last* time you forgot we existed, you've attempted to get home on time, the kids have seen a bit more of you, you sit there and work after we've gone to bed, not in the office – but do you know something? You're starting to slip again. I can see it. It's like history repeating, but not for a second time – for the hundredth time. You've actually been home so little over the past forty-eight hours, Liam hasn't even had a chance to *tell* you that you missed his match. So, I don't know any more. I don't know if I can put up with you disappointing me again. I don't know if I can keep defending you to the kids. Because what exactly am I defending, Colm? You can't even get it together for your daughter when she almost dies in a car crash.'

Healy closed his eyes, rubbing at them.

In his head, he saw the woman in the red coat.

He saw the knife at Naughton's throat.

'We've been together twenty years,' Gemma continued, turning in her chair so that her back was almost towards him, 'and after twenty years, you know a person pretty well. So I get it, Colm, believe me. I understand that these cases get their claws into you, that you walk into these places and see the sort of crap that ordinary people won't get to see in their entire life, let alone every day of the week. I've listened to you late at night, when you're drunk, ranting about some kid who got killed and how you're going to destroy the person who did it. I've seen the files you've left around the house, full of pictures I'll never get out of my head. I've seen it in your face on the rare times when we take the kids out at weekends, because even then you're not with us, you're some-where else, glazed over and thinking about some murder. I get it, Colm. It's your job. You're the last bastion for these people; you're the one that speaks for them and gets them the justice they deserve. I understand it, because you've told me over and over and over again, ever since you joined the Met.' She readjusted herself in the chair and gripped Leanne's hand even tighter. 'You're a good man, Colm. There are lots of days when I absolutely loathe you, but you do the right things for the right reasons, at least, and – in my calmer moments – I always come to realize that that's more than a lot of people do. But I'm telling you this now so it doesn't come as a surprise when it happens: if you go on like this, you're going to turn around one day and it's going to be you, alone, and I won't be here, and neither will any of the kids. You'll just be someone who was in our lives for a time. To you, we'll just be faces in a photograph.'

You're the one that gets them the justice they deserve.

For some reason, of all the things Gemma said to him that night, it was those ten words that stuck with Healy the most. On any other case, that may have been true – but on this one he wasn't so sure who deserved justice. It wasn't Thomas Coventry. Hard as it was for Healy to admit, as the days passed, as Naughton drifted back to her other cases and Healy returned to the admin and office politics he hated, he found it hard to feel anything at all for a low-level gangster who'd stolen, violated and hurt. And he found it even harder to feel anything after he began looking into Cara Coben's account of the physical violence she'd said Coventry had inflicted upon her: Naughton got a warrant for her medical records, and in them they found a parade of injuries – a broken arm, a fractured wrist, a deep cut around the eye, bruising under the clothes that never quite seemed to fade – that pointed lucidly to an abuser.

Why would Healy want justice for a man like that?

Why would anyone?

And yet, aside from the fact that forensics had swept the house for evidence of where Coben might have gone and had found nothing, it was impossible for Healy and Naughton to let the case go. Even as it drifted back to cold storage, they would still think about it, still talk about it when they were alone in the office or beside one another at the coffee machine in the kitchen. It wasn't just that a nameless, seemingly untraceable woman had held a knife to a police officer's throat. It wasn't just that Healy could still see the echoes of those moments in Naughton's face sometimes as he looked up from his desk and spotted her, staring into space. Instead, it was that, while Cara Coben was a victim, she may also have been a killer, or at the very least an accomplice; and it was that two women – one of them with long-established roots in London that should have been hard to walk away from – had upped sticks and simply vanished.

They couldn't find Coben.

And they couldn't find the woman in the red coat.

Now

Healy trudges back up to the house, the rain getting heavier with every step. He's feeling irritated. He tells himself it's Raker who's got to him, all the stupid bloody questions. He tells himself it's this backwater village where he has no contact with anyone, no one to talk to, nothing decent to watch, or to read, or to eat, just whatever he can find among the crap in the library or on the shelves in the Co-op. He tells himself it's working on a fishing trawler with a guy who barely communicates and his gobshite son whose lights Healy wants to punch out.

But it's none of those things.

Not really.

Deep down, he knows the actual reason he's irritated: he deceived the only person he can really count on any more, the man who knows the truth about him, who aids him financially, who instantly drops everything to help him start over when things get complicated, or risky, or dangerous. Raker is the man that insulates him.

And Healy has lied to him.

The thing with his family, following their lives through Instagram, is a small act. It's an act of almost no consequence whatsoever. He never posts anything, he only looks. And even if someone does, for whatever reason, try and follow the trail from @MichaelSanderson16386 to the IP address of the library, it still won't be obvious who the account belongs to out in the real world. Healy lives twelve miles away and only visits the library once a week – and, anyway, there are no cameras anywhere in the town. He knows because he's checked. If someone comes looking, they'll literally have to sit outside the library all week, watching every single face.

There's only a very slim chance he'll ever be found.

And, yet, there's still a chance.

Because the problem is, that's not the only lie that Healy has told Raker – he just can't work out whether the second lie is worse than the first. What it definitely is, is another small crack in the window-pane. When Raker asks him, like clockwork, every single week on the phone, 'What have you been up to?', Healy always says the same thing: 'The usual.' Or, 'Nothing much.' Or, 'You know how it is by now, Raker: just another week trapped on a boat that stinks of fish with the Chuckle Brothers.' He makes light of it all because, for the most part, his week is boring. It's repetitive. He wants to hear about Raker's life, the cases he's working or things that have been happening to him, not relive the meagre details of his own.

But he also wants to move the conversation away from himself.

He doesn't want to have to linger on his guilt.

Because the Instagram thing isn't the only reason he uses the computer at the library. After he's looked at what his boys are doing, after he's wallowed in the pain of seeing Gemma and the life she's carved out with someone new, he stays online.

He does Google searches.

He reads things.

He prints them off and cuts them out.

He knows Raker would disapprove because Raker has asked him to stay below the surface, to not do anything stupid that could compromise them both. He's said it repeatedly, like a mantra, because he knows Healy has a history of obstinacy; of not responding well to orders or ultimatums, even when they're meant to help him.

But it's hard for Healy to stop now.

It's gone too far already.

Because, just like in the last house he lived, in the last village, under the last assumed name, he's kept himself sane by challenging himself, by going back to his days as a cop. In his spare time, he goes hunting for cases – unsolveds, things that have slipped through the cracks – and prints out everything he can find on them. He grabs books that might be relevant, buys magazines and newspapers. He goes back to a time in his life when he was at his happiest, not just because his family was still around him, not just because he existed as a person and not as a fading memory, but because when he had cases, he was worth something. He was a cop, a detective, he had a calling, something he excelled at. He was tethered to something that counted.

Some of the cases are local, and he's just trying to build a picture of what happened and whether anything was missed. Others are further afield, ones that spark his interest. He doesn't know what he will do with any breakthroughs he might make, he just knows the cases keep him fired up and help him get through the boredom of his days on the trawler and his evenings alone at home.

And somewhere among the cuttings and the printouts, and buried somewhere in the memory of a computer at the library – despite Healy always making a point of deleting his history – will be the evidence of his search for answers in another case.

A case, unlike the others, that did actually belong to him once.

A case he's been working hard the last few weeks.

A case involving a woman in a red coat.

Thirteen Years Ago

One Sunday evening, almost eight weeks later, Healy was watching a movie at home with Gemma and the kids – a crappy horror film that the boys had chosen – when he suddenly thought of something. He'd been making a big effort since Gemma's speech at the hospital, and he'd wondered often if, in sacrificing something of himself at work, he'd cost himself the ability to see the Coventry case clearly, or the other cases his teams were working. He didn't want to be forgotten by his wife and kids, didn't want them to be those faces in a photograph Gemma talked of, but it felt increasingly like there was a trade-off: the more he committed himself to his family, the more time he spent with them, the more he seemed to be losing his instincts as an investigator.

He waited until the end of the movie, not following the plot at all in the last thirty minutes. And then, when the kids drifted back up to their rooms, Leanne still on crutches, Gemma telling him she was going to bed, Healy said he wasn't tired and would join her later. He kept the volume of the television up to make it sound like he was watching the football, but went through to his office and scooped up his laptop.

Back on the sofa, he logged into the HOLMES database.

Healy put in a search for 'red coat'.

As the results loaded, he thought back to that day at the baths, to the coat the woman had been wearing: the zips, the poppers, the knives she'd hidden in it, the gloves. There could have been other things too, squirrelled away in other parts of the jacket, but it was obvious at the time that the coat wasn't just a way to keep warm: it was an important part of who she was, her identity, and, crucially, the way in which – whatever her motivation for doing so – she'd helped protect and defend Cara Coben. Healy had looked at it that day and, in his head, had called it an *armoury*. And afterwards, in the fallout, as he and Naughton pursued all the obvious leads – the interview with Cara Coben, her laptop, her phone, her ATM card, even the CCTV – he'd pushed the relevance of the coat to the back of his mind.

And maybe it really *wasn't* relevant.

Or maybe it was.

He looked at the results. Red coats were listed as items in the inventories of hundreds of crimes. People had been killed in them. Murderers were wearing them. Witnesses had worn them, or described seeing them, or they'd been left behind by suspects or victims. Blood, saliva, semen, hairs and carpet fibres: they'd all been found on red coats. The parameters were too wide for the search to be effective.

Healy started again.

This time he put in a search for 'red coat' but added some additional terms to the enquiry – 'zips, pockets, knife, gloves' – and hit Return. His laptop chugged away.

He thought about Rosa Naughton again, about the subtle ways in which she'd changed since the incident at the baths. She'd become quieter, a little less confident. He also noticed she'd stopped bulking up. He'd asked her about the competition in the spring, the one she'd talked about in the car, the one she got her body in shape for every year, and she made an excuse about picking up an injury, and how it was going to make it impossible to do what she needed. He asked her what the injury was and she said it was a sore back, but then – a few days later – Healy asked her how her back was, and she looked at him as if she didn't know what he was talking about. A couple of days after that, he got her alone in a meeting room and asked her whether she needed to see someone, speak to someone, about what had taken place.

She said no.

He wondered afterwards, briefly, whether to go to his DCI, and suggest to him some time off for her might be good, but he didn't trust the DCI when it came to Rosa: he was one of the arseholes Healy had heard making fun of Naughton in the toilets that day, so how much was he going to care about her well-being?

He studied the search results on his laptop.

There were twenty-seven hits now, and none included Thomas Coventry's name: that was because no one had mentioned a red coat before Healy and Naughton met Raynold Yintley at the house Marie Havendish had rented in Tottenham. The red coat had only become relevant when Healy himself saw the woman wearing it at the baths, and, until tonight, he'd never thought to base an entire line of enquiry around that single item of clothing. It had been entered into the system simply as something the woman had been dressed in, and hadn't been used to try to track her down. Even then, its importance remained questionable. This whole search was, at its heart, based on desperation: they had little else to focus on in their hunt for answers.

So now you're hunting for a fucking coat.

Healy's gaze went down the list.

Immediately, he found himself discarding another group of eight cases, where the reference to a red coat wasn't relevant to an actual suspect or victim. He dumped another four after that, and then another seven. That left eight: seven were possibly relevant to the search for Marie Havendish, but none of the coats mentioned had zips, only open pockets, so he set them all aside and zeroed in on the one remaining case.

He felt an instant hit of adrenalin.

A 42-year-old man from Camberwell called Gary Crunn had gone to his local pub two years ago and, at the end of the night, somewhere between the pub and his house, he had vanished. The case shared some similarities with Thomas Coventry's: Crunn had kicked his wife out three months before he disappeared and immediately moved his girlfriend – who he'd been seeing over the course of the final four months of his marriage – in with him. Just like with Coventry, it was the new girlfriend who'd reported Crunn missing. And, again, as in the Coventry case, police interviewed the girlfriend in the days after, to see if she might have been involved in whatever had happened to Crunn, before dismissing her as a suspect. When Healy clicked on the interview transcript and read through it, the girlfriend – named April Rolley – came across as measured and detailed, and her answers were very credible.

Just like Marie Havendish.

And, just like Havendish, April Rolley had a red coat. That was the search term that had brought Healy here, and now he read the passage in which those two words appeared: a neighbour, who didn't really know Crunn and his girlfriend but who was spoken to by detectives all the same, said he saw a woman in a red coat come back and forth to the house several times on the day Gary Crunn vanished. He'd described the coat precisely – had remembered the zips on it, high on the breast – but, for the cops, it was a minor detail. They'd already talked to Rolley and rejected her as irrelevant.

Healy moved on through the report.

Once again, just like Thomas Coventry, Crunn had a criminal record, albeit a minor one. A six-month ban for drink-driving.

Receiving and selling some stolen PlayStations. An arrest for being drunk and disorderly outside Stamford Bridge. The accompanying notes – both on the arrests and on the disappearance – were in the bland, impassive language of a police report, but Healy had been a cop long enough to read between the lines: Crunn wasn't like Coventry – a middleweight criminal, whose smarts at least extended far enough for him to mostly stay off the police's radar. Instead, Crunn was just a Neanderthal, a battering ram; he was the type of prick who you'd only have to look at the wrong way before he was losing his mind and threatening to chin you.

Healy switched his attention to Crunn's ex-wife.

Her name was Patricia Burcey.

'Risha' for short.

When the police asked her whether she'd heard from Crunn recently, she reminded them that he'd kicked her out three months before and moved his new girlfriend in: 'Given that, why the hell do you think Gary would want to speak to me?'

But there was something else in her interview.

An echo.

In fact, one section mirrored so closely what Cara Coben had said to Naughton and Healy about Thomas Coventry, it was like Healy was back in Coben's living room again:

He would push me around. I fractured my wrist once when he shoved me out of the door at the back of our house. I broke my fingers when I tried to shield my face from a punch. He was a violent piece of shit. But the physical stuff, that was really just the sideshow: what really got him off was playing with my head. Gaslighting, I guess they call it now.

It was almost word for word what Coben had said about Coventry. It may even have *been* word for word, like a part that both Coben and Risha Burcey had learned, a performance they'd been prepped for when the cops came calling. Their answers were saying, *I know that you think I've got something to do with this, but look how honest I'm being about not caring what happened to him. Would I be this honest if I'd actually killed him? Would I implicate myself like this?* It was crude, but it had worked: in both cases the ex-wives' roles in the disappearances were completely dismissed.

And, as he looked at the single photograph of April Rolley, he felt another big charge of electricity: she had a short blonde bob and very bright, very blue eyes; she was wearing fake eyelashes, a thick swipe of mascara and tons of bronze foundation.

Next to her nose was a small, pale mole.

The database was a piece of code, a program, still not powerful enough to see subtle physical differences, which was why no one at the Met had been able to link Coventry's and Crunn's disappearances – or the girlfriends they'd had.

But Healy could see the likeness clearly.

These weren't two different girlfriends.

They were the same person.

He picked up his phone and texted Naughton. He had no idea what she did on a Sunday evening, still wasn't sure if she lived with someone or lived alone, because she'd never talked about it. But after the text was sent, he sat and stared at the picture of the woman – one version of her with mousy, greying hair, dull brown eyes, looking older and more diffident, the other with blonde hair and blue eyes, caked in make-up, confident, younger – and hoped Naughton would call him straight back.

As he waited, he switched to Chrome and did a Google

search for April Rolley. The spelling of the surname was unusual enough to help narrow the number of hits. There were no social media profiles for anyone of that name, and a lot of the hits were based entirely on the search term 'April', but on the second page he found something. It was a single Facebook post by someone called James Robertson.

en.gb.facebook.com > James Robertson > Posts

James Robertson – Posts | Facebook

James Robertson . . . Betting night at AJ's . . . good evening . . . four hundred quid . . . drunk . . . **April Rolley**

Healy clicked on the link. It took him through to James Robertson's Facebook profile. His wall was locked but the photograph – and the post – were viewable.

The picture was two years old, taken six weeks before Gary Crunn vanished. It was of a group of twelve people – eight men, four women, all in their late thirties or early forties – at some low-rent poker night in someone's garage. A piece of green baize had been laid out on a table, chips scattered across it, and one of the men was in a tuxedo.

In the accompanying caption, Robertson had written:

Betting night at AJ's! Proper good evening with the usual crew. Won a bit of dosh, lost a lot more (four hundred quid). Thanks to all these nonces for a great time, especially the Archbishop of Banterbury Ian 'Shit Legs' Stevens who got so drunk he fell over his own feet and April Rolley who brought the whisky we got pissed on! 😂😂😂

And then he tagged everyone in the post, except for April Rolley, who had no Facebook profile of her own. Rolley was at the very edge of the photograph, as if she was trying to sneak out of it or disappear behind Gary Crunn, who was next to her.

Healy used Command + to zoom in on her.

She was dressed in a cream blouse with a V-shaped neckline. At her throat, she wore a chain.

It was hard to make it out because it was thin, the pendant small, but as she'd stepped back from Crunn, her arm still at his waist, her blouse had shifted to reveal it. Healy zoomed in again and leaned closer to the screen: the pendant was unusual, a red square with two black letters on it. The letters were tiny, but looked a bit like initials.

NB?

Just then, his phone started buzzing.

It was Naughton.

'Rosa,' he said, trying to keep his voice down. 'Thanks for calling me back.'

'Is everything okay, Boss?'

'Yeah,' Healy said, looking at the pendant at Rolley's throat.

MR?

'I've found something,' he continued.

'Okay.' Naughton sounded confused. 'What have you found?'

'Marie Havendish. This isn't her first one.'

'What do you mean?'

'I mean, it's not the first time she's made someone disappear. It's not the first time she's played the role of girlfriend. And I don't think it's the first time she's helped a wife get . . .' He stopped. Get what? Payback? Revenge? What they felt they deserved from surviving a long, abusive relationship? 'There's another case, two years ago.'

'Are you for real?'

And then he realized he'd forgotten to check something: had any money been taken from Crunn? It didn't take long to find the answer: it hadn't, because he'd had nothing in savings, but Healy had a feeling, a strong gut instinct, that *something* would have been taken from Crunn. This case mirrored the Coventry one in so many ways it just seemed impossible that for Risha Burcey, the wife, and April Rolley, the girlfriend who was working to help her, there hadn't been some financial recompense too.

'Let's meet before work tomorrow,' Healy said, looking at the picture of Rolley again at the edge of the photograph taken at the betting night. She didn't want to be captured. She didn't want to be seen at all.

'Sure,' Naughton said. 'What you thinking, 9 a.m.?'

But this time, Healy didn't hear.

Because his gaze was back on the chain that Rolley had at her throat: the red square with two black initials on it. Suddenly, he was thinking about the woman he'd faced in the baths, the woman who'd held a knife to Naughton's neck and been so completely in control of the situation, so focused, had such clarity of purpose, that he'd wondered to himself about her past.

He'd wondered if she had once been a soldier.

And now he knew that he was right: because he recognized the red square with the two black letters on it now – and he knew for sure they weren't *NB* or *MR*.

They were *MP*.

The pendant was a replica of an army badge.

Military Police.

Now

He's still thinking about the woman in the red coat as he reaches the house. Opening the gate to the driveway, he remembers the night he realized she was ex-army.

The next morning, he'd got Naughton to put in some calls, and the chase – their desire to discover who this woman really was – filled her with an energy that Healy hadn't seen since the incident at the baths. He had the old Rosa back all of a sudden, smart, unyielding, a rocket of a cop laser-focused on finding the answers they sought. And she found them too. It took another three days before the guy she talked to at the Special Investigations Branch – the Royal Military Police's equivalent of CID – managed to join up the dots for them and send over a file on one of their former soldiers. 'I remember her,' he told Naughton at the time. 'She was here when I first joined the RMP. She was in the SIB then, but before that she worked in the CPU.' The Close Protection Unit: the branch of the RMP that specialized in protecting people – royals, cabinet ministers – at high risk of assassination, kidnap or terrorism. When Naughton told Healy that, he was pretty sure they both had the same picture in their heads: the panic button installed in Cara Coben's bathroom. The woman had still been working protection, even six years after she left the army.

Healy snaps back into the present and pushes the gate closed again. It moans on its hinges and then clicks into place. As he gets closer to the house, the security light springs into life, and he starts fumbling around in his pockets for his keys. The weather has got even worse, which doesn't help: a storm so ferocious it feels like pellets are being fired at him, and with his hood up he can barely hear anything except the fierce, relentless crackle of rain.

He finds his keys and lets himself in.

As he closes the door, and the rain and the wind are both reduced to a threatening hiss, he thinks about the woman again.

Her name was Callie Overton.

Forty-one. Five feet eleven. Her natural hair colour was black. The day he'd met her at the baths, that had been how she looked. He can still remember tiny details from her file, even thirteen years on. She weighed ten stone, one pound, and she was born and raised in Birmingham, and was married for four years to another soldier, until he died in a car accident while out on a week's leave.

Healy fills up the kettle.

The wind whips up even more, making the windows creak, and as he stands there for a moment, watching it boil, he slowly becomes aware of something off to his left. He turns, fractionally, staring into the shadows in the corner, into the space next to a farmhouse dresser, trying to figure out what it is he thinks he's seen.

And then he realizes.

But, by then, it's too late.

Thirteen Years Ago

Callie Overton was renting a top-floor flat on Romford Road in Stratford, which was presumably how she'd managed to get to Cara Coben's house so quickly after Coben had pushed the panic alarm that day. The properties were less than two miles apart.

Naughton did one pass in the car, Healy in the passenger seat, and then did a second, but slower. The reality, though, was that there wasn't much to see: two small second-floor windows under an overhanging roof, both with metal blinds, both sets of blinds twisted shut. It was 6.30 a.m. in late March – freezing cold, the sun not up yet – and there were no lights on inside, so it was possible she was still asleep.

But she could have been awake.

She could easily have been watching them.

They left the car in a space one street away from Romford Road, then headed back around on foot. They didn't talk much, didn't need to. They knew all about Callie Overton now, her history, the potential danger she posed, so neither of them needed reminding of the risks and Healy could sense that both their silences were born out of the same thing: nervousness. He'd brought extra manpower – just in case things went south – and an armed-response team was stationed less than a minute from the flat. Healy had toyed with the idea of bringing the team with him as back-up but something had stopped him: maybe pride, maybe the desire to be the one to put the handcuffs on Overton himself – or maybe because he knew, if the team put Overton face down on the floor the second she opened the door, he would lose any chance he might have to build a rapport with her. If he was going to get her to talk, he had to get her to trust him. She wasn't going to do that with a gun in her face.

As they approached the property, Naughton removed the front-door key from her pocket. The evening before, she'd driven to the rental agency in Blackwall – who looked after all three flats in the building – and had picked it up. There, she'd talked to the guy who had let the flat to Overton. He said she'd been in there for six months and they'd had zero complaints: she'd had good references, she was polite, she always paid her rent on time, and they'd heard nothing from her in the entire twelve months she'd been living there.

Healy looked up at the top windows again. Still shut, still no lights on. Naughton unlocked the door and then paused.

'Are you okay?' she asked him.

He nodded. 'Let's go.'

Naughton led the way through to a hallway with a black and white chequerboard floor. The ground-floor flat was to their left, the staircase to their right. They headed up the stairs quietly, helped by the carpet underfoot. The building creaked around them, contracting in the cold, which helped disguise their approach. Inside the first-floor flat, they could hear breakfast radio as they passed – conversation, the sounds of activity.

There was just silence on the second floor.

They stopped outside the door, white and peeling, a brass 2 in the middle of it, and looked at each other. Healy nodded again, Naughton nodded back, and he took out his radio, ready to call in the armed-response team immediately if needed. Naughton knocked twice. There was no noise from inside, not even the slightest, gentlest creak.

'Ms Overton?' Naughton said, her voice confident, strong.

Nothing.

'Ms Overton, this is the police. Can you come to the door, please?'

Again, nothing.

Naughton knocked for a second time, for much longer, and, as she did, Healy heard a door opening on the next floor down. He stepped to the banister and looked over the railing: a man in his twenties, dressed in a vest and boxers, was searching for the source of the noise. Healy flashed him his warrant card and gestured for him to go back inside his flat. As soon as he did, Naughton knocked again – harder.

'Ms Overton, open up – or we'll have to.'

They gave it another thirty seconds and then Naughton stepped up to the door and slid in the key she'd been given by the rental agency. Healy readied the search warrant, removing it from his jacket pocket and unfolding it so that they could show it to Overton the second they had the door open.

Healy watched across Naughton's shoulder as the door bumped away from its frame with a soft click.

Neither of them moved as the light from the landing leaked in across a small, narrow hallway. On the right were two doors; on the left was a third. On the wall, just inside, was a chain of brass coat hooks. There were no coats on it, no clothing at all.

'Ms Overton?' Naughton said again.

This time, he could hear the apprehension in Rosa's voice, could feel anxiety fizzing inside himself, but as she turned to him briefly, as he raised his eyebrows, silently asking her the question that he knew he had to as her commanding officer – *Do you want me to go in first?* – he got his answer immediately. Naughton shook her head. This had to be her.

These were ghosts she needed to exorcize.

Healy followed Naughton into the flat, his eyes darting between the doorways. It smelled pleasant, of perfume or maybe shampoo, and through the first door he could see a bathroom. A basin, a toilet, a bath. There were shelves with nothing on them; as he paused for a moment, he saw there was no moisture in there either, no steam, no sense the bathroom had been used recently. The toilet was flushed, the tiles spotless.

She's cleaned up.

It was the same in the bedroom.

She's gone.

There was furniture in there – a bed frame, a mattress, an old oak wardrobe, a chest of drawers – but it was shabby and looked like it had come as part of the flat. The drawers were all open, hanging at a downward slant, and they were all empty. The wardrobe door was only partly ajar, but Healy didn't doubt it would be the same.

Naughton looked back at him for the first time.

The kitchen had been cleared out and cleaned too, and then they reached a living room. It was surprisingly big, with a long window looking out across rooftops to the green square and skeletal trees of West Ham Park.

There was a sofa and a side table, both marked by age, and an old television on an even older stand. Some DVDs had been left behind, and some books on the shelf above. Healy wandered across, looking at the books. It was an eclectic mix: romances, thrillers, some sci-fi and horror, history, autobiographies, even plant and animal encyclopedias. As he ran a finger along the creased spines, he thought back to the start of the case, to Thomas Coventry's house: not to the tooth they'd found – it seemed pretty obvious now that it had been knocked out of his mouth in an attack on him, and the attacker was Callie Overton – but to, of all things, the movies that Coventry had kept on his shelves. He'd had no books at all – the dope probably hadn't read a whole chapter of anything in his entire life – but even his taste in films had been awful: copycat cockney gangster shite, on repeat. But not here: as he looked at the well-thumbed books, at the long row of classic films, Healy wondered if they could have been Overton's, and somehow he felt certain that they were. These books, these films, they were information; even the horror novels, even the most lightweight John Hughes comedies, could be used to build a view of the world, to give a different angle on it, to accumulate knowledge.

And Overton was a soldier.

Information and knowledge were a weapon.

'We'll never find her,' Healy said quietly.

Naughton turned, frowning.

'She knew we were coming.'

'That's impossible,' Naughton said. 'How could she know?'

'She's seriously smart, that's how.'

'We can find her, Boss.'

He looked at Naughton, and then back at the bookcase. 'I saw this thing once,' he said, 'on TV – one of those wildlife documentary channels – all about elephants. These scientists in the States had been studying them, and they found out that elephants can communicate danger through seismic waves. They use their feet to create these vibrations in the earth that can be heard twenty miles away.' He stepped up to the glass, looked out. 'That's what we're dealing with here. We're dealing with someone who can hear the vibrations in the earth. She can hear the danger coming.'

Naughton didn't say anything, but Healy could see her reflection in the glass, the outline of her face, and for the first time he realized she'd lost a little faith in him.

She thought he'd given up.
But this wasn't giving up.
It was realism.
'We'll only find her,' he said, 'if she wants to be found.'

Now

She shifts in the shadows at the side of the dresser.

From where he is, Healy can see her, but not clearly: he's only got a single light on – above the cooker hood – and that's at the other end of the room from her. She's in black tonight, not red. It's hard to know where her jacket ends and her jeans begin: he can hardly see anything of her, just a hint of a face, her skin a pale grey.

His heart is beating fast.

He's scared.

The obvious first question should have been, 'How did you find me?' but he's already answered that. He's answered it, over and over in his head, since he lied to Raker. She's here because of what he's been doing at the library: not just using the Internet to trawl Instagram for photographs of a family he no longer has; not just using it to look at newspapers, or to print out interesting cases he finds with Google, or to try to think about unsolveds that have slipped through the cracks, as if he's still a cop and not just a fisherman hiding out at the end of the world. No, she's here because he's been at the library reacquainting himself with her case – one that he was never able to close, and whose resolution was left dangling like a thread in the wind. He wanted only a taste of it – just a tiny, innocuous taste to keep him sane and focused – because, without some sense of purpose, of being good at something, some days it feels like the walls are falling in.

And a taste is all it's taken to bring her here.

'What did I do?' he says finally.

She doesn't respond for a moment.

'What mistake did I make?'

'Your Google search of my name took you to a website someone had

created about unsolved cases.' She speaks softly. It's been so long since he's heard her voice, he can't remember if she sounds any different, but he thinks the same thing now as he recalled thinking after they found out who she was: she was born and raised in Birmingham, but she has no accent. He wonders if it's something she's trained herself to do to the point where she no longer needs to think about it, or if she's deliberately suppressing her accent, even now. He can see her shrug, see a very slight tilt of her shoulders. 'That website you went to was created by me. Every time someone like you visits it, it sends an alert to me and logs an IP address.'

Healy smiles to himself, frightened as he is and ridiculous as it feels on his face: after lying to Raker, he'd convinced himself that – even if someone would think to look for him, given that he was dead; even if someone had the inclination to try and trace an IP address – no journalist would ever sit outside a library in a tiny village in north Wales for a week and watch every single face that came and went on the off chance it might be a dead man. Plus, no sane editor would indulge them.

But that's the problem.

Callie Overton isn't a journalist.

And patience is just another of her weapons.

A hand comes out of the shadows at the side of the dresser. Pinched between the thumb and forefinger is Healy's passport, her thumb propping up the stiff cover so that he can see which page she's on: his photograph, his fake name and history.

'Marcus Savage,' she says. The kettle has finished boiling and, except for the rain on the roof and an occasional, sudden burst of wind, it's silent in the house. She looks at Healy. 'It seems like neither of us are who we really are.'

Finally, she moves, tearing herself from the shadows. She still has black hair, but it's much longer now, although hard to tell exactly how long: she's French-braided it into two, tightly plaited tails, then tied the tails together at the back, presumably to keep it away from her face. She's fifty-four now – he knows that for certain – but she looks younger: it's her eyes, he thinks, blue as tropical water, and her physical condition.

Low as the light in the kitchen is, he can see how in shape she is, the lines of her clothing showing no hint of fat — just brawn, just muscle.

There are two black zips on the jacket.

Both of them are open.

She stops at the kitchen table. 'Marcus Savage,' she says again, the corner of her lips angled in amusement. She turns to him. 'You don't look like a Marcus . . .'

He doesn't know what to say to that.

Doesn't want to say the wrong thing.

She frightens him.

She starts to leaf through the passport again, its pages empty. No stamps. No visits anywhere. It's just a prop, an emergency cord, and she knows it. 'This is good work, though,' she says. 'Professional.' She leaves it on the edge of the table. 'Seen a lot of this stuff in my time, and whoever did this for you, he's got some skill.'

There's a pause as they look at each other.

And then, quietly, Healy asks, 'Why did you come here?'

'Why did I come here?' she repeats, ripping her eyes away from Healy and taking in the kitchen, the fake passport, the life he's built for himself here, in secret. 'I came here because, as a rule, I always look my enemies in the face before I kill them.'

Thirteen Years Ago

They did a forensic sweep of the flat but there was nothing to find: they already knew who had rented it, knew her personal details, had her military file and her background. And, while techs were dusting for prints and looking for trace evidence – anything that might help them find Callie Overton – Healy and Naughton headed to Risha Burcey's home in Clerkenwell. Her life had mirrored Cara Coben's, the suffering she'd experienced, the violence, it was just the husband – Gary Crunn – who was different.

But they were already too late.

Burcey was gone, just the same as Coben: she'd dropped everything and, with Overton's help, had disappeared. In the following weeks, Naughton put out alerts on anything Burcey might return to, and a month later, those same alerts hadn't gone off once. She hadn't returned home. She hadn't touched her bank account. She hadn't turned up to work. No texts or calls had been made from her mobile phone. Like Coben, she'd likely been an accessory to murder, perhaps even been there at the time her husband was killed, and, like Coben, the moment she'd become exposed, the moment Healy and Naughton had closed in, Overton had instigated her escape.

They couldn't find the women.

They couldn't find Callie Overton.

And they still had no answers.

Now

'I'm not your enemy,' Healy says.

Overton smiles. 'Then why were you looking for me?'

'I was just . . .' Healy stops. 'I've been thinking a lot about old cases, about my old life, and I thought about you, and . . .' He stops again. Is he just making it worse?

'Your old life?' Overton purses her lips as if she's thinking, as if those three words hold some deeper meaning, which, of course, they do. She knows who he is.

'Even if I'd found something –'

'You wouldn't have been able to tell anyone?' she cuts in.

He looks at her and then at her jacket. They are maybe only six feet apart now and in one of the pockets, just above the level of the zip's ebony teeth, he can see the arc of something shiny and dark grey.

It's the handle of a knife.

'No,' he says. 'I wouldn't be able to tell anyone.'

'Because you're supposed to be dead?'

Healy nods.

'What about your friend, David Raker?'

'He doesn't know I'm doing this.'

She eyes him suspiciously.

'It's the truth,' he assures her.

'Isn't he the whole reason you're here? He's the guy that pays your rent, he's the guy that pays the bills here. You go down the hill there to call him once a week.' She frowns, her gaze fixed on him, intense, un-wavering. 'Why would you do that?'

She meant, why would he betray Raker's trust.

Healy blinks.

Because this is what I do, he thinks. I fuck up.

Instead, he says, 'I don't know.'

Her eyes linger on his for a moment and then, unexpectedly, she pulls a chair out from the table. She gestures to the kettle. 'I'll take mine black with one sugar.'

Healy glances at the kettle. Is she joking?

She kicks out another chair from under the table, pushing it towards him, and says, 'I prefer coffee – but tea is okay.'

He makes her a coffee.

As he does, he can feel her watching him closely, studying every move, partly because she's looking for tricks, plays, stupid things he might do – like trying to drop something in her drink – and partly, he imagines, because she's spent so long doing this: it's been thirteen years since she disappeared into the ether, never found despite Naughton relentlessly trying in the months after they turned up at her flat.

He puts the coffee down on the table in front of her, then backs away. She nods towards the chair she's pushed out for him. It's right in the middle of the kitchen, an island in the centre of the room, and an arm's length away from the table, the worktops, and even further from the door. He sits down, feeling exposed, as if he's on trial – which is the point. He knows it; she knows it. For a second, they just stare at each other, and then she says, 'You know what the irony of this situation is, "Marcus"?' She sips the coffee and nods at him, telling him it tastes good. 'The thing with Cara Coben, it was over. Everyone had moved on. No one was looking for Thomas Coventry any more and no one gave a shit what had happened to him. A man like that – he's just human waste. So why start trying to find him again?'

'We were trying to find you.'

'Why?'

'Marie Havendish had just vanished.'

'Exactly. But you didn't know that until you decided to go back to Coventry's disappearance. That's when you found out about Havendish, because I didn't dump all traces of the Havendish ID until after I was

351

sure the investigation into Coventry had fizzled out. If you'd just left Coventry to rot, like he deserved to, we wouldn't be here. I'd be Callie Overton and Cara Coben would still have the life I won for her.'

'You "won" for her?'

She pauses, watching Healy.

'Do you believe everyone deserves justice?' she asks.

'I was a cop. Justice is fundamental to the –'

'Don't give me the rulebook answer. Do you believe it?'

He hesitates, thinking of Thomas Coventry, of all the people throughout his time as a cop who he had to try and do the right thing by, despite loathing who they were. He looks at her. 'Some people deserve to rot in hell for what they've done. But that doesn't change things. If a crime's been committed against them –'

'So you were crushed that Coventry didn't get found?'

'Not crushed, no.'

'Did you even lose one night's sleep over him?'

'That case kept me awake –'

'Not the case. Coventry.'

They stare at each other for a moment.

Healy shakes his head. 'No.'

She picks up her coffee cup because she's made her point, and, as she drinks, her eyes stay on him, two perfect blue marbles cutting him in two from the other side of the kitchen. When she's done, she says, 'Thomas Coventry was a fucking brute.'

It's the first time her voice has risen even a little.

'He beat her, he tormented her, he trapped her in that house, made her feel worthless, made her feel scared to even do the basic things human beings were built to do, like breathe.' Overton pauses, seeing if Healy is taking any of this in. 'I mean it,' she says, coming forward at the table. 'There were nights when he would grab Cara by the throat and choke her because she had a cold and kept sniffing. All this crap I heard afterwards, about him being some low-level criminal – like he was a joke, a figure of fun – that might have been true, he might have shat

352

himself every time he stood in front of another man stronger and more powerful than him, but with women, he was as bad as anyone I've seen. He was a beast. I knew it the first time I met Cara at that AA meeting she used to run, and I sure as hell knew it after that.' She moves the coffee cup on the table, caught for a moment somewhere else, then she looks up again. 'So what do you think? Did Coventry deserve justice?'

Healy says nothing.

It feels like there isn't a right answer.

Overton leans back in her chair, those eyes still on him, and then she reaches into the zip pocket on her left breast and removes the knife. Healy's heart shifts in his chest. Initially, the knife is folded, the blade concealed, but – with her forefinger – she touches a lever on the grip and the blade springs open. It's small, maybe two inches, maybe a little more, but it looks sharp as a razor and glints in the dull light.

She sets it down on the table in front of her and says, 'You know, in a weird way, all of this is actually quite refreshing. I can admit to what I want here without worrying about the consequences. And it's been a long time since I could do that.'

'You met Coben at that AA group?' Healy asks her, trying to redirect things, trying not to let Overton linger on the reason she's had to spend the past thirteen years in hiding.

'My name's Callie, and I'm an alcoholic.' She smiles, but she's not amused. For the first time, Healy even thinks she looks a little vulnerable. 'I've been an alcoholic since I was nineteen. It's why I joined the army: I needed to stop, I needed to gain control of my life, needed something that could focus my attention elsewhere. So, yeah, that's where I met her. After the army, I moved to London, and I tried different AA groups all over the city, but I never felt at home until I started going to the one Cara ran.'

She looks at the knife.

'I was married for four years,' she says, her fingers tapping out a rhythm on the grip. 'I expect you know that. It would have been in my file. My husband was in the army too. He died in a car accident while *he was out on leave.' She looks up from the knife: there's something in her face, a hint of what's coming, and it freezes Healy's blood. 'That car was perfectly fine in the days before that. We'd just had it serviced.'*

The rest hangs in the air.

'You killed him?'

'No,' she says. 'The car killed him.'

'But you messed with the car?'

She shrugs. 'It was subtle enough never to get noticed but it was enough to be cataclysmic when you drove at the speeds he did.' She stops tapping her finger. 'He was a violent piece of shit too. I could defend myself, I could fight back, I was trained – but he still dominated me. Physically, I could put up a fight, but mentally? He destroyed me. I had an unhappy childhood, a terrible father, and he played on all of that, brought it all back to the surface. He wasn't educated, but he was clever. He was a master manipulator. And so my levels at work dropped. Every day I stayed married to that prick, I became a worse soldier. That's no good at the best of times, but it's definitely no good when you're a woman. You have to work twice as hard to get even a quarter of the recognition, and he was grinding me into paste. He was ruining me.'

There's a distance to her now, a sadness that Healy – despite everything – feels drawn to. But it doesn't stay there long. A few seconds later, she's shaken it from her face. 'When I came out of the army, I kept thinking to myself, "I wonder how many other women there are like me." I kept thinking, "I, at least, had the ability to physically defend myself. Most women wouldn't even have that much."' She draws her coffee towards her and finishes what's left, then she pushes it across the table, her eyes falling on Healy again. 'That was how it began.'

He waits for a moment and then says, 'How many?'

'How many women have I saved?'

'How many men have you killed?'

Overton shrugs. 'Who cares?'

'Bad as they were, those men had families.'

'And, in most of these cases, those families just stood there and did

354

nothing while their sons tormented those women, belittled them, beat the living shit out of them.' Her voice is perfectly steady, even measured, but Healy can hear a burning anger thrumming in her words. 'I left the army when I was thirty-five, so I've been doing this nineteen years. You can't even begin to imagine the scope of what I've done. You don't know how much this has helped these women. This is bigger, more important work than all of the cases I took on in the sixteen years I was in the RMP. You only know about two of the women — Cara and Risha. Those are the only two times I've ever been forced to resettle a victim. But I would resettle them all, on repeat — for ever — if it meant they were safe and they got what they deserved.'

'What they deserved?'

'Freedom,' she says. 'And money.'

Healy frowns. 'But you only took twenty grand from Thomas Coventry, and Gary Crunn had no cash to his name at all. How can any of this be about money?'

'Because some of the men weren't like Gary Crunn.'

The air seems to chill because it's obvious what she's saying: some of the men were rich. Very rich. Healy says, 'So you take the money and then — what? — pool it?'

She nods. 'It gets shared around equally. Plus, there's property, estate, all of that sort of thing: it's why I get rid of the men before the divorce has gone through.'

Because then everything still goes to the partner.

'We normally sit on the dead properties for a year, because if you sell them too soon, cops like you start seeing it as suspicious. That's what we were doing with Coventry's place. We'd been waiting. Did you know it was only about two weeks away from being signed over to Cara when you and your partner turned up to talk to her that day?' She flashes Healy a look. She's annoyed, even now. 'Once it became hers, we were going to sell it. We could have netted about three hundred and fifty grand from Coventry. And then there's the place Cara was living in when you went to interview her. Obviously that was one of mine too — somewhere

I've sent a lot of women for safekeeping in their first couple of years alone. My plan was to keep her there until the money from Coventry's place came through. But, thanks to you, I had to abandon that house as well – so that was another four hundred grand down the drain. You cost me seven hundred and fifty grand.'

'Do the women ever meet each other?'

'No, never.'

'You just divide it all out?'

'I'm a regular Communist,' she says, then unexpectedly moves. She picks her knife up, holds it in her palm and then walks around the kitchen table, standing in front of it. Healy pushes back on his chair, the legs scraping against the wooden floor.

He doesn't know what she's going to do.

But he can hear his pulse thumping.

He can feel his heart in his throat.

'In a way,' she says, head tilted slightly, watching him closely, 'you should be grateful you killed yourself off seven years ago. Do you know why that is, Colm?'

She emphasizes his real name, almost spits it out.

He shakes his head.

'Because if you were still "alive" and you started looking into me like this and you were actually getting somewhere, I really would have to kill you.'

He swallows.

'Don't ever look for me again,' she says.

And then she comes towards Healy and he sucks in a breath, ready for her to tell him she's joking, playing with him, that she's going to kill him anyway.

But she doesn't.

She walks right past him.

And then she vanishes into the night.

PART THREE
The Daughter

Thirteen Years Ago

At the end of May – four months after what happened at the public baths – Healy was called into a meeting with his chief inspector, where he was told that Naughton was moving boroughs, to the Major Incident Team in Islington and Camden. It blindsided him: he and Rosa had got close after the Callie Overton case, unsuccessful as it was, and, as Healy sat and listened to the DCI, he couldn't help but feel hurt that she hadn't mentioned anything. Afterwards, as he returned to his desk and tried to concentrate on the paperwork in front of him, the hurt slowly turned to anger.

That night, as he was leaving, he bumped into Naughton outside the entrance to the station. She'd been out all day on a case. As they ran into each other, almost literally bouncing off each other's chests, Naughton started laughing and said, 'Sorry, Boss, didn't see you there. It's because you're so thin now.'

She meant it as a compliment, even though it wasn't true: since the beginning of April, Healy had been trying to lose some weight, forcing down shite like salad and couscous at every meal. He'd managed to shift nine pounds so far, but the worst thing was, he could hardly even see it – and yet every pound had been like pulling teeth. He hated the food, hated dieting, hated giving up all the things he loved. Deep down, he knew it was part of the reason he was feeling so irritated: it wasn't just Naughton leaving and not telling him, it was the diet and how it felt like an endless punishment.

'I'll see you tomorrow,' he said in response.

She frowned. 'Is everything okay?'

He paused there, wondering whether to say anything.

'Boss?'

'Why didn't you tell me you were leaving, Rosa?'

He thought he'd managed not to sound too annoyed – but she could tell he was pissed off because her smile instantly dissolved.

'I'm sorry,' she said.

'Yeah, me too.'

She took a long breath.

'What, it was a big secret, is that it?'

She shook her head. 'No.'

'Then what?'

'I just . . .' She stopped, looked down at her feet, clearly unable to hold his gaze. 'You've been brilliant to me, Boss. I've learned such a lot from you. You trusted me, my instincts on cases. I'll never forget that.' And then she looked up again. 'But since . . . I guess since . . .' She paused, didn't know how to articulate herself. 'Since that thing at the baths, since she held that knife to my throat, I just . . . I just . . .' She faded out again.

'You just what?'

She swallowed. 'Every time I look at you now, I see that moment. It's not your fault. If it hadn't been for you, for what you said to her, I might not have made it out of there alive. But when I look at you, Boss, all I see is those minutes in the baths. I see her telling you to wait ten minutes and then dragging me off into the darkness.'

Tears glinted in her eyes.

'I'm sorry, Boss,' she said softly, 'but you're a reminder.'

She sniffed.

Wiped her eyes.

'You're a reminder of the worst day of my life.'

Now

It's the end of October and the weather has set in.

Healy makes his way down the slope to the phone booth. In the intervening weeks, since Callie Overton came to the house, Healy has thought many times about confessing to what he did, to what happened, but he always stops short. Every week, when Raker asks him if anyone has been asking questions – if anything has changed – Healy always says no, nothing has changed.

It's the same.

Exactly the same.

And then, afterwards, he walks back up the hill to the loneliness of the house, stares at the spot at the kitchen table where Overton sat, and lets the guilt eat him up. He lets it consume him like an animal, a feeding frenzy that lasts until all he has left is a deep, profound hollowness. And then the next day, he gets the bus into the town along the coast, and he goes to the library there, and he looks at his family online, at all the latest Instagram posts of their lives. And on the ride back, as the sun goes down and autumn starts to bite, he lets the hollowness eat away at him again.

Tonight, after Healy puts the fifty-pence piece in and dials Raker's number, Raker is a couple of minutes late calling him back.

'Sorry,' he says, after Healy picks up.

'Is everything all right?'

'It's McCaskell.'

It takes Healy a couple of seconds to catch up: Connor McCaskell, the tabloid journalist that had been sniffing around Raker's life. He's been quiet for over a year.

'What about him?' Healy asks.

'Have you seen a paper this week?'

'No. I'm going into town tomorrow on the bus. I usually pick up a newspaper after I've been to the library to grab some books.' And then he stops himself, not wanting to accidentally say what's in his head.

When I'm at the library I use the computer.

On the computer, I compromise us.

'Why?' he manages, forcing the word out.

'That Snatcher stuff I was talking about has hit the media. It took longer than I thought, but it's out there now. Police aren't connecting the crimes of the Snatcher to what Gerry Stein did – they're not saying it's a copycat, or that the two men are connected in any way – but that hasn't stopped the tabloids from making the leap.'

Shit, Healy thinks.

'So, I don't need you losing your rag with me,' Raker continues, and Healy knows exactly what's coming, 'but is there anything at all here that could burn us?'

Healy's heart is hammering in his chest.

He can taste the words on his tongue, the truth about what he's been up to: looking at photos on Instagram, doing Google searches, reading up on cases then pretending to work them like he's still an actual cop – and then visiting the website that brought Callie Overton to his house, to this existence no one but he and Raker were meant to know about.

Instead, he says, 'No.'

'There's nothing?'

'No,' he repeats.

'Okay, good,' Raker says, 'because McCaskell called me today for the first time in months – and if he comes at me, and he will, I need to make sure we're secure.'

Healy tries to say something but the words get stuck in his throat.

'Healy?'

'I hear you,' is all he can manage.

Raker moves on to other things, a trip he's got planned in the new year, but Healy is only half listening: 'I'm flying out to New York, *because it's halfway. It'll be nice to see her. I mean, it'll be the first time I've seen her since what happened in Yorkshire.' Raker pauses, and at the mention of Yorkshire, Healy tunes back in: it was there that the village disappeared. It was the case Raker worked over three years ago that almost cost him his life – and the life of an ex-cop called Joline Kader.*

'Wait, you're flying out to New York to see her?' he asks.

'Sometime in the spring, yeah. Probably May.'

He remembers that Kader lives in Los Angeles.

'Nice work if you can get it,' he says, but his thoughts are drifting again.

Raker stops talking.

He can sense something's up.

'Are you sure everything's okay there, Healy?'

'Yeah,' Healy says, 'it's fine.' And then he tries to think of something else they can talk about and his thoughts lodge on the favour he asked Raker for last month.

The flowers he wanted put on a grave.

'Did you do that thing for me?' Healy asks.

'Yes, of course I did.'

Healy swallows. It's trickier than it should be because the guilt has lodged at the back of his throat and it's making it hard to breathe.

'I think Gemma and the boys had been there,' Raker says.

'Well, it was the ten-year anniversary a few weeks back.'

Ten years since his daughter was murdered.

He thinks of the car accident she was in a few years before that, when Healy had been in the middle of the search for Callie Overton. That should have been a warning to him. That should have been the moment he pulled Leanne in and never let her go. But he hadn't. Slowly – in the years that followed – he let her drift again. And then another killer, on another case, ripped her away for good.

I'm sorry, Lee, he thinks.

I'm so sorry I couldn't protect you from the world.

'Gemma wrote a nice note,' Raker is saying. 'I took a photo for you. I'll show you next time I'm up there. Anyway, I bought Leanne daisies, because I remember you said she liked those.' Raker pauses, waiting for Healy to say something, but Healy can't think of what to say: he has tears in his eyes, and he's not sure if it's this small kindness that Raker has done for him or the memory of Leanne's death.

And then he stands there, the rain dotting against the phone box, and thinks, *I wish I could have my time again. I would do so many things differently. I wouldn't make the same stupid mistakes, and say and do the same hurtful things. I would hold on to the moments that mattered, to the people that mattered, and never let them go.*

I would love my family more.

I would be a better husband.

I would be the dad, every day, that I should have been.

Thirteen Years Ago

One morning, a few weeks after Rosa Naughton left to start her new job, Healy found himself alone in the house with Leanne. It was his day off, and to start with he didn't even realize she was home. He thought she'd left earlier for a shift at the supermarket, so when she wandered in, Healy was taken aback.

'Lee?' he said. 'Why are you still home?'

But it was obvious why: she looked absolutely terrible. Her eyes were running, her nose was crimson and had begun to crust, she was pale and was breathing hard.

'You look awful.'

Leanne rolled her eyes. 'Thanks, Dad.'

She went to one of the cupboards, searching for cereal.

'Let me make you breakfast, honey.'

She turned towards Healy, surprised.

'I think I know how to pour a bowl of cereal,' he said, smiling.

She stood there for a moment, still staring at him, her eyes red, what she was thinking projected across her face: *What's going on here?*

'What, a dad can't look after his daughter?'

'Are you having some kind of breakdown?'

He laughed. 'Why would you say that?'

'You've never offered to make me breakfast before, ever.'

That wasn't true, he was certain of it, but when he tried to remember the last time he'd made any of the kids a meal – when he'd done anything for them that wasn't some pre-arranged obligation – he came up blank. He looked at Leanne from across the breakfast bar, a seventeen-year-old daughter that he'd allowed to drift so far from him that she was confused when he offered to pour out a bowl of Frosties for her. Was this who he was now? Was this how far from the shore he'd become marooned? Was Leanne going to turn around to him in six months, or a year, or two, or ten, and say the same thing to him that Rosa Naughton had? *When I look at you, all I see is a reminder of the worst time in my life. You're just a reminder of what a dad should have been. You're just an empty space where a parent should have been standing.*

All we are to you are faces in a photograph.

'You know I love you, Lee, right?'

Leanne's expression changed again.

She was even more confused now.

She probably *did* think he was having a breakdown.

'My work,' he said softly, sliding his hand further across the breakfast bar, as if he were reaching for her, 'my work is overwhelming sometimes. I love it, mostly, and I feel like it's a calling – like something I was *born* to do. But I don't want you to ever think that . . .' He faded out. He wasn't good at this sort of thing. He wasn't one for big speeches, even when it mattered most. 'I just want you to know that I love you, Lee.'

She eyed him, still silent.

'Whatever mistakes I've made, that's never changed. It never *will* change. I've let you down in the past, your brothers too. Your mum. I've let you all down. I never meant to, but I know I have.' He stopped. He could feel the emotion building and it was cutting into his voice. 'You're my daughter. You're my baby, even at seventeen. I would go to the ends of the earth for you, Lee, if that was what you asked me to do.'

For a long time, Leanne didn't move, maybe because she

didn't know how to react to any of this. He didn't talk like this to them. He didn't say these things. He felt them, he just never articulated them.

But then, finally, she pushed herself away from the worktop, blinking as if she were awakening from some dream, and then blinked again as if she was worried it might all be a trick.

'Okay,' she said, simply.

'I really love you, Lee. I do. I love you so much.'

She nodded.

They stared at each other, and then Leanne suddenly reached into the cupboard, pulled out a box of Frosties and put it on the worktop next to Healy.

'I like lots of milk,' she said.

Healy broke out into a smile.

And then he reached over to her, and she let him take her in his arms – and in the quiet of the house, as she sniffed against his chest, he held on to his beautiful girl.

CASE #4
Sleeper

I

Joline Kader slid her iPad and book into the back of the seat in front and then looked out of the window, across the asphalt, at a plane taxiing in from the runway.

She felt tired.

It was partly because she'd just celebrated her seventy-first birthday and, as if a switch had been flicked on somewhere inside her, everything had begun hurting: her bones felt heavy in a way they hadn't before, her muscles were stiffer, the serious injuries she'd sustained to her neck and head almost four years ago had begun throbbing a little more whenever she hoisted herself off the mattress in the mornings. It was old age – of course it was; she was realistic about that – but she was still in good shape, still trim, and her last check-up, a couple of weeks before, had delivered a clean bill of health, so she was hardly on her way out. The complete opposite, in fact. So she suspected none of that was the real reason she felt tired. The real reason was that, over the past couple of months, her son, Ethan, had told her that he and his wife, Claire, had been having a few problems: not huge stuff, not insurmountable issues yet, but problems nonetheless.

'What do you mean by "problems"?' she'd asked him on the phone.

'I'll tell you next time I see you, Mom.'

'Sweetheart, you live in Oakland.'

She meant she lived in LA, four hundred miles away, and there were no immediate plans on the horizon for them to come down to her in Seal Beach or for her to fly up. Ethan had paused on the line for a moment and, in the background, Jo had been able to hear her granddaughter Maisie. She was five. Suddenly, the idea of Ethan and Claire splitting up, of Maisie having to spend the rest of her life shuffling back and forth between them, had crashed against Jo like a wave. She'd wanted to say to her son, *Please don't make any rash decisions. Think about it. Talk it out.* But she didn't. She knew she had to bite her tongue, that the worst thing she could do now was interfere. So she told Ethan that she was always at the end of a phone, or on the other side of a video screen, and she left it. And, as the days had passed, as she awaited an update from her son that didn't come, it had begun to play on her mind more and more to the point where, the last few days, she'd hardly slept.

She looked at her reflection in the window. It was imperfect, but she could see the worry in her face. It was in the green of her eyes, behind the blobs of light that formed in the lenses of her glasses, under the fringe of her bob that was now more grey than black. She was five-nine, weighed about 140 pounds, but – for a brief moment – she seemed smaller: the airplane seat had compressed her somehow, making her look hunched.

'Would you like a newspaper?'

Jo looked up at one of the cabin crew, a good-looking guy in his twenties. He was holding out a copy of the *LA Times*. 'Sure,' she said, smiling at him. 'Thank you.'

She set it down on her lap. On the front page, the main story was about a mass shooting outside a Walmart in Rosewood. Sixteen dead. Thirty injured. Jo had watched it unfold the previous night on TV as she'd been packing, but the photograph on the front of the *Times* really seemed to bring it home: it was a shot, taken low to the ground, showing a row of bodies under sheets.

She started to leaf through the pages, trying to think about something other than Ethan and Claire, and as she got to page five, her cell pinged.

> Landed in NYC. It's hotter than the surface of the sun. Looking forward to catching up tomorrow. D x

She tapped out a reply.

> It's only the start of May, Raker. You should come in August. Man up! 😄 Just about to take off x

She got a response almost immediately.

> I'm a big fan of warm weather, believe me, but currently waiting for a taxi in the world's longest queue and there's no shade. Even you would be sweating it out in this and we both know you have ice for blood 😊 What time are you due in? x

Jo smiled:

> 5.5 hour flight. 3 hour time difference. Leave at 1.30pm, get in at 10pm. Cheeseburgers and beer will need to be consumed tomorrow. I know a place x

The cabin crew started to walk the aisles, asking people to switch their electronic devices to airplane mode. As Jo pocketed her cell, she thought of the last time she'd seen David Raker in the flesh. It was under very different circumstances: he'd been looking into the disappearance of an entire village in Yorkshire, England, and after twenty-eight years with the LA Sheriff's Department and LAPD, and then another twelve teaching at UCI, she'd been newly retired. Physically, at least. Psychologically and emotionally, her head was still in the game, haunted by a case she'd never been able to solve. Eventually, David's search for the villagers and her unsolved became shackled to one another, and the two of them ended up in the same place: a hunting ground. The escape from it had almost cost Jo her life, and if David hadn't been there, maybe it would have done. So, in the four years since, they'd kept in touch, by text, by email and video, and towards the end of last year had hatched a plan to meet. Jo had offered to fly to London, but David had said that wasn't fair, so he suggested they meet in New York. It was five and a half hours on a plane for Jo, just over seven for him, but David told her he didn't mind: he said he loved New York, had spent months there working when he was a journalist, and had been meaning to go back for a while.

'Kader?'

She looked up from her phone.

An attractive man in his late sixties – tall and slim, blue eyes under the peak of a baseball cap, his clean-shaven face marked with a scar at the top of his right cheek – was looking between her and the empty seat beside her. He smiled for a moment, and then started frowning, as if her lack of response had made him less certain of himself. Jo looked at him: she recognized him in return, the blue eyes and the scar like markers, and she knew instantly he was someone from her old life – at the LASD or, after that, at the LAPD – but she couldn't think of his name. He seemed to become conscious of holding up the last of the passengers trying to file on to the plane, so he stepped into the gap next to her. And then, as he moved, it came to her, and she felt embarrassed that it had taken her so long to recognize him.

'Gerald *Rivers*?'

The man smiled again. 'Yeah,' he said, and held out his hand to her. 'Yeah, it's me.' They shook. He'd lost so much weight: that was why Jo hadn't put it together. 'You look great,' he said. '*Really* good. What's your secret? Bathing in virgin's blood?'

374

Jo laughed. 'You look good too.'

'Yeah,' he said, 'who'd have thought that dropping eighty-one pounds would not only make you feel better but *also* stop your former partners from recognizing you?'

He patted his belly.

'I'm really sorry about that,' Jo said.

'Don't be. You aren't the first, and you won't be the last.'

Jo watched him as he checked his phone for his seat number. She couldn't get over how much weight he'd lost. He looked better now than he'd done when they'd worked together – briefly – in the late eighties at the LA Sheriff's Department. Then, he'd been grossly overweight, his diet was bad, his skin even worse; he'd been going through a divorce too, which had made him edgy and quick to anger for a time. Jo remembered how, when he got frustrated, his face would flush crimson, like all the blood in his body had rushed to his head. Some of the guys had nicknamed him 'Red' Rivers, but Jo had never called him that: it wasn't just because she realized he was conscious of it, hated it, and was being crushed daily by the aggression of his wife's expensive, ball-breaking attorney; it was also that, in the eighties, even into the early nineties, Jo had no power in the department. For a long time, she'd been the LASD's only female detective and that turned every day into a battle. Rivers might have had a nickname he didn't like, but his opinion had got heard; his instincts had been trusted. For Jo, it was completely different. Every single day, she had to scale Everest – and, if she made it to base camp, that was a good day.

'Would you mind if I sat here?' Rivers asked her.

Jo had brought her earphones and a book and had been hoping for five hours of peace and quiet, not conversation. But then she remembered how Rivers had been one of the only detectives at the LASD who'd never made a comment about her sex. Most men in the department had seen her as a woman first and a cop second, but Rivers had never seemed bothered. They'd talked about other stuff: politics and baseball and music – Rivers, like Jo, had been a big Marvin Gaye fan – and how they both longed to live by the ocean when they called time on their careers.

'Sure, Gerald.'

He double-checked with one of the cabin crew but there were spaces all along the plane, and Rivers was now the only passenger who hadn't taken his seat yet – so whoever had been due to sit next to Jo, if anyone actually had, wasn't coming. Rivers put his bag into the overhead locker and collapsed into the empty seat. As he did, he noticed the folded copy of the *LA Times* and the book in the seat pocket.

'Shoot,' he said. 'I really hope I haven't screwed up your plans.'

Jo held up a hand. 'You haven't.'

Rivers smiled again. 'So what has it been – like, thirty years?'

'Maybe more,' Jo said.

'Yeah, it could be.' He paused, thinking, his finger tapping out a rhythm on the top of the seat in front. 'I mean, I went to Denver after my divorce, so that must have been – what? – 1990. I was out there until I retired. So, yeah, thirty-two years.'

'A long time.'

Rivers nodded. 'A real long time.'

'Isn't Denver where your kids were living?'

'Kid, yeah,' he said, and there was a flash of something in his face. Jo watched him, but not too closely, unsure if he wanted to speak about it. 'You always did have a good memory,' he said to her. 'Yeah, my son lived there. He worked at the zoo.'

'Right. I think he was still studying when we were partners.'

But she'd noted something.

He'd used *lived* not *live*; *worked* not *work*.

He was talking about his son in the past tense.

2

Eventually, Rivers shrugged. 'My boy, he, uh . . .' A beat. 'He died.'

'Shit. I'm so sorry, Gerald. When?'

'January 14th, 2012. My ex-wife was also living out in Colorado at the time, but Ed was our only child. So when he died . . .' Rivers ground to a halt again. 'I guess it felt like there was nothing to stay in Denver for any more. All of my family are back here – my parents were both alive then; my sister lives in Santa Clarita. Literally, the only reason I ever transferred out of the LASD was because I wanted to be closer to Ed. It was like this dull ache being so far away from him all the time, and after the divorce, after Marian – that's my ex – moved out there, I knew if I wasn't there too, she'd start to subtly manipulate him – try and turn him against me. That was why I left you all.'

He made it sound like the Sheriff's Department had been a family at the time, but it had never felt like that to Jo. And even if it had been some kind of family, it was the worst kind – fractious and difficult, combative and painful.

'Ed was the only reason I was in Denver,' Rivers went on, quieter now. 'After I buried him, there was nothing else keeping me there – so that was why I came back.'

'I'm real sorry, Gerald.'

'Thanks.'

'How did he die?'

'He got shot outside a gas station.' He shrugged again, but

everything seemed a little slower, a little more fractured and broken. 'Never found the asshole who did it.'

'It was just random?'

'Guy in a ski mask went into the gas station, got the attendant to empty out the register, shot her once in the shoulder, here.' He pointed to a spot, high up on the right-hand side of his body, under the collarbone. 'Attendant survived, but as the robber exited, Ed stumbled into him. They literally bumped against one another because Ed was on his way in. He'd filled his SUV up and gone around to the side – where the restrooms were – to take a leak. He didn't know the robbery was even going on because he was in the can. First time he realizes what's gone down is when he walks into this guy. He'd already paid for the gas. All he was going back in for was a candy bar. Anyway, the robber thinks Ed's trying to attack him, trying to go for his gun, and the robber, he just . . . he pushes Ed away, then he just . . .'

Shoots him.

Rivers's voice crumbled at the last part.

Jo put a hand on to his arm. 'I really am so sorry, Gerald.' She didn't know what else to say.

'Thanks, Jo,' he said.

She wasn't sure if Rivers, or anyone else for that matter, had – in all her years as a cop – ever called her 'Jo', or even 'Joline'. It was 'Kader', or whatever name they dreamed up behind her back. Occasionally, a cop she'd hated called Greg Landa would sing 'Jolene', the Dolly Parton song, to her, changing the lyrics to suit whatever putdown he had for her that day, but all of that felt like a lifetime ago. It made her realize how much time had passed since she'd last seen Gerald Rivers. And not only that: it made her realize how much time had passed since she'd last been a detective.

It was nineteen years. But it felt like ninety.

'So what are you heading out to New York for?' Rivers asked.

Jo could see the hint of tears in his eyes, but again she tried not to make a big deal of it, facing forward for a moment to give him a chance to wipe the evidence of them away. After he was done, she said, 'I'm meeting a friend of mine from London.'

'Cool. Are you retired?'

'Yeah. This'll be my seventh year. You?'

'Eighth. How are you finding it?'

'It's been nice,' she said, and realized how non-committal it sounded. But that was the truth of it: it *had* been nice – she met with friends, she did Pilates classes and went swimming in the ocean; she was part of a book club in Seal Beach, hiked in the Santa Ana Mountains with a group of LAPD retirees, and even went back to UCI on occasion to deliver a lecture. All of it would have been better if Ira was still alive and she had someone to share it with, but she'd made a life for herself and it worked. Yet, hard as it was to understand, the moment she retired as a detective, she left a part of herself behind, a part that no lecture at UCI could replace, a part that no comfortable retirement could mimic. So that was why it was only ever nice: frustrating, stressful and harrowing as police work could be, it had been everything to her, the blood in her veins, and she'd been good at it. Apart from the day Ethan was born and the day Ira died, Jo never experienced lower lows or higher highs than as a cop.

The safety video started playing.

She watched it for a while, the cabin crew demonstrating the parts that they were supposed to – clipping belts shut, and pointing towards strip lights, and showing how to attach an oxygen mask – and then it was over, and the plane started to inch out of its stand. Jo said to Rivers, 'What about you? Retirement keeping you busy?'

He shrugged. 'Busy enough. I joined a book club.'

'Yeah? I don't remember you being the reading type, Gerald.'

'I wasn't. But I guess I am now.'

She smiled. 'It's a rite of passage at our age.'

'I like it. It's a nice place to meet people.'

Jo nodded this time, because she could read between the lines. He was on his own, he obviously hadn't remarried, and he'd figured out the same thing as her: it was all too easy to drift into seclusion when you were alone.

They were both quiet for a moment as the plane taxied out to the runway, and then Jo looked over and saw that Rivers was changing his watch to New York time and realized that she'd never asked him why he was making the trip out to the east coast. He smiled as soon as she asked the question, but the expression sat awkwardly on his face: there was no joy in the smile, no sense this trip was anything except unpleasant.

'You should check your newspaper,' he said, pointing to the *Times*.

Jo frowned.

'Page eight,' Rivers added.

Jo reached forward to the seat pocket and took out the copy of the *Times*. She started flicking through the pages. As she did, the plane began accelerating along the runway. Just as the wheels left the ground – the plane fractionally tilting as it traded smooth blacktop for fresh air – she found it. It was buried in the corner, unillustrated with any sort of photograph – just a headline, a byline and four succinct paragraphs.

L.A. FATHER SEEKS JUSTICE FOR SON 10 YEARS LATER

BY CLARA DONNELLY | STAFF WRITER

The father of a 41-year-old veterinarian, killed in a gas station robbery ten years ago, is heading to New York today in an attempt to close the book on what has been the most painful chapter of his life.

Gerald Rivers of Panorama City, a former homicide detective in the LA Sheriff's Department and a three-decade law-enforcement veteran, has spent over ten years trying to find out who killed his son, Edward, in Denver, Co. Edward, a primate specialist at the zoo in the city, was shot in the head as he entered the gas station by a man in a ski mask, and – despite numerous appeals down the years, and countless false leads – until four months ago, Gerald, and Edward's mother, Marian, had accepted that they would never find out who pulled the trigger.

But then a cold-case team in New York – led by Lieutenant Amy Houser and retired NYPD detective Frank Travis – stepped in. They were working a separate case, a seven-year-old jewelry store robbery on Manhattan's Lower East Side – and it was that search that led them to Aron Stavis, 54, a prolific, LA-born thief who had already served an 8-year term at Terminal Island, Ca., after holding up a bank in West Hollywood in 1991. Back then, Stavis's DNA was never taken by the LA Sheriff's Department, but this time Houser and her team in New York made no mistake. 'And then we fed his DNA profile through the computer,' Houser says, 'and we got an instant match for the DNA taken from the scene of a gas station robbery in Denver in 2012.'

Now, finally, as Stavis goes on trial in New York for stealing $1.1m worth of diamonds – and a Denver PD spokesperson confirmed to the *Times* that Stavis will go on trial in Colorado for murder immediately afterwards – Gerald Rivers might finally be able to find some closure. 'It's been a long road,' he says, 'and I miss Ed so much, every day. But maybe, in a small way, this will help us move on with our lives.'

Jo looked up from the paper.

'I don't know what to say, Gerald.'

Rivers just shrugged again. 'What *can* you say? At least they found the asshole. That's a step in the right direction.' He was having to talk louder, because of the drone of the plane, and he seemed to be aware of it. He dropped his voice a little, leaned in closer to Jo, and said, 'Stavis still denies that he shot Ed.'

'The DNA says otherwise.'

Rivers opened his hands out.

Jo asked, 'Why the hell didn't we collect his DNA back in '91?'

By *we* she meant the Sheriff's Department. If they'd collected Aron Stavis's DNA in 1991, the year he held up the bank in West Hollywood, Rivers would have known who had murdered his son in a matter of days because Denver PD would have got a match for Stavis on the computer. Instead, Rivers had had to wait another ten years.

'I don't know,' Rivers said. 'I guess maybe because DNA evidence was still so new back then, so collection would have been patchy. I mean, if memory serves, there was only one DNA lab in the whole of California in 1991, and that was over in Orange County.'

'That was the only one west of the Mississippi,' Jo said.

'For real?'

'Funny what you remember, but I remember that.'

The revelation seemed to sadden Rivers even more.

The plane had slowed its acceleration now, the high-pitched moan of the engines dropping away as the pilot eased back on the throttle. From her window, Jo could see

Downtown, its brown, grey and black knot of skyscrapers, the sky still blue above the ridges of the Santa Monica Mountains in the distance but the city beneath that shrouded in a low-level blanket of smog. As they banked to the right and crossed the river, they passed over the concrete braids of the interstate, the confluence of the Santa Ana, Golden State, Pomona and Santa Monica freeways. A memory flickered at the back of her head, an image from the front seat of a cruiser, as she and Rivers – in the short, four-month period they were partnered – pursued a suspect into East LA.

Rivers had always let her drive.

It seemed like a small thing now, but it had been massive back then: no man she had been partnered with before that had ever trusted her to drive, let alone take the wheel in a high-speed pursuit. It made her feel even worse for Rivers, for what he was flying cross-country for, and she reached over and put a hand on his arm again.

'I really am so sorry, Gerald,' she said once more.

'Thanks, Jo. That means a lot.'

They landed at JFK five and a half hours later.

She and Rivers walked off the plane and out to the carousels together. They hadn't talked much for the second half of the flight – two hours in, Rivers admitted he was feeling tired, closed his eyes and fell asleep – but they'd done enough catching up to keep them going, and Jo was pleased for the break. There was only so much conversation you could have with someone you hadn't seen for thirty years.

'Well, it was great to see you again, Gerald,' Jo said. Her luggage had been one of the first off the plane, and as she hauled it from the belt and released the handle, she turned to him. 'Good luck with everything. I hope you get what you want tomorrow.'

'Thanks, Jo,' Rivers said.

He offered his hand, but then Jo thought, *What the hell?* and stepped in to hug him. He hugged her back hard, as if she were the last piece of dry land for miles, and then she broke off and, as an awkward pause settled between them, she said, 'Well, I'll be seeing you.'

'Yeah. See you around, Jo. You stay safe.'

She headed out of the terminal.

3

David had booked them both rooms at the Library Hotel on Madison, but by the time Jo had checked in it was after 11.30 p.m., so she decided against sending him a text to let him know she'd arrived. His body clock was still going to be on London time, which meant he wasn't going to appreciate a 4.30 a.m. wake-up call.

It was too late for room service, so she dumped her suitcase on to the bed and then asked the night manager if there were any diners nearby still serving. He suggested one on 41st Street called Pippin Red's, so Jo took her iPad and headed a couple of blocks east. The night was still warm, the streets still busy, and even though it was after midnight by the time she got to the door of the diner, she had to wait for a table because the place was packed. Five minutes later, a waiter took her to a booth at the back of the room, with views out over the crosswalks at Lexington. As she watched people move from kerb to kerb, she thought of Gerald Rivers again. Something had stayed with her after they'd parted ways, a deep, immovable sadness for him. It wasn't just for the way he'd lost his son, for ten years of unanswered questions he'd had to face; it was also for the grief he carried, so embedded in him – his skin, his voice – it was as overt as the scar he had on his cheek. Jo knew why Rivers's suffering had affected her so much: it reminded her of her own, of the months and years after Ira had died. Her husband had been dead a lot longer than Rivers's son had, but the pain never went away. It became greyer, like the light at dusk – but it never vanished.

The waiter came back and Jo ordered a Philly cheese wrap with extra pickles and a black coffee, and then logged on to the WiFi. She checked her Facebook page and saw that she had over thirty notifications, but she didn't bother cycling through them for now, going to her emails instead. There were quite a few there too but none that needed any immediate action. That was one of the things about being retired: everything moved at a different pace. Emails, the Internet, even things like DNA and multi-agency databases, were relatively late additions to her career as a cop. She became a police officer in 1975: DNA evidence didn't get used in a US court for the first time until 1987; she was still using a typewriter to fill out the boxes on crime-scene reports in 1992; and – a year later – the Homicide squad at the LASD still only had two computers for the entire floor. But as soon as technology became more prevalent, and especially when it became the norm, it seemed to alter the flow of her work: things like emails and cellphones created a kind of artificial urgency, an environment where everyone needed – and expected – answers immediately. Sometimes answers *did* come quickly, and you could wrap up cases within days. Most of the time, though, cases were complicated and frustrating and undisciplined. They went where they went and you just had to hold on to the reins. So that was one part she *did* like about retirement: she missed the buzz of casework, but she definitely didn't miss the pressure of having to respond to every tiny request.

With her earphones in, and the sound of the diner reduced to a low hum, she carried on watching a documentary she'd downloaded about the Donner Party, a group of pioneers who, in 1846, set out for California from Missouri. Eighty-seven of them left but only forty-eight survived. Jo had just got to the part of the story that she most vividly remembered from high school: the claims, and counterclaims, of cannibalism, and whether any of the party resorted to eating other people.

But, after a while, good as the documentary was, she realized that she'd begun to drift in her thoughts, back to Gerald Rivers, back to his son, to his grief and anger.

She pressed Pause as the waiter brought out her food, and, after taking a bite of the cheese steak, she switched to Google and put in a search for 'Ed Rivers Denver shooting'.

The top hit was a *Denver Post* story.

It was an archived version of the original article that had run in the paper the day after the shooting at the gas station. She went through it but there was nothing new, just a parade of facts that tallied with what Gerald Rivers had already told her on the plane. She looked at the photograph accompanying the story – a shot of the gas station with police tape in the foreground – and then at an inset: the face of Ed Rivers looked back at her. He was handsome, square jawed, well groomed. He looked a little like Rivers, particularly around the eyes and nose, and Jo imagined Gerald – or, perhaps, his ex-wife – had chosen this picture because it showed their son as he would want to be remembered: young, happy, healthy, with everything ahead of him.

It was the face of a 41-year-old in his prime.

As she ate, still looking at the photograph of Ed Rivers, she thought of Ethan, who, in terms of age, was in the same ballpark. She thought again, painfully, of the last call she'd had with her son, where he'd told her about the problems he was having at home. It was nothing compared to what Gerald and his ex-wife had been through with Ed, but it made Jo realize how far away from her Ethan was, certainly physically, and in this moment, emotionally too. If he'd lived closer, she could at least have called around to see him, she could have heard him speak, seen the fine movements in his face and got an idea of how he was *really* doing. If there was one thing she'd learned as a cop, it was how to read people, and how every minor shift in a facial expression held its own little truth. But that was impossible on the phone – hard, even when the two of them used FaceTime – and, right now, she felt that distance keener than ever.

Trying to blink away the frustration and worry, her gaze went to the right-hand side of the article about Ed Rivers, where a series of related links cascaded downward:

- DENVER PD RELEASE SKETCH OF
  SHOOTER IN GAS STATION ROBBERY

- DENVER PD: 'NO NEW LEADS' ON
  GAS STATION KILLER 'SO FAR'

- ATTENDANT IN GAS STATION ROBBERY WAKES,
  GIVES COPS MORE DETAILS OF KILLER

- FAMILY APPEAL FOR WITNESSES ON
  5 YEAR ANNIVERSARY OF SON'S MURDER

- SUSPECT IN 10-YEAR-OLD DENVER MURDER
  TO FINALLY FACE JUSTICE IN NEW YORK

Jo clicked on the last one.

Much of the story she already knew. Background on the killer himself, Aron Stavis, was limited to what was already in the public domain, but it hinted at a disrupted childhood, it made mention of the eight-year stretch – between 1991 and 1999 – he'd served at Terminal Island after the bank job in West Hollywood, and then it came full circle to the diamond robbery, carried out here on the Lower East Side seven years ago, where he'd made off with $1.1 million of stones. Thanks to the work of the Cold Case Squad at the NYPD, Stavis was eventually found and charged, and that was when his DNA connected him to DNA swabbed at the scene in Denver.

What was interesting to Jo, however, was how Stavis had pleaded guilty to the diamond heist but vehemently denied having anything to do with Ed Rivers's killing. 'That thing in Denver is *bullshit*!' he screamed into the gallery after his arraignment was over. 'I never killed no one in my entire *life*!' But, according to the *Post*, who had a source at Denver PD, there was some uncertainty about that. A cell mate of Stavis's died in what prison authorities referred to as 'suspicious circumstances' while Stavis was doing his stretch at Terminal Island, although investigations by the LAPD were never able to conclusively prove Stavis was behind it and the Denver cops didn't have much more than that to go on; and then an ex-girlfriend of Stavis's in Denver, where he'd lived between 2007 and 2013 – crucially coinciding with the year that Ed Rivers was killed in the city – claimed that, as well as being violent towards her, she'd heard Stavis on the phone to a friend one night, bragging about 'popping some preppy for just getting in my way'. It was easy to describe Ed Rivers's style as 'preppy': his friends said he always wore a tie and blazer to work, even in the heat of summer, and a woman he dated for a while in the late 2000s said his favourite pants were pale blue chinos.

It was also impossible to argue with the DNA evidence. Stavis's saliva was dotted all over the plastic shield separating the teller from the customers, presumably because he'd been screaming instructions at the teller as he'd ordered her to clean out the register. The same ex-girlfriend who possibly overheard Stavis bragging about killing Ed Rivers also claimed that Stavis's favourite item of clothing were white Nike high-tops. 'He wore them constantly, one pair after the next,' she told cops. And in the video from the store, although the angle was 'less than ideal' according to Denver PD, the gunman was wearing a pair of denims, a black hoodie with *Corton* printed on it, and a pair of white Nike high-tops.

And yet . . . Jo leaned back in the booth. Something still bothered her, and it wasn't just Stavis's insistence that he'd never killed anyone. That *did* rankle with her, but only because – in her experience – suspects tended to display that level of fervour when they genuinely felt they'd been wronged. The vast majority of criminals were, weird as it sounded, pragmatic: they knew when they were cornered and had no way out. It was exactly the reason that Stavis would have pleaded guilty to stealing the diamonds. But only a tiny fraction of the criminals she'd arrested and charged in her years as a detective were happy to take the fall for a crime that they'd never committed.

There was something else too.

A small thing, but there in the background.

In 1991, Stavis robbed a bank in West Hollywood. In 2015, he stole diamonds worth $1.1 million from a store on the Lower East Side. Those were big jobs, with big risks and potentially massive rewards; they weren't some spur-of-the-moment stick-up at a gas station, where the maximum you were going to make off with was two or three hundred bucks. It was possible, of course, that Stavis had just been desperate: desperate for cash, for food, for drugs. But during that period, according to what Jo could work out, he was gain-fully employed, as a labourer on a construction project in the Downtown area. His employment history was spotty, which seemed to suggest he was constantly being drawn back into crime – much of which had clearly gone below the radar – yet, at the time of the gas station shooting, he had a steady job.

Knowing that, would he go and rob a gas station?

And if he had – and all the evidence pointed categorically towards him being there, and being the man behind the mask – was there a more complex explanation?

Could he have carried out the job for some other reason?

Blackmail? Revenge?

Could he have *known* Ed Rivers?

For a second, Jo had a moment of clarity: *What am I doing?* This wasn't her case, she wasn't even a *cop* any more. She was already having trouble sleeping, and she didn't need another reason to be awake at night. Because that was what would happen here if she wasn't careful: the conditioned part of her brain, the detective, the trained pursuer of loose ends and unresolved leads, would find something amiss and never let go of it. So she eyed the arrest photograph of Aron Stavis in the news story: his grey skin, his unkempt hair, his dark brown eyes.

And then she went back to her food.

To her documentary.

To her retirement.

4

She got back to the hotel at 1 a.m., had a shower, and then lay on the bed in a robe and watched the last twenty minutes of *Psycho*. As Vera Miles went down the steps into the cellar for the final reveal, Jo thought of Ira. It was always this part that reminded her of her husband because the first time she ever saw the movie was at a drive-in in North Hollywood, and when Lila Crane turned Mrs Bates around, Jo had sucked in a breath and then glanced at Ira, who had been watching her the whole time, waiting for her reaction. It was one of his favourite films, so he'd known what was coming, but although he was amused, he also reached for her and took her hand in his, and that moment had always stuck: it was the first time Jo realized she was in love with Ira.

After the movie was over, she read for twenty minutes, trying to make herself tired, but when she slipped under the covers and turned out the light, she spent the next hour wide awake, staring into the darkness. She thought about Ethan, and about Claire. She imagined them in their home in Oakland, arguing with one another; she pictured Maisie in the background, still too young to properly understand what was going on, but bright enough and old enough to know that something definitely wasn't right. And then her thoughts began to shift back to that night at the drive-in with Ira, to Ira's death – and then finally to Gerald Rivers, to Ed Rivers and to the man accused of killing him.

Sitting up in bed, she grabbed her iPad from the nightstand and went back through her history, eventually ending up at the last story in the *Denver Post* that she'd read at the diner. On the right-hand side was a waterfall of related links, including some she'd seen the first time. Her gaze landed on one in the middle.

- ATTENDANT IN GAS STATION ROBBERY WAKES, GIVES COPS MORE DETAILS OF KILLER

She clicked on it.

It turned out that the attendant at the gas station, a woman called Hermione Suza, had been shot in the shoulder but the bullet had splintered on impact and part of it had lodged under her breastplate and perforated her lung. What should have been a relatively straightforward procedure to remove a slug from a shoulder joint turned into a traumatic four-hour ordeal in the OR, and then two more days on a ventilator.

Jo read the story.

ATTENDANT IN GAS STATION ROBBERY WAKES UP

Hermione Suza able to give cops more details of killer

BY SEB GRUNDY | CRIME REPORTER

The attendant who was shot during a fatal robbery at a Conoco gas station in Globeville on Saturday night has woken up. Hermione Suza, 24, was shot in the shoulder on the same night that Ed Rivers, 41, a veterinarian at Denver Zoo, was murdered by a masked gunman. The gunman, yet to be identified, shot Rivers in the face while exiting the gas station 7-Eleven, fatally injuring him. The killer made off with just $329 – but the impact of that night has been infinitely bigger for the family of Mr Rivers, particularly his father Gerald and mother Marian.

But now detectives from Denver PD are hopeful for a breakthrough after Ms Suza was able to provide them with new information about the masked killer, including a detailed description of the clothes he was wearing. 'These are details that just aren't apparent on the instore video,' says lead detective Craig Dominguez.

The gunman, already described as being white or Hispanic, about six feet tall and between 180 and 190 pounds, was wearing blue jeans, a pair of white Nike high-tops and a black hooded top with the word 'Corton' written across it. The top is where Denver PD's interest now lies: 'As far as we've been able to ascertain, Corton isn't a brand name, it's not the name of a clothing line, it's not a band or place,' says Detective Dominguez, 'which potentially makes it unique to our suspect. Is it an item of clothing that he himself has made? Is the word "Corton" in some way important to him? Is it a family name? These are questions we need answers to, and we're appealing to the public for help in this.'

Crucially, though, Ms Suza has been able to give Dominguez and his team another useful lead in relation to the Corton top: 'She believes that, on the sleeve of the top, she saw a series of numbers, like the kind of readout you might see on your alarm clock at home: four digits with a colon between the first two numbers and the last. So, do you know anyone in Denver with a top like that? Have you seen these tops on sale anywhere? Have you made these tops for someone? These are hugely important questions that can help us bring the killer of Ed Rivers to justice – but we need the public's help to do that.'

Jo read over the article again, and then put 'Corton' into a Google search. All she got back were results for a place in England. She read up a little more about it, just in case, but it seemed incredibly unlikely this had anything to do with a town in the UK. She changed tack and tried 'Corton Denver' – nothing – and then 'Corton Colorado' – nothing again – and, finally, 'Corton United States', and this time she got a link to a two-line Wikipedia article on an unincorporated township in

West Virginia. Just to be sure, she dropped into Google Maps to check it out: it was a scattering of eight or nine buildings on a bend of the Elk River, about thirty-one miles north-east of Charleston.

Again, it seemed unlikely this was where answers lay.

And why are you even looking for answers?

Tapping out a rhythm with her finger, Jo asked herself the same question a second time. The answers had already been found: the man who shot and killed Ed Rivers – whose DNA was all over the gas station where the crime took place – was going to be standing up in a New York courtroom in only a few hours' time.

Forget it. Go to sleep.

She switched off the iPad and stared at the blackness of the screen. She knew it wasn't her fight – she knew it wasn't even a fight, because the cops already had their man – but those same tiny anomalies had got their claws into her now and wouldn't let go. Why would Aron Stavis so vehemently deny he'd killed Ed Rivers but accept his fate when it came to the diamond heist? Jo seriously doubted it was because he knew his sentence would be less for the theft than it was for the murder. He'd gone into the jewellery store with a gun, had pointed it in the manager's face and threatened to use it, so, despite pleading out, he was still guilty of a Class B felony and that meant – combined with the price of the diamonds he'd stolen – he was likely to be looking at the higher end when it came to sentencing: fifteen years if he was lucky; twenty if he wasn't.

If he got twenty years, he'd be seventy-four by the time he got out.

Jo was still tapping out a beat with her finger. The more she did, the more she argued herself around: maybe it *was* possible he was thinking about the sentencing side of things.

If he got out of prison at seventy-four, in theory he'd still have some life left to live. With good behaviour, or a lesser sentence because he'd pled, it was possible he might even be in his mid sixties – or younger – when he saw daylight again. But if he admitted to the murder, all of that was gone: he'd get fifteen-plus years for the jewels and then another twenty-five to life for the murder, and that really would mean that he'd never be getting out.

All of that made more sense than the reason for him robbing the gas station in Denver in the first place, though. That was another anomaly that didn't sit right with her, and this one she couldn't rationalize as easily. Would a guy like Aron Stavis, who had made off with half the contents of a West Hollywood bank vault in 1991, and then diamonds worth $1.1 million seven years ago – plus whatever jobs he'd pulled in between, given his sporadic work history – *really* stoop to holding up a gas station for three hundred bucks in cash? Again, anything was possible, but the more Jo thought about it, the more unconvinced she became. And the fact that it didn't fit Stavis's MO *and* he was so emphatic that he'd never killed anyone only added to her suspicions.

Switching on her iPad again, Jo went back to Google and put in a search for Hermione Suza. There were a few stories related to the gas station robbery at the top, but halfway down the first page was what she was looking for: a social media profile.

Jo clicked on Suza's Instagram page.

It was the same woman Jo had seen in the newspaper stories, albeit ten years older. She had two children now, from the looks of things, and was married. Jo scrolled down the page for a while but most of the posts were about her, her husband and their two girls, so she returned to the top, where Suza's Instagram handle was.

Jo grabbed her phone and went to her own Instagram. That, and Facebook, were her only brushes with social media. But although a lot of her friends and old colleagues used Facebook, no one Jo knew – except for Ethan and Claire – used Instagram. It was why her profile was still basically a shell: she'd only posted twice, in early 2016, shortly after she'd retired, when Ethan had persuaded her to create an account so they could all see what each other was up to. Now she just used it to look at photographs that Ethan and Claire posted of Maisie.

She tapped on the little arrow in the top right.

And then she paused. *What the hell are you doing?*

Outside, a police siren wailed in the distance, its red and blue lightbar casting colour across buildings further down Madison. Jo watched it for a while as it slowly faded, first the red and blue, then the sound – then she turned back to her cellphone.

She wrote a message to Suza, introducing herself and some of her history, and then explained that she was a friend of Ed Rivers's father and just wanted to ask her some questions as an interested observer of the case. That last part was an expansion of the truth, but Jo didn't worry too much: in all likelihood, Suza would never respond anyway, not least because Jo's DM would lodge itself in message requests, away from the main inbox. Also, she felt it likely that Suza just wanted to forget being shot, being questioned by police and the memories of everything following that night.

Once the message was sent, she switched off her phone and her iPad, set them down on the nightstand and then closed her eyes as the room returned to darkness.

5

She finally fell asleep at 6 a.m. and then, what seemed like seconds later, her phone buzzed on the nightstand. She reached for it, her eyes gritty, her body aching, and saw that she hadn't been asleep for seconds at all: it was now after 10 a.m., sun was pouring through the blinds in narrow sheets of light, and she'd missed a whole bunch of texts.

Two were from David Raker.

> Good morning! Hope you got in okay last night. Just wondered where and what time you wanted to meet? x
>
> PS: I'm going for a run first, so no hurry.

There was a WhatsApp from Ethan, asking her what she was going to get up to on her first morning in New York, along with a selfie of Maisie helping Claire make breakfast. Jo went to that message first: Claire and Maisie were smiling for the camera, both of them in aprons, Maisie's hands plastered in pancake mixture and her mouth smeared with what looked like peanut butter. Ethan was right at the edge of the shot, eyes and part of his mouth visible, as he took the portrait of the three of them. Jo smiled at the sight of them all, almost feeling tearful as she stared at their faces.

Everything seemed so perfect.

There was nothing for her to worry about here.

She replied, telling them they looked like they were having so much fun, that Maisie and Claire looked beautiful together and she missed them all so much, and then said that she'd only just woken up and was about to arrange to meet David. After that, she closed WhatsApp, switched her focus to Messages – and then stopped.

There was a *1* next to her Instagram app.

Jo sat up straighter, grabbed her glasses and went to her DMs – but she already knew what was waiting for her there. She never used Instagram, never got reactions to posts she'd made or direct messages she'd sent, because she didn't post anything or send anything. For her, Instagram had purely become a watching brief.

Until last night.

She opened the reply from Hermione Suza.

Dear Jo. I'm at work. You can call me if you like.

Under that, she'd left a number.

Jo knew the 303 area code was Denver, but she put that and the rest of the number that Suza had sent her into Google to see where Hermione worked.

The answer was an insurance company.

Jo hit Dial and, after a couple of rings, someone picked up.

'Good morning, this is Hermione, how can I help you today?'

'Hermione, this is Joline Kader. I sent you a message on Instagram.'

'Oh,' Suza said. 'Yes, of course.'

'Are you okay to talk?'

'Yes, it's cool. I don't officially start until eight thirty.'

Jo glanced at the clock on the nightstand and saw that it was ten past ten. Denver was two hours behind New York, so that meant she had twenty minutes to figure this out.

Whatever *this* was.

'I really appreciate it,' Jo said, and then launched into a quick repetition of the things she'd written in the Instagram message. 'Gerald Rivers was an old partner of mine when he lived out in LA – and I told him that I'd look into a few things for him.'

It was a lie, but not one Jo felt bad for telling.

Now she was here, with Suza on the phone, she could feel the faint hum in her blood that she'd missed for so long. She'd loved being a detective, and this was why.

The belief that something wasn't right.

And then the hunt for what it was.

In police work, the chase was everything.

'I thought that Stavis guy was in court today?' Suza asked.

'He is, he is. I just wanted to talk to you about your memories of that night at the gas station.' Jo reached over and picked up a notepad with the hotel's name and logo at the top. 'Specifically, I was very interested in your description of the gunman.'

'My description of him?'

'I realize it was a long time ago now, but according to what I've read, you told the cops in Denver that the gunman had a number printed on his hoodie?'

'Yeah, it was like a digital readout kind of thing.'

'Like the numbers on an alarm clock?'

'Right.'

'I didn't see it mentioned in any of the stories I've been reading online, but did you recall at the time – or even after – what any of those numbers were?'

'No,' Suza responded. 'It all happened so quick. We had a plastic shield on the counter but it was really just there for show. If a customer wanted, they could easily get their arm in and around it; they could grab you if you weren't careful. And that's what happened with that guy. He came in, waving the gun around, and I was shit-scared. He told me to clear out the register and put the money in a bag for him, but I was just so damn nervous. I kept dropping bills on the counter the whole time. So he thought I was doing it all on purpose, he got frustrated with me, and that was when he snatched the bag back and shot me.' Suza paused and Jo could hear her swallow. Jo wondered if she was wiping away tears. 'I only saw the numbers on his sleeve as I was about to hit the floor, because he reached in and grabbed what else he could from the register.'

'But not the specific numbers printed on it?'

'No, sorry.'

'It's okay.'

'I was on the verge of blacking out at that point.'

'I understand.' On her iPad, Jo had brought up the story about Hermione Suza that she'd read the previous evening. 'Did you tell the cops anything else that night?'

'Like what?'

'I don't know. Maybe you told them something about the shooter – the way he sounded or looked: an accent, a speech impediment, a mole on his face or a crooked tooth. Maybe you told them something like that, but they didn't deem it important, so didn't ask you about it again. That can happen. I know it did back when I was a cop.'

That was another half-truth: there *were* cops who dismissed certain memories a witness might have, either because they believed that witness was too traumatized, or too confused, or too unreliable, or it just didn't fit neatly into the narrative – but it was rare. Most cops, and certainly Jo, had taken everything a witness gave them and noted all of it down, even if a witness's recall might have been skewed by the kind of catastrophic event Hermione Suza had experienced in that gas station. Only then did you start getting to the heart of what mattered, to the lead that found you your suspect.

'No,' Suza said eventually. 'No, there was nothing like that.'

'Nothing distinctive about him?'

'The shooter? No. He was wearing that mask.'

Jo looked at the notepad. It was still blank.

'Are you saying you don't think the shooter was this Stavis guy?' Suza asked, and Jo realized her mistake, realized she'd sown this seed with the question about the shooter's physical appearance, and that – as much as she'd loved being a cop, and had always believed she'd been a good one – she was older now, rusty and out of practice.

'No,' she replied, 'Stavis is the shooter.'

'I always wondered if it had something to do with drugs,' Suza said.

Jo paused. 'Drugs? Why?'

'Oh, it was just that we were beside the interstate there and these guys used to come off the freeway and deal right next to us. There was this, like, patch of land, kind of a dumping ground, I guess, full of long grass and trash. They used to deal in there.'

Jo went to Google Maps and dropped into Street View, at the location of the gas station. In the ten years since Ed Rivers's murder, the area looked like it had been given a make-over: the gas station was still there, but where the patch of land might once have been, there was now a Carl's Jr, a Starbucks and a Dick's Sporting Goods.

'So why did you think it might be about drugs?' she asked Suza.

'I don't know. It was just a thought that came to me at the time. It wasn't that I saw anything – nothing like that. Most of the time, I didn't hear anything either. It was in their interests to remain quiet. I suppose that's how it works. But sometimes things would start up. You'd hear some shouting – cars would pull up and there would be raised voices. Once, I remember shots being fired.'

'That must have been scary.'

'It was, yeah, but I grew up in a neighbourhood where that sort of thing would happen all the time. Shouting. Gunshots. Cops turning up in the middle of the night.'

'So you were used to it?'

'I don't know about "used to it", but I'd seen a lot of it before. When I did the night shift we'd shut the gas station up at 11 p.m. – so customers couldn't come inside, you know? They'd have to pay through the window – and some of the other people I worked with, for them, that was when things got serious. When the sun went down and the dealers came out, for them it was, like, what do you call it? Hunkering down. But for me, I always found the night shift way more comforting because, even with the sun down and the dealers out, no one could get in. I tended to get more nervous when the gas station was actually *open*, because people could just wander in whenever they liked and, like I say, our protection at the counter was an absolute joke. If I'd been on the night shift and Rivers had arrived after 11 p.m., none of this would have happened.'

'So I imagine the dealers came into the gas station a lot *before* 11 p.m.?'

'Oh yeah, all the time.'

'Do you ever recall Aron Stavis coming in?'

'If he did,' Suza said, 'I don't remember.'

The question had been a long shot: Stavis wasn't charged with the gas station robbery until this year, so Jo was asking Suza to go back over a decade and put Stavis in context, at her place of work, *before* the night of the shooting. She would have served hundreds of thousands of people during the four years that she worked there.

The other thing was that, as far as anyone knew, Stavis had no history of drug use and had never dealt. It was possible both those things were hidden in the big employment gaps

404

he had, or when it wasn't exactly clear where, and even which city, he'd been living at the time. His path across the country, from LA to Phoenix, to Denver, to Chicago and then on to New York, via a single-year spell in Pittsburgh, had been laid out for the press when he'd been charged with the diamond heist, but cops at the NYPD had to admit that they didn't have a complete, unabridged biography for him. Even Stavis himself couldn't recall every place he'd been to and settled in. But Jo's gut told her, whatever else Stavis had been into, drugs was likely to have been way down the list: he eventually got caught for both the bank job and jewellery-store robbery, but not until afterwards – and you didn't pull off crimes like those if you were scrambling around for your latest fix.

But still.

Drug dealers congregating close to the gas station, coming *into* the 7-Eleven all the time – could there be something here that the cops had missed? And if so, what?

Or are you just getting desperate now?

Jo rubbed at her eyes. She felt tired.

'Are you still there?' Suza asked.

'I am. Sorry. I was just thinking.' On her iPad, Google Street View was still up, her screen filled with the frozen image of Carl's Jr, Starbucks and Dick's. 'Just a couple more questions. Did you ever tell Denver PD about the fact that the patch of land next to the gas station was being used by drug dealers?'

'I did, yeah.'

'And what did they say?'

'I don't remember exactly. They just said they'd look into it.'

'Okay.'

'After the shooting, they stopped. The dealers, I mean. It was like they were there – then they weren't.'

'You mean, the dealers stopped coming to that spot?'

'Yeah, that patch of land.'

'How soon after the shooting did they stop coming?'

'Really soon. Days.'

Jo looked at her notes. It wasn't necessarily suspicious: if the dealers saw cops all over the gas station that night, and saw them returning in the days after, they weren't going to chance coming to a patch of land literally yards away to sell drugs. Perhaps they moved somewhere else temporarily after the shooting, to wait until the heat died down and the investigation ran its course. But that didn't explain why they didn't come back. Could the temporary location have proved better than the patch of land next to the gas station? More traffic, longer sight lines? Jo wrote the idea down and circled it, but it really did feel like she was drifting.

What was the point of any of this?

What was she hoping to achieve?

For the first time, she started to feel a little foolish, so she set the notepad and pen back on the nightstand, thanked Hermione Suza for her time and hung up.

Another text from David had come through.

> You ready to rock and roll? I'm at a bookshop on the corner of
> 45th and 6th, so I can meet you in Bryant Park if that suits? x

She said that was fine and then hit the shower.

Afterwards, as she sat on the edge of the bed, drying her hair, she went back to her iPad. When she'd texted David the day before, she'd joked about cheeseburgers and beer, and had told him she knew a place. She wanted to check it was still open as it had been five years since she'd last been to New York, and restaurants opened and closed faster here than they did in LA. But it was still there, on the corner of 53rd and 9th, a burger joint called Marlito's Way that did the best milkshakes Jo had ever had.

After her hair was dry and she'd finished getting ready, she picked up her iPad again and started closing tabs in Chrome. The last one, open from earlier, was for the story in the *Denver Post* about Hermione Suza waking after two days on a ventilator.

Jo stopped.

The right-hand side of the screen wasn't the only place with links to connected stories: there were more links at the foot of the article too – and one in particular caught her eye.

- ZOMBIE DRUG 'SWEEPING' THROUGH DENVER

She tapped on it and waited for it to load.

The story was four years old, published six years after the shooting at the gas station. On the surface, because of the timing discrepancy, it shouldn't have had any relevance to the murder of Ed Rivers, or what Hermione Suza had told Jo about the drug dealers that used to gather out in the long grass just across the street from the gas station 7-Eleven. But then Jo started reading.

ZOMBIE DRUG 'SWEEPING' THROUGH DENVER

'Sleep cut' responsible for up to 40 deaths in a month, cops say

BY AISHA TYLER | CRIME REPORTER

Police authorities issued a city-wide alert yesterday to the dangers of so-called 'tranq dope', a relatively new cut of heroin – brought in from cities on the east coast such as Philadelphia – which has slowly infiltrated Denver and could now be behind as many as 40 deaths in a month.

Originating in Puerto Rico, police believe tranq dope has actually been on the US mainland for a while – perhaps longer than ten years – and that the major cities, Denver included, have been exposed to it for almost as long. But it's the recent explosion of cases that has really brought the dangers of the drug home and forced authorities to act.

It had been in US cities for a decade, at least; that meant it was in Denver *before* the death of Ed Rivers. It meant tranq dope could easily have been sold by the dealers on the patch of land next to the gas station. But as Jo processed that, she tried to think rationally: *so what?* So what if one particular drug was being sold over another? What did any of this mean? What might it have meant for Ed Rivers? She had this strong, almost overwhelming sense that something wasn't right here – about the shooting, about the guy they'd charged with it, about the entire case – and, as she saw the words *tranq dope*, *zombie drug* and *sleep cut*, a spark of recollection flared at the back of her head.

She just couldn't figure out what.

But then she got to the third paragraph.

Cops believe tranq dope has been sold along the I-70, possibly for years, because its location means dealers can come almost into the heart of the city and exit quickly to the east and west. Its proximity to the north–south I-25 at Globeville also makes it ideal selling territory.

Globeville. Jo didn't know Denver well – but when she checked her notes she remembered that Globeville was the neighbourhood in which the gas station had been located. Even if she hadn't known that, though, the confirmation was already in the first line of the paragraph: Hermione Suza had said the drug dealers used to come in off the interstate, and this was corroborated by the article.

Except that wasn't what had caught Jo's eye.

It was something directly below it.

In order to bulk out their product, so that they can make more money at less cost to themselves, drug dealers use 'cutting agents' – things like baking soda, powdered milk and sugar; even substances like rat poison and over-the-counter pills – which are similarly coloured, and with the same texture, as real heroin. Heroin can also be cut with other drugs, including highly dangerous opioids like Fentanyl. However, one of the key ingredients in tranq dope – and the reason it has been nicknamed the 'sleep cut' – is xylazine, an anaesthetic. In the medical field, xylazine is most often used by veterinary doctors as a sedative.

Jo stared at the last sentence, hardly able to breathe. Dope was being sold next to the gas station, and the cut was bulked with an animal anaesthetic – an anaesthetic that dealers would only be able to get hold of if they found a vet willing to supply it.

A vet like Ed Rivers.

6

It took Jo a few moments to find David Raker, then she spotted him, on the other side of Bryant Park, under the shade of a tree.

He was talking to someone.

A woman in her late thirties.

As Jo approached the table, David saw her and broke out into a smile, and as he stood, the woman he'd been talking to turned around and Jo could see that she was pretty, bright-eyed, but had a scar on the side of her face that looked quite new.

'Detective Kader,' he joked, and gave Jo a big hug.

'How you doing, honey?' Jo replied, squeezing him back.

He was half a foot taller than her at least, wider, stronger, but what she'd liked about David from the start was that, big and well-built as he was, it never felt like it. His physical strength was just a thing he hid in the background. His work could be dangerous, and she knew that he'd had to – literally, in some cases – fight to survive, but he rarely showed that side of himself. His strength was in his eyes, in how he thought, in the way he spoke and sometimes didn't.

It reminded her of Ira, of his calm intelligence.

In fact, she'd thought often since he saved her life in that hunting ground that – if she'd been just a few years younger – she could have had a thing for David Raker.

'Jo, this is Rebekah,' he said, introducing the woman.

Jo shook her hand. 'It's nice to meet you, Rebekah.'

'It's lovely to meet you too.' She had an English accent,

like David, although it sounded like it had dulled over time, and Jo suspected she'd lived in the States for a while. Getting up, Rebekah looked at Jo and said, 'Well, it sounds from David like you've got a lot of catching up to do, so . . .' She stopped and looked at David, and Jo noticed for the first time that Rebekah was holding a business card that David must have handed her. 'I'll be in touch,' she said to David – although Jo could see some uncertainty in her face.

'There's no pressure,' David said.

Rebekah smiled. 'Thank you.'

'You're welcome. It was nice to meet you.'

'And you,' she replied, looking at the business card again – and then she said goodbye to them both and headed out, under the trees, in the direction of 42nd Street.

'You making friends already?' Jo asked.

'We just got chatting.'

'You going to expense this whole trip?'

'No, it's not like that, I promise you. I didn't come to New York to pitch for work. We just got talking and she said her mother disappeared when she was still a kid. But she was living in the UK at the time, so, even if she calls me, I won't be expensing another US trip.'

'Maybe her mom came to the US too.'

'Maybe. It doesn't sound like it, though.'

Jo eyed him. 'You've got the buzz, Raker.'

'The buzz?'

'You've got the scent of a case.'

He rocked his head from side to side, still amused. 'Well, she has to *want* me to find her mum first, and then we'll see.' And then his gaze fell on Jo, and it was like he could see into her head. 'Hold on, is that expression telling me I'm not the only one?'

Jo shrugged.

411

'Aren't you supposed to be retired, Kader?'

'Retirement's boring.'

David laughed.

'Buy me a coffee,' Jo said, 'and I'll tell you all about it.'

'So you think this Ed Rivers guy supplied the xylazine to these dealers?'

Jo looked up from her iced coffee. It was the middle of the day and, although they were in the shade, the heat was oppressive. She picked up her cup and swirled the ice around, watching the cubes clink against one another – and then she glanced at David and said, 'At this point, I'm not sure it makes much difference what I think.'

'It makes a difference if you're right.'

'It's a bit late now, isn't it?'

'Not for Aron Stavis it isn't. He's on trial for this diamond heist today, and he's going down for that – and that's fair enough. But after this is over, he's going to be put in the dock in Denver for a crime he might not have even committed, or, at the very least, someone else was equally complicit in. You have to tell someone.'

She nodded.

'So *are* you going to tell someone?'

'This isn't enough to stop the train.'

'What do you mean?'

'I mean, it's all just circumstantial. It's hearsay. None of this is going to stand up in court once a lawyer gets hold of it. Not when it's up against actual DNA evidence that can put Stavis *at* the scene of that gas station robbery.' Jo paused, thinking, and could see David was doing the same. He picked up the pen that was lying next to his notebook and started rolling it back and forth, the plastic rattling against the metal table. 'If Ed Rivers *was* supplying those dealers with xylazine from the zoo', Jo continued, 'would he really drop the drugs off to them at the same place they're selling? I mean, the more I think about it, the more that makes no sense *at all*. The dealers are going to have to cut the xylazine in with the dope – and they're not going to do *that* in the middle of some grass at the side of the interstate.'

'Unlikely,' David said, 'unless they were especially careless.'

'No one's that careless. Take delivery there and they'd have thousands of bucks worth of cutting agent sitting right beside them while they were busy selling eight balls.'

'Doesn't mean Rivers wasn't the supplier, though.'

'No.'

'Doesn't mean he wasn't at that petrol station for a reason.'

'No,' Jo repeated, 'it doesn't.'

'I mean, did he even *live* in that area of Denver? Did he have any reason at all to be passing through that part of the city? Because, if he didn't – if he lived miles away – but he still went out of his way to stop there, it seems suspicious.'

Jo realized she hadn't checked where Ed Rivers had lived, so searched for the answer on her phone. Inside a minute, she'd found it: Rivers had lived in Thornton, which was about ten miles north of Downtown. When she went to Maps and checked the possible routes home he might have taken from the zoo, her heart sank: two possible routes were flagged up, both crossed the I-70 – and one passed right by the gas station in Globeville. His decision to stop for gas there and use the restroom was, therefore, perfectly reasonable.

Except, even if the gas part made sense, why use the restroom? It was only a twelve-mile drive from the zoo to his home. Less than twenty-five minutes. It seemed highly unlikely a healthy 41-year-old wouldn't be able to make a journey that brief without having to stop for a bathroom break on the way. So could the restrooms be key to this somehow? She closed her phone and explained to David what she'd just found out.

'Do you know his medical history?'

She shook her head. 'No.'

'Maybe he had a problem that meant he couldn't make the drive in one go. Or he had to rush out of work at the end of the day and didn't get to go to the toilet back at the zoo.'

'Maybe. But everything I've read about him so far describes him as a healthy guy.'

'So maybe him using the toilet there is just background noise. Irrelevant. Maybe you need to consider instead that it wasn't just the dealers who were close to that petrol station.'

'What do you mean?'

'I mean, maybe the trap house was nearby too.'

The trap house: the place the xylazine would get dropped off.

'Maybe that explains why he went to the gas station,' David continued. 'He came from the zoo, he went to the trap house first, he spent some time there sorting out whatever he needed to sort, including getting his money, and then as he's on his way back to the interstate, he thinks, "I need petrol and I could do with the bathroom." So that's why he stops and does both.'

Jo felt another buzz of excitement.

'I'm guessing you don't have access to his phone records?' David asked.

'No, nothing like that. I've got no access to anything.'

'So you don't know if anyone called him in the minutes before he ended up at that petrol station?' David was still rolling the pen, his face mirroring Jo's: they were in this now – deep in it – trying to work out the angles and the things that mattered.

'No,' Jo admitted. 'But it's reasonable to suppose that, if

someone *did* call him just before he went to that gas station, maybe to arrange to meet there, and that call – and that caller – was directly related to his murder, we wouldn't have had to wait a decade before someone was charged with killing him. What I mean is, cops miss stuff sometimes, but they're not dumb. If someone phoned Ed Rivers and asked him to meet at the gas station, and then Ed Rivers got shot in the head shortly after he did so, you have your suspect. Instead, it took them ten years to get to Aron Stavis.'

'Yeah.' David nodded. 'Yeah, that's a fair point.'

They looked at each other for a moment.

'Have you ever thought it could just be random?' David asked.

'You mean, he was just unlucky?'

'Wrong place, wrong time.' David shrugged. 'I lived in America for a while. You live here permanently. We both know this sort of thing happens all the time.'

'True.'

He eyed her. 'You don't think it's possible?'

'It's possible,' Jo said. 'In fact, when you look at everything, it's probably more likely than not, but I don't know . . . This drug thing bothers me. Six years *after* the murder, that area – and others along the interstate – are identified as being hotbeds for tranq dope. Tranq dope is heroin cut with animal anaesthetic. Ed Rivers works in a zoo and he's a doctor so has access to that shit. And he just happened to be at the gas station right next to the place where the tranq dope was being dealt the night he was murdered.' She paused, took a breath. 'My gut tells me it's too many coincidences.'

David agreed. 'You haven't seen the video of that night?'

'From the gas station? No, like I say, I don't have anything.'

'But his dad said Ed was shot as the robber exited the 7-Eleven?'

'Yeah. He said they literally bumped into one another.'

'That doesn't suggest pre-planning.'

David meant, if the robber was using the gas station stick-up as a cover for the real reason he was there – to kill Ed Rivers – why not wait until Rivers came inside or appeared out on the forecourt before shooting him? Why basically stumble into him? Why make it more complicated and messy and not give yourself a clear shot?

'Maybe the robber wanted it to look random,' she said.

'If he did, it sounds like he did a good job,' David responded, rolling his pen between his thumb and finger now. 'Okay, if we run with the idea that this was a premeditated murder made to look like a random robbery-gone-wrong, then the question is, who would have wanted Ed Rivers dead?'

'Not the people he was selling to.'

'No. Because why cut off your own supply?'

Jo looked down at her notepad, to the scribbles she'd made the night before and this morning. 'Unless, of course, the people he was selling to had found a newer and cheaper xylazine supplier . . .' But she knew, deep down, that wasn't how these things tended to work. You didn't kill off a supply line, even if you weren't using it any more, and especially not for something like xylazine, which, unlike baking soda or sugar, wasn't sitting on shelves in a Walmart.

'Could Rivers have been about to compromise the dealers somehow?' David asked, but, almost as soon as he said it, he grimaced and Jo understood why: he knew, like Jo did, that if Ed Rivers had been about to turn on the dealers, and especially if he'd been in contact with the cops already, it would have come out in stories about his death. And if Rivers *had* been talking to them, Denver PD would have automatically had a list of potential suspects too. Drug dealers, in Jo's experience, weren't hard to track down if you talked to the right people on the street, and it was a whole lot easier if someone handed you a list of names and addresses. Yet the cops hadn't charged anyone with Ed Rivers's killing for another ten years, and, when they did, their guy was a man with no previous drug convictions.

Both of them seemed to become aware then that they'd wandered off the path. Their instincts as investigators had automatically drawn them deep into the shadows – where the unanswered questions lay – when this was supposed to be a chance for two friends from opposite sides of the world to catch up for a few days. As soon as they became aware that they were both thinking the same thing, David smiled, and then so did Jo, and she said, 'I'm really sorry, David. This isn't what we came here for.'

'No need to apologize. My brain is feeling flexed.'

Jo laughed. 'I don't know what it is about this case.'

'I do. You feel like something's not right with it.'

She nodded. 'I just can't prove anything.'

'No,' David said. 'But if I know you, you will.'

7

They went to the place Jo knew on 53rd Street and ate cheese-burgers. The A/C was on full blast and they sat at the back, behind a tinted window, looking out at a series of black metal fire escapes zigzagging across the buildings opposite.

As they ate, Jo told David about Ethan, about the problems that he and Claire were having – even if she didn't know, specifically, what those problems were – and then she talked about the things she was filling her retirement with. In return, David told her about the last big case he'd taken on – the search for a man who had disappeared inside his own home – and, although she could tell he'd stopped short of telling her everything, it was obvious that it had got to him. She could tell as well that it was *still* getting to him. Some cases were like that: they got their nails into you and, even once they'd released their grip, the marks remained behind, unable to heal.

Just before lunch was over, David got a call on his cellphone – on the display she saw a UK number – and as he checked who it was, his expression immediately dropped: 'Urgh. Shit.'

'What is it?'

'It's a journalist called Connor McCaskell. He won't leave me alone.'

'What does he want?'

'He thinks he's got the whiff of a story.'

'He thinks he does – or he has?'

David smiled, but not with any humour, and rocked his

head from side to side as if sizing up the question. 'An old friend of mine, Colm. He died a few years back . . .'

The cellphone was still humming in his hands.

He seemed lost for a moment, staring at the screen, and Jo wasn't sure if he was thinking about the journalist or the friend. But then he stirred. 'It's about my friend.'

And then he killed the call.

'Sorry about that,' he said, pressing his lips together.

'Is there anything I can do to help?'

'No,' David responded. 'This is something I have to figure out for myself.'

After lunch, they walked to the Seventh Avenue subway station, then got the B down to Bryant Park. As they ambled back to the hotel, the twenty-year age difference between them was starting to become starker: David was still energized, still talking, animatedly, about another, entirely different case now – not one of his own, but one he'd been called about: the family of a London Underground worker, who'd been murdered by the worker's best friend – and although Jo was listening, she was feeling exhausted. The lack of sleep the night before didn't help – she was basically running on only four hours' worth of fuel – and neither did the fact that it was in the high eighties and brutally humid. But it wasn't just her disturbed sleep pattern or the weather. It wasn't even that her muscles ached and her back hurt. It was that she was emotionally drained, her head weary, her eyes gritty, from thinking about Ed Rivers.

Back at the hotel, she said, 'What time do you want to meet tonight?'

David eyed her for a second. 'Are you okay?'

'Yeah, just tired is all.'

His eyes stayed on her.

'I didn't sleep well last night,' she added.

'Are you sure you want to go out tonight?'

'Of course.'

'We don't have to.'

'No, I want to.'

'This isn't supposed to be an endurance test, Kader.'

She smiled. 'I know it isn't.'

'We can just eat here if you'd prefer.'

She looked along the flank of the hotel – they had an in-house restaurant, with tables out on the street – and then up three floors to where her room's window was.

'Actually,' she said, 'you know what? That would be nice.'

'I'll book a table, then. What time?'

'Eight, eight thirty?'

She looked at her watch. It was three thirty.

That gave her plenty of time to sleep.

'Perfect,' David said. 'Go and rest up, detective.'

She slept like the dead and didn't wake up again until after 7 p.m. When she finally stirred, she lay there for a while, looking up at the ceiling, before scooping up her cellphone and sending a text to Ethan, telling him about her day. Flipping back the covers, she shuffled through to the bathroom, her bones and muscles stiff from sleeping, and ran the shower.

Afterwards, she checked her cell again: David had texted her to say that the earliest table he could get was at nine and did she want to meet for a drink first. They agreed on eight thirty, which gave her an hour to get ready.

Plenty of time.

She grabbed her iPad.

As the sun started to burn out above the city and the light in the room slowly dwindled, Jo spent thirty minutes going back through the things she'd already been over. She checked and rechecked everything, skim-reading every story she'd already absorbed. Next, she started clicking on related links, especially if they were stories she hadn't yet been through. Some were affiliated only because they shared a few keywords; others had a more obvious connection – they were stories about robberies, or drugs, or the *Post* believed there were similar, city-wide implications for whatever the article was about, in the same way that the arrival of tranq dope had sparked a red alert for Denver authorities.

By the end, she had nothing new.

She realized she was working at a disadvantage, that without access to things like cellphone records and transcripts, and contact with the families and witnesses – to even a basic police report – there was no way to know if she'd overlooked something big. *Maybe something they'd brought up in the trial today.* It was only the first day, so it was likely nothing had been achieved beyond the opening arguments – and maybe not even that much; court cases moved as slow as icebergs most of the time – but she went online and checked anyway. There was some reporting on the Aron Stavis case but not much on what had actually happened in court, which suggested Jo was right: if the defence or prosecution was hiding some revelation that would either exonerate or incarcerate Stavis, it wasn't going to be presented for days, perhaps weeks, and that meant stories about the Stavis case were going to be small – or not run for now at all.

She switched tack, going back to the night of the robbery, to her notes, and to the man in the mask who'd shot Ed Rivers. White or Hispanic. Six feet tall. Between 180 and 190 pounds. All of that was worthless information, even back then. It might have meant something if the camera at the gas station had been good enough to pick out an eye colour, or the shade of any hair that might have been straying out from under the neckline of the mask. Or maybe marks on the skin, blemishes, bruises, tattoos – anything, basically, that could help to identify someone. But the camera wasn't that good. Certainly from the stills of the suspect that had run in the newspapers, it appeared low resolution; worse, in one of the stories where Denver PD had appealed for information on the shooter, the *Post* had mentioned that the video ran at five frames per second. That was slow even ten years ago, and it meant footage was going to be staccato, and – unless cops lucked out and one of those five frames per second caught the shooter at a perfect angle – unlikely to help in pinpointing the man. Which just left his clothes.

The blue jeans.

The white Nike high-tops.

And the black hoodie with *Corton* written on it.

Jo did a Google Images search and tried to locate the very best picture Denver PD had released of the suspect. Downloading the highest-resolution version she could find, she then went to YouTube and searched for the Rivers murder there. She'd been hoping for news stories from the time, or references to it in crime shows on TV.

There was none of either.

'Well, that makes things simpler,' she said bitterly.

It was the camera shot or nothing.

She opened up the image and zoomed in on the masked man, trying one last time to see if there was anything notable about his eyes or his mouth, about the exposed skin at his neck or hands. Even if there was, she had her doubts whether the quality of the picture would allow her to see it: the shooter's eyes were more like tiny grey smudges, his mouth a flat, featureless line; there was only a sliver of skin visible between the hood of his top and the bottom of the mask, and both his hands were gloved and on the gun.

Her eyes went to his top again.

Corton.

What did that mean?

The lettering was in either a yellow or a pale green – it was hard to tell exactly as the colours were so washed out – and the font was in an old-fashioned, embellished style, the kind of thing you might find in handwritten manuscripts from three hundred years ago. The *r* in the middle had an elaborate tail on its left-hand side and the *C* and the *t* were gilded with a series of additional flourishes.

The stylized design of the lettering had to be deliberate – had to mean something – but in all her searches, the name *Corton* led nowhere, so even if the style *was* conscious, what difference did it make if she didn't know what *Corton* meant or was? Just to be sure, she put it into Google again, but she got back the exact same results. It was possible she was calling this wrong but, in her gut, she just didn't feel this had anything to do with a few houses on the bend of a minor river in West Virginia, and certainly nothing to do with a town in England. Again, she forced herself to click through the pages of search results, just to be absolutely certain, but nothing caught her attention. There weren't even any social media accounts for people with the name. *Corton* appeared to be a total dead end.

That was what bothered her.

If it meant nothing, why put it on a top like that? Because it *had* to have been specifically made for the person wearing it, maybe even a complete one-off. It wasn't a brand name. It wasn't something you could get in Target or Macy's. If he'd got it on the Internet, there'd be a trail somewhere. If those tops had *ever* been on sale, there would be a record of it somewhere; someone would have come forward and told the cops what *Corton* meant, or where the top had come from. And yet there had been no follow-ups in any press stories about the hoodie, despite the cops appealing for information.

Jo sighed and slumped back on the bed. She glanced at her watch – 8.08 p.m. – and then got up and went to the bathroom to clean her teeth. As she did, she stared at her reflection in the mirror and thought of Aron Stavis. *It's time to just let it go, Kader.* Stavis's DNA was all over that scene at the gas station. He had a history of armed robbery. And he was living in Denver at the time.

Just accept it was him.

She finished brushing, put on a light dusting of make-up, then returned to the bed. On her iPad, the screen still showed the same shot of the masked man.

Aron Stavis.

It's Aron Stavis.

Jo looked at the hoodie again, at the elaborate tails on the letters, at the way they mimicked the handwritten characters of old manuscripts.

Move on, meet David, forget it.

Forget Stavis, forget all of . . .

She stopped. Leaned in closer to the iPad.

Her heart started beating a little faster as she pinch-zoomed into where *Corton* was printed on the hoodie – and then pinch-zoomed a second time, to the *C.*

She dragged the image across to the *t.*

'Shit,' she said quietly.

She leaned back from the screen, staring at the *t,* at its ornate design, at the bright yellow-green flow of its twists and angles as they sang out of the blackness of the hooded top. Except, for the first time, she realized it might not actually *be* a *t.* It might not be a *C* at the start either.

In fact, it might not even have said *Corton* at all.

8

A dizzying spike of adrenalin hit her.

Going back to Google, Jo swapped out the *C* and *t* for a *G* and *f*. *Gorfon* didn't make a whole lot of sense either, but the more Jo looked at the design, at the font, at its flourishes, the more she felt she might be right. And if she was, this whole lead had been worked incorrectly from the start.

The intricacy of the font had hidden the real word.

She hit Return.

As she quickly scrolled through the results, top to bottom, she realized only the first one was relevant:

cabrillobeachsoccer.com > about > gorfon hernandez

In Memory of Gorfon Hernandez

The idea for Cabrillo Beach Soccer ... the death of **Gorfon** ... inmates at Terminal Island ... friends and former prisoners ...

Terminal Island.

That was where Aron Stavis had served his eight-year sentence for the bank job in West Hollywood. Jo had been to TI many times, had wound her way along Seaside Avenue, past the huge cranes and even bigger warehouses, all the way down to the barriers at the end of the peninsula that marked out a different sort of building: one hidden behind vast, sand-coloured concrete and bolstered with helixes of razor wire.

Cabrillo Beach was just across Los Angeles Harbor from

Terminal Island. Jo didn't know that side of the water as well, but she'd been down to San Pedro once to interview a suspect who'd lived in an apartment looking out at Cabrillo's sands.

She clicked on the link.

The homepage for the Cabrillo Beach Soccer Club was easy to navigate and she was quickly able to work out the basics. The club had been set up in 1999 by a Baptist minister called Emilia Fuentes as a place for former offenders to come and meet other people who'd been in prison, while taking part in a beach soccer match. According to the bio, the club had started with just five members, but now – on any given night – there were as many as thirty. Jo paused on the pictures laced throughout the story of the soccer club's founding: some of them went all the way back to 1999 – but she didn't see anyone she recognized.

She went back to the top.

There were links to two other pages.

One was a Contact page. She checked it, very quickly: it had an email address for Emilia Fuentes, a cell number, and the street address for her church in San Pedro. If you wanted to come along on Monday and Thursday nights and play soccer on the beach with other club members, it said you had to get in touch with Fuentes first.

The other page was dedicated to Gorfon Hernandez.

He'd been twenty-four and had already 'served three years for drug convictions' at the time of his death. It didn't take long for Jo to find out why there was a page about him: he was Emilia Fuentes's nephew and the reason the Cabrillo Beach Soccer Club was established in the first place. Hernandez had hanged himself in 1993, four days after being arrested and charged again, this time for selling ecstasy tablets at a bar in Redondo Beach. It was likely, given his history and how strict the drug laws were in California in the early to mid nineties, that Hernandez would have gone down for at least another four or five years – perhaps more if he was unlucky. Beside that information was a photo of Hernandez in the green of the Mexican national team, no more than ten years of age.

In the text, it said he'd loved soccer and used to play with his brothers and his Aunt Emilia on Cabrillo Beach. So that was where the idea had come from: to help other ex-cons from lapsing and returning to a life of crime, through sport and social events, and what appeared to be some sort of impromptu counselling service that Fuentes had set up at the church, and in a tent at the beach after matches were over.

At the bottom of the page were more photographs.

It was mostly guys in the middle of playing soccer matches, or standing around at barbecues – but there was one of an entire group, posing for the camera, in a line.

The caption underneath said that these were the 'original' five members of the soccer club, and that the photo had been captured shortly after its inception in 1999. The shot had clearly been taken on film, which meant it must have been scanned from a physical version at some point: the very fine hairs, damage marks and creases at the corners confirmed as much, indicating it had been in a drawer somewhere, perhaps for a long time. The shot wasn't completely in focus either, so, even without the age damage, there was an irritating blur to it. Faces were visible, and so too were the black hoodies the members of the club were wearing, but both the fine detail in the men's expressions and the printed *Gorfon* on their chests – even though it was in bright yellow – were much harder to see than they should have been. Certainly, there was no hope of seeing the alarm-clock-style number sequence on the sleeve, which Hermione Suza identified as having been printed on the hoodie.

427

Jo leaned in, studying the faces more closely.

That was when she recognized him.

Aron Stavis.

Even though he was out of focus, she knew it was him. He was on the left, twenty-three years younger than the man who'd been in a New York courtroom today, charged with stealing over a million dollars' worth of jewellery-store diamonds. At this point, he must have just got out of Terminal Island after the bank job in West Hollywood.

He was one of the founding members of the club.

She looked at the others.

Emilia Fuentes was easy to pick out because she was the only woman and her photo was on the contact page – but the other three men Jo hadn't seen before.

Or have I?

Her attention had snagged on a man standing directly to Fuentes's right. It was hard to be certain given the quality of the scanned photo, but he looked to be in his early twenties, had black hair and a light covering of dark stubble. He was Hispanic, like Fuentes, like all of the group except Aron Stavis. Where did she know him from?

She checked the time.

She was meant to have met David five minutes ago.

Very quickly, she grabbed her cellphone off the bed, went to the Contact page of the website and dialled Emilia Fuentes's number.

It started ringing.

She waited, toes tapping out a nervous beat against the carpet, her attention back on the Gorfon Hernandez memorial page and the guy to Emilia Fuentes's right.

Who are you?

Where would I know you from?

'Hello?'

Jo tuned back in. 'Is that Reverend Fuentes?'

'Yes, it is.'

'My name's Joline Kader. I'm a . . .' She paused. *I'm a what? I'm not a detective any more. I'm just an old woman chasing after a feeling.* 'I used to be a cop with the Sheriff's Department and LAPD and, at the moment, I'm out in New York following the trial of Aron Stavis. I understand that you might have known Aron at one time?'

A pause on the line.

'Yes, I knew him. What is this concerning?'

'I wanted to ask you about a picture on your website.'

'My website?'

'Your Cabrillo Beach Soccer Club page.'

'Oh, I see.' Another pause. 'What about it?'

'There's a photograph that I'm interested in.' Jo pulled the iPad closer to her, then glanced at the time in the corner: 8.37. Seven minutes late now. Switching her attention back to Fuentes, she said, 'It's the one of the five founding members of your group that you posted to the Gorfon Hernandez memorial page. Do you recall that one?'

'Yes,' Fuentes replied. 'Yes, of course.'

'I was just interested in knowing who the others were in that photograph. I can see that one of them's Aron, and obviously you're there too. Who are the others?'

'Sorry, who did you say you were again?'

She reintroduced herself and some of her history, trying to be as detailed and convincing as possible, because she could feel Fuentes closing up on her. Jo didn't blame her: she was being asked to give out the names of men she'd known – perhaps been friends with – to a stranger at the other end of a phone line.

After Jo was finished, as she waited for Fuentes – hoping that she'd done enough – she used her iPad to send David a text, apologizing and telling him she was going to be a few minutes late; and just as the text sent, she heard Fuentes take a long breath.

She waited some more, but Fuentes still didn't say anything.

Finally, softly, Jo prompted her: 'Reverend?'

'Two of them are no longer with us,' came the response. Jo felt a momentary buzz: she'd decided to trust Jo enough to tell her. 'Erik is the one that's immediately to the left of me. He, unfortunately, returned to prison five or six years after the picture was taken: a stupid lapse on his part; a drink-driving thing that put a little girl in the hospital and her mom . . .' She stopped, but Jo could guess the rest of it: *in the morgue.*

She looked at the picture of the group.

Erik wasn't the one she wanted.

'Anyway,' Fuentes went on, 'he died up at Victorville last year. The one on *his* left is Alex.' Jo looked at the next man along. This wasn't the one she wanted either, but she didn't interrupt. She'd got Fuentes onside now and needed her to stay that way. 'He still came to the group all the way up until his death, maybe . . . oooh, I don't know: three, four years ago. Bowel cancer. It was very sad. Alex really was a shining example to all of us – after he got out of prison, he retrained as an electrician.'

Jo's eyes fell on the final face.

I recognize you. I know I'm right.

'And the final man in that shot?' she prompted.

'That was Craig,' Fuentes said.

Craig.

Did she know a Craig?

'He'd been in prison too?' Jo asked.

'No, not Craig, no. Craig was just a member of my church who liked the idea of giving these men a second chance. Of course, it helped that he loved his soccer, as I –'

But Jo had stopped listening.

Craig.

She grabbed her notebook off the nightstand and flicked through some of the notes she'd made over the past day. And then, a couple of pages back, she found him.

Everything else in the room slipped away.

Craig Dominguez.

That was why she recognized him.

He was the lead detective on the gas station robbery.

9

Jo didn't talk to David about what she'd found out – not that evening, not on either of the two full days they spent together after that. She just tried to forget it for a while, tried to enjoy the meals they had, the bottles of wine they shared, the installation they went to at the Met, on Bosch, and at the Museum of the Moving Image, where David had been keen to see an exhibition on the film-noir director Robert Hosterlitz.

On the last night, they sat in the corner of the rooftop bar at the Library and drank cocktails, and both of them got a little drunk. By the time they finally got to bed, it was 3.30 a.m. But then the next morning, as they shared a cab to JFK, both of them nursing hangovers of varying severity, he finally turned to her and said, 'It's time to 'fess up, Kader.'

She frowned. 'What do you mean?'

'I know you haven't let go of that petrol station thing.'

This time, she smiled.

'You know I was happy to be a sounding board, right?'

'I know.' She nodded, looking out through the front, to the cars jammed up on the expressway ahead. 'I guess I just wanted *not* to think about it for a while – maybe figured, if I gave it some time and distance, things would pull into focus.'

'And have they?'

'No,' she said. 'Or yes. Or maybe. I don't know.'

She spent the next ten minutes filling David in on what she'd found out forty-eight hours ago – the Cabrillo Beach Soccer Club, the founding members, the Gorfon memorial, and the fact that Aron Stavis wasn't the only connection to those hoodies.

'So you think this cop, Dominguez, is involved in the murder of Ed Rivers?' he asked her.

'I don't know.'

'You're thinking – what? – that he might have framed Aron Stavis?' He was deliberately keeping his voice down so that the driver couldn't hear.

She shrugged. 'He knew Stavis from way back.'

'That's not the question I asked.'

Jo smiled again. 'I know it isn't.'

'This isn't court. You don't have to prove it for me to believe you.'

'Put it this way,' she said. 'I think we have to consider it.'

'That this cop framed Aron Stavis?'

'Yes.'

'Which means – what? – Craig Dominguez carried out the robbery?'

'Not necessarily, but it's certainly possible.'

'And he killed Ed Rivers deliberately?'

'It stands to reason.'

Jo paused for a moment, thinking about where Ed Rivers would fit in to all of this. He could still have been the supplier of the xylazine, but maybe Dominguez was the middle man. Maybe he was the guy who went to the trap houses to drop off the drug: that felt a better fit than a veterinarian doing the legwork. Interacting with drug dealers wasn't for the faint-hearted and nothing she'd seen of Ed Rivers's history suggested he was a man who had the experience and courage to walk right into the lion's den and demand cash for a ton of stolen cutting agent. Dominguez, on the other hand, was a veteran cop, so that was *exactly* the sort of work he could do in his sleep. It didn't make it any less risky, but he would know how to protect himself, would know the game and the way it was played, *and* the potential dangers. And if Jo was to run this whole thing to its natural conclusion, then it felt likely that Dominguez's role as middle man was also one of protection: not just of the drugs, or the flow of money, but as a shield for Rivers as well. Rivers was his supplier, his source of income, so if Rivers ever started to feel the heat from the law, for whatever reason – a slip-up, some stupid mistake – Dominguez was in a position to make those lapses go away. And yet, if that were true, something had gone wrong. The relationship had broken down.

And Ed Rivers had ended up with a bullet in his head.

'So what would Dominguez's motive be for killing Rivers?' David said.

Jo glanced at him. Again, just like on the first day, when they'd talked about the case, it felt like he was following the conversation she'd been having with herself.

'Something must have changed,' she said.

'Between Dominguez and Rivers?'

'Yeah. The arrangement got screwed up somehow.'

They were both quiet for a moment.

'I'm convinced Dominguez is a part of this, though,' Jo said after a while. 'I just keep thinking about something Hermione Suza said to me on the phone when I called her: she said that, after Rivers was murdered, the dealers never came back to that patch of land – like, *ever*. Literally, the cops cleared the scene and then it was like the whole place got washed down with Clorox. No one ever used it to push drugs again.'

'So you're saying the dealers were *told* not to come back?'

'I'm saying, in all my years as a cop, I never once heard of a dealer who didn't get desperate enough to return to a place that worked for them before, no matter how risky it might

434

have gotten. The fact that these dealers didn't return there at all says to me that someone powerful, someone high up – someone with the ability to make or break these people's livelihoods – issued an edict telling them to find somewhere else to sling dope. I'm not saying Dominguez is, *was*, the man in charge . . .' Jo went to the pocket of a thin cotton jacket she'd brought with her for the flight and wriggled out her notebook. 'I think the man in charge was a guy called Jermaine Washington.' She turned some pages. 'I read about him online the other night. Denver PD have been after him for years: they know he's the kingpin, the guy at the head of this tranq dope operation, but they can't make anything stick. So, in that context, it makes sense that Dominguez would be the middle man, supplying the cutting agent to Washington's people, and so would have had a vested interest in not having the gas station murder connected to product *he* was helping put on to the streets. So he says to Jermaine Washington, "Move your people somewhere else," and Washington takes the advice.'

'What I don't get,' David said, 'is that Denver PD *knew* Ed Rivers was a vet at the zoo, so would have access to xylazine, and they knew dope was being sold next to the gas station, but they didn't put two and two together?' He was frowning. 'I'm sure Dominguez could have suppressed *some* information, but he couldn't suppress it all.'

'The reason is the timings didn't match up.'

'What do you mean?'

'See, here's the thing: Denver authorities didn't start going to the press about tranq dope until six years *after* Ed Rivers was killed. So at the time Rivers was shot, cops knew drugs were being sold on that patch of land, because Hermione Suza told them in interviews, but not what *type* of drugs. Tranq dope was around then, and the cops would have heard

435

talk of it on the street, I'm sure, but it wasn't big. More likely, they would have figured that the drugs sold on that patch of land were the same drugs being sold everywhere else – dope, pills, rock, ice, all the normal sort of crap.'

'And then by the time tranq dope became public knowledge . . .'

'The case was done. The murder of Ed Rivers was ancient history.'

'So no one would have made that connection.'

'No,' Jo said. 'Not to Rivers, not to his murder.'

Ahead of them, the traffic had started to move again.

'So what are you going to do?' David asked.

'About which part?'

'Are you going to give this information to someone?'

'There's nothing to give.'

'I get it. It's circumstantial. But someone needs to hear it.'

Jo looked at him. 'What I know in my gut isn't the same as what I can prove – and, anyway, there are still too many questions. If I go to someone with this, I don't want to be laughed out the room as the crazy old woman who still thinks she's a cop.'

'You'll never stop being a cop, Jo.'

'You know what I mean.'

David shrugged. 'Even on a closed case, there are always questions.'

'Not this many. I mean, right at the end of the phone call I had with this Reverend Emilia Fuentes – after she told me it was Craig Dominguez in that picture – I suddenly remembered to ask her about the numbers they printed on the sleeve of the hoodie.'

'You mean, what they meant?'

'Right.' She paused. 'She said, there *weren't* any numbers.'

David frowned. 'What are you talking about?'

'She said, on the sleeves of those hoodies, they never printed any numbers. There was no alarm-clock-style design on it; no four-digit readout. It was just the word *Gorfon* on the chest, nothing else. That was the only thing Fuentes said they printed on there. So either Hermione Suza was mistaken when she told the cops about those numbers – or she lied.'

David nodded to himself, taking the new information in.

'And do you think she's a liar?' he asked.

'No, I don't. But she got that wrong. Way wrong.'

'Or she didn't.'

Jo looked up, could see his brain working. 'What do you mean?'

'I mean, she'd just been shot in the shoulder, right?'

'Right.'

'I've been thinking about this ever since you described what happened to her: from what the newspapers reported, it sounds like she saw the sleeve design *after* she was shot.' He'd posed it as a question, and Jo nodded, confirming that was what she'd read. It was like looking in the mirror: she saw the same look in his eyes that she'd seen in her own two days ago, as she sat in her hotel room reading about the gas station robbery – and she knew that David had something: maybe not a breakthrough, maybe not an answer, but some small ghost of an idea.

'What's on your mind, Raker?' she asked.

'She's been shot in the shoulder and she's hurt, badly, because the injury is much more serious than it appears. So it's possible she's mistaken. It's possible she thinks she's seeing something that isn't actually there, because her body is in shock, her blood is rushing to her core, she's hit the floor and she's woozy. But why see this particular thing? Why see an alarm-clock-style printout on the sleeve of a hoodie? It's so

437

specific, that's what bothers me. It's such a *crazily* specific thing to even mention.'

'Which makes you more certain it's true?'

David opened his hands out. 'It just seems such a bizarre thing to make up. And then this Reverend Fuentes tells you that there *weren't* any numbers on the hoodie sleeve.'

Jo's eyes narrowed. 'So?'

They stared at each other for a moment.

And then she got it. 'Our gunman reached *around* the plastic window on the counter,' she said. 'He reached in to shoot her.' Jo looked down at her notebook and flipped back to some of the ideas she'd written down at the start. 'Hermione Suza said there wasn't a lot of space at the side of the plastic shield, but there was enough space to get a hand past.'

David smiled at her. 'Exactly.'

'When he reached around to shoot her,' Jo continued, 'when his arm went through that narrow gap at the side, his hoodie got caught on the edge of the window.'

'And in that split second . . .'

'It yanked the sleeve up his arm,' Jo muttered.

'Suza was in shock, she was likely in excruciating pain, her vision was probably blurring at that point, it was affecting her sight, all of her functions. So for her account to be ever so slightly off – that's understandable.'

Again, they just stared at each other.

'I don't think that number was printed on a sleeve,' David said.

'No,' Jo replied. 'It was tattooed on the gunman's arm.'

10

The cab dropped Jo off at Terminal 8 first.

She and David hugged in the back of the taxi, holding each other for a moment as she thanked him for flying out to the States, he thanked her for three great days, and she started apologizing for letting the Ed Rivers killing loom so large in her thinking the entire time. But David stopped her before she'd finished: 'Never apologize for doing what's right.'

She smiled. 'I'll let you know what I decide.'

'I'll look forward to it, Detective Kader.'

She headed inside the terminal, and – after checking in and passing security – she found a seat in a quiet spot, next to a gate that didn't have a flight assigned to it, and made a call to the west coast. It was to a cop that had worked for Jo at the LAPD called Trae Burrows. After the call with Burrows was over, Jo logged into the WiFi and put in a search for 'Craig Dominguez'.

She'd already read up about Dominguez after finding out he was the man in the photograph. He'd been nineteen in that picture, and – sometime shortly after it was taken – had moved to Denver to join a programme run by the National Park Service to train rangers. There was no information online about why he then decided to make the switch to police work, or when, or even if he actually became a qualified ranger at all; there was also no information about how long it took him to become a detective at Denver PD. But the oldest image Jo was able to find of him was from 2007 – he'd been behind a bank of microphones, talking to the press about a murder outside a strip mall in the south of the city – which suggested to her that he couldn't have stuck it out at the Park Service for more than a couple of years.

This time, though, she wasn't looking for stories that featured quotes from him, or the cases at the Denver PD that he'd led, she was simply conducting an image search.

She was looking for a tattoo.

She scrolled down the walls of pictures.

A lot of the time, Dominguez was standing behind a nest of microphones, putting the message out about the crime he was investigating, flanked by members of a family in mourning. In most of the images in Google, he appeared trim and smartly dressed, a good-looking, dark-haired man in his thirties – that shot from 2007 was the earliest, by far, that she could find of him, and the only one of him in his twenties – and a man who was likely, because of that, to have been used by the DPD to their advantage. Cynical as it was, good looks made bad news more palatable.

A lot of the pictures were from the same cases because they had gone so big: the hunt for a serial killer; the murder of an African American woman by a white supremacist; the rape and murder of two teenage boys. In all three cases he had a parka on, the crimes occurring over the winter months when the snow struck Colorado.

But in a few photos from some other, smaller cases, he was in a shirt.

In one he had his sleeves rolled up.

Jo opened the image in a new tab. This time, he wasn't on press duty, he was actually working a crime scene, talking to a forensic tech at the front of a walk-up in downtown Denver. He was pointing to something on a floor further up – beyond the range of the image the camera captured – and the edge of his right arm was exposed.

Jo felt a surge of electricity.

He had a tattoo.

The image's size was listed as 800 pixels by 533, so the second she started to zoom in, the quality began to break up. She backed out again slowly, pinch-zooming in reverse until she felt she had the best balance between magnification and quality.

Around her, the noise of the airport faded away.

The angle on the tattoo wasn't perfect, but she could see enough: it was on his right arm – the same as the gunman at the gas station – and there were four numbers on the skin. Black or dark blue, inked into the underside, starting a couple of inches from the wrist.

They weren't traditional numbers, though.

They were roman numerals.

XXVI.

Jo tried to think of the relevance, to Dominguez, to the murder of Ed Rivers, to anything else she'd discovered over the past few days, and eventually ended up back at the brief, incomplete biography of Dominguez she'd written down in her notebook.

XXVI. Twenty-six.

She worked back through what she knew about him and then returned to the earliest picture she'd found of him, in 2007, at the scene of a murder at a strip mall. He was already a detective by then, so it was safe to assume he'd been working major crimes for a while before that, because no commanding officer was going to put a complete rookie in charge of a homicide investigation. So he'd been a detective for a year by 2007 – maybe slightly less, maybe a little longer – and at minimum, before that, would have spent four years as a patrol officer – likely more – before being allowed to take the detective's exam. If he spent a year, or eighteen months, with the National Park Service, it tallied with the move from LA to Denver in 1999 or 2000.

Which meant the *26* tattoo could refer to an age.

The age he first became a detective.

Just then, Jo's cellphone started buzzing.

She grabbed it from her pocket and looked at the number. She didn't have it logged and didn't recognize it – but she had a feeling that she knew who was calling.

She pushed Answer.

'Hello?'

'It's me.'

She was right: it was Trae Burrows, the detective she'd called earlier. Burrows had worked for Jo for seven years at the LAPD when Jo had switched from the Sheriff's Department and been made lieutenant there. Trae was a good cop and a good person, but she'd made one bad call on an arrest in East Hollywood in the late nineties that had almost cost her her career. The brass had wanted to push the nuclear button, but Jo had managed to talk them back from the edge: she rated Trae, her temperament, the discipline she'd shown up until then with her cases, and Jo assured her captain and commander that they would never see Trae make the same mistake again. And then she got Trae in a room and repeated those same things to her, and added something else: she'd put her neck on the line for Trae and, if Trae ever screwed up and got heavy-handed with a suspect again, Jo would be at the very front of the queue with a pink slip. But Trae never did screw up – and, when Jo retired, Trae pulled her aside at a party they threw for her, and said she owed Jo her entire career.

Now Jo was calling in some of that debt.

'How you doing, Trae?'

'I'm good,' she said, and Jo could hear that Trae was out

on a street: there were cars in the background, horns. She was probably trying to fade into the melee: she didn't want to look like a cop talking on a burner, just a woman talking happily to a friend.

'Have you got something for me?' Jo asked.

'I don't want to send it. I don't want a trail.'

'I know. That's fine. Just read me what you've got.'

There was a pause as Trae presumably went to the notes or printouts she'd brought with her. Jo grabbed hold of her own notebook, then flipped to a fresh page.

'No hits on that alarm-clock tattoo anywhere,' Trae said. 'Literally, nothing. I put it through every database we've got and it came back with zero matches.'

'Okay.'

Jo looked down at the photograph of Dominguez on her iPad. The news wasn't all that surprising: she was already pretty sure that – fresh from being shot, in shock, terrified and confused – Hermione Suza's recollection of the tattoo's design had been skewed. And, anyway, the less Trae found, the more it helped to narrow the focus on Jo's number-one suspect: she believed more than ever that Craig Dominguez had been the one in the gas station that night, and the man who killed Ed Rivers – and because Dominguez didn't have an alarm-clock design tattooed on his arm, the lack of hits on the computer was, in a weird way, a win. She just wished she could ask Trae to go back to the database and put in a search for a *XXVI* tattoo, but it was too late to do it now.

'What about number tattoos on the right arm?'

'There's a shitload of them,' Trae said.

'I don't doubt it. Any in the same sort of ballpark?'

'Some,' Trae said. She paused, checking her notes. 'I ran them down, using some of the search parameters you suggested – white or Hispanic, 180 to 190 pounds, a connection to Denver – and there was one that came back that might be interesting.'

'Yeah?'

'Yeah, his name's William Marquis.'

Jo wrote down the name.

'I'll give you the basic overview,' Trae said. 'Forty-three, looks like a drifter. He's moved between cities frequently, so his list of former addresses is long, and in most of those places he's got into some sort of trouble: minor infractions mostly – shit like drinking in public or fishing without a licence. Given his record overall, though, I suspect that most of what he's gotten up to in these places, he's never been caught for.'

'Has he done time?'

'Yeah, twice. Aged eighteen, he held up a liquor store in Las Vegas and shot the owner twice in the leg. The owner didn't die, but he never walked again. Marquis served a dime in Nevada Ely State for that.' A dime was a ten-year sentence. 'Then, aged thirty-six – so, what, seven years ago? – he tried to rob a payday loan store in Denver, shot and killed one of the employees and injured another. I mean, this shit sounds pretty close to what you described to me.'

Trae meant the scene at the gas station.

And she was right: it did.

Jo looked at the photograph of Dominguez again, an anxiety forming in the pit of her stomach. *So much for narrowing the focus.* Had she called it wrong? Was Dominguez not a part of this after all? Were his links to Aron Stavis, first at Cabrillo Beach, and then when both of them just happened to end up living in Denver at the same time, simply coincidence? It felt way too *much* of a coincidence . . .

. . . *and yet.*

444

'So is this Marquis serving time again now?' Jo asked.

'Yeah. He made away with thirty-five g's, but was arrested the next day by state troopers close to the Wyoming border. He's up in Colorado State Pen doing LWOP.'

Life Without Parole.

'And this guy's got a number tattoo on his right arm?'

'He's actually got forty tattoos, but all of them except one are on his chest and back, including white supremacist tags, which is a nice touch. Anyway, the one on his right arm is four numbers – 1232 – which is apparently the day, month and year that his mother was born. In an interview he did with the DPD, he said . . .' Trae paused for a moment, presumably trying to find the right piece of paper. '"My mom was the only good person I ever had in my life." She was killed when he was eight years old.'

Marquis fit the profile perfectly: he had the history, he had the tattoo, he was living in Denver at the time of the robbery. Jo stared at the image of Dominguez again.

'There's something else as well,' Trae said.

Jo tuned back in. 'What?'

'That gas station you gave me the address for . . . I checked it against the address Marquis gave cops in Denver when they handed out some disturbing-the-peace beef to him. He was, uh, "playing his music excessively loudly at three in the morning, and repeatedly refused to turn it down." The neighbours called the cops on him. Anyway, like I said, I checked the gas station against his address and he lived real close to it.'

'How close?'

'Less than a mile away. He'd also been fired from his job washing plates in the kitchens of a diner somewhere downtown, about two weeks before – so, you know . . .'

He wasn't going to be earning.

And, suddenly, he'd have the motive to rob a gas station.

Jo's guts were all twisted up. She'd put in a search, while Trae was talking to her, for William Marquis and, from his arrest photograph, he looked as good a fit for the masked gunman as Dominguez did. So this thing was complicated again. She'd straightened it out, narrowed the focus, and now it had got even messier than before.

Worse, if the man who'd murdered Ed Rivers *was* William Marquis, then that unravelled everything in the background as well: the theory about Dominguez being the middle man, about Ed Rivers being the supplier. Because if Marquis was the gunman, it was just a random act of violence born out of his need for money.

'That's all I got,' Trae said.

'I appreciate it, Trae.'

'You got it. Stay safe, LT.'

She still called her Lieutenant, even now. But that was a lie. Jo wasn't her boss. She was a crazy old woman who still thought she was a cop, just like she'd told David.

Hanging up, Jo studied the images of Craig Dominguez and William Marquis, tabbing back and forth between their photos. It was difficult to see straight any more.

So she switched off her tablet.

Closed her eyes.

A few minutes later, she put everything back into her carry-on, and then went out to the main concourse and stood in a queue for coffee. The terminal was busy, the queue long, announcements and conversations and music coming from everywhere.

She got out her cell again, checking for messages. She had none. She typed out a WhatsApp to Ethan and sent her son a selfie she'd taken of her and David in Central Park, and then asked how they were. As the queue inched forward, she looked again at the photograph of Claire and Maisie making

446

pancakes that Ethan had sent a few days before. Jo smiled at the image, and then suddenly felt lost, untethered, far away from her family, far away from the career she'd once had and the instincts she'd relied on.

One of the baristas called her forward and she ordered a black coffee, paid for it and stood at the end of the counter, waiting. She went to her emails to see if there were any messages, and then to Facebook and the thirty-six notifications she hadn't checked.

She scrolled down the list of alerts, not expecting to find anything of any real interest – but, at the end, as her coffee was placed on the counter, something caught her eye.

Six days ago, she'd been tagged in a photograph.

The photograph was on a page called 'The Badge Never Dulls', which was the incredibly pretentious name for an LASD veterans group. A fellow Sheriff's detective called Gary Perez who she'd worked with in the mid-to-late eighties – and who'd died of a heart attack fourteen months ago, aged eighty-four – had invited her to join after he came to see a lecture she did at UCL in 2013. Gary had been one of the few men who'd actually treated her decently during that period of her career.

She studied the photo she'd been tagged in.

It was a group shot, taken in 1988, of the LASD detective squad. She was the only woman and was standing out to the side, one hand on the edge of a nearby desk, as if she feared she was going to be pushed out of the picture entirely. She looked at the younger version of herself: it must have been summer, because she had a thin cotton blouse on and had tied her hair up, which she'd always tended to do when the LA heat started to become too much. As if to confirm the time of year, almost all of the men were in short-sleeved shirts, and some of them – especially Greg Landa, a fat,

447

repugnant misogynist she'd been forced to look at every day for seven years – were marked with sweat, even though the A/C would have been on full blast.

'Ma'am, your coffee.'

Jo looked up, realizing she'd become distracted by the picture and that she was holding up the line. She apologized and, eyes switching between where she was going and the photograph of the detective squad, she headed back to the same corner of the terminal she'd chosen to sit in before – and, as she did, she noticed something small.

Something almost hidden in the shot.

A face she'd forgotten would be there.

He was at the opposite end of the photograph from her, almost leaning out of the frame. But not enough that Jo couldn't see that he was the only one of the male detectives wearing a long-sleeved dress shirt, and that – although he'd rolled up his sleeves in the heat – it was only to the halfway mark between his wrists and elbows.

And yet it was enough.

As Jo stared into the face of a young Gerald Rivers, his stance, the way his body was slightly turned, she saw what looked like a shadow cast against a spot on his arm.

His right arm.

Except it wasn't a shadow.

It was a tattoo.

11

It felt like she'd been hit by a train.

She tapped on the photograph and then pinch-zoomed in closer. The quality of the shot was poor, another scan of an old print, but she could clearly see four small numbers inked on to the underside of his arm, could see how rectangular their design was, how much like an alarm clock readout they were. It looked like the first digit was a zero, the second was a four, but she couldn't make out the two after that.

He killed his own son.

The enormity of that statement almost cleaved Jo in two, made her throat feel like it was closing and her stomach clench like a fist. *He shot and killed his own son.*

How could any father do that?

Why would he do it?

She was so consumed by what she was seeing, by the absolute depravity of it, by her immediate desire to try and weave the whole thing together into some sort of coherent narrative, that she hardly noticed when someone sat in the seat next to her.

But then the person's closeness to her finally registered.

She looked to her left.

Gerald Rivers smiled at her. 'Hey, Jo.'

Something pulsed in her throat. She looked around, trying to see if he was alone – her survival instincts immediately kicking in – but in this area of the terminal it was just the two of them. There was still no flight assigned to the gate they were at.

It was just her. And a killer.

How was he here?

How was he sitting beside her?

He should have been watching from the gallery at the trial of Aron Stavis, not at the airport waiting for a plane ride home. Gerald nodded once, as if he could hear what she was thinking, as if he knew she would want answers to those questions, and then one of his eyes started watering. A single tear trail broke from his eyelashes and began its escape down his cheek. He reached into the pocket of his pants and pulled out a folded handkerchief – and then slowly, almost gracefully, wiped the tear away.

'Damn eyes get so itchy,' he said.

Jo didn't respond and then she realized, on her lap, the photograph she'd been tagged in on the LASD Facebook group was still showing – and zoomed in on Rivers.

'Still, I'd take a weepy eye over the high blood pressure,' he went on, his gaze flicking to the photograph of his younger self on the tablet, 'over the cholesterol, and the constipation, and the constant fucking backache. It wears you out, Jo, doesn't it? My dad used to say, "Old age ain't for sissies," and, hell, now I know what he means.'

'What are you even doing here, Gerald?'

He dragged his carry-on luggage between his legs, as if frightened someone would steal it, then glanced at the photograph of himself again. He lingered there for a moment, caught in the memory, and when, finally, he ripped his gaze away from the picture, his eye had begun to water again. This time, Jo wasn't certain whether it was old age or emotion; Rivers used one of his fingers to brush the tears away and said: 'The call you made to Emilia Fuentes a couple of days ago. That was when we knew. She still talks to Dominguez – they're old pals; grew up together in LA – and, after you

450

were done asking Reverend Fuentes your questions, she called Dominguez wanting to know *why* you were asking questions about him. Dominguez fobs her off with some bullshit, then calls me. So last couple of days, I've been watching you and your detective pal.'

'Watching me?'

'From a distance.' Rivers shrugged. 'I figured if I got too close, either you would spot me, or your friend from England would. I've read about him. He seems a smart guy.'

'And now you're here.'

'Now I'm here.' He gave a forced smile, flat and inexpressive. 'I was supposed to fly back to LA tomorrow, but I managed to bring my flight forward twenty-four hours so you and I could have a little chat, Jo.' He checked his watch. 'We've got time, I think.'

'You want to chat about how you killed your own son?'

He winced a little and then pointed to the photograph on Jo's phone. 'Was it the tattoo?' He rolled up his sleeve and showed the tattoo to her: it had faded over time, been consumed by the wrinkles in his skin, by prominent blue veins just below the surface, by liver spots and freckling – but it was there. *04:59.* 'I always liked the one Dominguez got,' he said quietly, 'so I decided to get my own. But this one isn't anything to do with me being a cop: Craig's was a celebration of when he first became a detective; mine was a celebration of my son. This is the time Ed was born.'

04.59 a.m.

'Why now, Gerald? Because I've found out your secret?'

'To be honest,' he said, still speaking softly but playing with the handkerchief on his lap now, folding it and refolding it, 'I'm surprised I survived this long. The past ten years, I spent every day waiting for the truth to come out, but it never did. And then, when they finally tied Aron Stavis to it, when our back-up plan kicked in, I thought that was it. It was the end of it. Someone else was going to go down for what Craig and I did.'

'So it was Dominguez and you?'

He nodded.

'Not you and your son?'

He frowned. 'Me and Ed?'

'Ed wasn't the one that supplied the xylazine?'

Rivers pushed his lips together. 'No,' he said. 'No, Ed would never have gone for anything like that. Never. He was too moral, a really good kid; never into shit like that. No, the xylazine used to come from a vet that Craig was friendly with down in Colorado Springs. He'd order more in every month than he needed at the clinic, and then Craig or I would go back and forth along the I-25 to pick up the new shipment.'

'And then what?'

He shrugged. 'And then we'd sell it to Jermaine Washington.'

The kingpin the cops had been after for years.

'Why?' Jo asked.

'Why what?'

'Why were you selling cutting agent to a drug dealer?'

Rivers didn't reply for a moment, just heaved his shoulders. 'I don't know,' he said eventually, mutedly. 'It just started. I'd been in Denver a few years by then, but I knew Dominguez from back west. He was the son of a guy I used to go to school with.'

Jo got out her iPad.

'Are you confessing to me, Gerald?'

Rivers stopped folding the handkerchief.

'Because if it's a confession, I should record it.'

His eyes went to the tablet. 'And then what?'

'And then I hand the recording to the cops.'

He smiled and then began with the handkerchief again. 'Kader, if I wanted to get sweated in an interview room, I would have called the cops myself a decade ago.'

'So why follow me? Why change your flight? Why come up to me here? I want to hear the story, believe me, but there has to be an endgame, Gerald, you know that.'

'Someone has to pay.' He nodded. 'I get it.'

'Your son deserves justice.'

'Do you think I'll be getting him justice by going to prison? What am I going to serve at my age? Ten years if I'm lucky?' He shook his head. 'I'm not going to the pen, Jo. That's not justice. That's not why I followed you. It's not why I'm here right now.'

'So why *are* you here, Gerald?'

He gestured to the iPad. 'Press Record.'

She stared at him.

'I mean it: press Record. Let's do this.'

'And then what?'

'And then you do what you want.'

She eyed him, trying to see through to what he meant. He was going to confess to her and let her record it – but he was going to make sure he never went to prison.

That meant he only had one exit left.

'You going to kill yourself in an airport, Gerald?'

He smirked.

'You think suicide is better than going to prison?'

'Depends where you end up after you've done it,' he said.

And then he looked at her, and he blinked once, and another tear ran down his cheek – and this time Jo saw clearly that it didn't have anything to do with him being old.

He was crying.

'Just press Record,' he said quietly, 'and I'll tell you everything.'

12

'Dominguez always wanted to be a cop,' Rivers said, looking at Jo.

It was twenty-five minutes until they boarded.

'Like I say, I knew his old man. But Craig ran into a bit of local trouble back in LA – was a bit heavy-handed with a woman in a bar one night, and *she* happened to have a brother who worked in Robbery-Homicide, and he told Dominguez that, although no charges were brought, he would make it his life's work to ensure Craig never became a cop there. So, one thing led to another, we talked, and I told him he should come out to Denver.' Rivers looked down at the iPad which Jo was holding next to him: numbers were turning on it and the audio waves were still moving, despite his silence, picking up the residual sounds of the terminal. 'I guess I took advantage. I mean, I could see him for what he was . . .'

'Which was what?'

'He was the type of kid who would let a little bit of power go to his head. That made him easy to manipulate. He was too cocky, especially when he finally became a detective; he thought he could get away with whatever shit he liked, and then suddenly he was in it deep, and I had a million different things over him, and there was no way for him to get out. It was stay in or go to prison. And as you know, cops don't do so well inside.'

'So you were already involved in drugs before he ever came out to Denver?'

Rivers nodded. 'A little bit of everything. It started small, just to earn more – a little to top up the wages. Marian, my ex, Ed's mom, she was a lawyer, so she always had a shit-ton of money. It was hard to compete with that. She and her partner would buy Ed a bunch of stuff that I never could – things for the house, weekends away for him and the girlfriends he had, all this crap – and, over time, that sort of thing starts to work. They grew close. Ed began to spend more time with them and less with me.'

'So you brought Dominguez in on what you were doing?'

He nodded.

'Why? Why split what you were earning off the books?'

'Like I told you earlier, Craig got friendly with a vet in Colorado Springs, and it just developed from there. He told me he thought the vet was up to something – that he was selling prescription drugs on the side – but, before he went too deep down the rabbit hole of *investigating* this vet, I told Craig we could *use* him. Dominguez wasn't keen to start with but you flash the dollar bills and most people can be per-suaded. So I brought Dominguez on for access to the vet, and cos I needed a layer of insulation.'

'A fall guy if the heat got too much.'

'Exactly. But in the end, we grew close. It was good for a few years – we had a good thing going – and then, just like that, it went to shit.' He grimaced and squeezed his eyes shut, as if he didn't want to have to dredge up the memory. 'We'd just taken this shipment of xylazine from the vet. I'd been down to collect it and had stored it in a lock-up I had; it was where we always put the drugs after we got them. Anyway, by that point, it had been going on for so long – we'd been sell-ing to Jermaine Washington for so many months – that I guess I got a little sloppy. I forgot that some of Ed's things from his childhood, all this crap I'd brought out to Denver when I moved, was in a box in there. Worse than that, I forgot that I'd *told* Ed about it. So, one day, because Marian has spent the whole day talking about all these things he got up to as a kid, he decides he wants to go through the box; he comes to my house – I gave him a key, because I wanted him to come and go as he pleased; for it to feel like a home, you know? – and he grabs the key for the lock-up off the rack. At this point, I'm at work. I have no idea.'

'And he finds the xylazine in the lock-up.'

'Right. And there's a *shitload* of it in there, so it would have looked suspicious even if he didn't deal with that stuff every day of his life. But, being a vet, he knew. He looked at all the bottles of it there, on the floor of the lock-up, and he knew there was no good reason for me to have it. And he knew the only way that I could get *hold* of that amount of it was either through seizing it or paying some doctor willing to sell.'

Rivers ground to a halt.

Again, the sounds of the terminal faded back in: every time Rivers spoke, they seemed to vanish, and it was just Jo and him; every time he paused, she remembered where they were again. She glanced at the clock: fifteen minutes until they boarded.

'Ed,' Rivers said finally, his voice small, the name of his child barely forming on his tongue. 'Ed just went absolutely fucking nuts. I tried to lie to him, but he just saw right through me. I tried to blame it on Dominguez, like some amateur-hour con artist, but he didn't buy it. He said to me, "You own up to this shit, Dad, or I'll tell the cops myself."' Rivers swallowed, forced another smile, his face haunted by the ghosts of heartache, and pain, and guilt. 'It's like I said: cops, we don't do well in prison. If I went to prison, I'd have lasted five minutes. I'd have been ripped to pieces. A guy I knew, second year I was in Denver, he went down for planting

456

evidence, then got his throat cut while he was on the can, second day he was inside.' He shook his head. 'I just couldn't do it . . .'

'So you killed your own son instead?'

'I didn't . . . It wasn't . . .' But then he paused; shook his head again. 'No,' he muttered. 'There's no excuses. Not any more.'

Over the tannoy, their flight was announced.

'How did Aron Stavis's DNA end up at the scene?' Jo asked.

'We put it there a couple of days before.'

'You and Dominguez?'

'Yeah.'

'How?'

'One day, a few weeks before Ed found the xylazine, Dominguez turned up at this homicide – some guy shot in the middle of a street, broad daylight – and, when he went around talking to some of the locals, he came face to face with Aron Stavis.'

'Stavis didn't recognize him?'

'From the Cabrillo Beach Soccer Club? No. I mean, by then, it had been, like, ten years since they'd seen one another. Plus, it's one of those weird, random events that just doesn't compute. They knew each other a little back in LA – they were both founding members of that soccer club – but Dominguez said they were never best buds, never went out drinking, or spent time together socially, and they never used surnames at the soccer club. So a decade later, Stavis just isn't expecting Dominguez to be there, in Denver, on his door-step. But Dominguez said, even when he introduced himself and showed Stavis his badge, it still didn't seem to click with him.' Rivers took a breath, readying himself for the next part. 'A few weeks later, Ed finds the xylazine and he's just cranking up the pressure the whole time, and I know in that moment that the two of us, we're never going to be the same again. If I hand myself in, it's still not going to be the same. If I go to prison, if I even *survive* in there, Ed and me, we're never going to heal the rift, not quite. He'll never trust me. There'll be a distance that I was already struggling to close, before he ever found those fucking drugs. His mom will cut him off from me; I'll have nothing. I'll have nothing after – so what difference does it make if I got nothing now? That was my thinking.'

The bleakness of that statement was absolute.

Jo couldn't think of a single thing to say.

'So I told Dominguez what needed to be done,' Rivers said.

Jo glanced at the time.

Ten minutes to boarding.

'And that's when we come up with the idea of making it look like a robbery, and that's when he tells me about Stavis. Craig says, "There's this guy I knew back in LA who's living here now, and he's got a history. He served time for a bank job." And so I go to Stavis's house, pretending to be follow-ing up on questions about the murder they had in his street, and instead – the minute he goes to make me a coffee – I ask if I can use the bathroom. I grab his toothbrush.' Rivers paused, his eye watering again. He put his handkerchief to it and then continued: 'A few days later, Dominguez and I come up with a play, and I'm in that gas station. When the attendant isn't looking, I use the brush on the plastic screen, on the counter, on some of the shelves right at the front.'

'And the cops never checked?'

'You mean, the instore video?'

'Yeah. They never went back over the previous days to when you were there?'

458

'Dominguez made sure he landed the case – even made sure he was in the area when the call went out about Ed – and he handled all of that. I was in there, on video, two days before – by the time Dominguez had finished, half of the tape from that day had corrupted. But no one checked, anyway. Craig worked the case, slowly, methodically, the way he normally would. In her witness statement, the attendant that worked there – Hermione Suza – said *exactly* what we hoped she would. Shooting her, shooting Ed as he was coming *into* the store, it was all part of the plan: it made it look desperate.'

'How did you get Ed to the gas station?'

'I called him. Told him to meet me there.'

'As simple as that.'

'It wasn't *simple*,' Rivers responded, and for the first time he raised his voice. He was lashing out at Jo because the pain was like a weight he couldn't shift; even as he confessed, even as he admitted to the terrible sin he'd committed that could never be unwritten. 'He was barely talking to me at that point,' Rivers said, his voice more stilled now. 'He'd given me a deadline of four days to admit to the cops what I'd done, or he said he was going to do it himself. So when I called him, the first thing he said was, "Have you been to the cops yet?" And I told him I hadn't, that I was going to go in the morning, and as I lied to him about that, I cried, and he could hear me crying, and that was why he agreed to meet me there, I think. It was on his way home, the emotion was real, I said I needed to explain some things: all of it made him come.'

Rivers blinked back tears.

Jo glanced at the iPad, at the numbers still ticking over, and filled in the rest of that night. Gerald Rivers killed Ed, Hermione Suza was injured, and the cop who would be looking at the cellphone records for Ed, to track his movements and his calls over the previous days, was the same cop who would be going through the instore tapes.

Craig Dominguez.

And even if, for whatever reason, someone else on Dominguez's team happened to see the call Gerald Rivers had made to his son that night, before Ed left the zoo for the gas station, who would have thought it was suspicious? A father calling his son – especially a father who, afterwards, was grieving so hard for his boy – was never going to raise an alarm. Gerald was instantly in the clear.

There was another announcement for their flight.

They had five minutes.

'Why wear the Gorfon top?' Jo asked.

'It was just a top Dominguez grabbed for me that afternoon when we were laying everything out at his place,' Rivers admitted. 'I didn't think much about it at the time – there was too much else going through my head – but afterwards it suddenly occurred to me that it might lead somewhere. But Craig was adamant it wouldn't. Back then, Reverend Fuentes hadn't set up the Cabrillo Beach Soccer Club website with Gorfon Hernandez's name attached to it, and there were no pictures online of the so-called "founding members". So Dominguez said to me, "It won't lead nowhere. If anything, it'll just have everyone going around in circles." First, the font was basically illegible – it looks more like *Corton* than *Gorfon* – which was the angle Dominguez pushed during the investigation. Second, no one in LA was hearing about a gas station robbery in Denver. This sort of shit happens in America hundreds of times a day, so it wasn't going to make the national news. There was no danger of Fuentes or anyone else out on the west coast seeing the video from the store. And then, by the time – what, five, six years later? – Fuentes sets up her website, the shooting has been long forgotten, anyway. It's a cold case at the back of a filing cabinet. No one ever put it together, no one ever got anywhere with that top – until you just asked me about it, here, today.'

'What about the tranq dope being sold next to the gas station?'

'What about it?'

'Was that why you asked Ed to meet you there? So, if anyone went digging, if they put it all together like I did, and they heard about people dealing next to the gas station and all along the interstate, they'd finger Ed as being the xylazine supplier?'

'Yes.'

'They'd think that gas station was a regular haunt for him, right? Somewhere he was familiar with, somewhere he'd conducted business. Of *course* he'd be there.'

'Yes,' Rivers said again, a profound sadness in his face.

'And that was why all the dealers cleared out afterwards?'

He nodded.

'You tipped them off. Told them the cops had them under surveillance – maybe something like that. You didn't want them anywhere near the scene, because although Dominguez was lead on the case, other cops would be working it, and they might get some bright idea about going down to that patch of land and asking hard questions.'

Finally, a third time, he said, 'Yes.'

And then something flickered in Rivers's face, and Jo thought she knew what it was: they were at the end, and he'd expected this confession to feel different. He'd let go of ten years' worth of secrets, come out from under the crushing weight of his own guilt, and yet the landscape hadn't changed. It wasn't any better. It wasn't sunlit.

It was just the same dark shadows.

Jo stopped the recording and said to Rivers, 'I can hold off on this. If you're going to do now what you should have done back then, and walk into a police station – either when we get back to LA or back in Denver – and tell them everything, I will give you time to do that, Gerald. But the clock is ticking. I'm not waiting four days . . .'

I'm not waiting the amount of time Ed gave you.

'I'm not going to prison, Jo.'

'You're not taking the easy way out, Gerald.' Above them, a voice on the tannoy announced that their flight had started boarding. 'I will call the cops here in New York, and I will call them in LA, but either way there's no escaping this. You're not going to the lockbox under your bed at home and eating a gun for what you did.'

'No,' he said, and looked at her. 'I'm not.'

And then his eyes started watering again – both of them now – and, for the first time, Jo noticed how much saliva had gathered in the corners of Rivers's mouth, how red his eyes were, how difficult he was finding it to breathe, and her belly squirmed.

Now she knew why his eyes were watering so much.

Now she knew what was really going on here.

'What did you take, Gerald?'

He smiled. 'Something to carry me on my way.'

His voice was breaking up.

'Were you ever going to board the plane?'

'No,' he wheezed, the colour of his cheeks changing – pink, red, mauve. It was like he was choking, struggling for air, and yet he didn't thrash around, didn't shift on his seat, didn't reach for her suddenly. He just looked at her, a man from another life.

A partner. A father.

A killer.

'I'm sorry, Ed,' he whispered. 'I'm so sorry.'

And then he was still.

13

Three weeks later, Ethan picked Jo up from Oakland airport.

She hugged her son hard as she came through the gate, holding on to him as if he might drift away. When they broke off, Ethan smiled and said, 'You okay, Mom?'

'Much better now, honey.'

'Claire's sorry for not coming as well, and especially that Maisie isn't here. Mais has got a birthday party this afternoon, which she was super excited about, and I was also super excited about' – he paused for comic effect – '*missing.* But they'll be back at the house by the time we get there, so you'll still get lots of time with them.'

Ethan took Jo's carry-on from her, while Jo looped her arm through her son's, and then they walked out to the parking lot. Literally the first thing Ethan asked about was Gerald Rivers: it had been all over the newspapers for days, and Jo had even been invited to appear on television, at the press conference that the Port Authority had laid on in the aftermath, alongside a detective from Denver PD.

She squeezed Ethan a little tighter as she recounted all that had happened, not just at JFK that day, but before, stretching all the way back to a gas station in Denver.

By the time they got to the car, she was done talking about Rivers, so as Ethan loaded her luggage into the trunk and she waited for him in the front, she took a long breath and prepared herself for whatever news was coming. When she'd talked to her son on the phone the previous night, he'd said that there were some things they had to discuss, and although she didn't pry, she knew it had to do with the marriage.

She could hear it in her son's voice, like a hum.

He climbed into the front.

She let him talk as they drove, although it wasn't about Claire and Maisie but about his job: he worked for a tech company in Santa Clara, doing something clever with websites, and had just been given a promotion. He told her about his new office: 'It's crazy, Mom. I'm on the fourth floor and it's got these huge windows on two sides with floor-to-ceiling glass. I get insane views across the water. Honestly, I'm sitting there most of the time thinking, "I'm sure they've made a mistake." Every time I get a knock on the door, I'm waiting for someone to come in and say, "Er, sorry, Ethan . . ."'

Jo smiled. 'They didn't make a mistake, honey.'

'I think you might be biased.'

'Maybe a little. But I'm so proud of you.'

'Thanks, Mom,' Ethan said, 'but I think we know who the real high achiever is in this family. I mean, you're that woman who was on CNN that time, weren't you?'

Jo laughed, and it felt good.

It felt right being here with her son, being close to the people she loved most in the world. She hadn't needed Gerald Rivers's confession to remind her of how she felt about her family, of how – as long as she had breath in her lungs – she'd never allow anything to happen to them, ever. But what Rivers had said had brought it into focus.

This was it.

These were the only moments in life that mattered.

They got to the house about forty minutes later. It was looking nice, neat, the garden manicured, the clapboards newly painted white. But when Ethan switched off the ignition, he didn't make a move to get out, instead turning in his seat to Jo, and she knew that this was what she'd come all this way for. There was a problem at the heart of her son's marriage, a lesion, and now she was about to find out what it was.

She steeled herself.

'You remember how difficult Maisie was, Mom?'

Jo frowned. 'What? She's always been such a good kid.'

'No, I mean, how difficult the birth was.'

'Oh, right.' Jo nodded. 'Yes, of course.' Claire had been in labour for thirty-two hours and, minutes from the end – just as it looked like the worst was finally over – Maisie's heart rate had dropped dangerously low and, for one terrible moment, Ethan and Claire had thought they'd lost their little girl. 'Of course I remember,' Jo added.

'Do you remember what I said to you at the time?'

'You said a lot of things, Eth.'

'I said, I never wanted Claire to go through it again.'

Jo nodded again. 'I remember that, yes.'

Just then, the front door of the house opened and Maisie came tearing out. As Jo erupted into a smile, waving furiously at her granddaughter, she opened her door, ready to grab Maisie and hug her and never let go.

A second later, Claire followed her daughter out, on to the porch.

And that was when Jo saw.

'I didn't want Claire to go through another pregnancy. I was so scared for her,' Ethan said, opening his own door. 'But Claire said we couldn't let fear control us.'

Jo grabbed her granddaughter.

'We fought about it, Mom.'

She squeezed Maisie tight.

'Wow, we fought about it in a way we've never fought about anything before . . .'

And then as Jo kissed Maisie's head, she looked across the

lawn towards Claire again. Her daughter-in-law waved at Jo and came down the steps, hand on her belly.

'But she was right,' Ethan said. 'We can't let fear control us.'

Jo felt tears well in her eyes.

'So, Granny, I guess you'd better come back again in five months.'

EPILOGUE
Ghosts

By the time I'd arrived in New York to meet Jo Kader, the stories about Gerry Stein had long since faded from view. As soon as the tabloids realized they could no longer string out an invented connection between him and the killer who'd terrorized London nine years before – and, more to the point, had helped those same newspapers sell thousands of extra copies as he did so – everything ground to a halt. The name of the Snatcher returned to where it had been for so long: just lines in a true-crime book; just a file buried at the back of a cabinet at the Met; just a person mostly erased from people's minds, except those of us – like me, like Healy – who were there when it was happening, who saw first-hand what he did, and who could never quite forget.

Stein eventually gave Dr Garrison the location of his friend Stevie O'Keefe, and once that was done, and the tabloids moved on from him and the Snatcher, tragic as the entire episode was, that should have been the end. But it wasn't. In fact, in a way, the opposite happened: the stories about Stein and his non-existent connection to the Snatcher proved to be a catalyst, a rejuvenating tonic that suddenly put energy into a man who'd been tracking me for a long time, but who I thought I'd got the better of.

Even as Jo and I spent time together in a city 3,500 miles from my own, the calls still kept coming to my phone. They kept coming when I got home too, and they were all from the same person: Connor McCaskell, the journalist from the *Daily Tribune* who, four years before, had caught the whiff of a story – the sense that I was hiding something; something to do with the person who was renting my dad's old place in south Devon – and who became fixated on finding the answer.

McCaskell was the reason we moved Healy out of that house in the first place, the reason he'd ended up in north Wales, under another assumed name, with another fake passport. And because McCaskell had been so quiet for so long, a part of me had allowed myself to believe that maybe he really *had* been defeated, that because he had nothing but suspicions, because he couldn't find a way to come after me with facts, he'd had to accept the inevitable and move on. But as the calls started coming again, as they became more frequent when I didn't answer and when I deleted his voice-mails without listening to them, I had to accept the reality: he hadn't ever gone away, he'd just retreated into the shadows. The Stein stories, the Snatcher stuff, it was like a shot of adrenalin: it reinstated his interest in me, and in being the man who would find out what I was hiding. He would show the world what he thought I was: not a person to be celebrated, not a person who brought people answers, who put his life on the line to try and do what was right – but, rather, a fraud, a charlatan, a liar.

Healy had told me there was nothing in his new life in north Wales that could cause us any problems, and I had to trust him on that. But it didn't mean I wasn't on high alert. McCaskell was coming for me, and this time I knew there would be no retreat.

He wasn't going back to the shadows again.

Not without his story.

A month after I got back from New York, Jo Kader video-called me and told me that she'd found out she was going to be a gran for a second time. We spoke at length about the Ed Rivers case, and then about kids, and family, and after we were finished I lay in bed that night, unable to sleep, and had a sudden compulsion to be close to my daughter, to the places I'd grown up in and to the memory of my parents that was written into them. I couldn't remember the last time I'd felt so drawn to my childhood, but I just had a sudden need to be closer to it, to the recollections of my mum and dad, to the life we'd had together; I wanted to return to the village I grew up in and walk the woods behind our old farm.

The next morning, I called Annabel and asked if she would mind me coming down for a couple of days, and she told me she and her seventeen-year-old half-sister Olivia would love to see me. Liv wasn't mine – at least, biologically – but I treated her just the same: her parents were both gone, so Annabel, almost twice as old as her sister, was her entire world; and as Annabel was mine, it made it easy for us to forge a tight unit.

I decided to get the train rather than drive, because I could relax that way and enjoy watching the world pass, but when I got to the Tube station at Ealing the next morning, I was met with delays on both lines. For a moment, I considered going back for the car and abandoning Plan A, but as heavy rain arrowed down between the roofs of the platforms, I decided to grab a coffee, find a ledge somewhere and wait it out.

Going to my phone, I started zipping through some of the emails I'd put off, and tried to answer as many as pos-sible. Before long, everything else started to fade out.

And then my phone erupted into life in my hand.

A London number I didn't recognize.

'David Raker,' I said, pushing Answer.

Around me, the noise of the station rushed back in.

'Oh, Mr Raker,' a female voice said. 'Hi, my name's, uh, my

name's Sue Clark.' A pause. She sounded nervous, a little fearful, as if she was worried that I might shut her down straight away. That told me immediately she was calling for help, because this was frequently the way my cases would start. I was the last resort when it came to their loved ones; after the last resort, there was nothing. That was what scared them. If I said no, there was nowhere else to go.

I tried to put her at ease. 'How can I help you, Sue?'

'It's my daughter, Cate.'

I levered my notebook out of my pocket.

'She and her husband, Aiden – they disappeared almost two and a half years ago. I don't know what . . .' She stopped. 'I don't know where else to go, or what to do.'

'It's okay,' I said gently. 'What happened to Cate and Aiden?'

'Have you heard of the Mystery of Gatton Hill?'

'No,' I responded. 'What's that?'

'That's what they call it on the Internet.'

'Call what?' I asked.

'What happened to Cate.' A moment's hesitation, and then I heard her take a long breath, as if she was fortifying herself. 'Ten seconds before the accident, their car got recorded on CCTV and everything was fine. They were laughing and happy. It was all perfectly normal, but then they . . . Aiden just . . .' She faded out. 'For whatever reason, Aiden lost control of the car – and they ended up plunging into a ninety-foot ravine.'

'This is the Gatton Hill you were talking about?'

'Yes.'

'Where's that?'

'In the Surrey Hills. A few miles south of the M25.'

I tried to imagine where this was going.

'Emergency services said the impact should have killed

them. And if the impact didn't, definitely the fire. The fire was . . . It was like an inferno. Pretty much as soon as the car landed in the ravine, it just . . .' I could hear her gently starting to sob. 'It just . . .'

'It burst into flames.'

'Yes.'

'I'm so sorry to hear that,' I said.

But it was getting harder to see how I could help if the answer she sought was why her daughter and son-in-law's car had suddenly left the road and gone down a ravine.

'I'm not exactly sure what you think I can do,' I said.

'What do you mean?'

'I mean, I find missing people. I'm not any kind of an expert when it comes to crash investigations. If you're looking for reasons why the car came off the road, I'd –'

'No,' she said. 'No, you don't understand.'

'Maybe spell it out for me.'

'It was on fire almost from the minute it landed.'

'Okay.'

'But when the fire engines and the police got there . . .' She stopped, took another long, broken breath. 'When they got there, they couldn't find Cate and Aiden inside.'

I frowned. 'Their bodies weren't in the car?'

'No,' Sue confirmed. 'It was completely empty.'

The next morning, I woke up early. It was a Saturday, so Annabel wasn't teaching and Liv didn't have school, and when I left the house, they were both still sound asleep. I headed out to the west of their home, where the roads rose up and across the edges of Dartmoor and did an eight-mile run. When I got back an hour later, they were still asleep, so I showered and changed, left them a note and then took Annabel's car and drove south, along the A38. Not long after that, I was winding my way across the rolling hills of the South Hams towards the place I grew up in on the Start Bay coast.

I parked almost on the seafront and did the short walk from one end of the village to the other, watching the waves idle gently against the shingle. Eventually, I started the climb out of the village, into the surrounding hills, where – at the crest – my parents' farm had been located. When I got there, I stopped at a set of steel gates and looked along a tarmac driveway: the farmhouse was still standing, but there was no farm here any more, just more houses, nine of them built all over fields my mum and dad had once kept cows on. Where one of the barns had once stood, the area had been cleared to make way for even more homes, the diggers paused for the weekend.

I played old memories of my childhood, of my mum talking to me about the things that she'd loved, like books and baking and animals, on the back porch of the farmhouse – the porch, eventually, where her heart had given in, and where Dad and I had found her, keeled over and still; and then I thought of my dad, before the end, before he weakened, when we played football in these fields, and he taught me how to milk a cow and fix an engine and fire a gun. For a second, I could hear the gunshots, the *pop-pop-pop* of the air rifles we used to fire at makeshift targets in the woods, and then I was moving again, around the old boundaries of the farm, towards the trees.

They didn't seem as tall as I remembered them being, perhaps because – as a seventeen-year-old – I'd only really been a child the last time I was here. But the woods still sprawled in the same way, a tangled mess of pathways, leading into a valley. I followed the cant of the hill down, all the time on the lookout for the Montgomery house, my discovery of which had sparked my father's questions in the last, dim days of his life.

As I continued on, I thought of Paul Conister, and particularly of Maggie, and wondered if she'd done anything after that last phone call I'd had with her, or whether that fear and heartache and regret that my dad had talked about still lingered in the rooms of her head. I thought of Healy – of what he'd become in the years since we faked his death – and whether our decision all that time ago might finally come back to haunt us in the shape of Connor McCaskell. I thought of Joline Kader, of the case she'd been working when we'd met in New York, and of how, in killing his own son, Gerald Rivers had ultimately been besieged by the spectres of his crime. And then, finally, I thought of the work I'd agreed to take on the day before, of how a husband and wife could vanish like apparitions from inside a burning car. Even without knowing Cate and Aiden Gascoigne at all, their story was imprinted on me. A day in, the questions were stalking my thoughts.

But then, for a time, those questions stopped.

It took me longer than I expected to find it, but eventually I stumbled across the Montgomery house almost by accident, its shell hidden by low, twisted branches, by vines as opaque as walls and earth as dense as concrete. To my disappointment, in the thirty-four years since I'd last stood in this spot, my dad alongside me, the two of us silent and staring in at the house, it hadn't just become swamped, it had almost completely disappeared.

Almost, but not quite.

Because I knew the house was still there, even if I couldn't see it.

Just like all ghosts.

Appendix

The following is an excerpt from an interview with David Raker, conducted by Sara Habib and Fabian Wilson on the *Echo World* podcast. *Echo World* explores crimes, including disappearances, and the way those crimes are reported in the media. Its episodes have been downloaded over 280 million times, and in 2020 the podcast won the prestigious Peabody Award for its series on the Night Stalker.

Sara Habib: Today's guest is a man that you probably won't know anything about – which is exactly the way he likes it. He's spent over ten years finding missing people in the UK – and, once, here in the US as well – and he's been directly involved in a number of high-profile cases that we've talked about on this podcast, including the Body Snatcher investigation and the mystery surrounding film-noir director Robert Hosterlitz. It gives us great pleasure to speak to him today from his home in London – David Raker, missing persons investigator, welcome to the *Echo World* podcast.

David Raker: Thank you for having me.

Fabian Wilson: David, what our listeners won't know is that we've actually spent quite a long time trying to get you on to this show. In fact, I checked my email chain this morning and I first dropped you a line back in 2017. I know you're not generally a fan of talking to the media, so can I ask what made you decide to speak to us?

David Raker: My friend Joline Kader.

Fabian Wilson: That's former LASD and LAPD detective Joline Kader, who regular listeners will remember we spoke to extensively during our Night Stalker series.

David Raker: Exactly. I was in New York with her recently and you guys came up in conversation and she sang your praises. She said you treated your stories – and, most importantly, the victims in the cases you cover – with reverence and exactly the right amount of dignity and respect. She said facts are important to you, that research drives what you do, not opportunism. Those are qualities that you don't see enough of in the reporting space. It's not that I'm against talking to the media – although it's not something I seek out – I'm just against talking to certain types of journalists.

Sara Habib: Do you think that has anything to do with the fact that you used to be a journalist yourself?

David Raker: Do you mean, can I spot a tabloid hack from a mile away?

Sara Habib: Well, it would be a useful skill to have!

David Raker: It would, you're right. Yes, I think that's a part of it. I'd like to think that, in terms of journalism, I was very much on your side of the fence: I took my stories extremely seriously and tried – to the best of my ability – to talk for the victims. Too much reporting is about the act and not the consequence. It's why we have – and by 'we' I mean 'society', and especially the media – this weird adoration for men like the Night Stalker. It's, like, 'Cool, look how many people he killed.' You've got websites that stick these men in a league table based on how many victims they had. Here in London, people talk about Jack the Ripper as if he were some scoundrel. I mean, we've got Jack the Ripper tours. He wasn't a rascal, he was a guy who butchered five innocent women – and most of us don't even know those women's names. We need to tilt the axis.

Fabian Wilson: Tilt the axis?

David Raker: We need to start speaking for, and about, the victims. When I listened to Jo talking to you about the Night Stalker, she barely even mentioned his actual name. I downloaded a few other episodes of your show and that's what you've done with other killers as well. That's how it should be. Their names *should* be forgotten. They don't deserve to be remembered. Only the victims and their families do.

Sara Habib: Let's talk about your switch to finding missing people. Can you tell us why you made the leap – and, also, are there any similarities to journalism?

David Raker: Answering the question in reverse, there are a lot of similarities to journalism. Responsible journalism, at least. Ultimately, you work a case in the same way you work a story: you get inside it, you live it, you breathe it, you find the truth. In terms of why I made the leap . . . It really came about because of Derryn.

Sara Habib: That's your late wife.

David Raker: Correct. She persuaded me to make the leap in the last few months of her life. I think she saw something in missing persons that would connect with me. And she was right.

Sara Habib: What is it that connects you to these cases?

David Raker: When Derryn died, it completely hollowed me out. I could barely breathe for months. So, in missing persons cases, it's the families that I connect with. It's the grief they're dealing with. I recognize so much of that suffering.

Fabian Wilson: But not all of it?

David Raker: Enough to make their case the most important thing in my life when I'm on it. But no, it's impossible to recognize all of what they're going through unless you've been there yourself. The way the families of missing people suffer, it's unique to them. The loss hurts in a way even a death of someone you love can't fully duplicate. The total lack of answers is terrible enough, but I've worked cases that seem to be impossible. A man disappearing inside a Tube train. A whole village vanishing. These aren't just cases without any answers, they're ones that don't seem to have any explanation at all.

Fabian Wilson: So, what's the most difficult case you've ever taken on?

David Raker: That's a tricky one to answer.

Fabian Wilson: In what way?

David Raker: Well, every case is different. Some are more complex than others but they're *all* complex. Physically, I suppose the case that cost me the most was the hunt for the Body Snatcher. I mean, my heart literally stopped at the end of that one.

Sara Habib: And emotionally?

David Raker: There's a couple. The search for the Ling family was one.

Sara Habib: That was where they all disappeared in the middle of dinner?

David Raker: Right.

Fabian Wilson: You ended up here in the States on that one, didn't you?

David Raker: I did, yeah. That journey was particularly emotional for me. When I talked about cases being complex, that's a prime example. It started out as one thing and became something else entirely: something that was very personal to me.

Sara Habib: You said there was another?

David Raker: Yeah, the other was when a woman who looked exactly like my dead wife walked into a police station. I have to be honest, that case almost broke me.

Sara Habib: So, do you regret taking it on?

David Raker: No.

Sara Habib: You never look back with any regrets at all?

David Raker: About taking on cases? No. When you bring families answers, there's nothing to regret. To me, those moments are like oxygen. It's how I breathe.

Acknowledgements

The Shadow at the Door is a very different project from the type of novel I normally write but I've loved every minute of piecing it together. I'm especially grateful to Maxine Hitchcock, my wonderful editor and publisher, who fully embraced the concept right from the second a draft landed in her inbox. (In a Raker-esque twist, that draft was literally the first time she knew anything about this book. I'd kept the whole thing secret until it was actually done, because I wasn't sure if the 'Four stories, four cases, one connection' idea would translate to the page.) Thank you as well to my brilliant agent and even more brilliant friend, Camilla Bolton, who reassured me that the idea *was* sound and that I *could* make it work. These two women are such a huge part of what makes the Raker books tick, and I'm so appreciative of their wisdom and support.

Wisdom, support and sheer, all-round brilliance also applies to the team at Michael Joseph and Penguin too: Rebecca Hilsdon, Beatrix McIntyre, Beth O'Rafferty, Jon Kennedy, Lee Motley, David Ettridge, Katie Williams, Olivia Thomas, Christina Ettridge, Deirdre O'Connell, Natasha Lanigan, Rachel Myers, Louise Blakemore, James Keyte and Laura Marlow. A very special mention to my brilliant copy-editor Caroline Pretty too, whose razor-sharp eye, trusty Raker Bible and brilliant timeline-unravelling has dug me out of so many holes over the last twelve years.

At Darley Anderson, a huge thank you to Mary Darby, Kristina Egan and Georgia Fuller in Foreign Rights, Sheila David in Film and TV, Jade Kavanagh and Rosanna Bellingham, who all do such an amazing job for me.

For keeping me sane and sharing the pain, thank you to my great writing pals Chris Ewan, Claire Douglas and Gilly Macmillan.

To my beautiful extended family – Mum, Dad, Lucy, Rich, Hannah, Sam, Boxie, Di, Delme, Kim, Declan, Nathan, Josh, Barry, Jo and John – thank you for all your love and support. And then there's my wife Sharlé and my daughter Erin, who get to spend every day of their lives with me and still have the good grace not to complain: I couldn't do any of this without you and I love you both so much.

Finally, to my wonderful readers: there's a reason this book is dedicated to you. Thank you for buying my books, for talking about them, for spreading the word, for all the lovely emails and social media messages, and for taking the David Raker novels to your heart. If it wasn't for you, none of this would be possible.